image comics presents

THE WALKING DEAD™

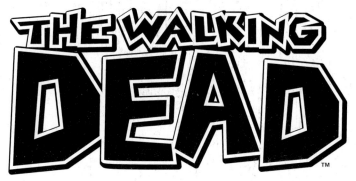

ROBERT KIRKMAN
CREATOR, WRITER

CHARLIE ADLARD
PENCILER, INKER

CLIFF RATHBURN
GRAY TONES

RUS WOOTON
LETTERER

CHARLIE ADLARD
&
DAVE STEWART
COVER

SEAN MACKIEWICZ
EDITOR

SKYBOUND™

For SKYBOUND ENTERTAINMENT

Robert Kirkman - CEO
J.J. Didde - President
Sean Mackiewicz - Editorial Director
Shawn Kirkham - Director of Business Development
Brian Huntington - Online Editorial Director
Helen Leigh - Office Manager
Lizzy Iverson - Administrative Assistant

For international rights inquiries,
please contact: foreign@skybound.com

WWW.SKYBOUND.COM

IMAGE COMICS, INC.
Robert Kirkman - chief operating officer
Erik Larsen - chief financial officer
Todd McFarlane - president
Marc Silvestri - chief executive officer
Jim Valentino - vice-president

Eric Stephenson - publisher
Ron Richards - director of business development
Jennifer de Guzman - pr & marketing director
Branwyn Bigglestone - accounts manager
Emily Miller - accounting assistant
Jamie Parreno - marketing assistant
Emilio Bautista - sales assistant
Jaemie Dudas - administrative assistant
Kevin Yuen - digital rights coordinator
Tyler Shainline - events coordinator
David Brothers - content manager
Jonathan Chan - production manager
Drew Gill - art director
Jana Cook - print manager
Monica Garcia - senior production artist
Vincent Kukua - production artist
Jenna Savage - production artist
Addison Duke - production artist
www.imagecomics.com

PRINTED IN THE USA

ISBN: 978-1-60706-818-1

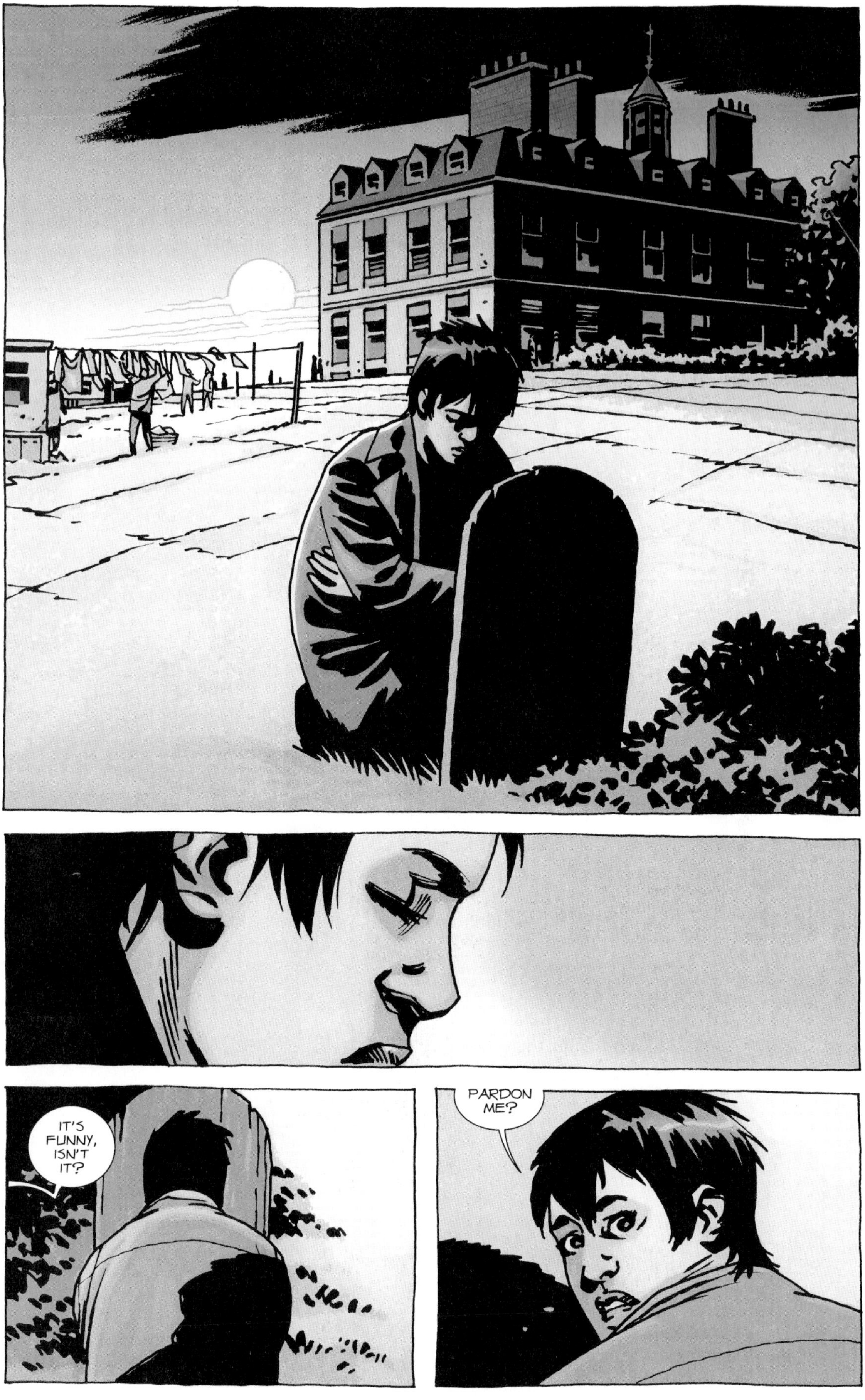
IT'S FUNNY, ISN'T IT?
PARDON ME?

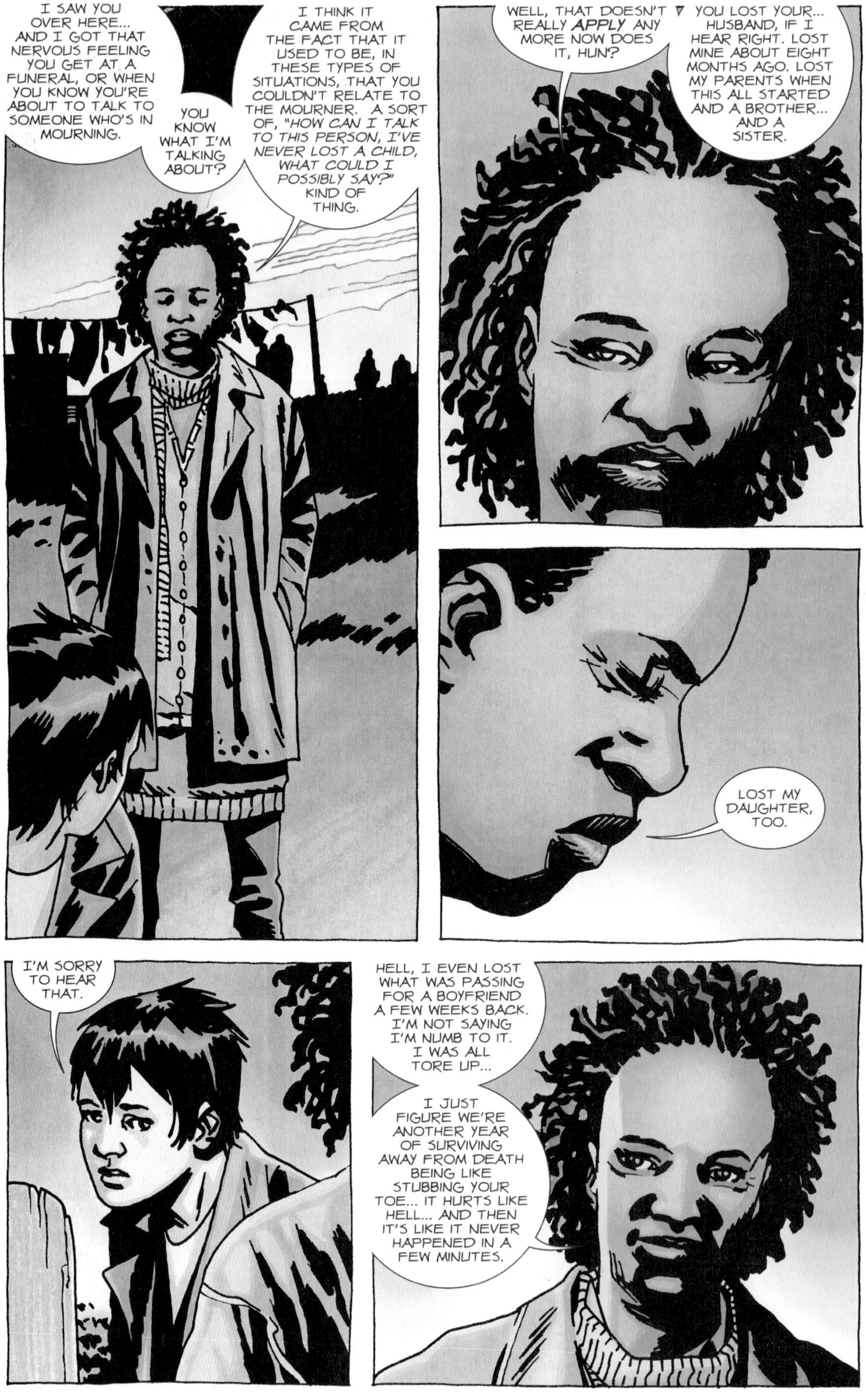

I SAW YOU OVER HERE... AND I GOT THAT NERVOUS FEELING YOU GET AT A FUNERAL, OR WHEN YOU KNOW YOU'RE ABOUT TO TALK TO SOMEONE WHO'S IN MOURNING.
YOU KNOW WHAT I'M TALKING ABOUT?
I THINK IT CAME FROM THE FACT THAT IT USED TO BE, IN THESE TYPES OF SITUATIONS, THAT YOU COULDN'T RELATE TO THE MOURNER. A SORT OF, "HOW CAN I TALK TO THIS PERSON, I'VE NEVER LOST A CHILD, WHAT COULD I POSSIBLY SAY?" KIND OF THING.
WELL, THAT DOESN'T REALLY APPLY ANY MORE NOW DOES IT, HUN?
YOU LOST YOUR... HUSBAND, IF I HEAR RIGHT. LOST MINE ABOUT EIGHT MONTHS AGO. LOST MY PARENTS WHEN THIS ALL STARTED AND A BROTHER... AND A SISTER.
LOST MY DAUGHTER, TOO.
I'M SORRY TO HEAR THAT.
HELL, I EVEN LOST WHAT WAS PASSING FOR A BOYFRIEND A FEW WEEKS BACK. I'M NOT SAYING I'M NUMB TO IT. I WAS ALL TORE UP...
I JUST FIGURE WE'RE ANOTHER YEAR OF SURVIVING AWAY FROM DEATH BEING LIKE STUBBING YOUR TOE... IT HURTS LIKE HELL... AND THEN IT'S LIKE IT NEVER HAPPENED IN A FEW MINUTES.

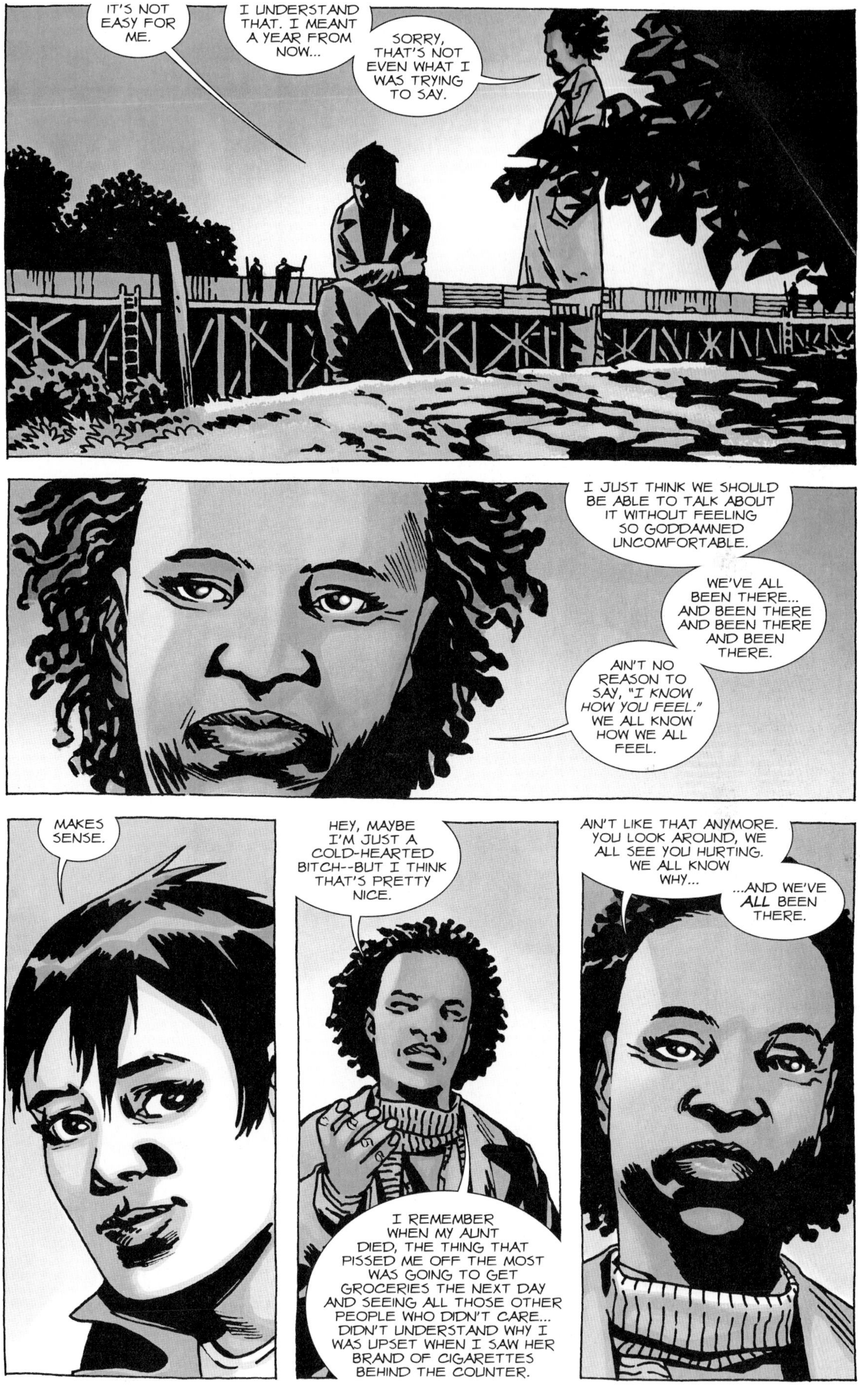
IT'S NOT EASY FOR ME.
I UNDERSTAND THAT. I MEANT A YEAR FROM NOW...
SORRY, THAT'S NOT EVEN WHAT I WAS TRYING TO SAY.
I JUST THINK WE SHOULD BE ABLE TO TALK ABOUT IT WITHOUT FEELING SO GODDAMNED UNCOMFORTABLE.
WE'VE ALL BEEN THERE... AND BEEN THERE AND BEEN THERE AND BEEN THERE.
AIN'T NO REASON TO SAY, "*I KNOW HOW YOU FEEL.*" WE ALL KNOW HOW WE ALL FEEL.
MAKES SENSE.
HEY, MAYBE I'M JUST A COLD-HEARTED BITCH--BUT I THINK THAT'S PRETTY NICE.
I REMEMBER WHEN MY AUNT DIED, THE THING THAT PISSED ME OFF THE MOST WAS GOING TO GET GROCERIES THE NEXT DAY AND SEEING ALL THOSE OTHER PEOPLE WHO DIDN'T CARE... DIDN'T UNDERSTAND WHY I WAS UPSET WHEN I SAW HER BRAND OF CIGARETTES BEHIND THE COUNTER.
AIN'T LIKE THAT ANYMORE. YOU LOOK AROUND, WE ALL SEE YOU HURTING. WE ALL KNOW WHY...
...AND WE'VE ***ALL*** BEEN THERE.

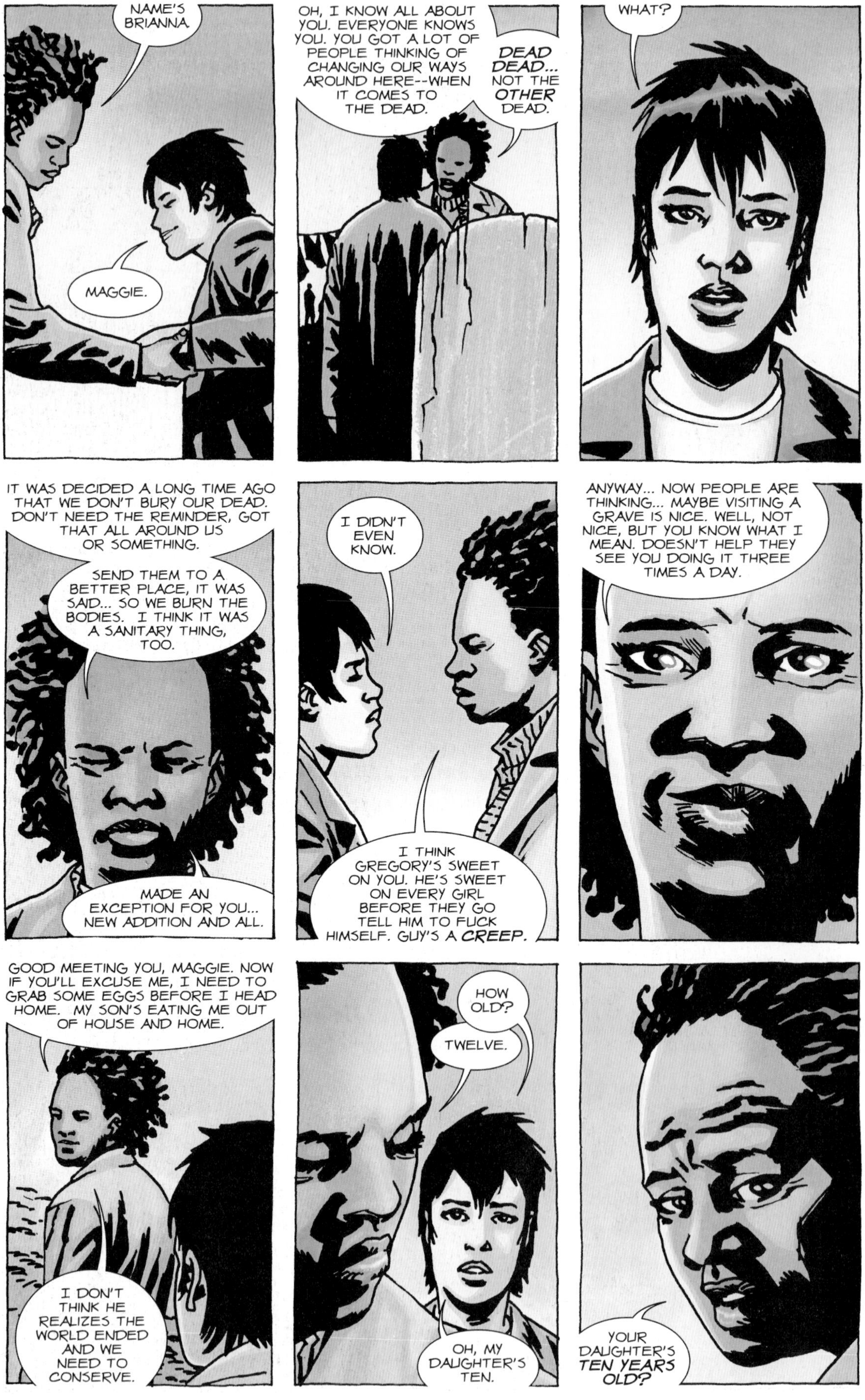
NAME'S BRIANNA.
MAGGIE.
OH, I KNOW ALL ABOUT YOU. EVERYONE KNOWS YOU. YOU GOT A LOT OF PEOPLE THINKING OF CHANGING OUR WAYS AROUND HERE--WHEN IT COMES TO THE DEAD.
DEAD DEAD... NOT THE OTHER DEAD.
WHAT?
IT WAS DECIDED A LONG TIME AGO THAT WE DON'T BURY OUR DEAD. DON'T NEED THE REMINDER, GOT THAT ALL AROUND US OR SOMETHING.
SEND THEM TO A BETTER PLACE, IT WAS SAID... SO WE BURN THE BODIES. I THINK IT WAS A SANITARY THING, TOO.
MADE AN EXCEPTION FOR YOU... NEW ADDITION AND ALL.
I DIDN'T EVEN KNOW.
I THINK GREGORY'S SWEET ON YOU. HE'S SWEET ON EVERY GIRL BEFORE THEY GO TELL HIM TO FUCK HIMSELF. GUY'S A CREEP.
ANYWAY... NOW PEOPLE ARE THINKING... MAYBE VISITING A GRAVE IS NICE. WELL, NOT NICE, BUT YOU KNOW WHAT I MEAN. DOESN'T HELP THEY SEE YOU DOING IT THREE TIMES A DAY.
GOOD MEETING YOU, MAGGIE. NOW IF YOU'LL EXCUSE ME, I NEED TO GRAB SOME EGGS BEFORE I HEAD HOME. MY SON'S EATING ME OUT OF HOUSE AND HOME.
I DON'T THINK HE REALIZES THE WORLD ENDED AND WE NEED TO CONSERVE.
HOW OLD?
TWELVE.
OH, MY DAUGHTER'S TEN.
YOUR DAUGHTER'S TEN YEARS OLD?

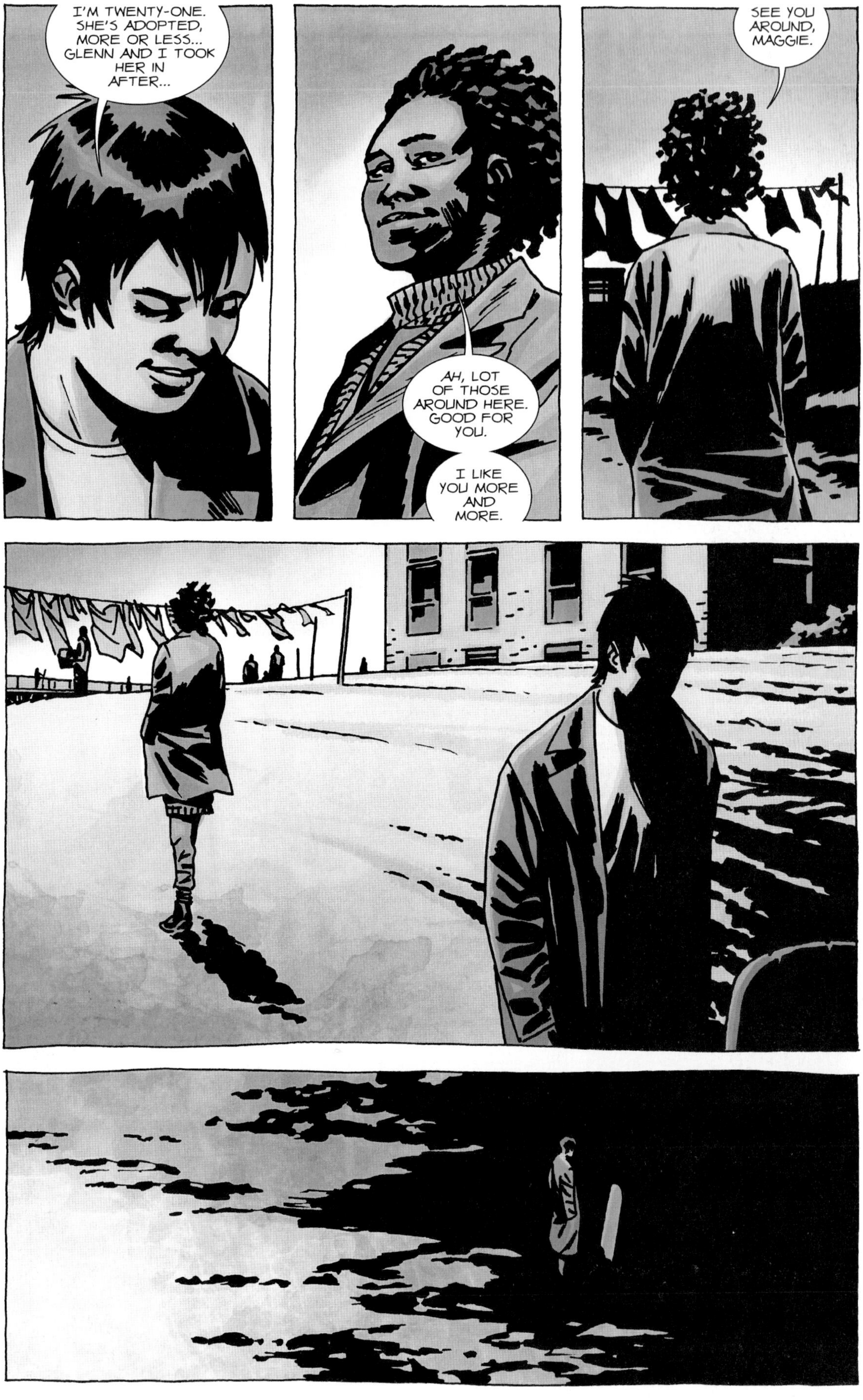
I'M TWENTY-ONE. SHE'S ADOPTED, MORE OR LESS... GLENN AND I TOOK HER IN AFTER...
AH, LOT OF THOSE AROUND HERE. GOOD FOR YOU.
I LIKE YOU MORE AND MORE.
SEE YOU AROUND, MAGGIE.

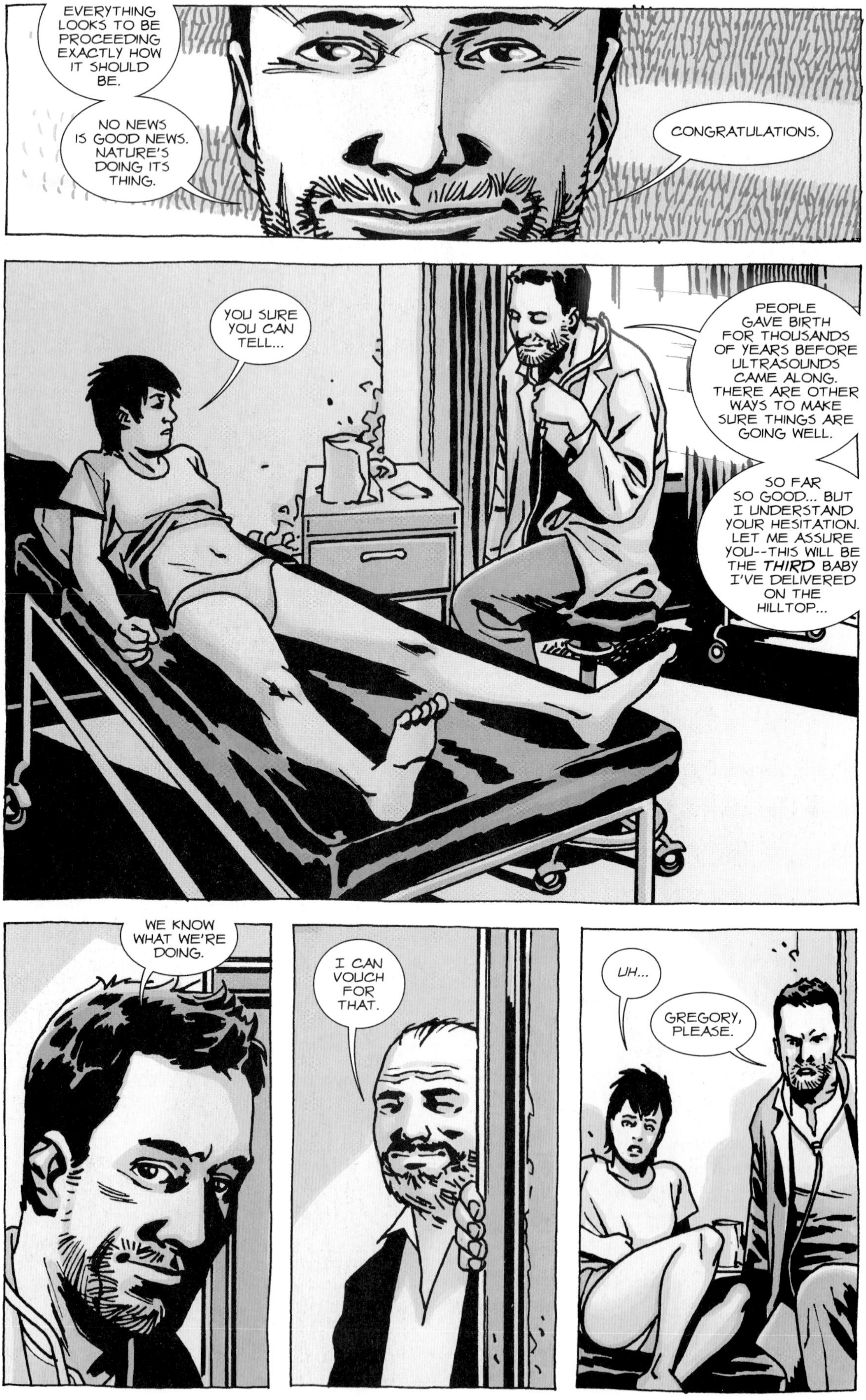
EVERYTHING LOOKS TO BE PROCEEDING EXACTLY HOW IT SHOULD BE.
NO NEWS IS GOOD NEWS. NATURE'S DOING ITS THING.
CONGRATULATIONS.
YOU SURE YOU CAN TELL...
PEOPLE GAVE BIRTH FOR THOUSANDS OF YEARS BEFORE ULTRASOUNDS CAME ALONG. THERE ARE OTHER WAYS TO MAKE SURE THINGS ARE GOING WELL.
SO FAR SO GOOD... BUT I UNDERSTAND YOUR HESITATION. LET ME ASSURE YOU--THIS WILL BE THE THIRD BABY I'VE DELIVERED ON THE HILLTOP...
WE KNOW WHAT WE'RE DOING.
I CAN VOUCH FOR THAT.
UH...
GREGORY, PLEASE.

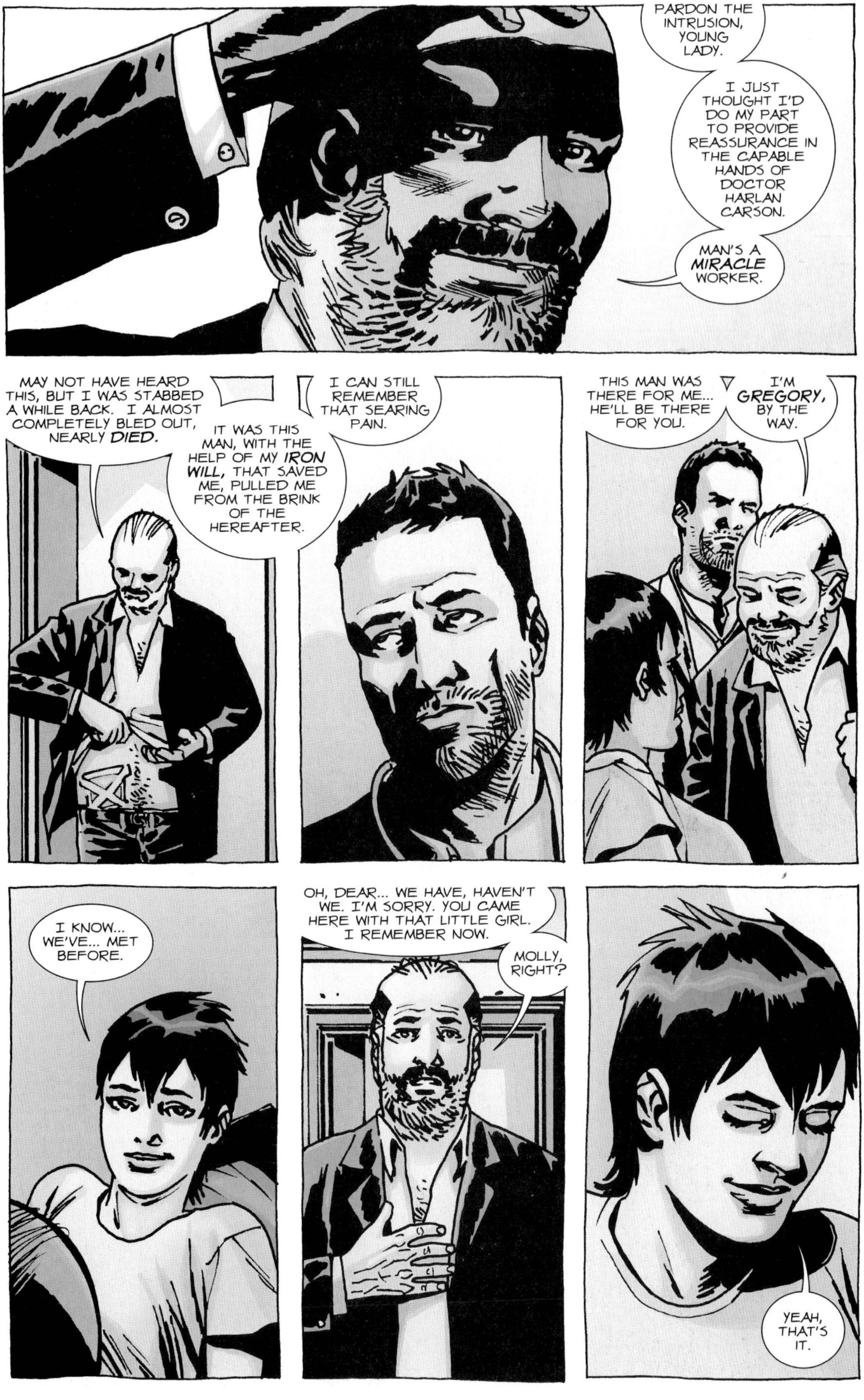
PARDON THE INTRUSION, YOUNG LADY.
I JUST THOUGHT I'D DO MY PART TO PROVIDE REASSURANCE IN THE CAPABLE HANDS OF DOCTOR HARLAN CARSON.
MAN'S A MIRACLE WORKER.
MAY NOT HAVE HEARD THIS, BUT I WAS STABBED A WHILE BACK. I ALMOST COMPLETELY BLED OUT, NEARLY DIED.
IT WAS THIS MAN, WITH THE HELP OF MY IRON WILL, THAT SAVED ME, PULLED ME FROM THE BRINK OF THE HEREAFTER.
I CAN STILL REMEMBER THAT SEARING PAIN.
THIS MAN WAS THERE FOR ME... HE'LL BE THERE FOR YOU.
I'M GREGORY, BY THE WAY.
I KNOW... WE'VE... MET BEFORE.
OH, DEAR... WE HAVE, HAVEN'T WE. I'M SORRY. YOU CAME HERE WITH THAT LITTLE GIRL. I REMEMBER NOW.
MOLLY, RIGHT?
YEAH, THAT'S IT.

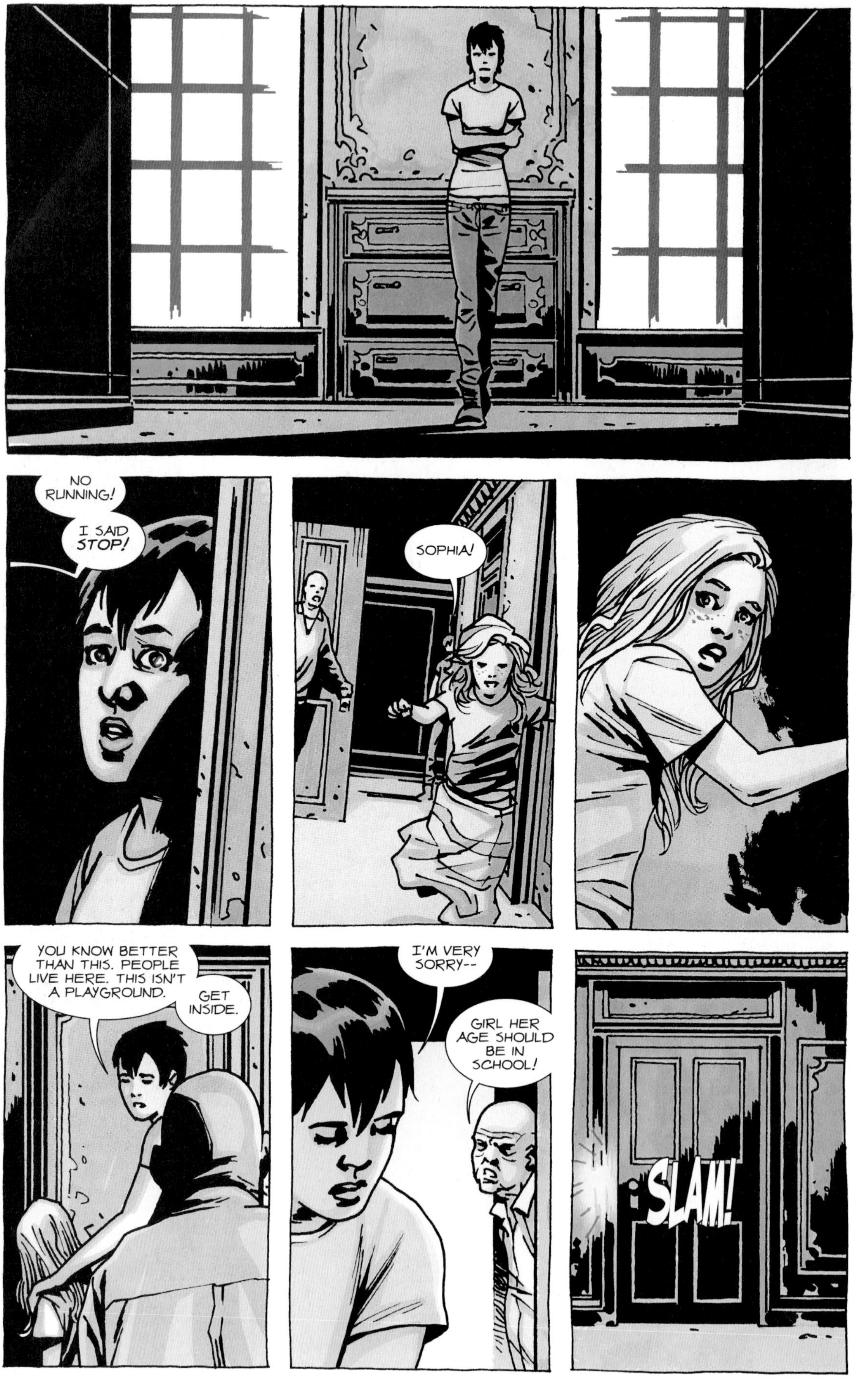
NO RUNNING!
I SAID STOP!
SOPHIA!
YOU KNOW BETTER THAN THIS. PEOPLE LIVE HERE. THIS ISN'T A PLAYGROUND.
GET INSIDE.
I'M VERY SORRY--
GIRL HER AGE SHOULD BE IN SCHOOL!
SLAM!

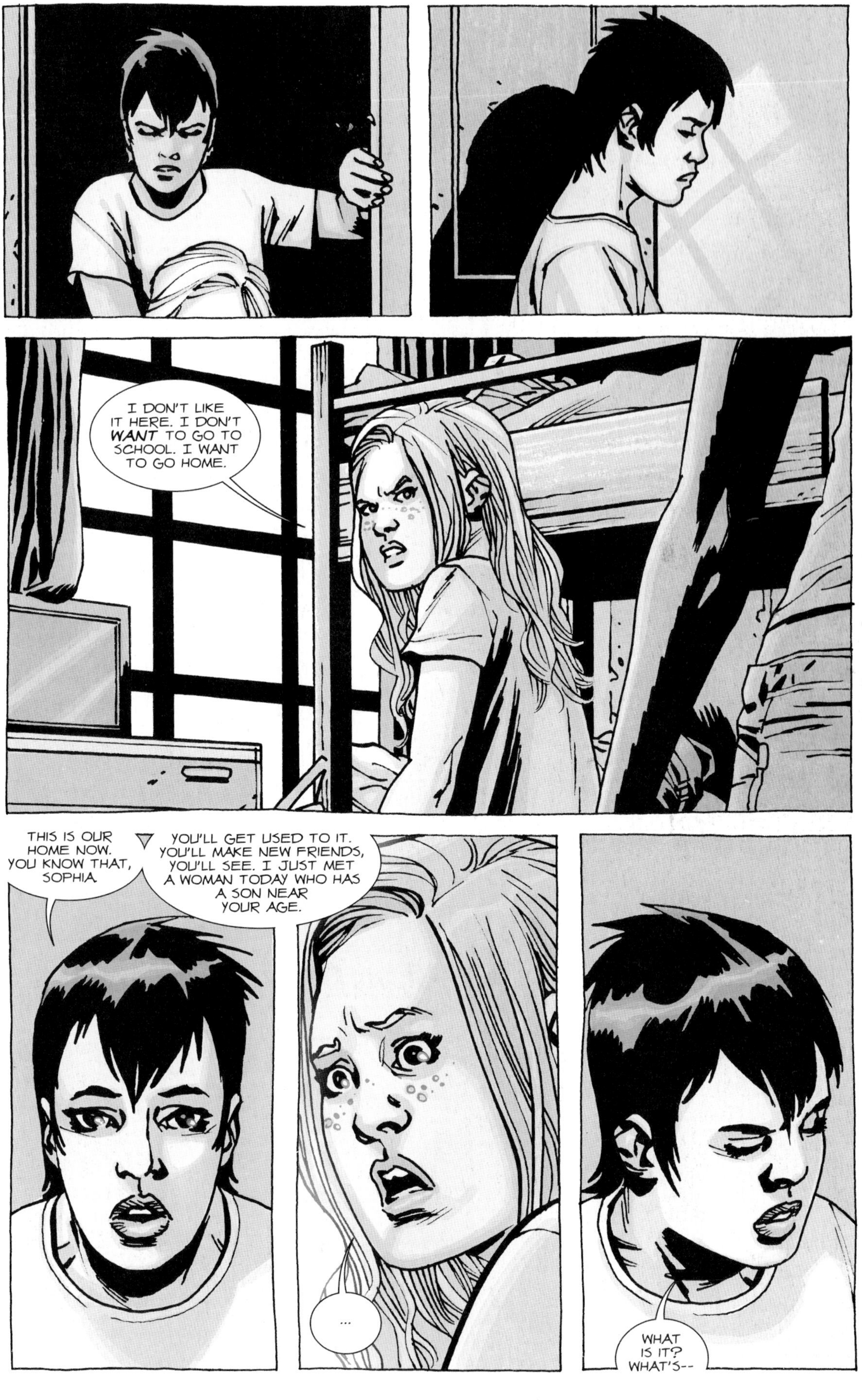
I DON'T LIKE IT HERE. I DON'T *WANT* TO GO TO SCHOOL. I WANT TO GO HOME.
THIS IS OUR HOME NOW. YOU KNOW THAT, SOPHIA.
YOU'LL GET USED TO IT. YOU'LL MAKE NEW FRIENDS, YOU'LL SEE. I JUST MET A WOMAN TODAY WHO HAS A SON NEAR YOUR AGE.
...
WHAT IS IT? WHAT'S--

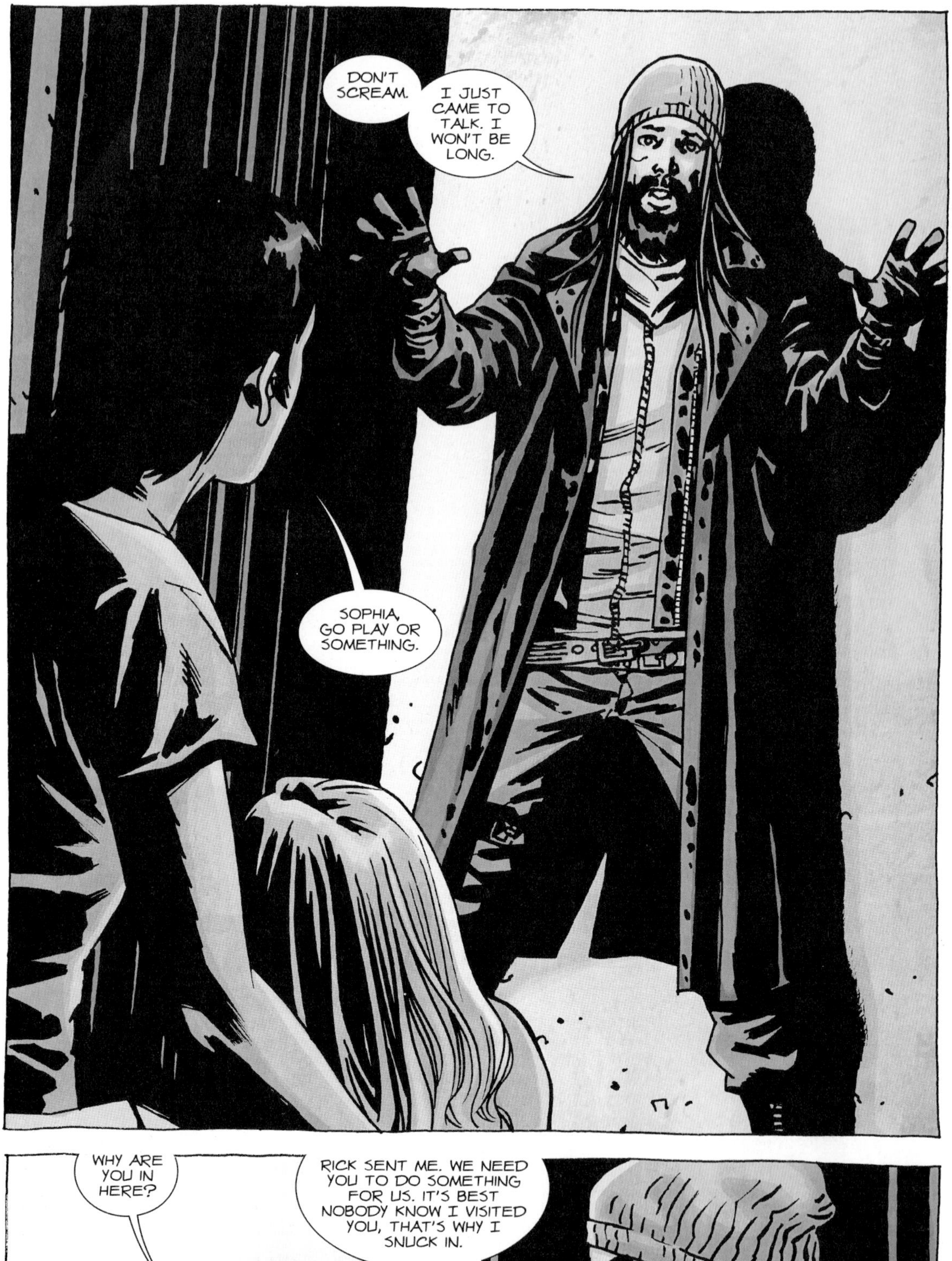
DON'T SCREAM.
I JUST CAME TO TALK. I WON'T BE LONG.
SOPHIA, GO PLAY OR SOMETHING.

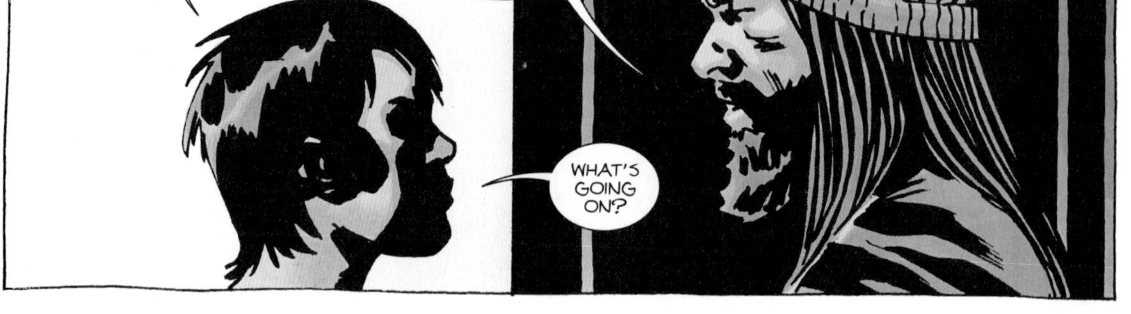
WHY ARE YOU IN HERE?
RICK SENT ME. WE NEED YOU TO DO SOMETHING FOR US. IT'S BEST NOBODY KNOW I VISITED YOU, THAT'S WHY I SNUCK IN.
WHAT'S GOING ON?

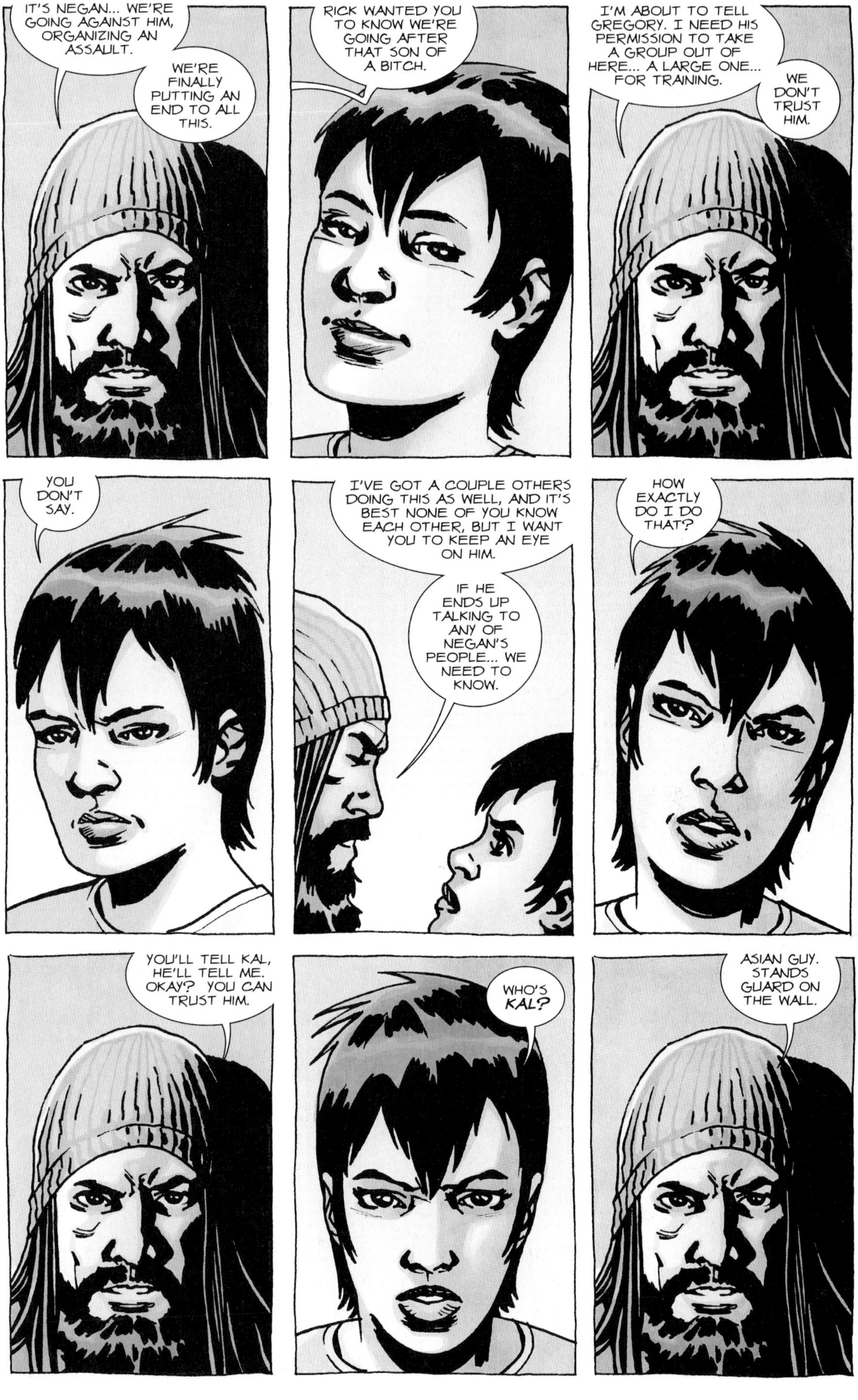

IT'S NEGAN... WE'RE GOING AGAINST HIM, ORGANIZING AN ASSAULT.
WE'RE FINALLY PUTTING AN END TO ALL THIS.
RICK WANTED YOU TO KNOW WE'RE GOING AFTER THAT SON OF A BITCH.
I'M ABOUT TO TELL GREGORY. I NEED HIS PERMISSION TO TAKE A GROUP OUT OF HERE... A LARGE ONE... FOR TRAINING.
WE DON'T TRUST HIM.
YOU DON'T SAY.
I'VE GOT A COUPLE OTHERS DOING THIS AS WELL, AND IT'S BEST NONE OF YOU KNOW EACH OTHER, BUT I WANT YOU TO KEEP AN EYE ON HIM.
IF HE ENDS UP TALKING TO ANY OF NEGAN'S PEOPLE... WE NEED TO KNOW.
HOW EXACTLY DO I DO THAT?
YOU'LL TELL KAL, HE'LL TELL ME. OKAY? YOU CAN TRUST HIM.
WHO'S *KAL?*
ASIAN GUY. STANDS GUARD ON THE WALL.

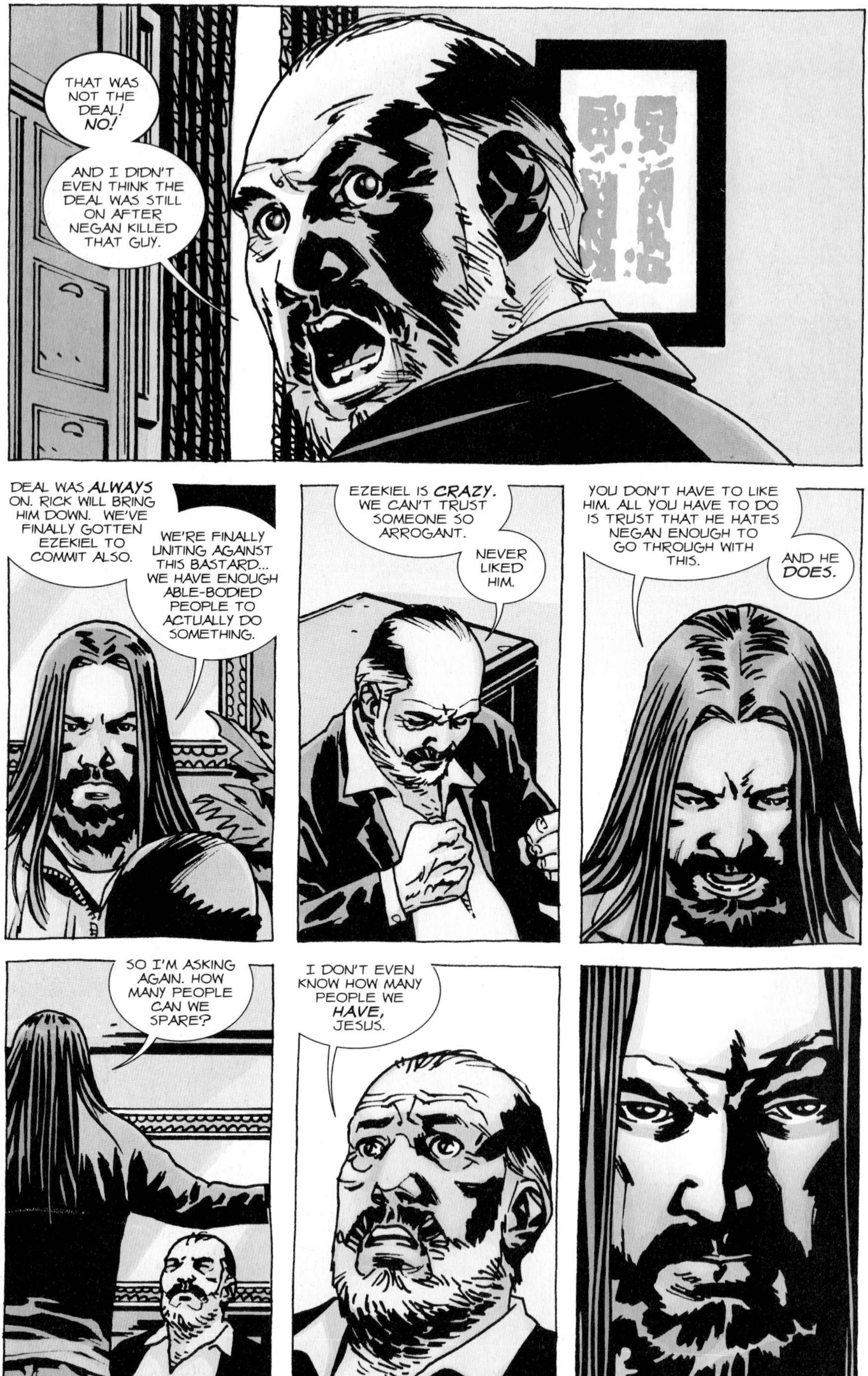
THAT WAS NOT THE DEAL! NO!
AND I DIDN'T EVEN THINK THE DEAL WAS STILL ON AFTER NEGAN KILLED THAT GUY.
DEAL WAS ALWAYS ON. RICK WILL BRING HIM DOWN. WE'VE FINALLY GOTTEN EZEKIEL TO COMMIT ALSO.
WE'RE FINALLY UNITING AGAINST THIS BASTARD... WE HAVE ENOUGH ABLE-BODIED PEOPLE TO ACTUALLY DO SOMETHING.
EZEKIEL IS CRAZY. WE CAN'T TRUST SOMEONE SO ARROGANT.
NEVER LIKED HIM.
YOU DON'T HAVE TO LIKE HIM. ALL YOU HAVE TO DO IS TRUST THAT HE HATES NEGAN ENOUGH TO GO THROUGH WITH THIS.
AND HE DOES.
SO I'M ASKING AGAIN. HOW MANY PEOPLE CAN WE SPARE?
I DON'T EVEN KNOW HOW MANY PEOPLE WE HAVE, JESUS.

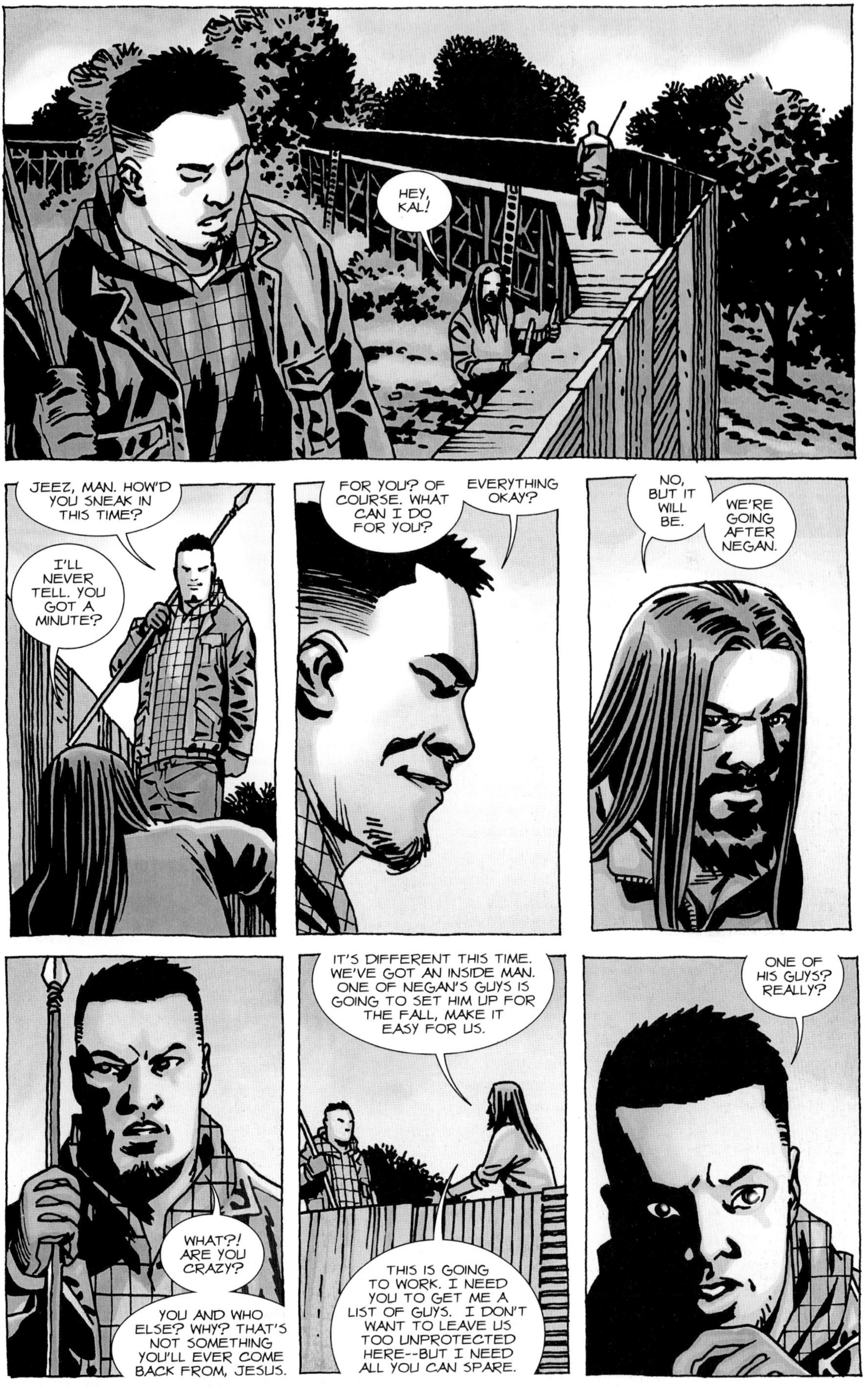
HEY, KAL!
JEEZ, MAN. HOW'D YOU SNEAK IN THIS TIME?
I'LL NEVER TELL. YOU GOT A MINUTE?
FOR YOU? OF COURSE. WHAT CAN I DO FOR YOU?
EVERYTHING OKAY?
NO, BUT IT WILL BE.
WE'RE GOING AFTER NEGAN.
WHAT?! ARE YOU CRAZY?
YOU AND WHO ELSE? WHY? THAT'S NOT SOMETHING YOU'LL EVER COME BACK FROM, JESUS.
IT'S DIFFERENT THIS TIME. WE'VE GOT AN INSIDE MAN. ONE OF NEGAN'S GUYS IS GOING TO SET HIM UP FOR THE FALL, MAKE IT EASY FOR US.
THIS IS GOING TO WORK. I NEED YOU TO GET ME A LIST OF GUYS. I DON'T WANT TO LEAVE US TOO UNPROTECTED HERE--BUT I NEED ALL YOU CAN SPARE.
ONE OF HIS GUYS? REALLY?

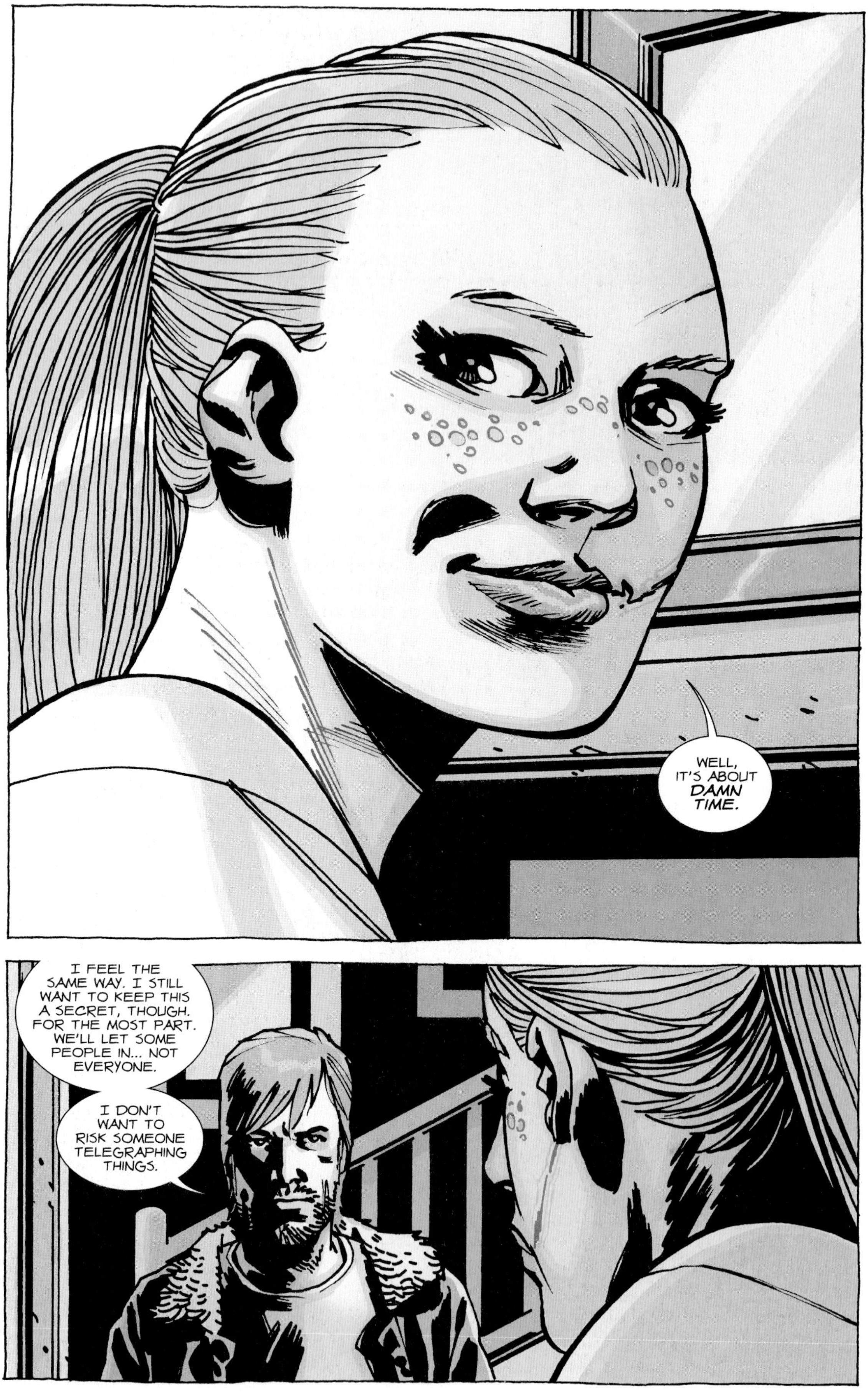
WELL, IT'S ABOUT DAMN TIME.
I FEEL THE SAME WAY. I STILL WANT TO KEEP THIS A SECRET, THOUGH. FOR THE MOST PART. WE'LL LET SOME PEOPLE IN... NOT EVERYONE.
I DON'T WANT TO RISK SOMEONE TELEGRAPHING THINGS.

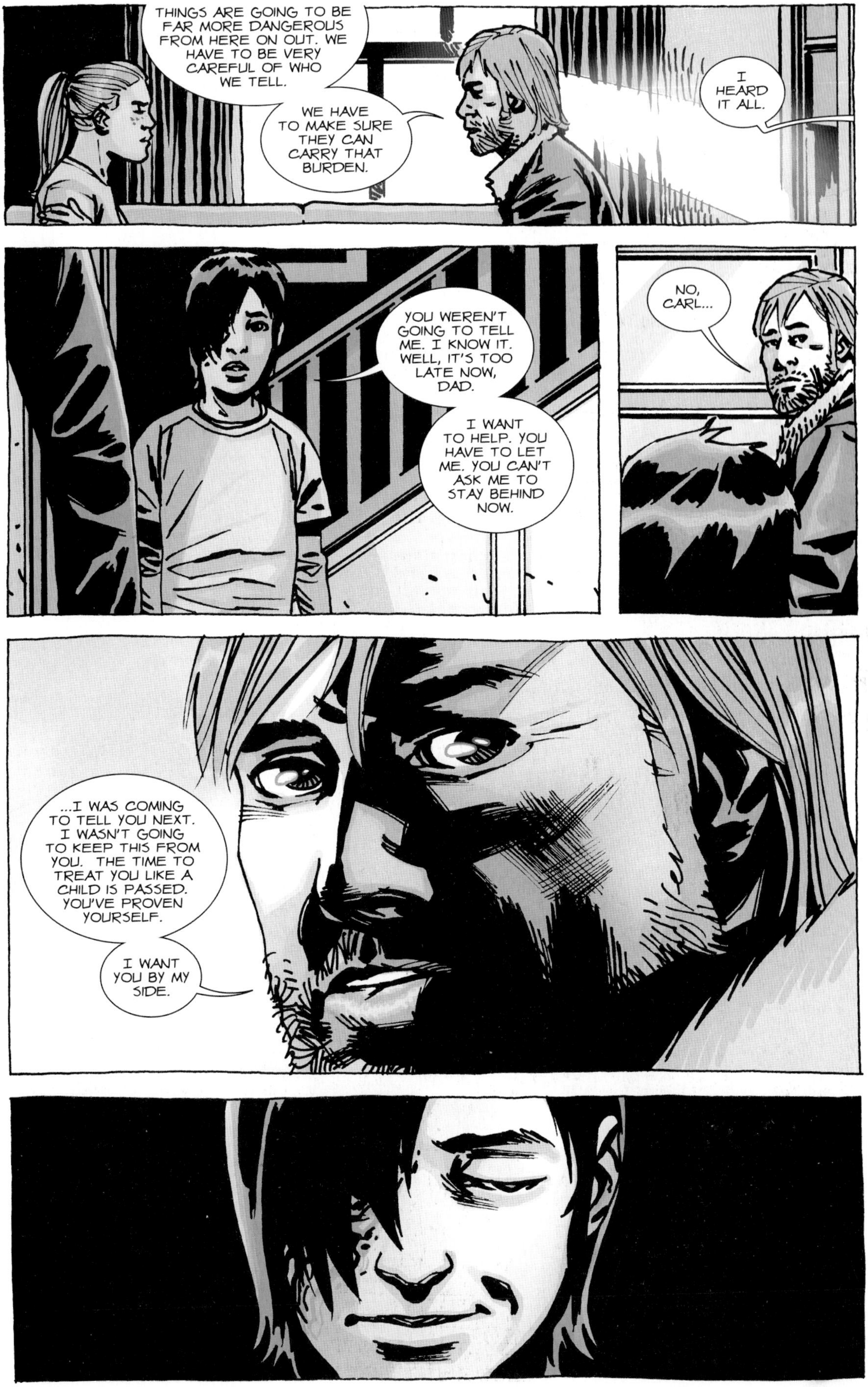
THINGS ARE GOING TO BE FAR MORE DANGEROUS FROM HERE ON OUT. WE HAVE TO BE VERY CAREFUL OF WHO WE TELL.
WE HAVE TO MAKE SURE THEY CAN CARRY THAT BURDEN.
I HEARD IT ALL.
YOU WEREN'T GOING TO TELL ME. I KNOW IT. WELL, IT'S TOO LATE NOW, DAD.
I WANT TO HELP. YOU HAVE TO LET ME. YOU CAN'T ASK ME TO STAY BEHIND NOW.
NO, CARL...
...I WAS COMING TO TELL YOU NEXT. I WASN'T GOING TO KEEP THIS FROM YOU. THE TIME TO TREAT YOU LIKE A CHILD IS PASSED. YOU'VE PROVEN YOURSELF.
I WANT YOU BY MY SIDE.

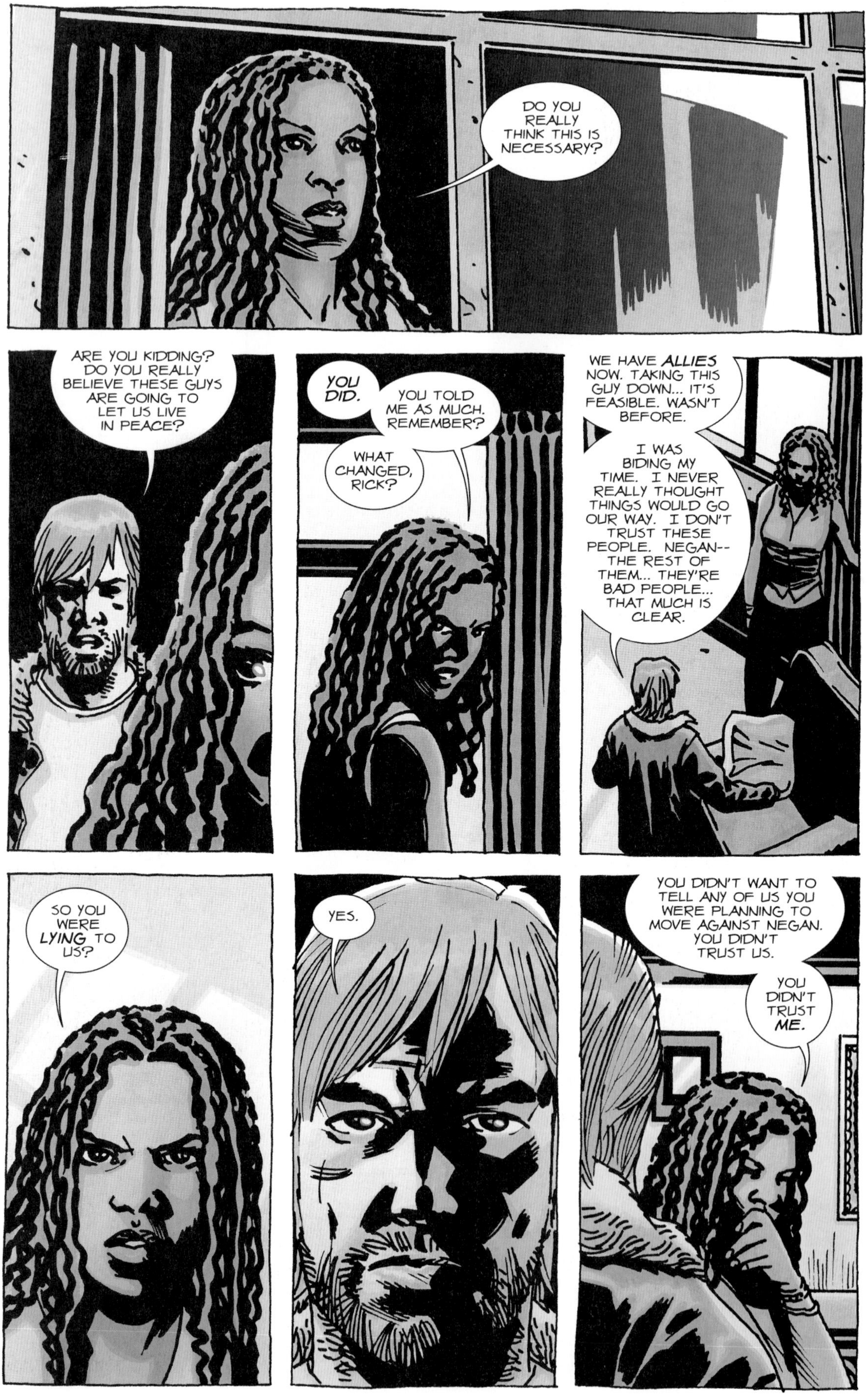
DO YOU REALLY THINK THIS IS NECESSARY?
ARE YOU KIDDING? DO YOU REALLY BELIEVE THESE GUYS ARE GOING TO LET US LIVE IN PEACE?
YOU DID.
YOU TOLD ME AS MUCH. REMEMBER?
WHAT CHANGED, RICK?
WE HAVE ALLIES NOW. TAKING THIS GUY DOWN... IT'S FEASIBLE. WASN'T BEFORE.
I WAS BIDING MY TIME. I NEVER REALLY THOUGHT THINGS WOULD GO OUR WAY. I DON'T TRUST THESE PEOPLE. NEGAN-- THE REST OF THEM... THEY'RE BAD PEOPLE... THAT MUCH IS CLEAR.
SO YOU WERE LYING TO US?
YES.
YOU DIDN'T WANT TO TELL ANY OF US YOU WERE PLANNING TO MOVE AGAINST NEGAN. YOU DIDN'T TRUST US.
YOU DIDN'T TRUST ME.

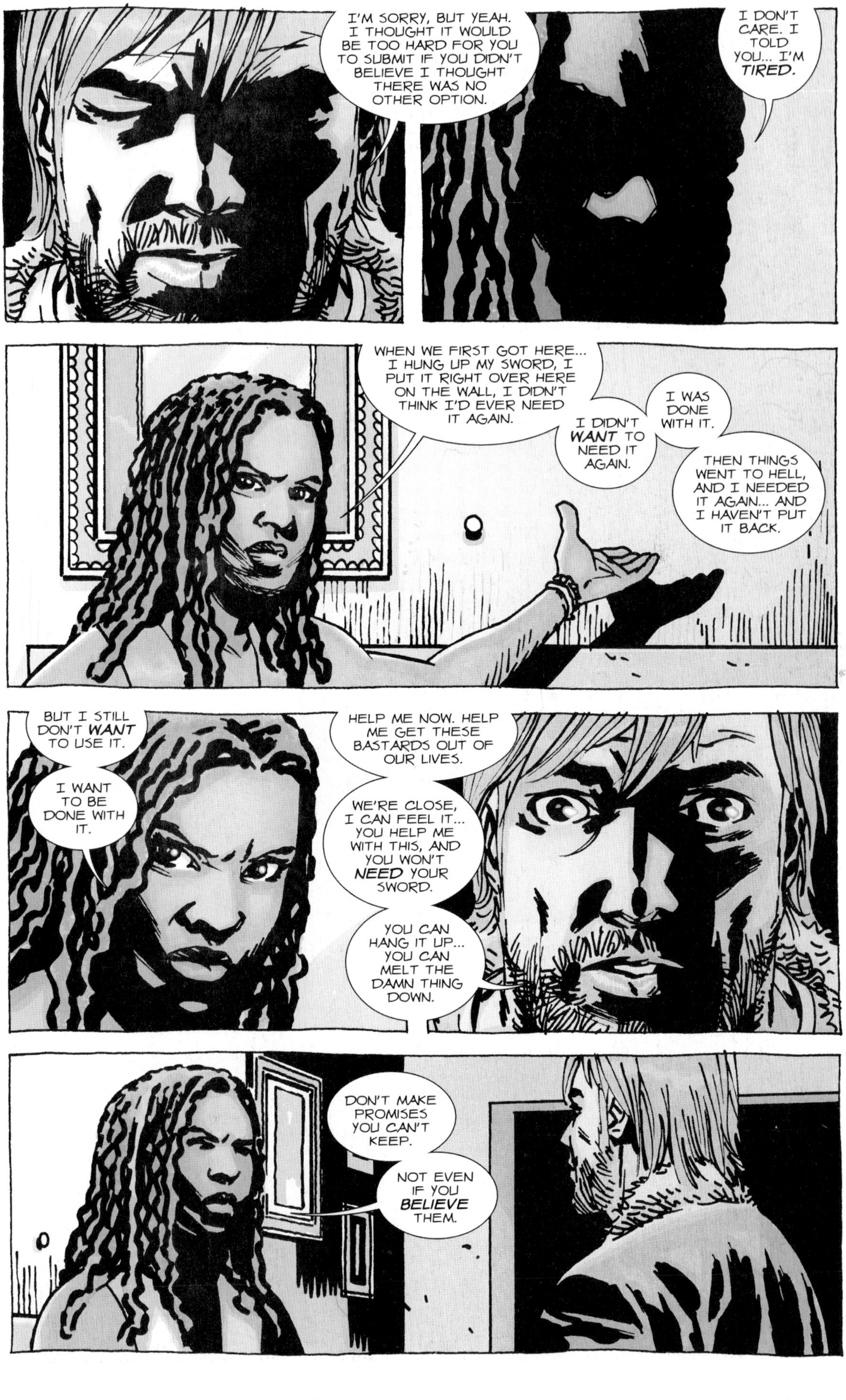
I'M SORRY, BUT YEAH. I THOUGHT IT WOULD BE TOO HARD FOR YOU TO SUBMIT IF YOU DIDN'T BELIEVE I THOUGHT THERE WAS NO OTHER OPTION.
I DON'T CARE. I TOLD YOU... I'M TIRED.
WHEN WE FIRST GOT HERE... I HUNG UP MY SWORD, I PUT IT RIGHT OVER HERE ON THE WALL, I DIDN'T THINK I'D EVER NEED IT AGAIN.
I DIDN'T WANT TO NEED IT AGAIN.
I WAS DONE WITH IT.
THEN THINGS WENT TO HELL, AND I NEEDED IT AGAIN... AND I HAVEN'T PUT IT BACK.
BUT I STILL DON'T WANT TO USE IT.
I WANT TO BE DONE WITH IT.
HELP ME NOW. HELP ME GET THESE BASTARDS OUT OF OUR LIVES.
WE'RE CLOSE, I CAN FEEL IT... YOU HELP ME WITH THIS, AND YOU WON'T NEED YOUR SWORD.
YOU CAN HANG IT UP... YOU CAN MELT THE DAMN THING DOWN.
DON'T MAKE PROMISES YOU CAN'T KEEP.
NOT EVEN IF YOU BELIEVE THEM.

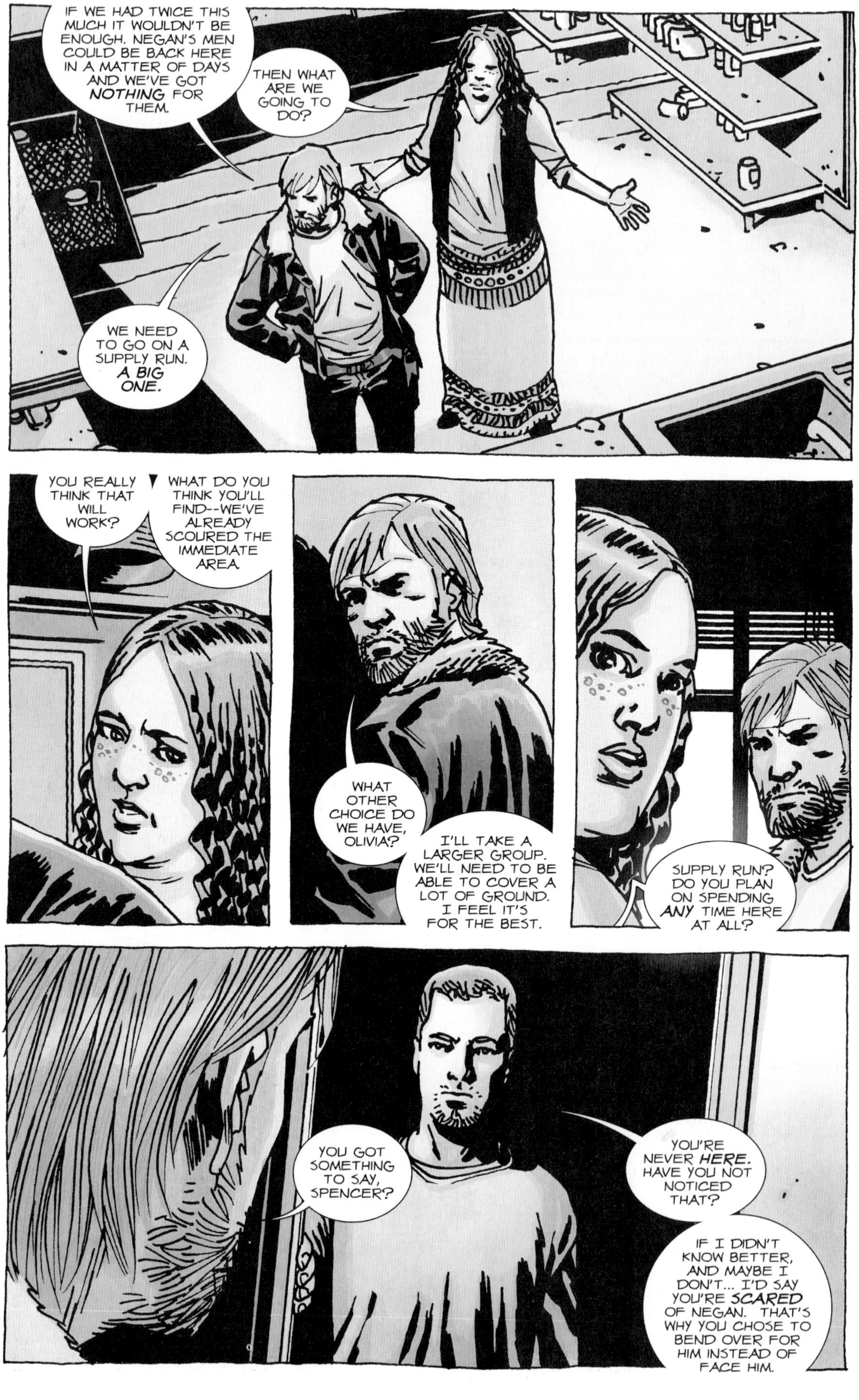
IF WE HAD TWICE THIS MUCH IT WOULDN'T BE ENOUGH. NEGAN'S MEN COULD BE BACK HERE IN A MATTER OF DAYS AND WE'VE GOT NOTHING FOR THEM.
THEN WHAT ARE WE GOING TO DO?
WE NEED TO GO ON A SUPPLY RUN. A BIG ONE.
YOU REALLY THINK THAT WILL WORK?
WHAT DO YOU THINK YOU'LL FIND--WE'VE ALREADY SCOURED THE IMMEDIATE AREA.
WHAT OTHER CHOICE DO WE HAVE, OLIVIA?
I'LL TAKE A LARGER GROUP. WE'LL NEED TO BE ABLE TO COVER A LOT OF GROUND. I FEEL IT'S FOR THE BEST.
SUPPLY RUN? DO YOU PLAN ON SPENDING ANY TIME HERE AT ALL?
YOU GOT SOMETHING TO SAY, SPENCER?
YOU'RE NEVER HERE. HAVE YOU NOT NOTICED THAT?
IF I DIDN'T KNOW BETTER, AND MAYBE I DON'T... I'D SAY YOU'RE SCARED OF NEGAN. THAT'S WHY YOU CHOSE TO BEND OVER FOR HIM INSTEAD OF FACE HIM.

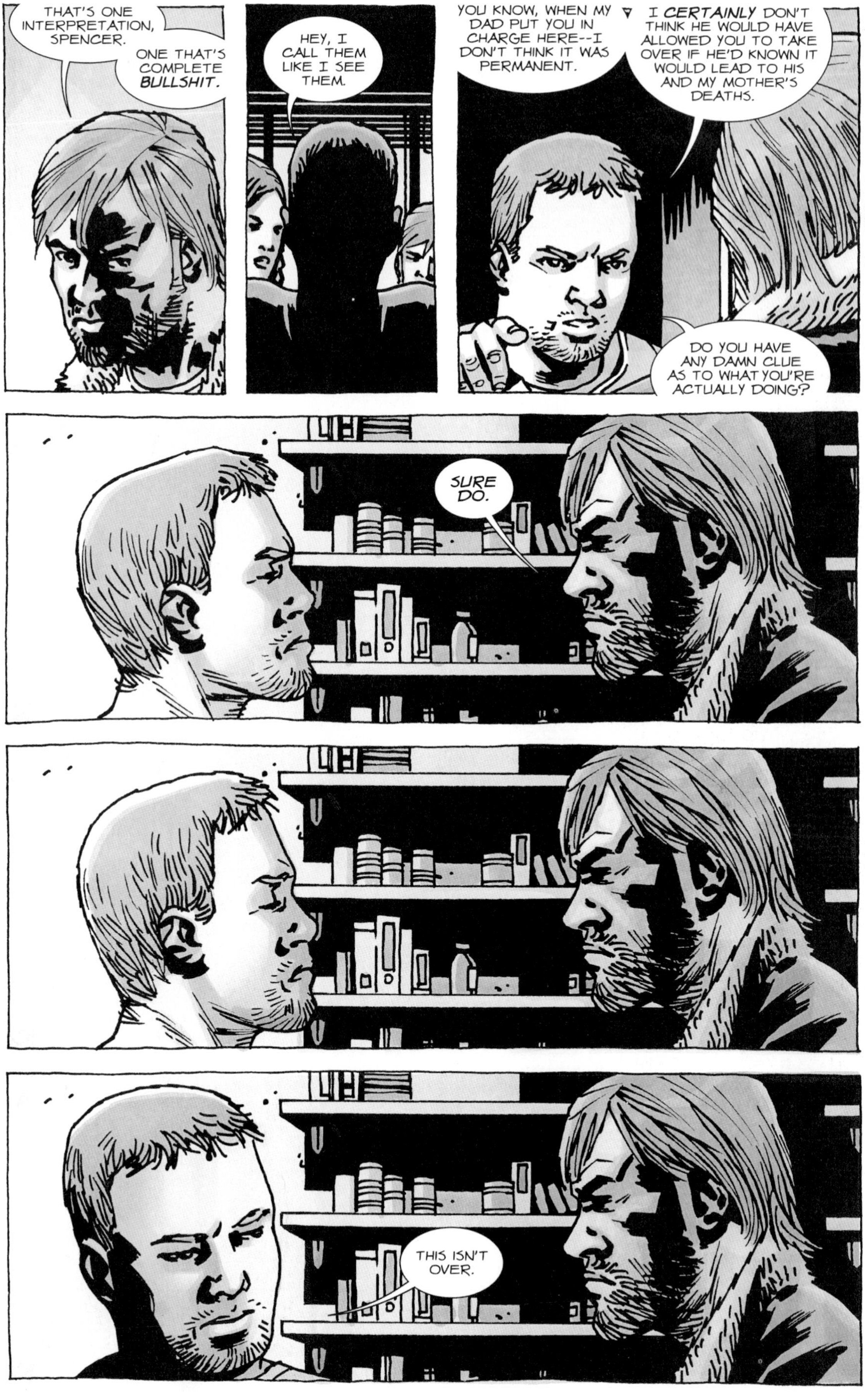
THAT'S ONE INTERPRETATION, SPENCER.
ONE THAT'S COMPLETE BULLSHIT.
HEY, I CALL THEM LIKE I SEE THEM.
YOU KNOW, WHEN MY DAD PUT YOU IN CHARGE HERE--I DON'T THINK IT WAS PERMANENT.
I CERTAINLY DON'T THINK HE WOULD HAVE ALLOWED YOU TO TAKE OVER IF HE'D KNOWN IT WOULD LEAD TO HIS AND MY MOTHER'S DEATHS.
DO YOU HAVE ANY DAMN CLUE AS TO WHAT YOU'RE ACTUALLY DOING?
SURE DO.
THIS ISN'T OVER.

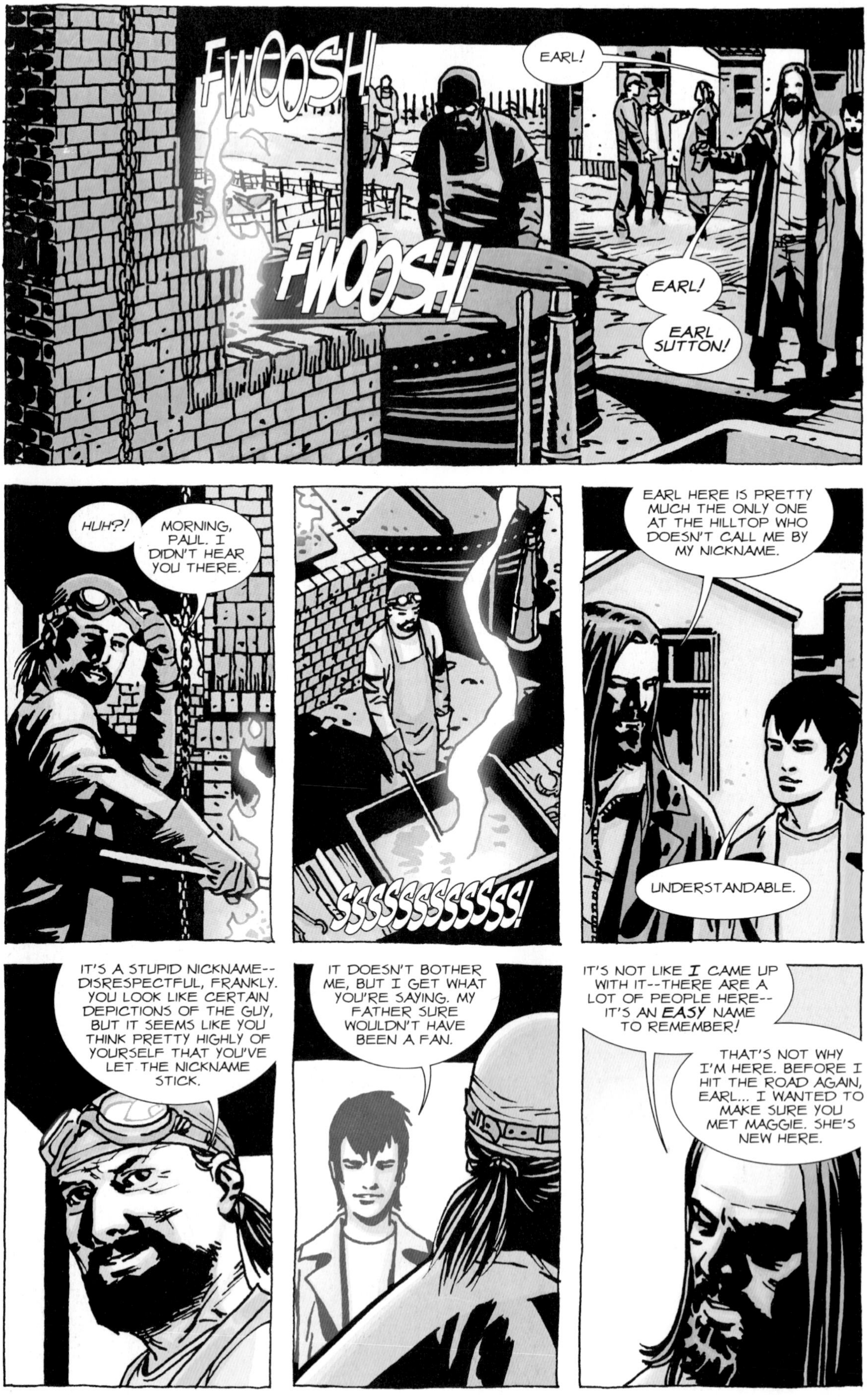
FWOOSH!
EARL!
FWOOSH!
EARL!
EARL SUTTON!
HUH?!
MORNING, PAUL. I DIDN'T HEAR YOU THERE.
SSSSSSSSSSSS!
EARL HERE IS PRETTY MUCH THE ONLY ONE AT THE HILLTOP WHO DOESN'T CALL ME BY MY NICKNAME.
UNDERSTANDABLE.
IT'S A STUPID NICKNAME-- DISRESPECTFUL, FRANKLY. YOU LOOK LIKE CERTAIN DEPICTIONS OF THE GUY, BUT IT SEEMS LIKE YOU THINK PRETTY HIGHLY OF YOURSELF THAT YOU'VE LET THE NICKNAME STICK.
IT DOESN'T BOTHER ME, BUT I GET WHAT YOU'RE SAYING. MY FATHER SURE WOULDN'T HAVE BEEN A FAN.
IT'S NOT LIKE *I* CAME UP WITH IT--THERE ARE A LOT OF PEOPLE HERE-- IT'S AN *EASY* NAME TO REMEMBER!
THAT'S NOT WHY I'M HERE. BEFORE I HIT THE ROAD AGAIN, EARL... I WANTED TO MAKE SURE YOU MET MAGGIE. SHE'S NEW HERE.

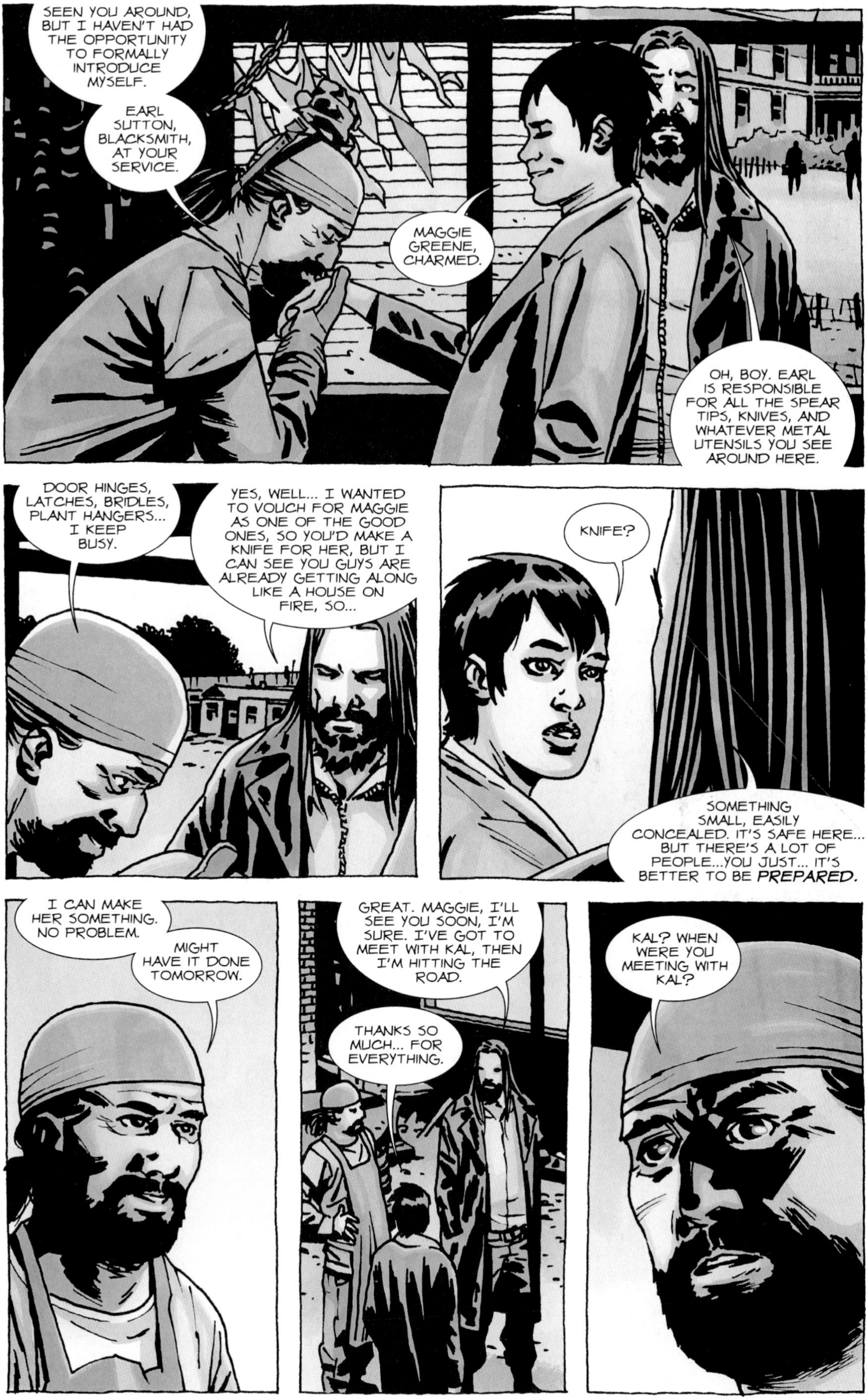
SEEN YOU AROUND, BUT I HAVEN'T HAD THE OPPORTUNITY TO FORMALLY INTRODUCE MYSELF.
EARL SUTTON, BLACKSMITH, AT YOUR SERVICE.
MAGGIE GREENE, CHARMED.
OH, BOY. EARL IS RESPONSIBLE FOR ALL THE SPEAR TIPS, KNIVES, AND WHATEVER METAL UTENSILS YOU SEE AROUND HERE.
DOOR HINGES, LATCHES, BRIDLES, PLANT HANGERS... I KEEP BUSY.
YES, WELL... I WANTED TO VOUCH FOR MAGGIE AS ONE OF THE GOOD ONES, SO YOU'D MAKE A KNIFE FOR HER, BUT I CAN SEE YOU GUYS ARE ALREADY GETTING ALONG LIKE A HOUSE ON FIRE, SO...
KNIFE?
SOMETHING SMALL, EASILY CONCEALED. IT'S SAFE HERE... BUT THERE'S A LOT OF PEOPLE...YOU JUST... IT'S BETTER TO BE *PREPARED.*
I CAN MAKE HER SOMETHING. NO PROBLEM.
MIGHT HAVE IT DONE TOMORROW.
GREAT. MAGGIE, I'LL SEE YOU SOON, I'M SURE. I'VE GOT TO MEET WITH KAL, THEN I'M HITTING THE ROAD.
THANKS SO MUCH... FOR EVERYTHING.
KAL? WHEN WERE YOU MEETING WITH KAL?

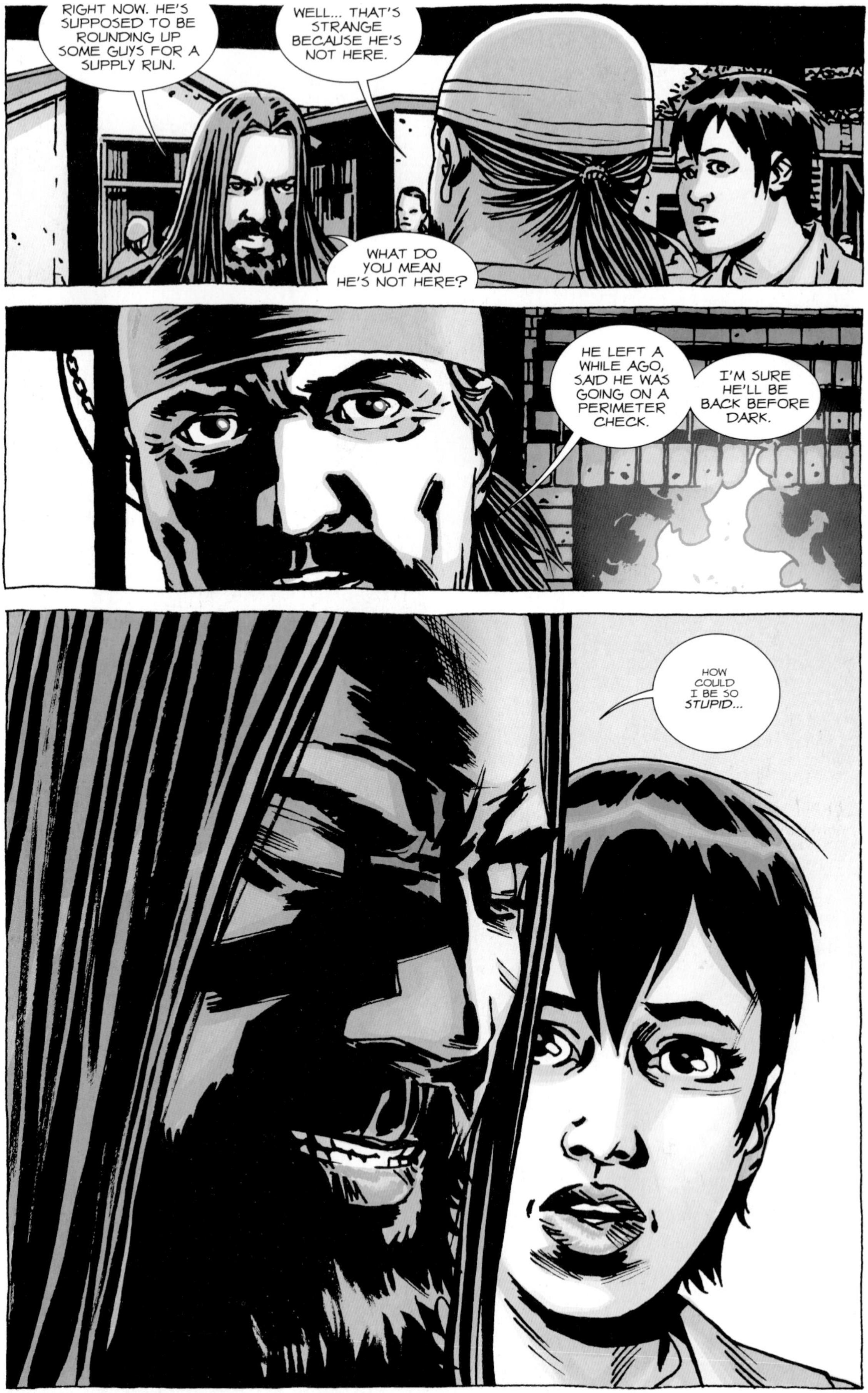

RIGHT NOW. HE'S SUPPOSED TO BE ROUNDING UP SOME GUYS FOR A SUPPLY RUN.
WELL... THAT'S STRANGE BECAUSE HE'S NOT HERE.
WHAT DO YOU MEAN HE'S NOT HERE?
HE LEFT A WHILE AGO, SAID HE WAS GOING ON A PERIMETER CHECK.
I'M SURE HE'LL BE BACK BEFORE DARK.
HOW COULD I BE SO *STUPID*...

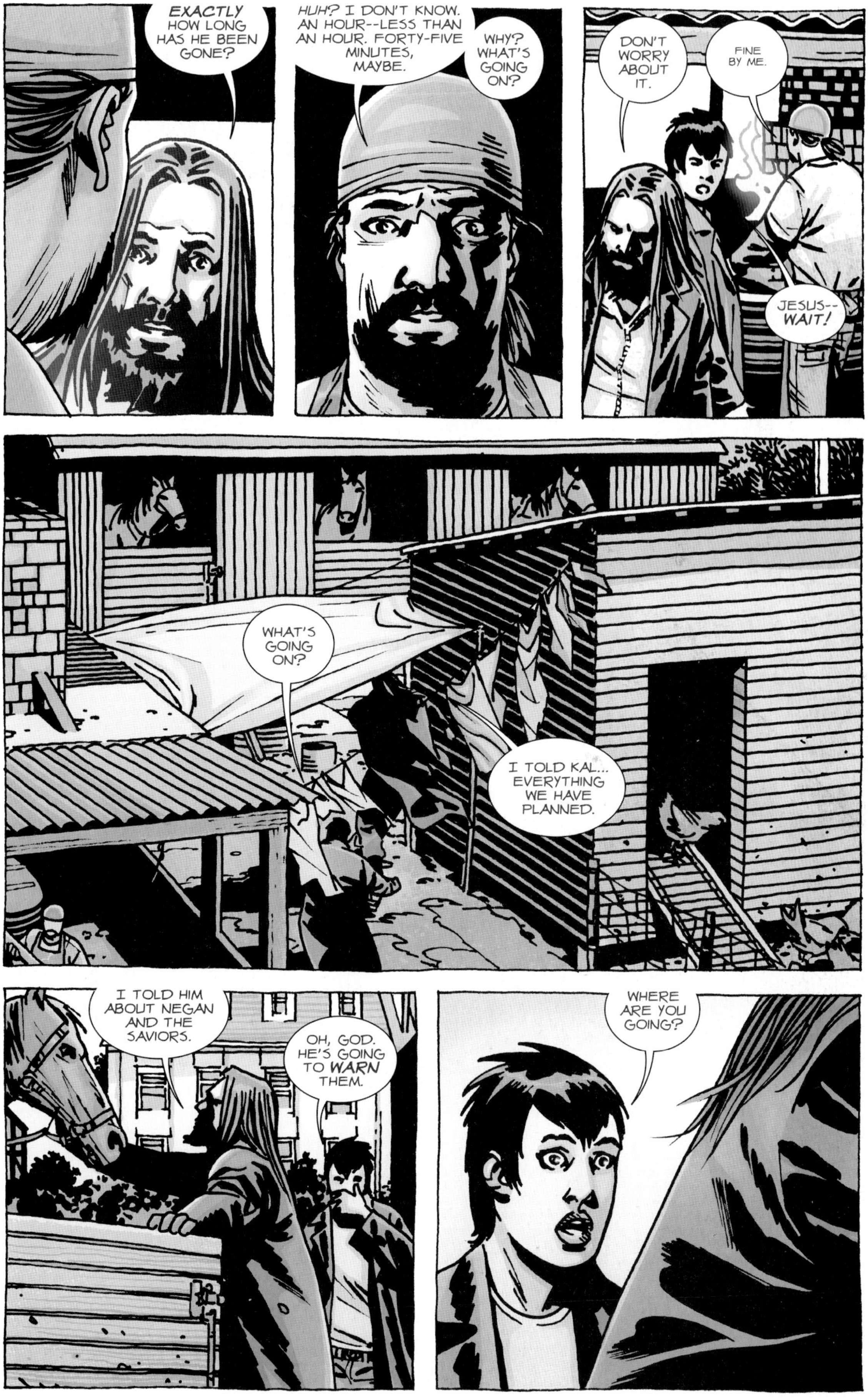

EXACTLY HOW LONG HAS HE BEEN GONE?
HUH? I DON'T KNOW. AN HOUR--LESS THAN AN HOUR. FORTY-FIVE MINUTES, MAYBE.
WHY? WHAT'S GOING ON?
DON'T WORRY ABOUT IT.
FINE BY ME.
JESUS-- WAIT!
WHAT'S GOING ON?
I TOLD KAL... EVERYTHING WE HAVE PLANNED.
I TOLD HIM ABOUT NEGAN AND THE SAVIORS.
OH, GOD. HE'S GOING TO WARN THEM.
WHERE ARE YOU GOING?

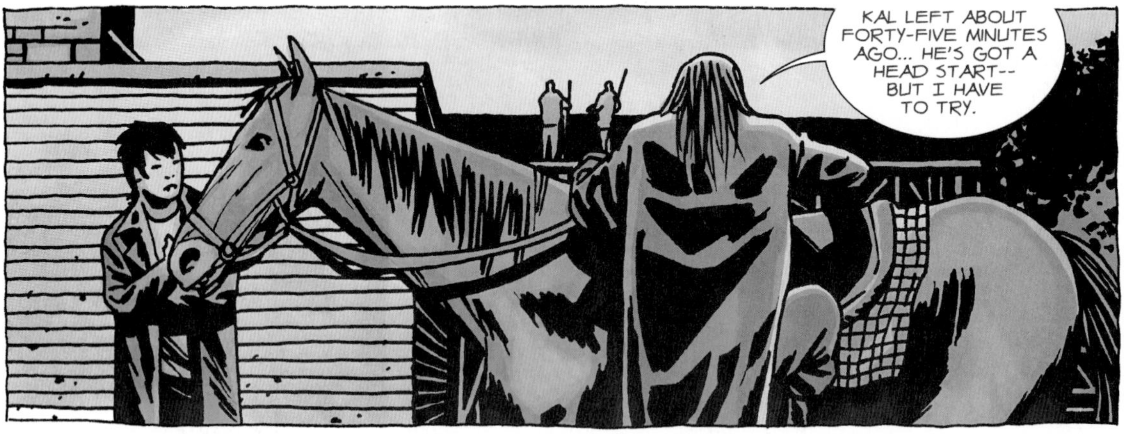
KAL LEFT ABOUT FORTY-FIVE MINUTES AGO... HE'S GOT A HEAD START-- BUT I HAVE TO TRY.

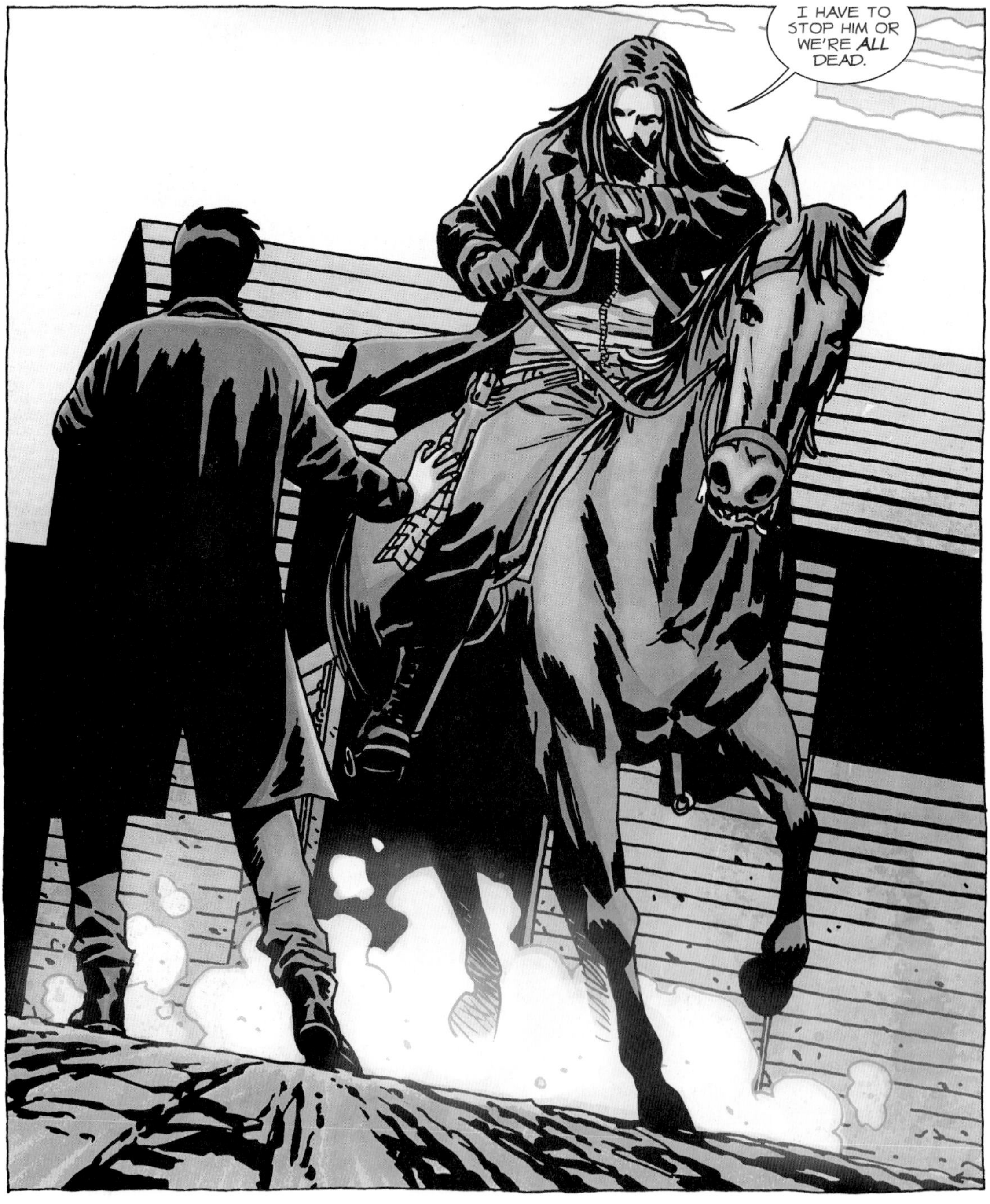
I HAVE TO STOP HIM OR WE'RE **ALL** DEAD.

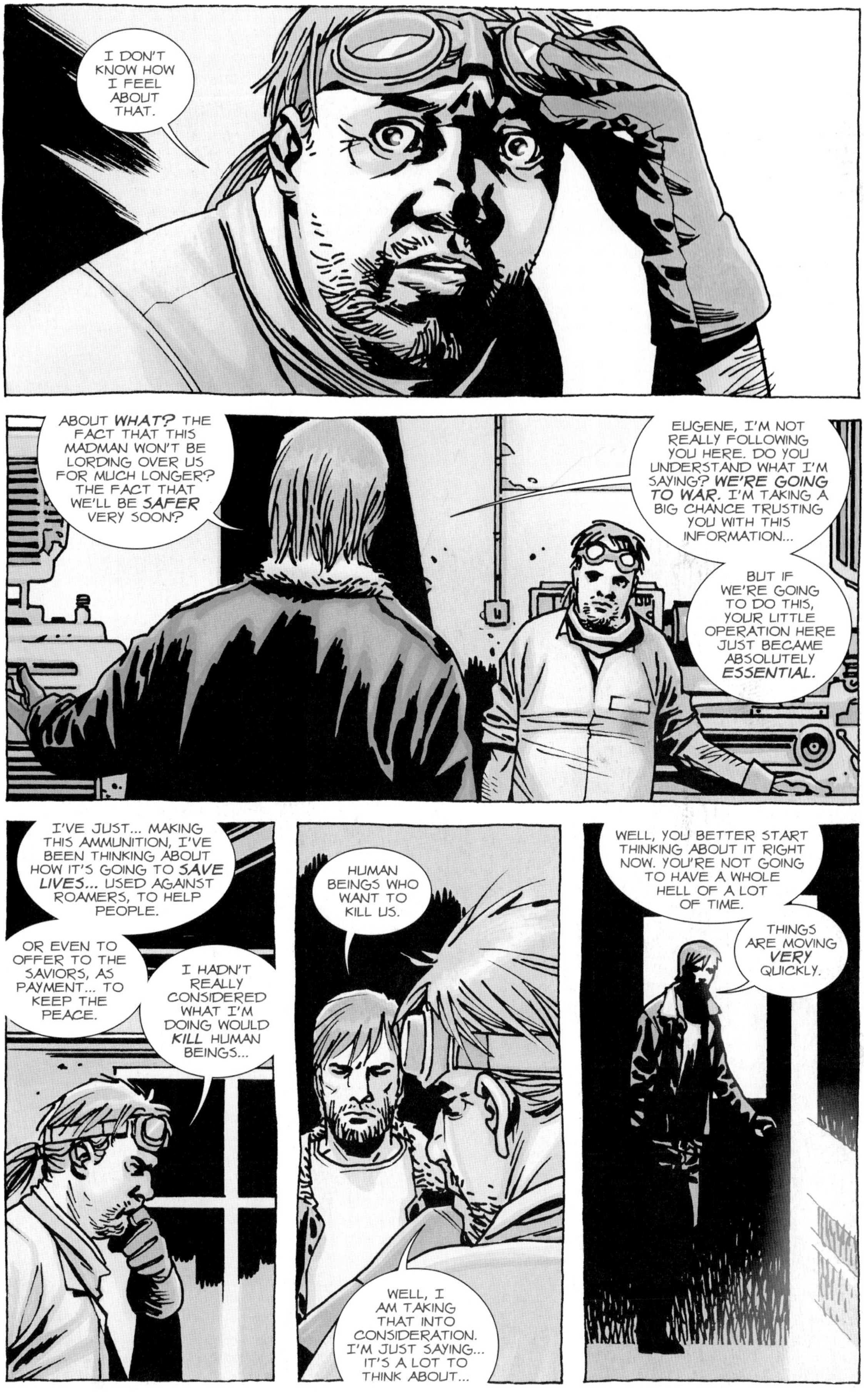
I DON'T KNOW HOW I FEEL ABOUT THAT.
ABOUT WHAT? THE FACT THAT THIS MADMAN WON'T BE LORDING OVER US FOR MUCH LONGER? THE FACT THAT WE'LL BE SAFER VERY SOON?
EUGENE, I'M NOT REALLY FOLLOWING YOU HERE. DO YOU UNDERSTAND WHAT I'M SAYING? WE'RE GOING TO WAR. I'M TAKING A BIG CHANCE TRUSTING YOU WITH THIS INFORMATION...
BUT IF WE'RE GOING TO DO THIS, YOUR LITTLE OPERATION HERE JUST BECAME ABSOLUTELY ESSENTIAL.
I'VE JUST... MAKING THIS AMMUNITION, I'VE BEEN THINKING ABOUT HOW IT'S GOING TO SAVE LIVES... USED AGAINST ROAMERS, TO HELP PEOPLE.
OR EVEN TO OFFER TO THE SAVIORS, AS PAYMENT... TO KEEP THE PEACE.
I HADN'T REALLY CONSIDERED WHAT I'M DOING WOULD KILL HUMAN BEINGS...
HUMAN BEINGS WHO WANT TO KILL US.
WELL, I AM TAKING THAT INTO CONSIDERATION. I'M JUST SAYING... IT'S A LOT TO THINK ABOUT...
WELL, YOU BETTER START THINKING ABOUT IT RIGHT NOW. YOU'RE NOT GOING TO HAVE A WHOLE HELL OF A LOT OF TIME.
THINGS ARE MOVING VERY QUICKLY.

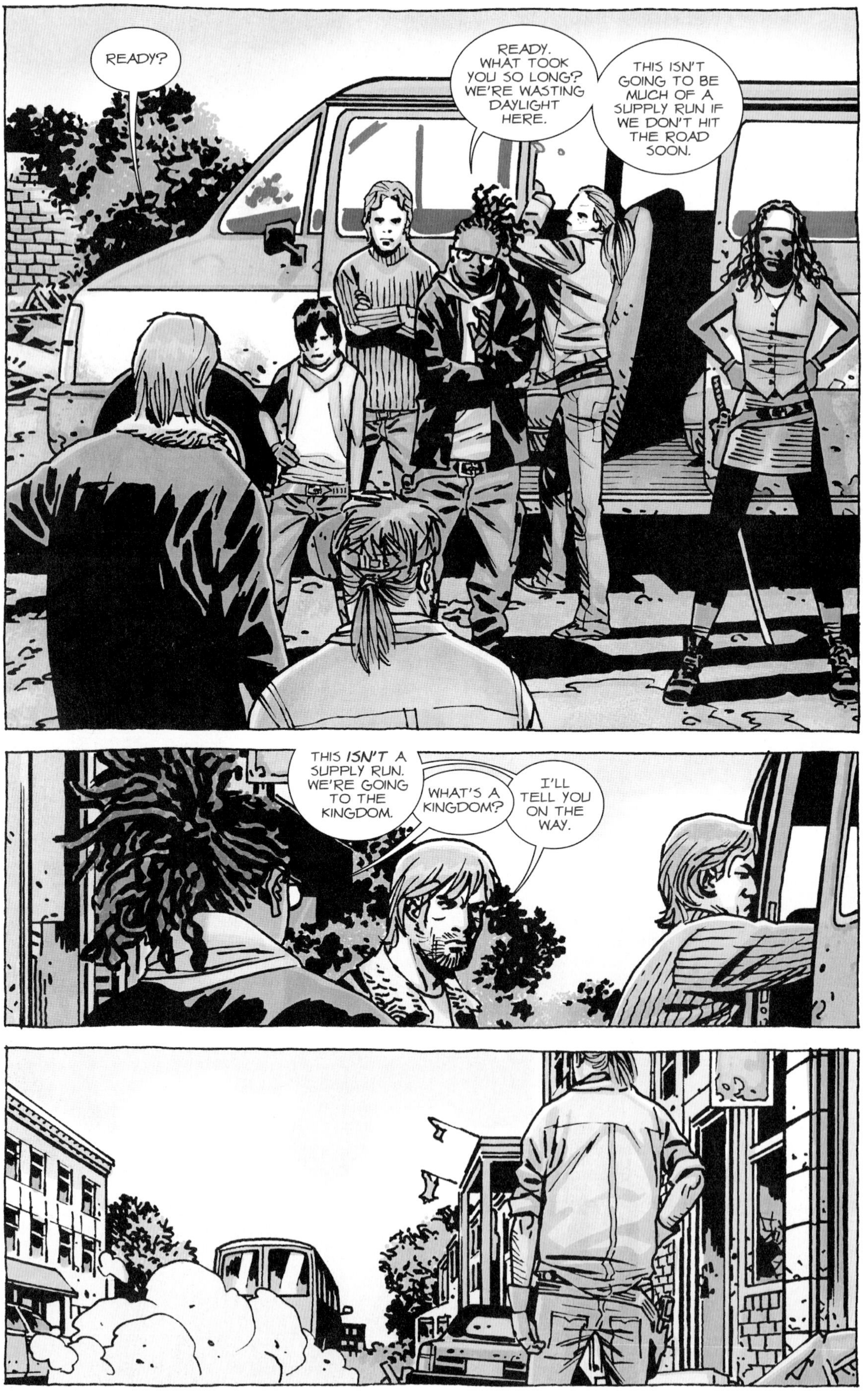
READY?
READY. WHAT TOOK YOU SO LONG? WE'RE WASTING DAYLIGHT HERE.
THIS ISN'T GOING TO BE MUCH OF A SUPPLY RUN IF WE DON'T HIT THE ROAD SOON.
THIS *ISN'T* A SUPPLY RUN. WE'RE GOING TO THE KINGDOM.
WHAT'S A KINGDOM?
I'LL TELL YOU ON THE WAY.

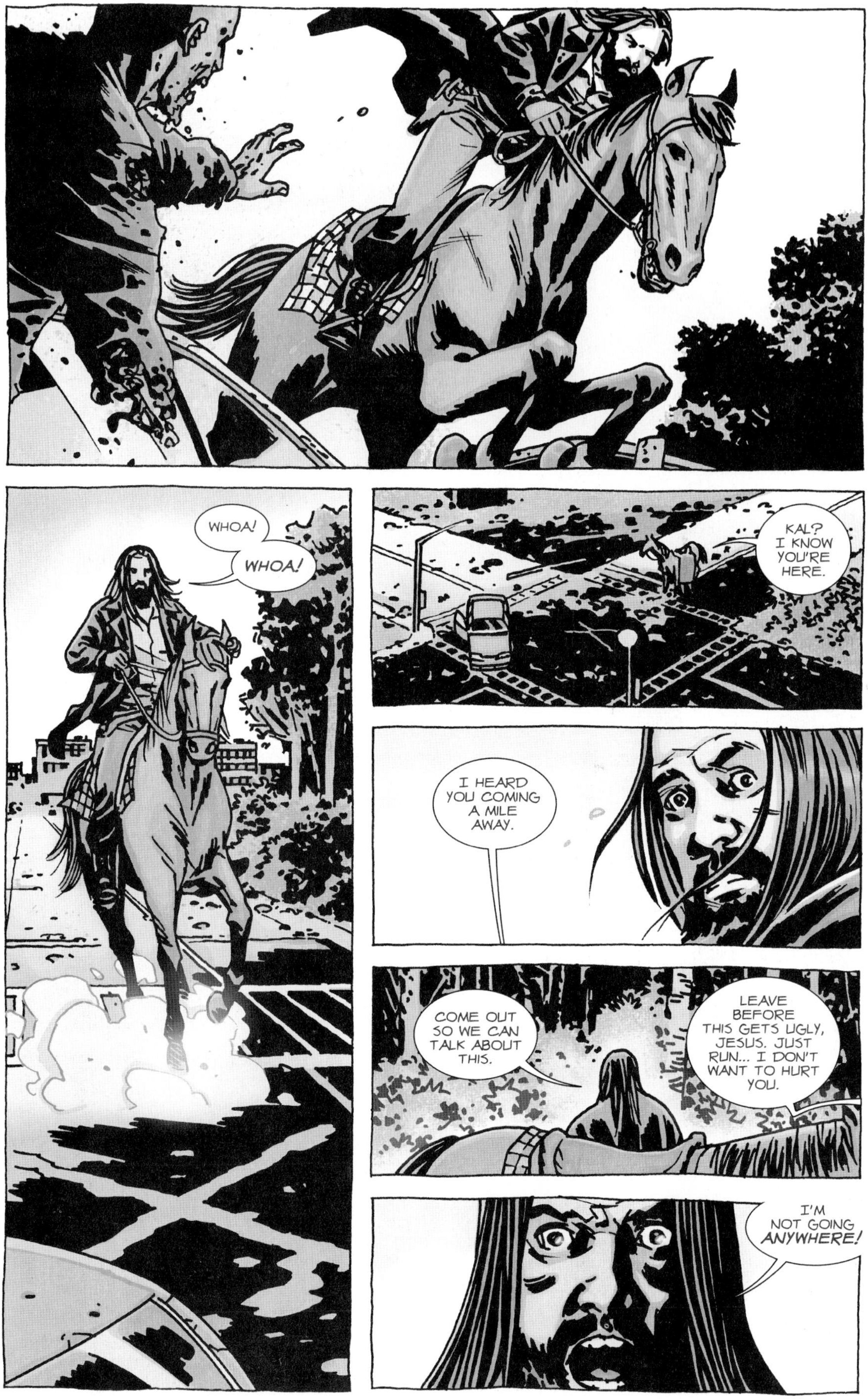
WHOA!
WHOA!
KAL? I KNOW YOU'RE HERE.
I HEARD YOU COMING A MILE AWAY.
COME OUT SO WE CAN TALK ABOUT THIS.
LEAVE BEFORE THIS GETS UGLY, JESUS. JUST RUN... I DON'T WANT TO HURT YOU.
I'M NOT GOING ANYWHERE!

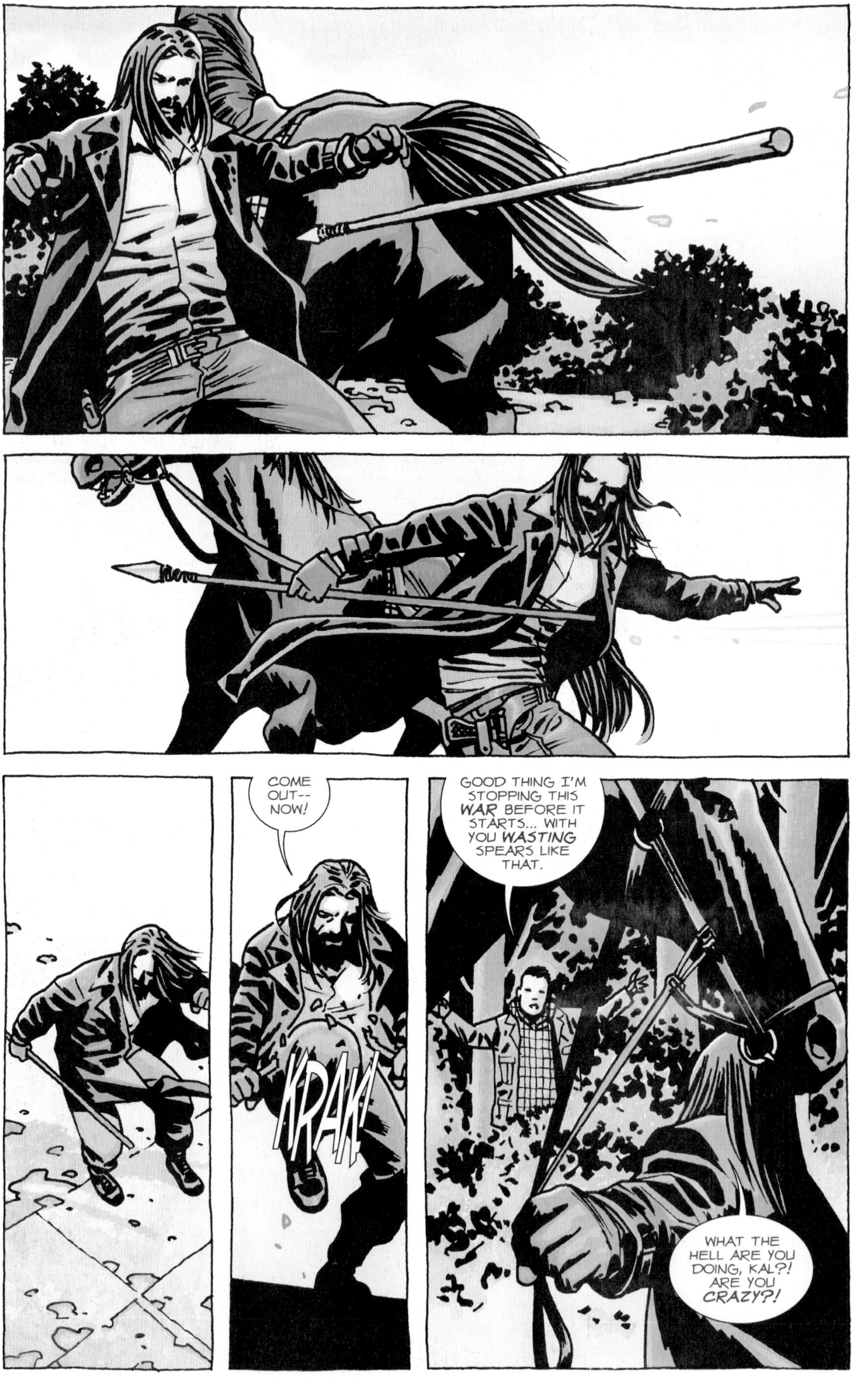
COME OUT-- NOW!
KRAK!
GOOD THING I'M STOPPING THIS WAR BEFORE IT STARTS... WITH YOU WASTING SPEARS LIKE THAT.
WHAT THE HELL ARE YOU DOING, KAL?! ARE YOU CRAZY?!

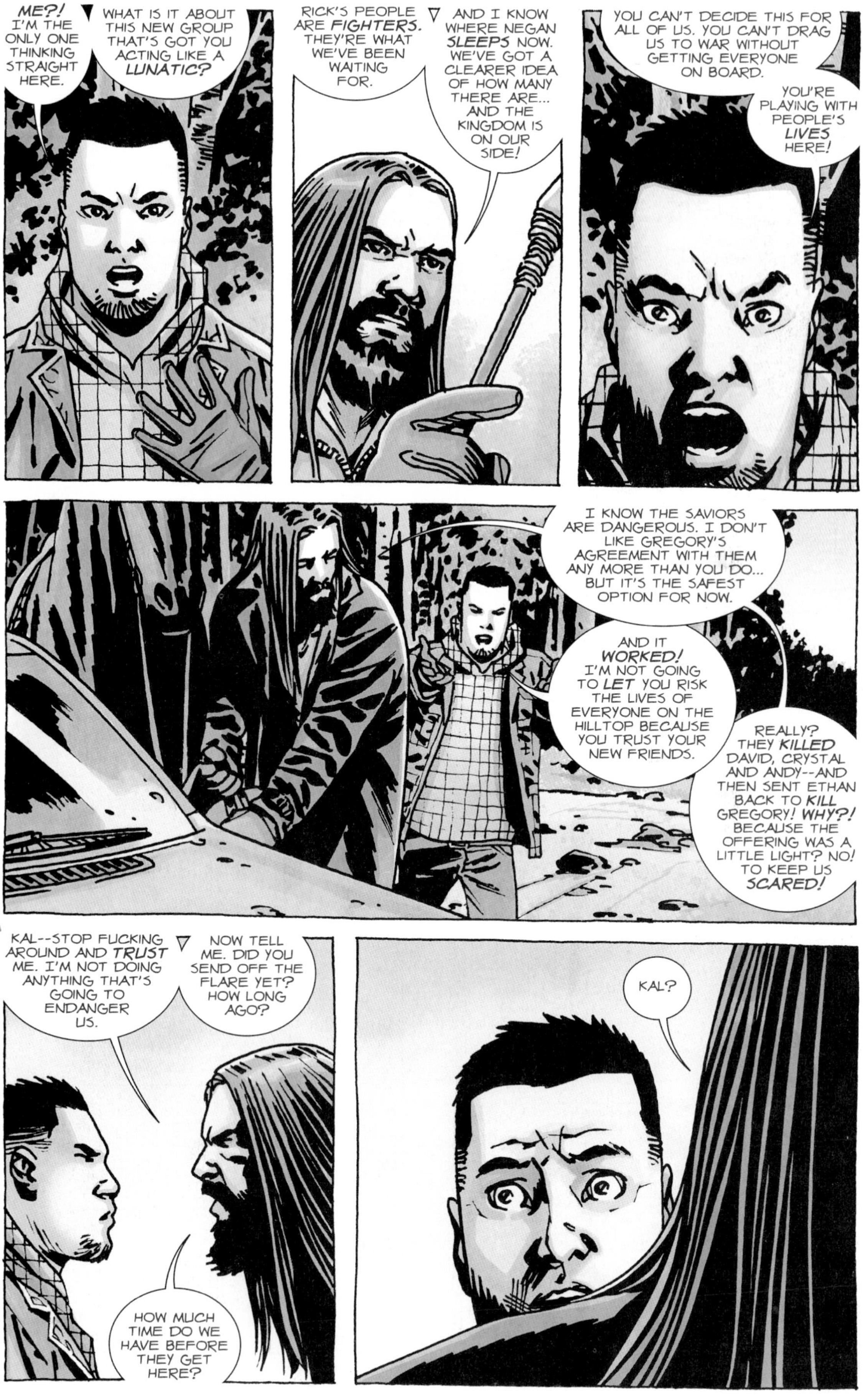
ME?! I'M THE ONLY ONE THINKING STRAIGHT HERE.
WHAT IS IT ABOUT THIS NEW GROUP THAT'S GOT YOU ACTING LIKE A LUNATIC?
RICK'S PEOPLE ARE FIGHTERS. THEY'RE WHAT WE'VE BEEN WAITING FOR.
AND I KNOW WHERE NEGAN SLEEPS NOW. WE'VE GOT A CLEARER IDEA OF HOW MANY THERE ARE... AND THE KINGDOM IS ON OUR SIDE!
YOU CAN'T DECIDE THIS FOR ALL OF US. YOU CAN'T DRAG US TO WAR WITHOUT GETTING EVERYONE ON BOARD.
YOU'RE PLAYING WITH PEOPLE'S LIVES HERE!
I KNOW THE SAVIORS ARE DANGEROUS. I DON'T LIKE GREGORY'S AGREEMENT WITH THEM ANY MORE THAN YOU DO... BUT IT'S THE SAFEST OPTION FOR NOW.
AND IT WORKED! I'M NOT GOING TO LET YOU RISK THE LIVES OF EVERYONE ON THE HILLTOP BECAUSE YOU TRUST YOUR NEW FRIENDS.
REALLY? THEY KILLED DAVID, CRYSTAL AND ANDY--AND THEN SENT ETHAN BACK TO KILL GREGORY! WHY?! BECAUSE THE OFFERING WAS A LITTLE LIGHT? NO! TO KEEP US SCARED!
KAL--STOP FUCKING AROUND AND TRUST ME. I'M NOT DOING ANYTHING THAT'S GOING TO ENDANGER US.
NOW TELL ME. DID YOU SEND OFF THE FLARE YET? HOW LONG AGO?
HOW MUCH TIME DO WE HAVE BEFORE THEY GET HERE?
KAL?

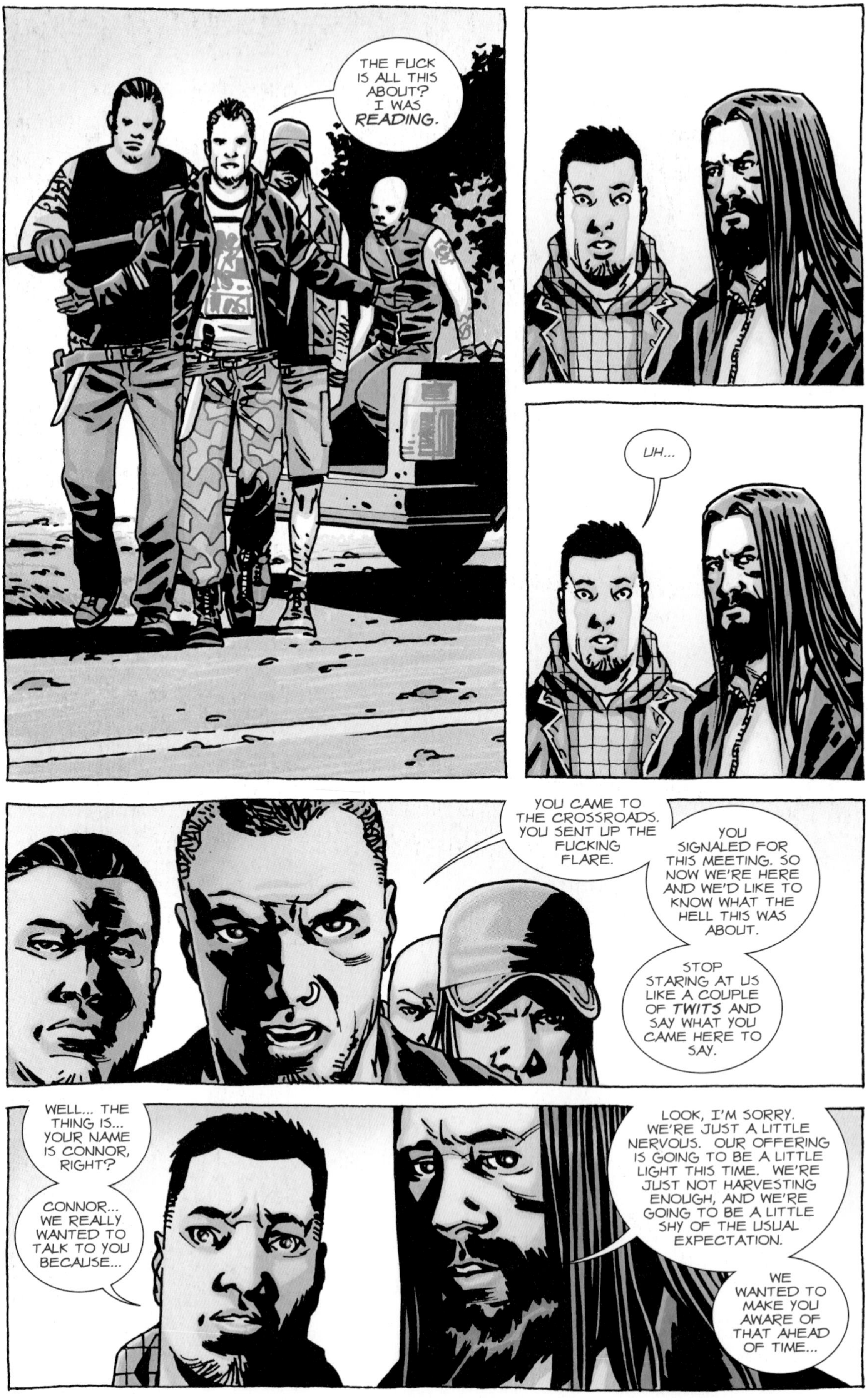
THE FUCK IS ALL THIS ABOUT? I WAS *READING*.
UH...
YOU CAME TO THE CROSSROADS. YOU SENT UP THE FUCKING FLARE.
YOU SIGNALED FOR THIS MEETING. SO NOW WE'RE HERE AND WE'D LIKE TO KNOW WHAT THE HELL THIS WAS ABOUT.
STOP STARING AT US LIKE A COUPLE OF *TWITS* AND SAY WHAT YOU CAME HERE TO SAY.
WELL... THE THING IS... YOUR NAME IS CONNOR, RIGHT?
CONNOR... WE REALLY WANTED TO TALK TO YOU BECAUSE...
LOOK, I'M SORRY. WE'RE JUST A LITTLE NERVOUS. OUR OFFERING IS GOING TO BE A LITTLE LIGHT THIS TIME. WE'RE JUST NOT HARVESTING ENOUGH, AND WE'RE GOING TO BE A LITTLE SHY OF THE USUAL EXPECTATION.
WE WANTED TO MAKE YOU AWARE OF THAT AHEAD OF TIME...

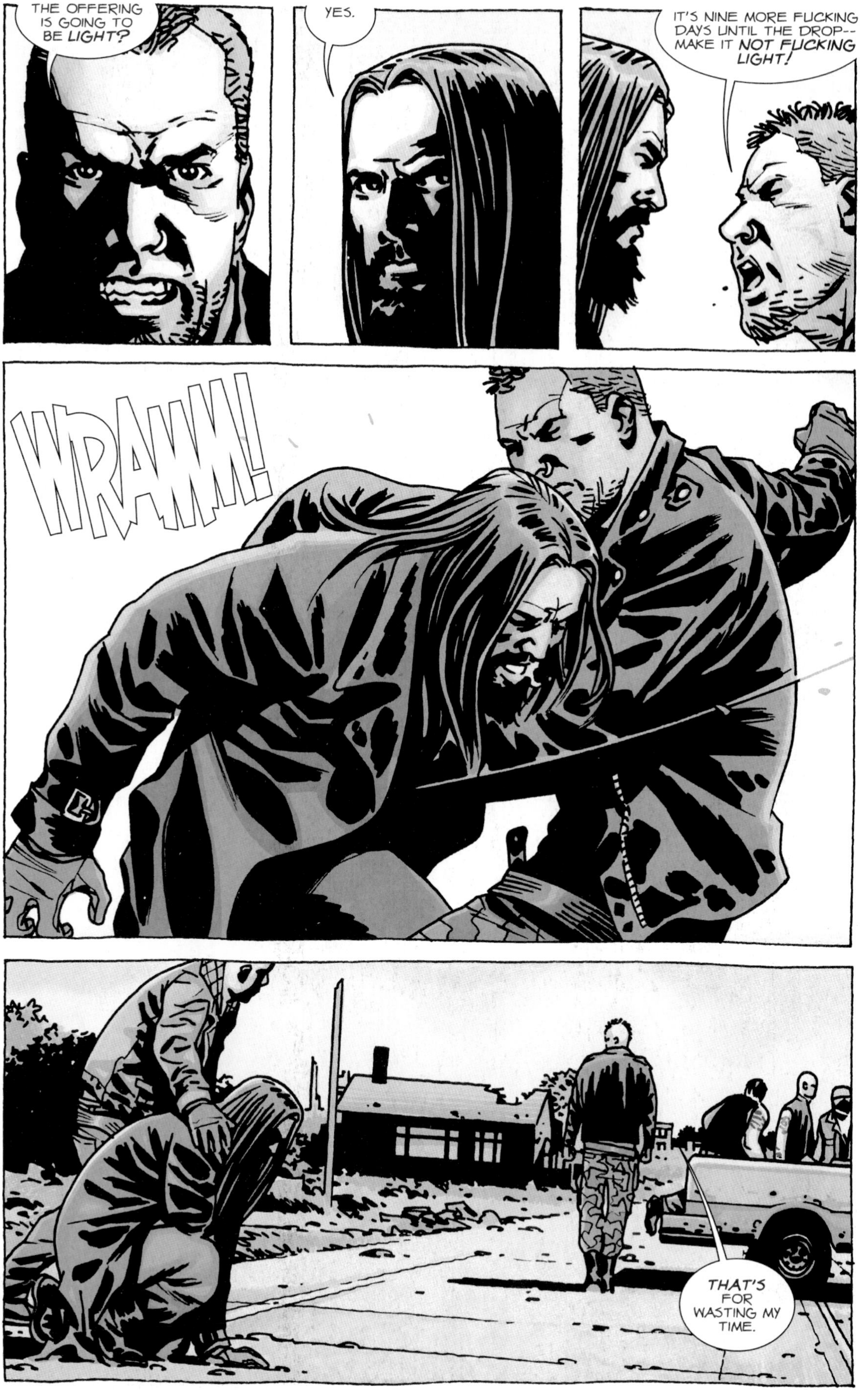
THE OFFERING IS GOING TO BE *LIGHT?*
YES.
IT'S NINE MORE FUCKING DAYS UNTIL THE DROP-- MAKE IT *NOT FUCKING LIGHT!*
WRAMM!
THAT'S FOR WASTING MY TIME.

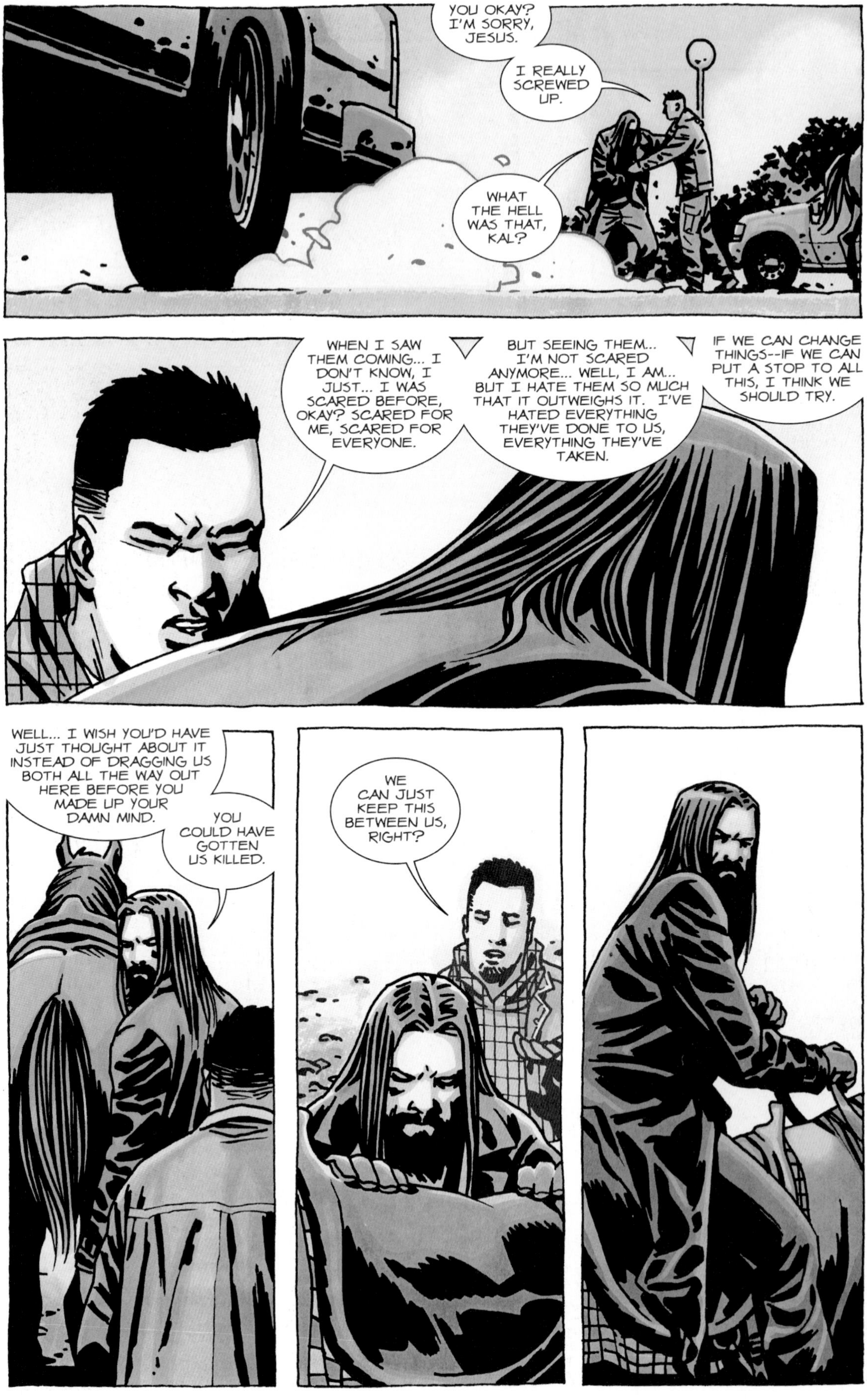
YOU OKAY? I'M SORRY, JESUS.
I REALLY SCREWED UP.
WHAT THE HELL WAS THAT, KAL?
WHEN I SAW THEM COMING... I DON'T KNOW, I JUST... I WAS SCARED BEFORE, OKAY? SCARED FOR ME, SCARED FOR EVERYONE.
BUT SEEING THEM... I'M NOT SCARED ANYMORE... WELL, I AM... BUT I HATE THEM SO MUCH THAT IT OUTWEIGHS IT. I'VE HATED EVERYTHING THEY'VE DONE TO US, EVERYTHING THEY'VE TAKEN.
IF WE CAN CHANGE THINGS--IF WE CAN PUT A STOP TO ALL THIS, I THINK WE SHOULD TRY.
WELL... I WISH YOU'D HAVE JUST THOUGHT ABOUT IT INSTEAD OF DRAGGING US BOTH ALL THE WAY OUT HERE BEFORE YOU MADE UP YOUR DAMN MIND.
YOU COULD HAVE GOTTEN US KILLED.
WE CAN JUST KEEP THIS BETWEEN US, RIGHT?

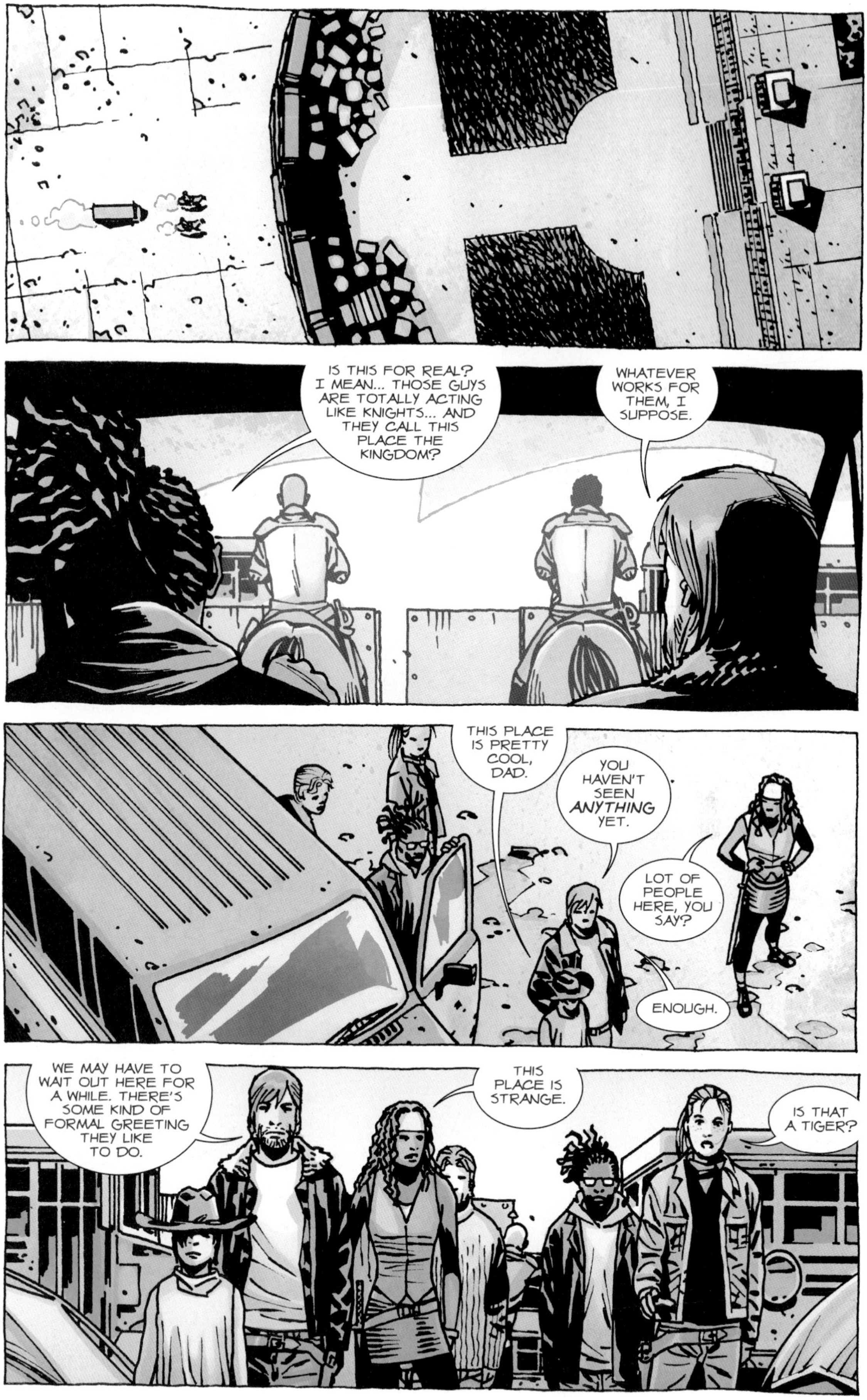
IS THIS FOR REAL? I MEAN... THOSE GUYS ARE TOTALLY ACTING LIKE KNIGHTS... AND THEY CALL THIS PLACE THE KINGDOM?
WHATEVER WORKS FOR THEM, I SUPPOSE.
THIS PLACE IS PRETTY COOL, DAD.
YOU HAVEN'T SEEN *ANYTHING* YET.
LOT OF PEOPLE HERE, YOU SAY?
ENOUGH.
WE MAY HAVE TO WAIT OUT HERE FOR A WHILE. THERE'S SOME KIND OF FORMAL GREETING THEY LIKE TO DO.
THIS PLACE IS STRANGE.
IS THAT A TIGER?

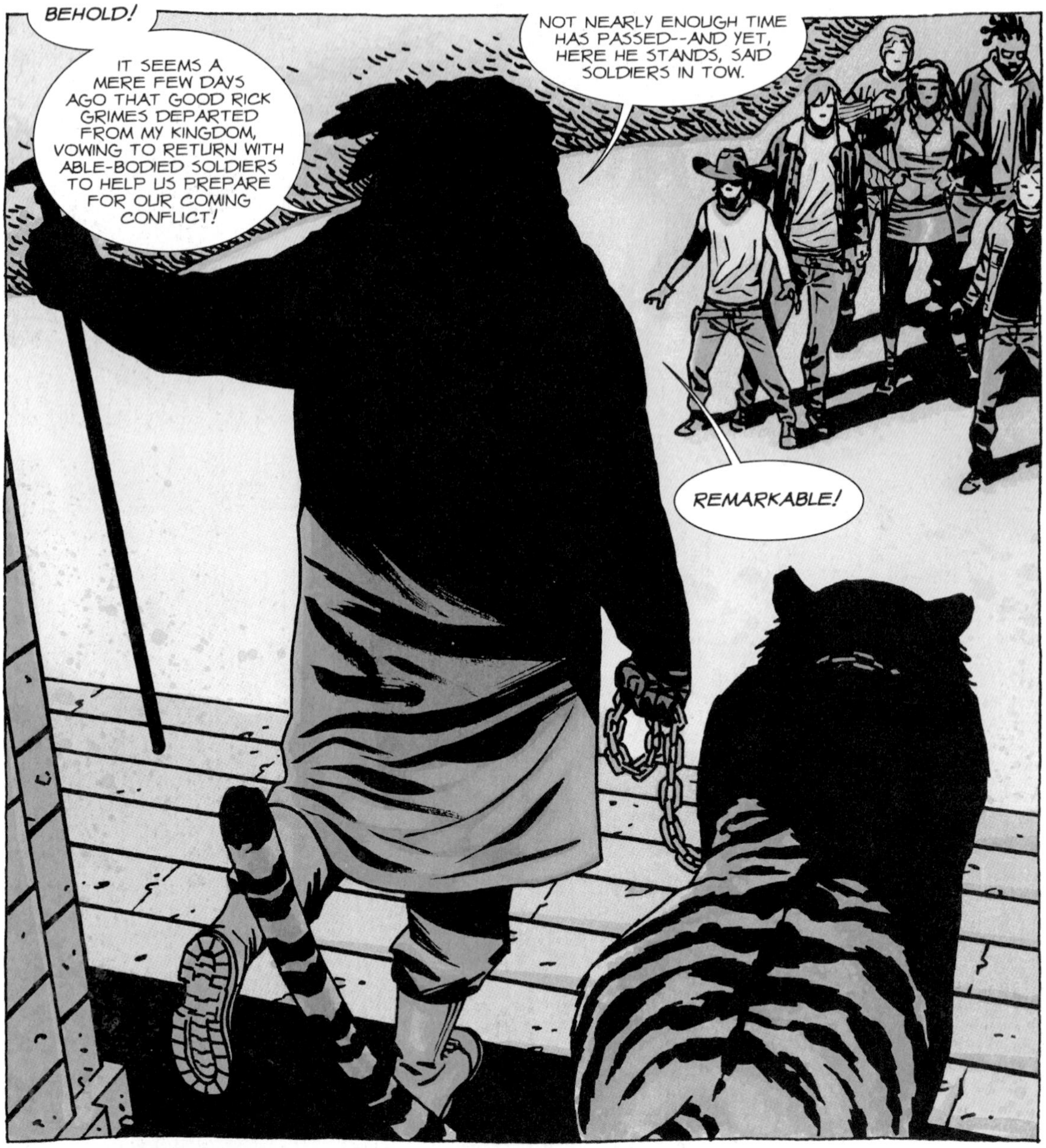
BEHOLD!
IT SEEMS A MERE FEW DAYS AGO THAT GOOD RICK GRIMES DEPARTED FROM MY KINGDOM, VOWING TO RETURN WITH ABLE-BODIED SOLDIERS TO HELP US PREPARE FOR OUR COMING CONFLICT!
NOT NEARLY ENOUGH TIME HAS PASSED--AND YET, HERE HE STANDS, SAID SOLDIERS IN TOW.
REMARKABLE!

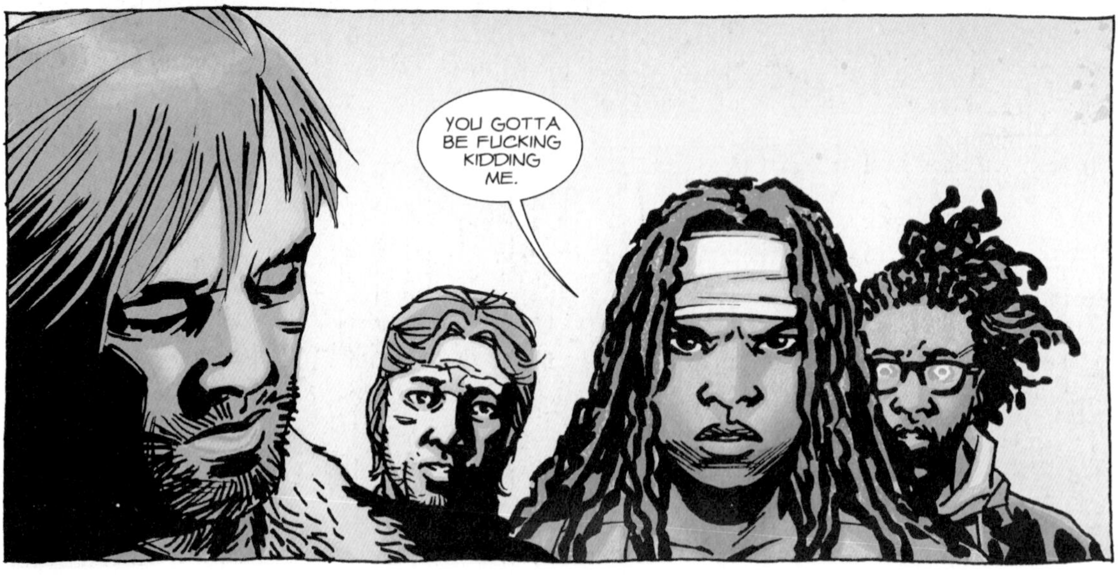
YOU GOTTA BE FUCKING KIDDING ME.

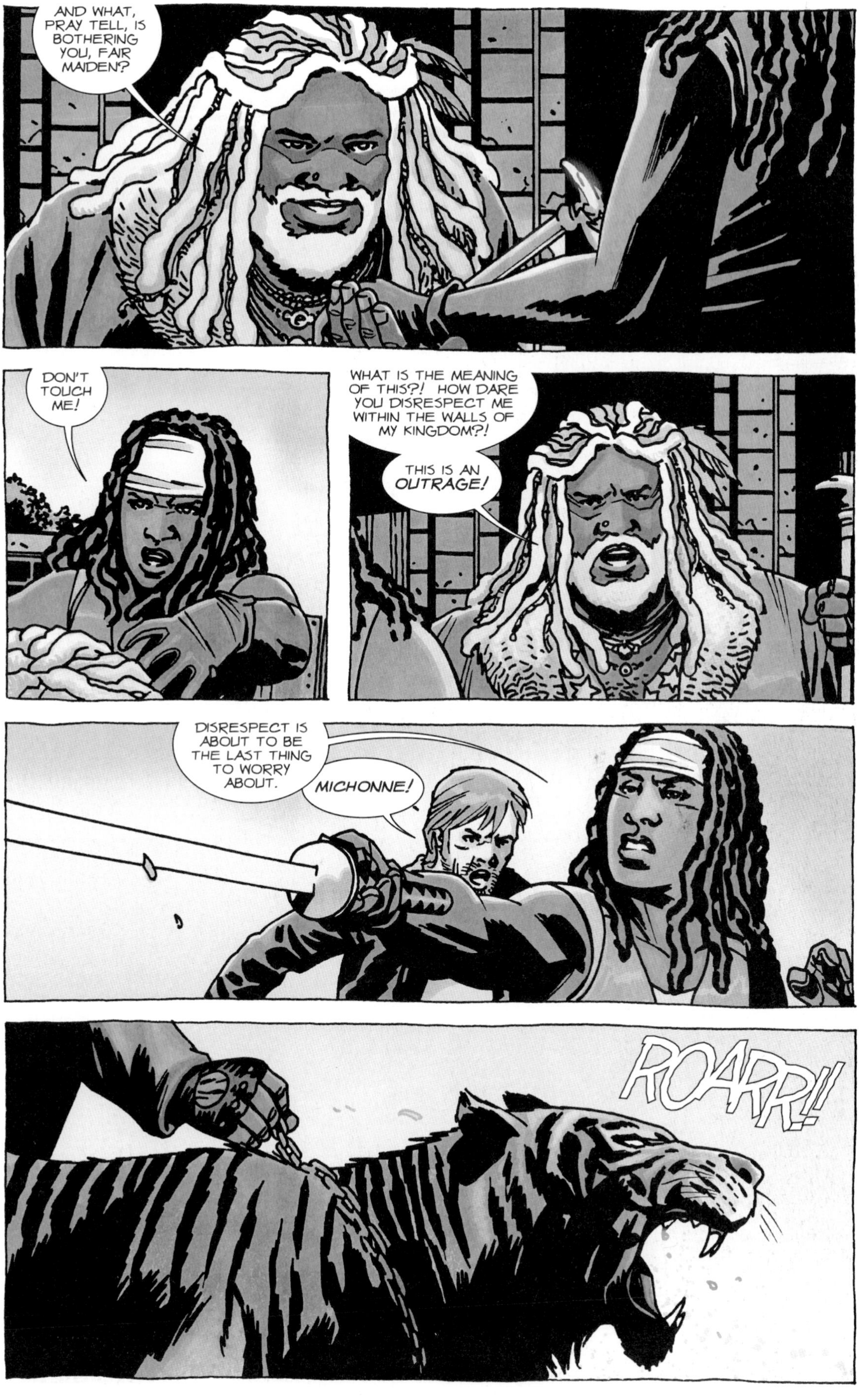
AND WHAT, PRAY TELL, IS BOTHERING YOU, FAIR MAIDEN?
DON'T TOUCH ME!
WHAT IS THE MEANING OF THIS?! HOW DARE YOU DISRESPECT ME WITHIN THE WALLS OF MY KINGDOM?!
THIS IS AN OUTRAGE!
DISRESPECT IS ABOUT TO BE THE LAST THING TO WORRY ABOUT.
MICHONNE!
ROARR!!

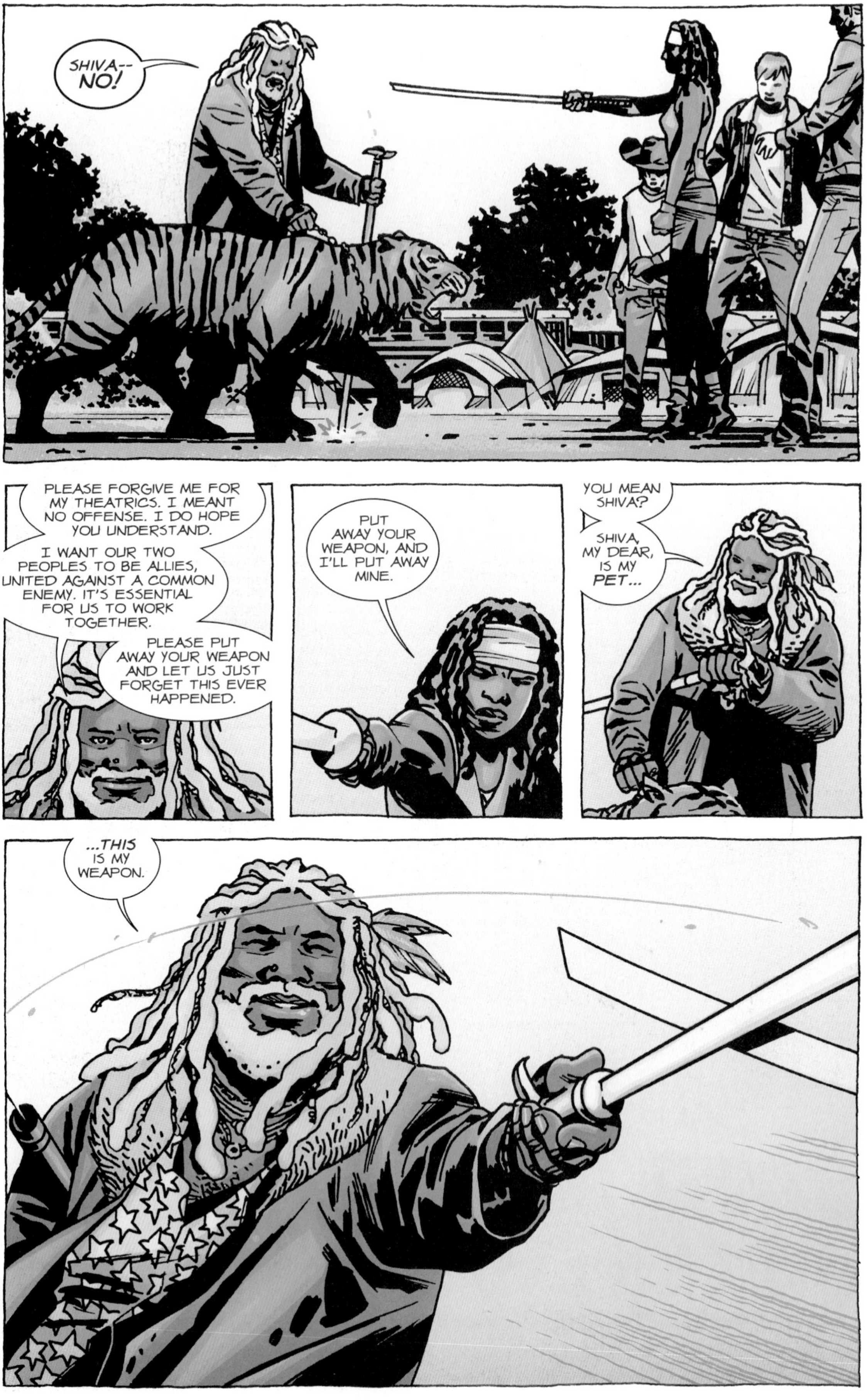
SHIVA-- NO!
PLEASE FORGIVE ME FOR MY THEATRICS. I MEANT NO OFFENSE. I DO HOPE YOU UNDERSTAND.
I WANT OUR TWO PEOPLES TO BE ALLIES, UNITED AGAINST A COMMON ENEMY. IT'S ESSENTIAL FOR US TO WORK TOGETHER.
PLEASE PUT AWAY YOUR WEAPON AND LET US JUST FORGET THIS EVER HAPPENED.
PUT AWAY YOUR WEAPON, AND I'LL PUT AWAY MINE.
YOU MEAN SHIVA?
SHIVA, MY DEAR, IS MY PET...
...THIS IS MY WEAPON.

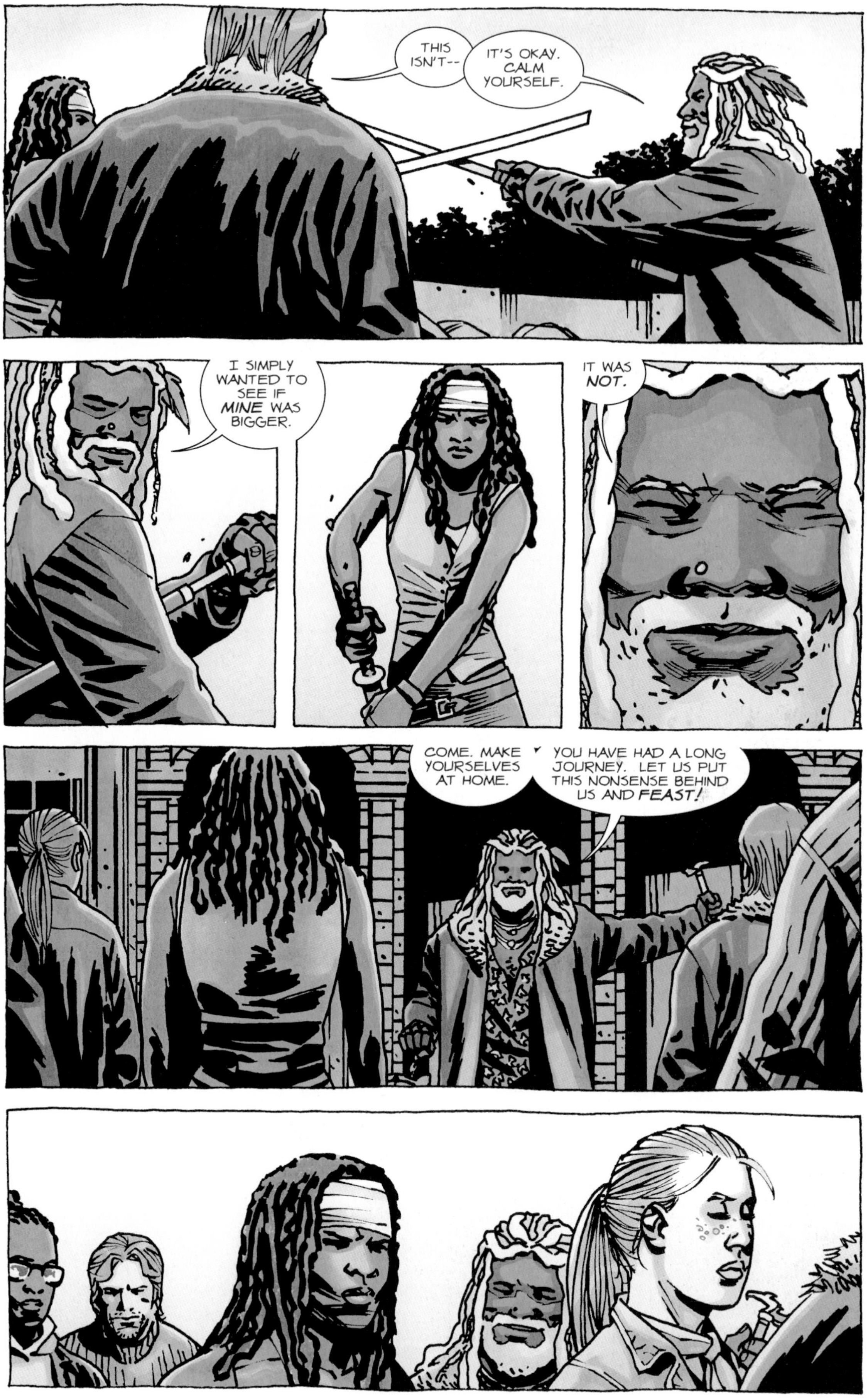
THIS ISN'T--
IT'S OKAY. CALM YOURSELF.
I SIMPLY WANTED TO SEE IF MINE WAS BIGGER.
IT WAS NOT.
COME. MAKE YOURSELVES AT HOME.
YOU HAVE HAD A LONG JOURNEY. LET US PUT THIS NONSENSE BEHIND US AND FEAST!

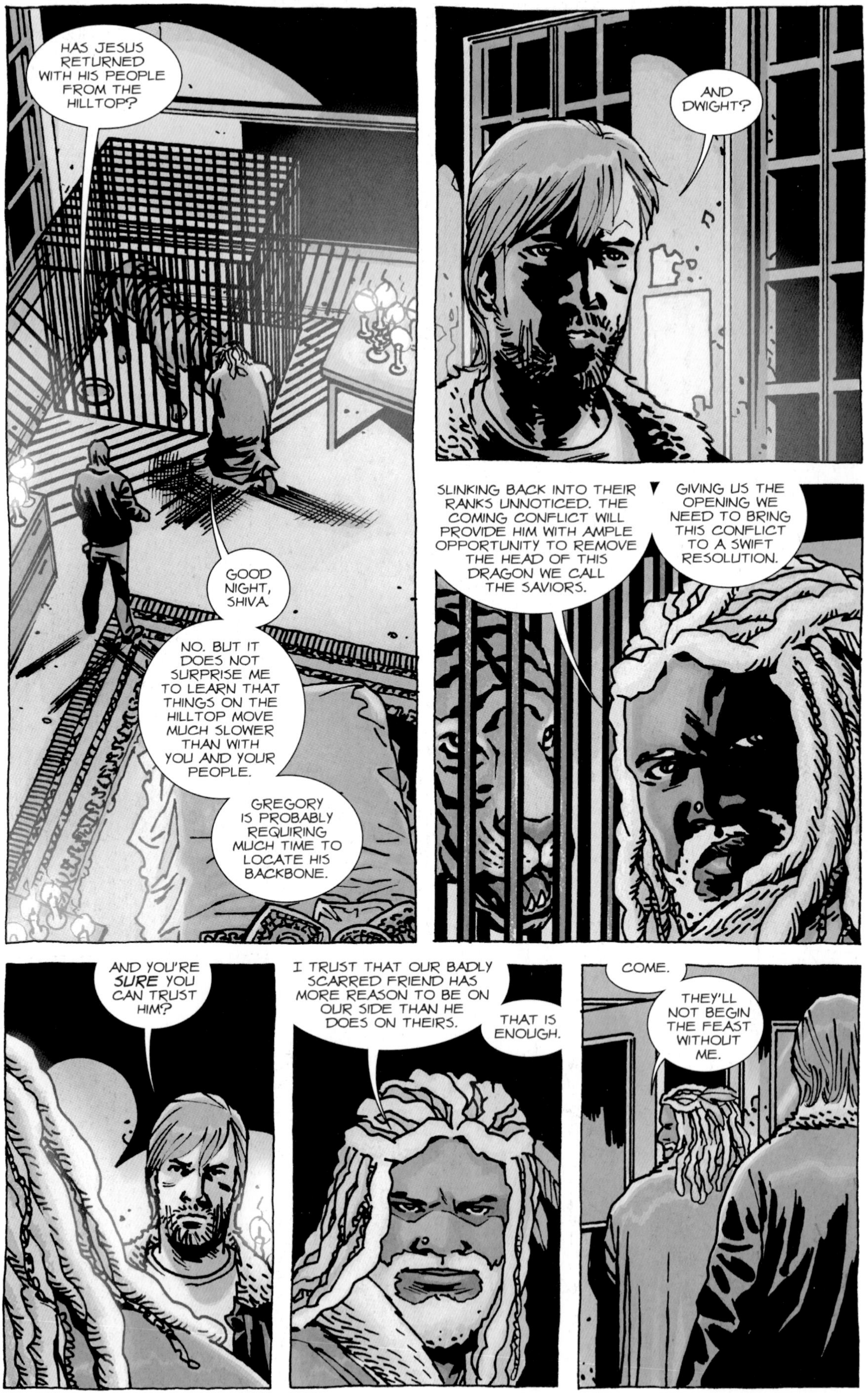
HAS JESUS RETURNED WITH HIS PEOPLE FROM THE HILLTOP?
GOOD NIGHT, SHIVA.
NO. BUT IT DOES NOT SURPRISE ME TO LEARN THAT THINGS ON THE HILLTOP MOVE MUCH SLOWER THAN WITH YOU AND YOUR PEOPLE.
GREGORY IS PROBABLY REQUIRING MUCH TIME TO LOCATE HIS BACKBONE.
AND DWIGHT?
SLINKING BACK INTO THEIR RANKS UNNOTICED. THE COMING CONFLICT WILL PROVIDE HIM WITH AMPLE OPPORTUNITY TO REMOVE THE HEAD OF THIS DRAGON WE CALL THE SAVIORS.
GIVING US THE OPENING WE NEED TO BRING THIS CONFLICT TO A SWIFT RESOLUTION.
AND YOU'RE *SURE* YOU CAN TRUST HIM?
I TRUST THAT OUR BADLY SCARRED FRIEND HAS MORE REASON TO BE ON OUR SIDE THAN HE DOES ON THEIRS.
THAT IS ENOUGH.
COME.
THEY'LL NOT BEGIN THE FEAST WITHOUT ME.

DINE! ENJOY THE BOAR WE'VE SLAUGHTERED IN YOUR HONOR!

EAT AND BE MERRY! FOR TOMORROW WE GO TO WAR!

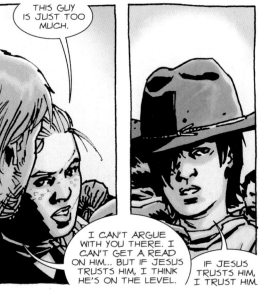

THIS GUY IS JUST TOO MUCH.

I CAN'T ARGUE WITH YOU THERE. I CAN'T GET A READ ON HIM... BUT IF JESUS TRUSTS HIM, I THINK HE'S ON THE LEVEL.

IF JESUS TRUSTS HIM, I TRUST HIM.

TO NEW FRIENDS-- AND THE END OF OLD ENEMIES.

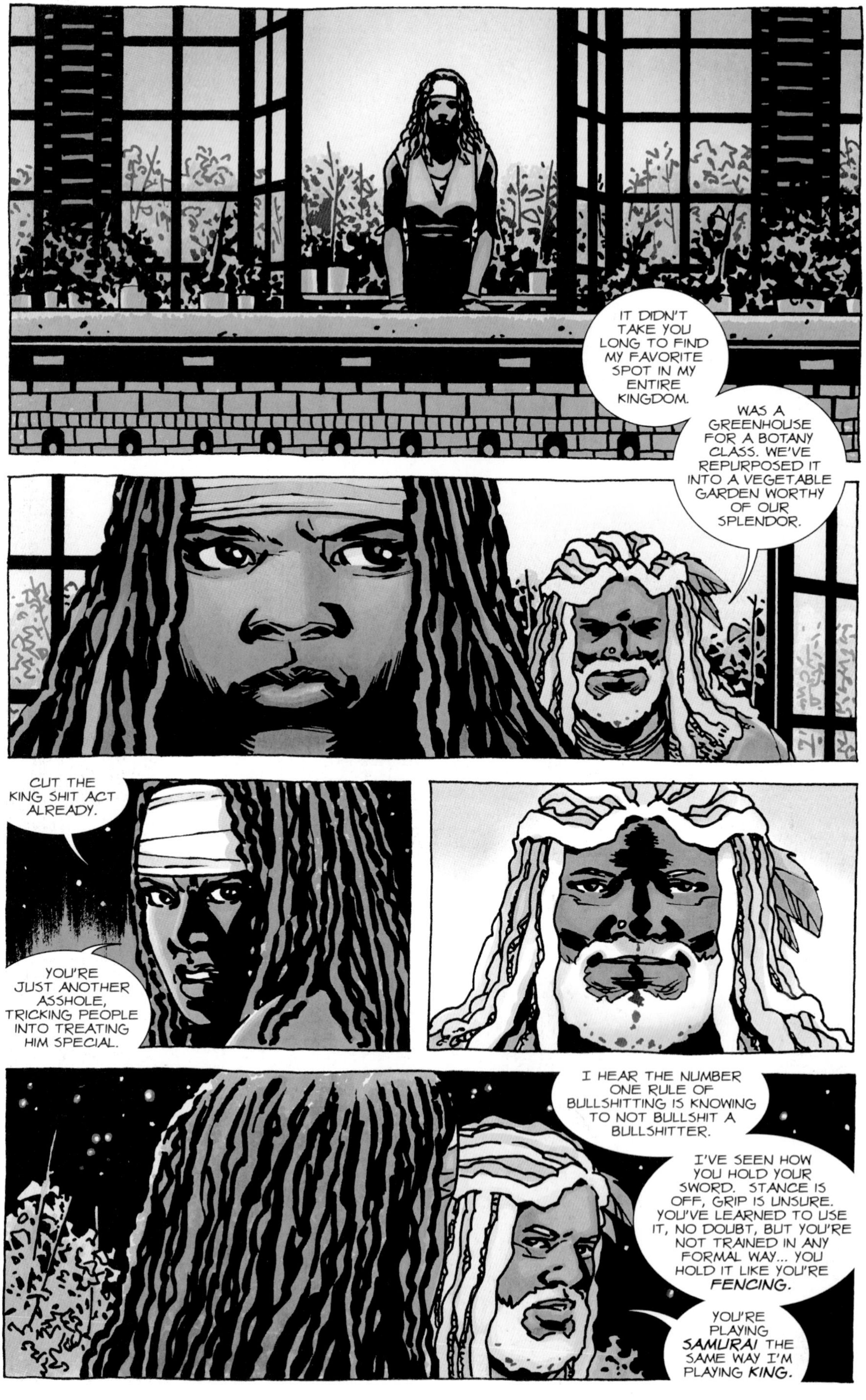
IT DIDN'T TAKE YOU LONG TO FIND MY FAVORITE SPOT IN MY ENTIRE KINGDOM.
WAS A GREENHOUSE FOR A BOTANY CLASS. WE'VE REPURPOSED IT INTO A VEGETABLE GARDEN WORTHY OF OUR SPLENDOR.
CUT THE KING SHIT ACT ALREADY.
YOU'RE JUST ANOTHER ASSHOLE, TRICKING PEOPLE INTO TREATING HIM SPECIAL.
I HEAR THE NUMBER ONE RULE OF BULLSHITTING IS KNOWING TO NOT BULLSHIT A BULLSHITTER.
I'VE SEEN HOW YOU HOLD YOUR SWORD. STANCE IS OFF, GRIP IS UNSURE. YOU'VE LEARNED TO USE IT, NO DOUBT, BUT YOU'RE NOT TRAINED IN ANY FORMAL WAY... YOU HOLD IT LIKE YOU'RE ***FENCING.***
YOU'RE PLAYING ***SAMURAI*** THE SAME WAY I'M PLAYING ***KING.***

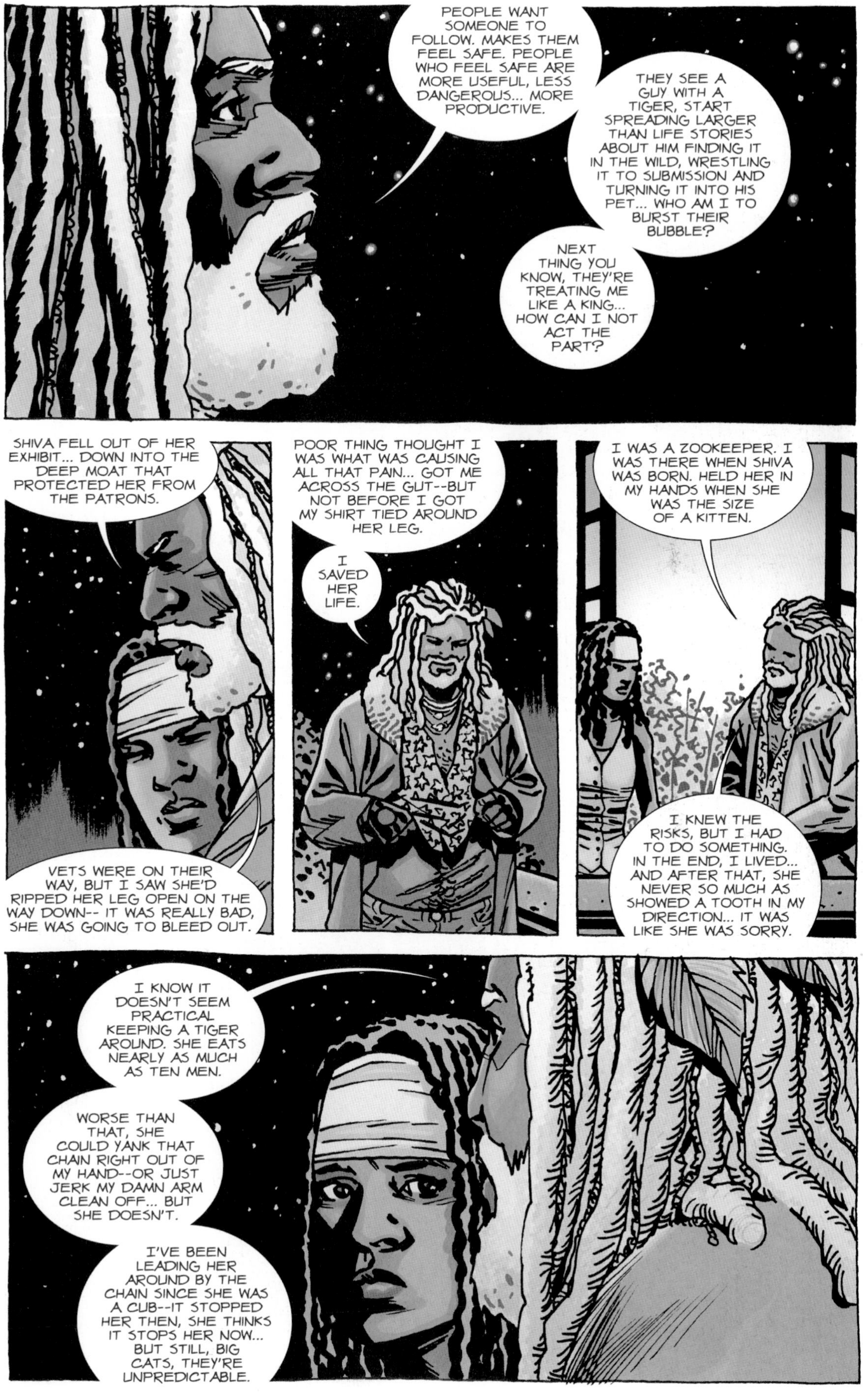
PEOPLE WANT SOMEONE TO FOLLOW. MAKES THEM FEEL SAFE. PEOPLE WHO FEEL SAFE ARE MORE USEFUL, LESS DANGEROUS... MORE PRODUCTIVE.
THEY SEE A GUY WITH A TIGER, START SPREADING LARGER THAN LIFE STORIES ABOUT HIM FINDING IT IN THE WILD, WRESTLING IT TO SUBMISSION AND TURNING IT INTO HIS PET... WHO AM I TO BURST THEIR BUBBLE?
NEXT THING YOU KNOW, THEY'RE TREATING ME LIKE A KING... HOW CAN I NOT ACT THE PART?
SHIVA FELL OUT OF HER EXHIBIT... DOWN INTO THE DEEP MOAT THAT PROTECTED HER FROM THE PATRONS.
VETS WERE ON THEIR WAY, BUT I SAW SHE'D RIPPED HER LEG OPEN ON THE WAY DOWN-- IT WAS REALLY BAD, SHE WAS GOING TO BLEED OUT.
POOR THING THOUGHT I WAS WHAT WAS CAUSING ALL THAT PAIN... GOT ME ACROSS THE GUT--BUT NOT BEFORE I GOT MY SHIRT TIED AROUND HER LEG.
I SAVED HER LIFE.
I WAS A ZOOKEEPER. I WAS THERE WHEN SHIVA WAS BORN. HELD HER IN MY HANDS WHEN SHE WAS THE SIZE OF A KITTEN.
I KNEW THE RISKS, BUT I HAD TO DO SOMETHING. IN THE END, I LIVED... AND AFTER THAT, SHE NEVER SO MUCH AS SHOWED A TOOTH IN MY DIRECTION... IT WAS LIKE SHE WAS SORRY.
I KNOW IT DOESN'T SEEM PRACTICAL KEEPING A TIGER AROUND. SHE EATS NEARLY AS MUCH AS TEN MEN.
WORSE THAN THAT, SHE COULD YANK THAT CHAIN RIGHT OUT OF MY HAND--OR JUST JERK MY DAMN ARM CLEAN OFF... BUT SHE DOESN'T.
I'VE BEEN LEADING HER AROUND BY THE CHAIN SINCE SHE WAS A CUB--IT STOPPED HER THEN, SHE THINKS IT STOPS HER NOW... BUT STILL, BIG CATS, THEY'RE UNPREDICTABLE.

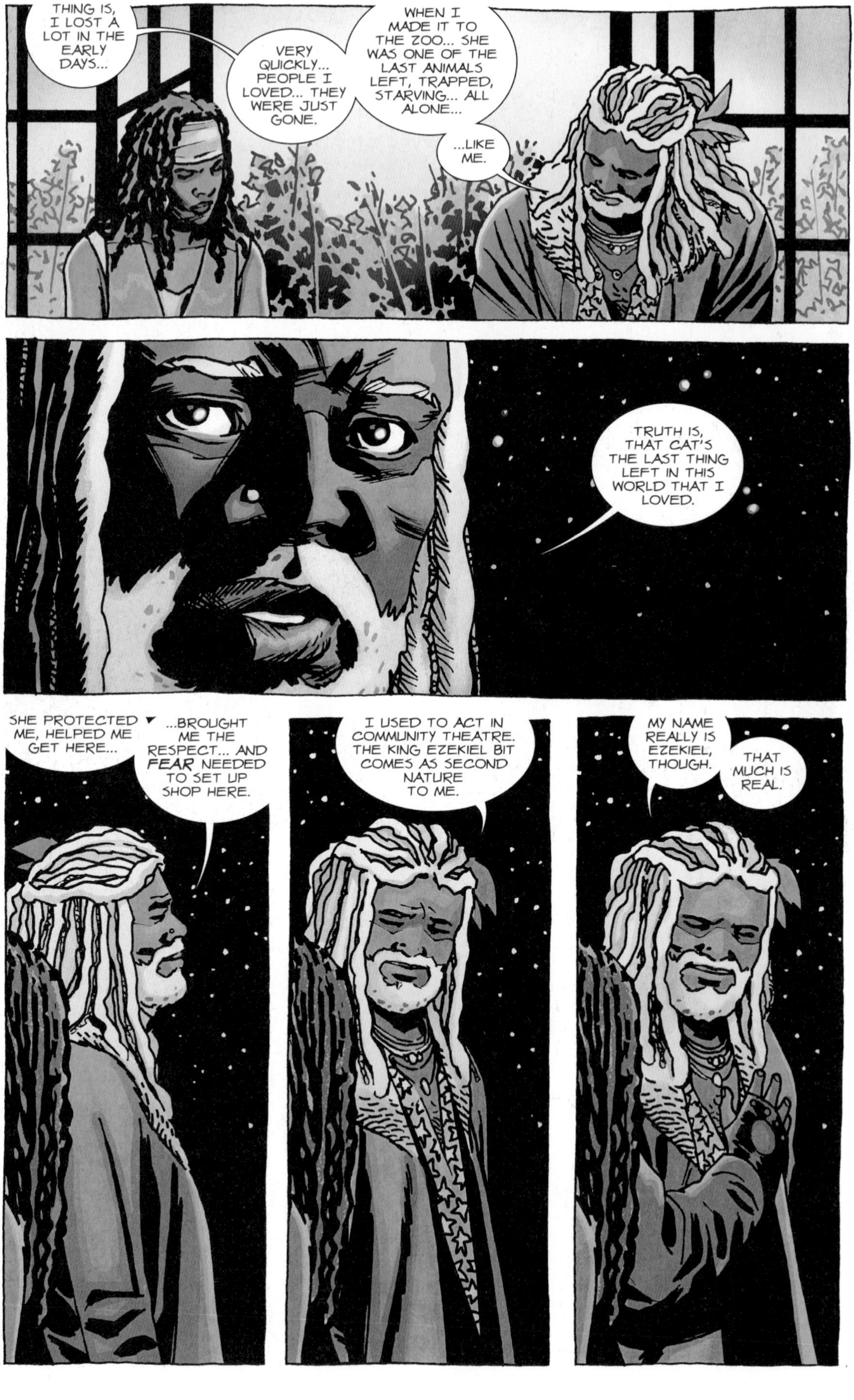
THING IS, I LOST A LOT IN THE EARLY DAYS...
VERY QUICKLY... PEOPLE I LOVED... THEY WERE JUST GONE.
WHEN I MADE IT TO THE ZOO... SHE WAS ONE OF THE LAST ANIMALS LEFT, TRAPPED, STARVING... ALL ALONE...
...LIKE ME.
TRUTH IS, THAT CAT'S THE LAST THING LEFT IN THIS WORLD THAT I LOVED.
SHE PROTECTED ME, HELPED ME GET HERE...
...BROUGHT ME THE RESPECT... AND FEAR NEEDED TO SET UP SHOP HERE.
I USED TO ACT IN COMMUNITY THEATRE. THE KING EZEKIEL BIT COMES AS SECOND NATURE TO ME.
MY NAME REALLY IS EZEKIEL, THOUGH.
THAT MUCH IS REAL.

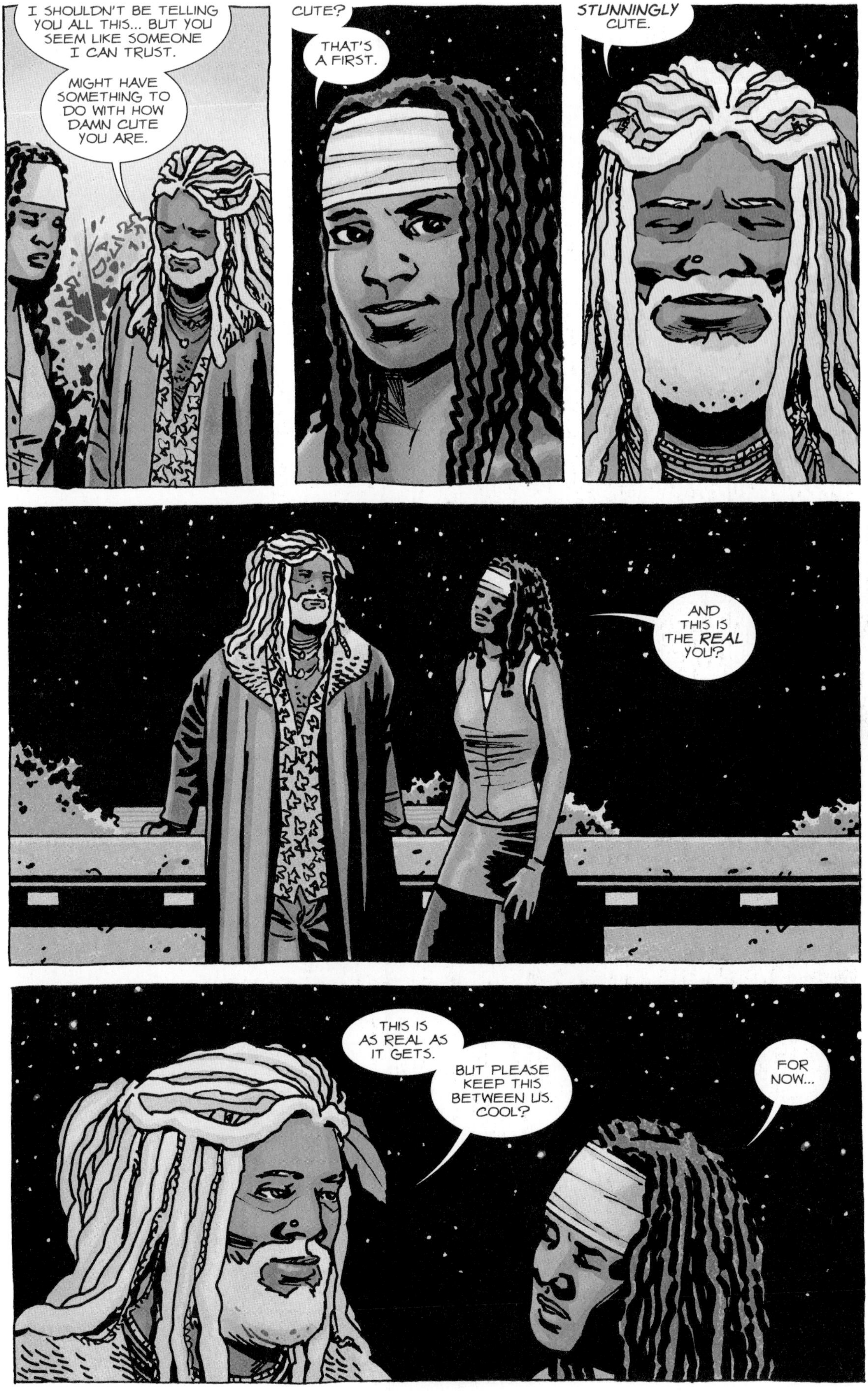
I SHOULDN'T BE TELLING YOU ALL THIS... BUT YOU SEEM LIKE SOMEONE I CAN TRUST.
MIGHT HAVE SOMETHING TO DO WITH HOW DAMN CUTE YOU ARE.
CUTE?
THAT'S A FIRST.
STUNNINGLY CUTE.
AND THIS IS THE REAL YOU?
THIS IS AS REAL AS IT GETS.
BUT PLEASE KEEP THIS BETWEEN US. COOL?
FOR NOW...

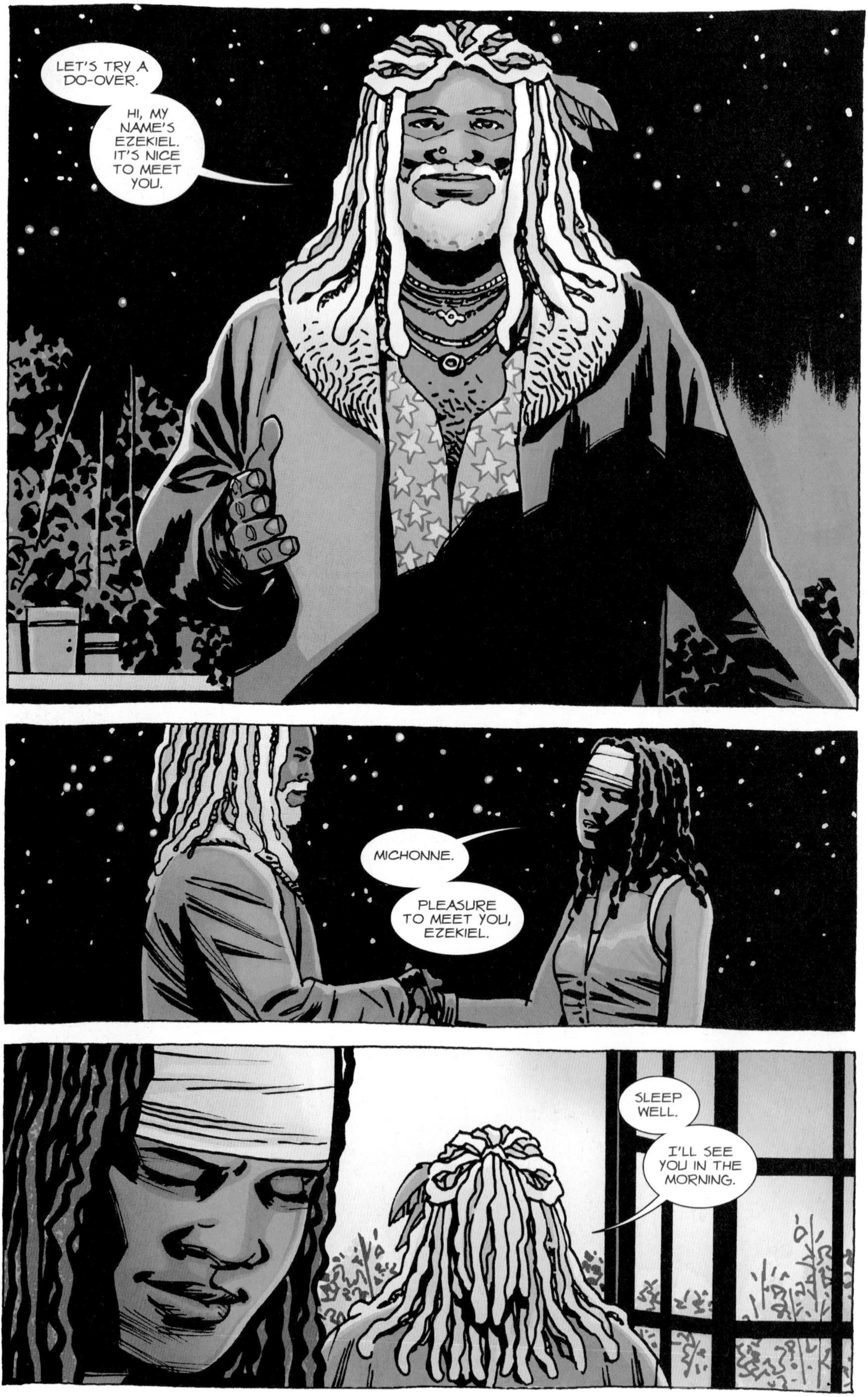
LET'S TRY A DO-OVER.
HI, MY NAME'S EZEKIEL. IT'S NICE TO MEET YOU.
MICHONNE.
PLEASURE TO MEET YOU, EZEKIEL.
SLEEP WELL.
I'LL SEE YOU IN THE MORNING.

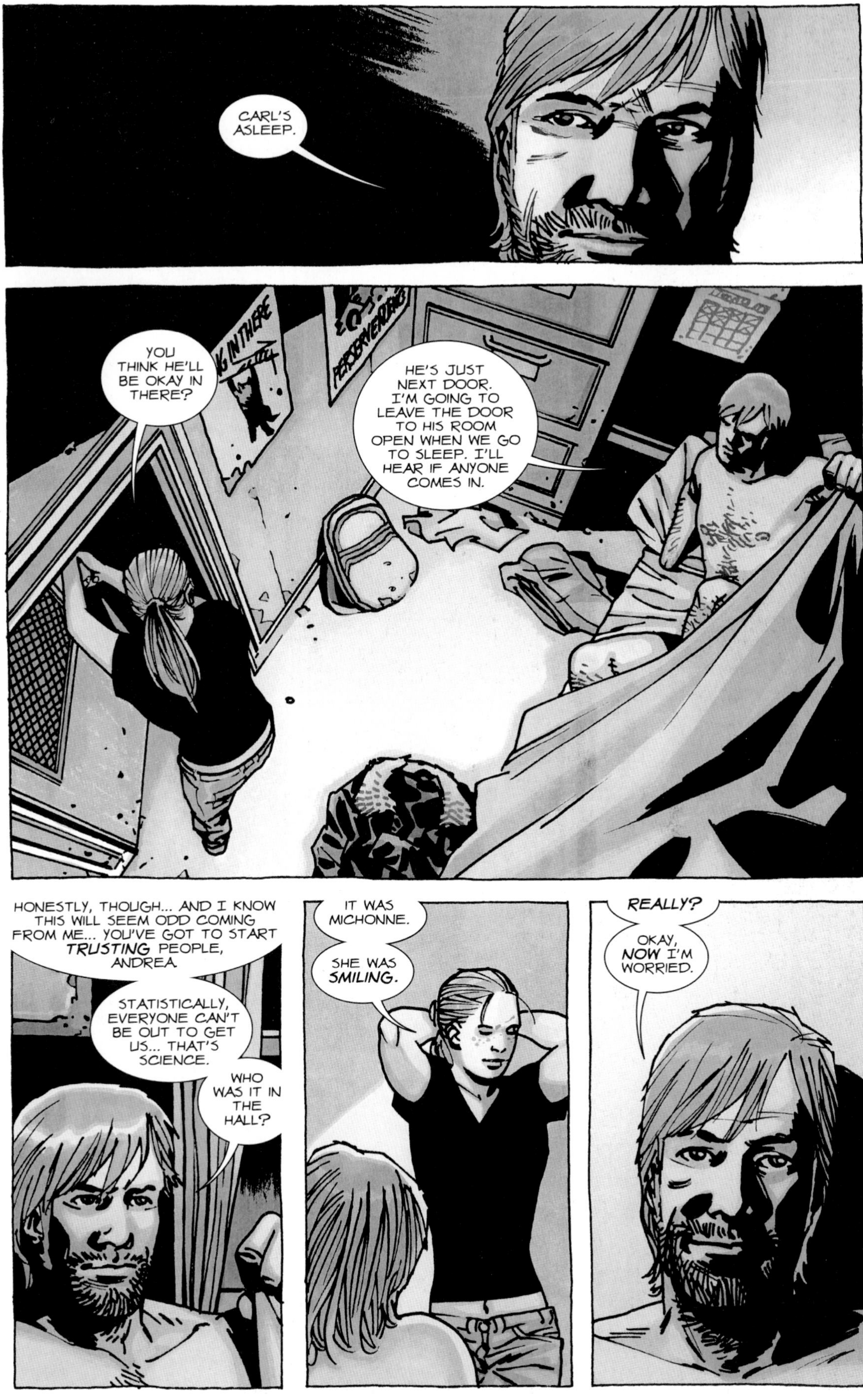
CARL'S ASLEEP.
YOU THINK HE'LL BE OKAY IN THERE?
HE'S JUST NEXT DOOR. I'M GOING TO LEAVE THE DOOR TO HIS ROOM OPEN WHEN WE GO TO SLEEP. I'LL HEAR IF ANYONE COMES IN.
HONESTLY, THOUGH... AND I KNOW THIS WILL SEEM ODD COMING FROM ME... YOU'VE GOT TO START TRUSTING PEOPLE, ANDREA.
STATISTICALLY, EVERYONE CAN'T BE OUT TO GET US... THAT'S SCIENCE.
WHO WAS IT IN THE HALL?
IT WAS MICHONNE.
SHE WAS SMILING.
REALLY?
OKAY, NOW I'M WORRIED.

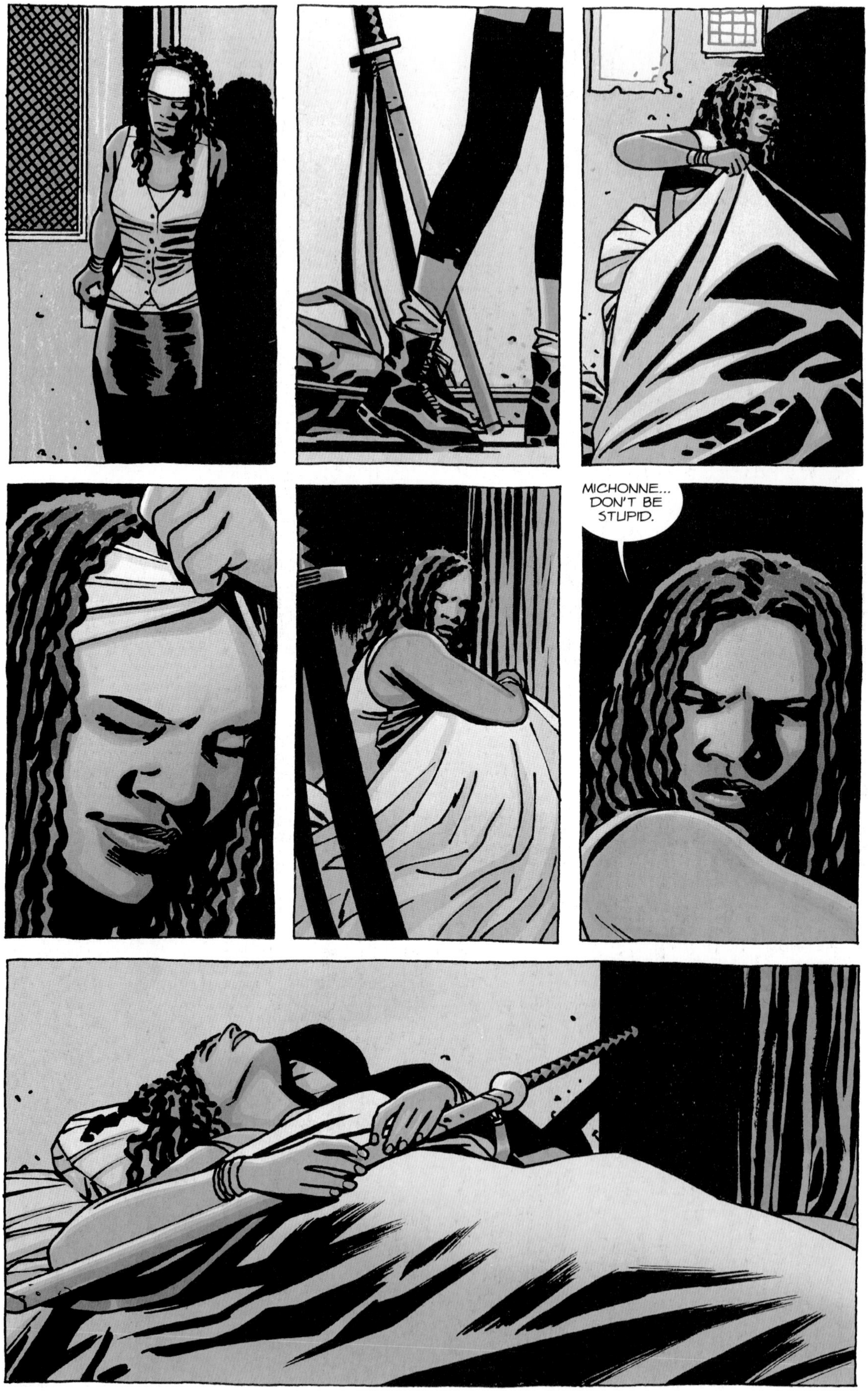
MICHONNE... DON'T BE STUPID.

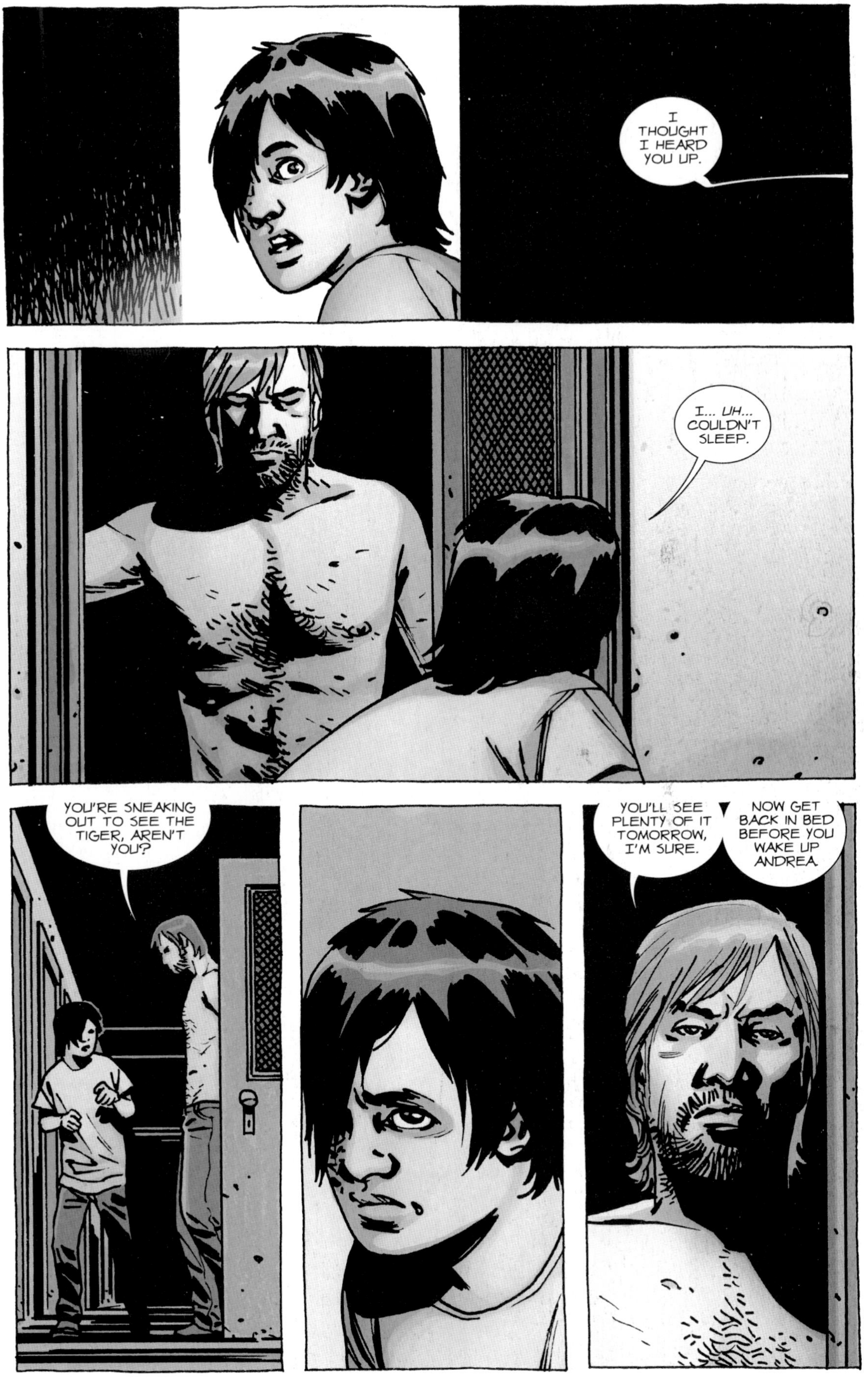
I THOUGHT I HEARD YOU UP.
I... UH... COULDN'T SLEEP.
YOU'RE SNEAKING OUT TO SEE THE TIGER, AREN'T YOU?
YOU'LL SEE PLENTY OF IT TOMORROW, I'M SURE.
NOW GET BACK IN BED BEFORE YOU WAKE UP ANDREA.

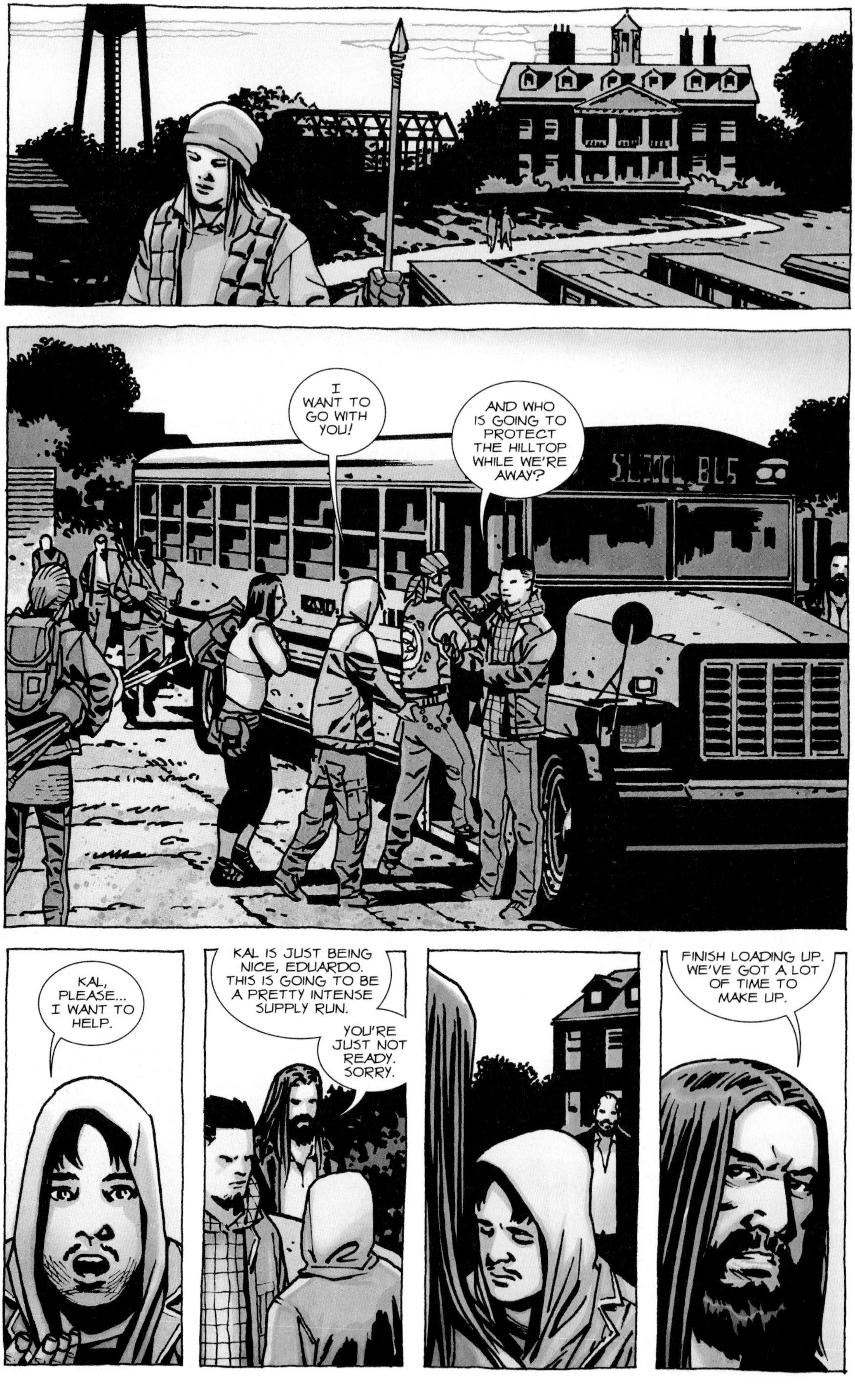

I WANT TO GO WITH YOU!
AND WHO IS GOING TO PROTECT THE HILLTOP WHILE WE'RE AWAY?
KAL, PLEASE... I WANT TO HELP.
KAL IS JUST BEING NICE, EDUARDO. THIS IS GOING TO BE A PRETTY INTENSE SUPPLY RUN.
YOU'RE JUST NOT READY. SORRY.
FINISH LOADING UP. WE'VE GOT A LOT OF TIME TO MAKE UP.

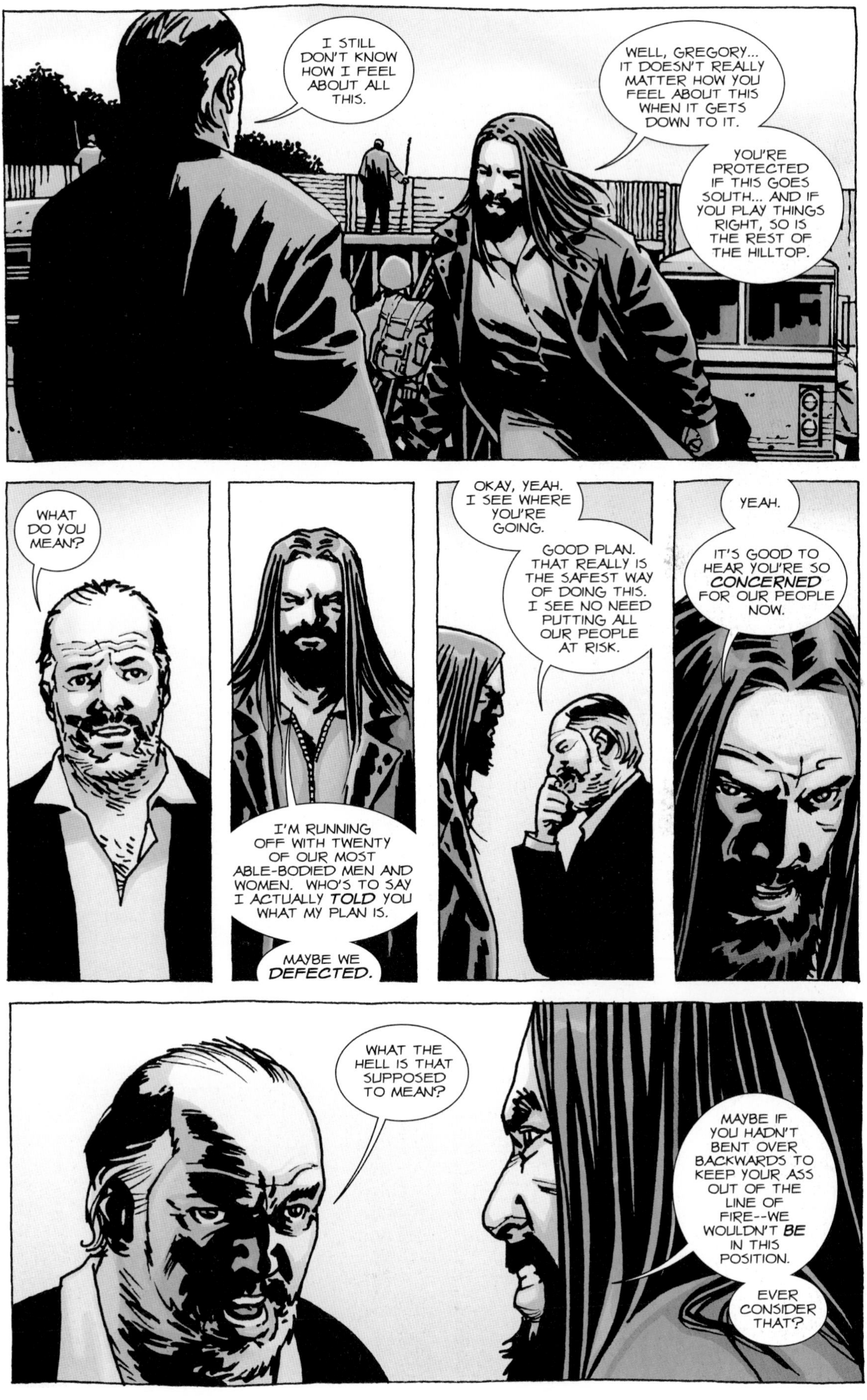
I STILL DON'T KNOW HOW I FEEL ABOUT ALL THIS.
WELL, GREGORY... IT DOESN'T REALLY MATTER HOW YOU FEEL ABOUT THIS WHEN IT GETS DOWN TO IT.
YOU'RE PROTECTED IF THIS GOES SOUTH... AND IF YOU PLAY THINGS RIGHT, SO IS THE REST OF THE HILLTOP.
WHAT DO YOU MEAN?
I'M RUNNING OFF WITH TWENTY OF OUR MOST ABLE-BODIED MEN AND WOMEN. WHO'S TO SAY I ACTUALLY **TOLD** YOU WHAT MY PLAN IS.
MAYBE WE **DEFECTED.**
OKAY, YEAH. I SEE WHERE YOU'RE GOING.
GOOD PLAN. THAT REALLY IS THE SAFEST WAY OF DOING THIS. I SEE NO NEED PUTTING ALL OUR PEOPLE AT RISK.
YEAH.
IT'S GOOD TO HEAR YOU'RE SO **CONCERNED** FOR OUR PEOPLE NOW.
WHAT THE HELL IS THAT SUPPOSED TO MEAN?
MAYBE IF YOU HADN'T BENT OVER BACKWARDS TO KEEP YOUR ASS OUT OF THE LINE OF FIRE--WE WOULDN'T **BE** IN THIS POSITION.
EVER CONSIDER THAT?

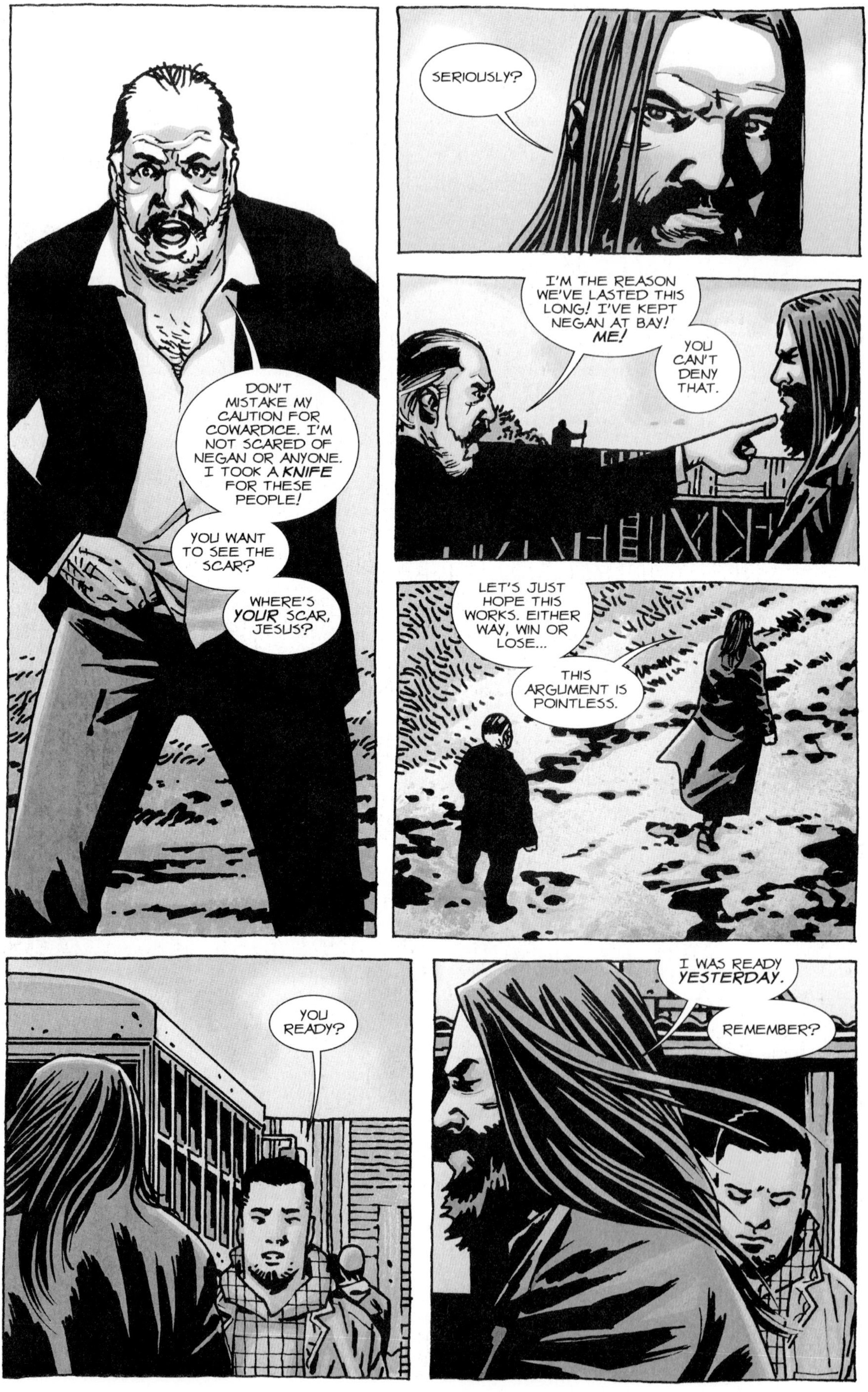
DON'T MISTAKE MY CAUTION FOR COWARDICE. I'M NOT SCARED OF NEGAN OR ANYONE. I TOOK A KNIFE FOR THESE PEOPLE!
YOU WANT TO SEE THE SCAR?
WHERE'S YOUR SCAR, JESUS?
SERIOUSLY?
I'M THE REASON WE'VE LASTED THIS LONG! I'VE KEPT NEGAN AT BAY! ME!
YOU CAN'T DENY THAT.
LET'S JUST HOPE THIS WORKS. EITHER WAY, WIN OR LOSE...
THIS ARGUMENT IS POINTLESS.
YOU READY?
I WAS READY YESTERDAY.
REMEMBER?

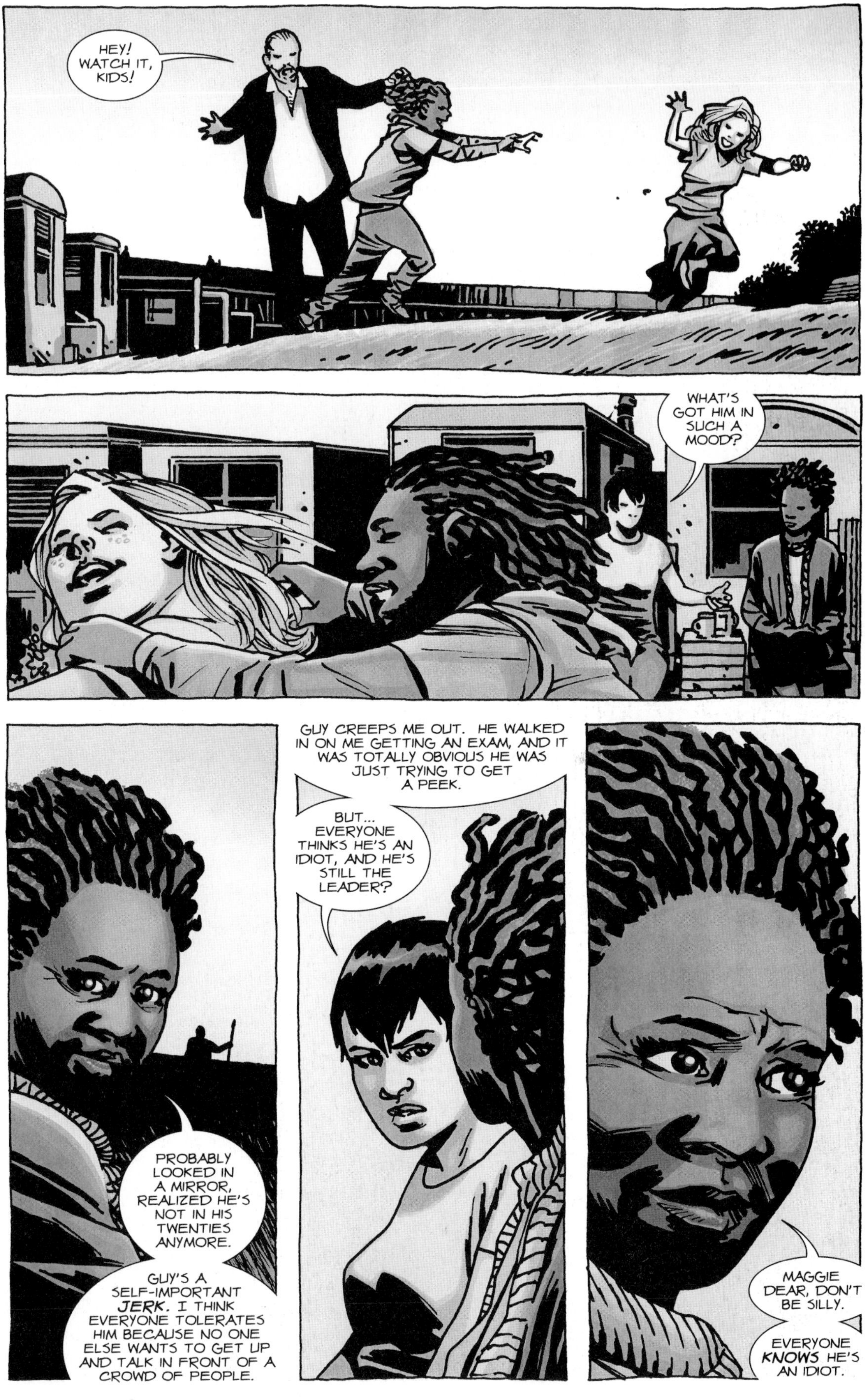
HEY! WATCH IT, KIDS!
WHAT'S GOT HIM IN SUCH A MOOD?
PROBABLY LOOKED IN A MIRROR, REALIZED HE'S NOT IN HIS TWENTIES ANYMORE.
GUY'S A SELF-IMPORTANT JERK. I THINK EVERYONE TOLERATES HIM BECAUSE NO ONE ELSE WANTS TO GET UP AND TALK IN FRONT OF A CROWD OF PEOPLE.
GUY CREEPS ME OUT. HE WALKED IN ON ME GETTING AN EXAM, AND IT WAS TOTALLY OBVIOUS HE WAS JUST TRYING TO GET A PEEK.
BUT... EVERYONE THINKS HE'S AN IDIOT, AND HE'S STILL THE LEADER?
MAGGIE DEAR, DON'T BE SILLY.
EVERYONE KNOWS HE'S AN IDIOT.

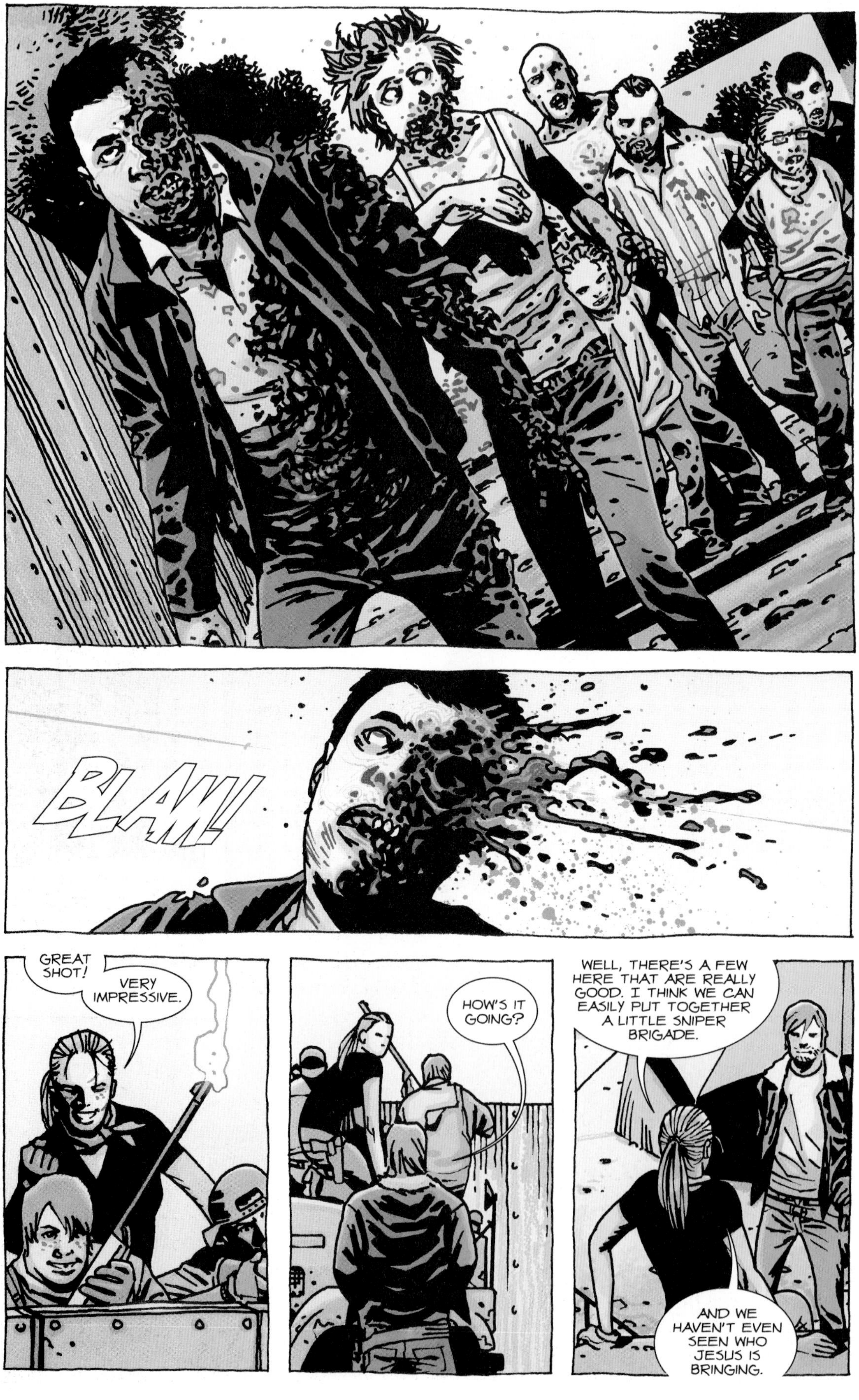
BLAM!
GREAT SHOT!
VERY IMPRESSIVE.
HOW'S IT GOING?
WELL, THERE'S A FEW HERE THAT ARE REALLY GOOD. I THINK WE CAN EASILY PUT TOGETHER A LITTLE SNIPER BRIGADE.
AND WE HAVEN'T EVEN SEEN WHO JESUS IS BRINGING.

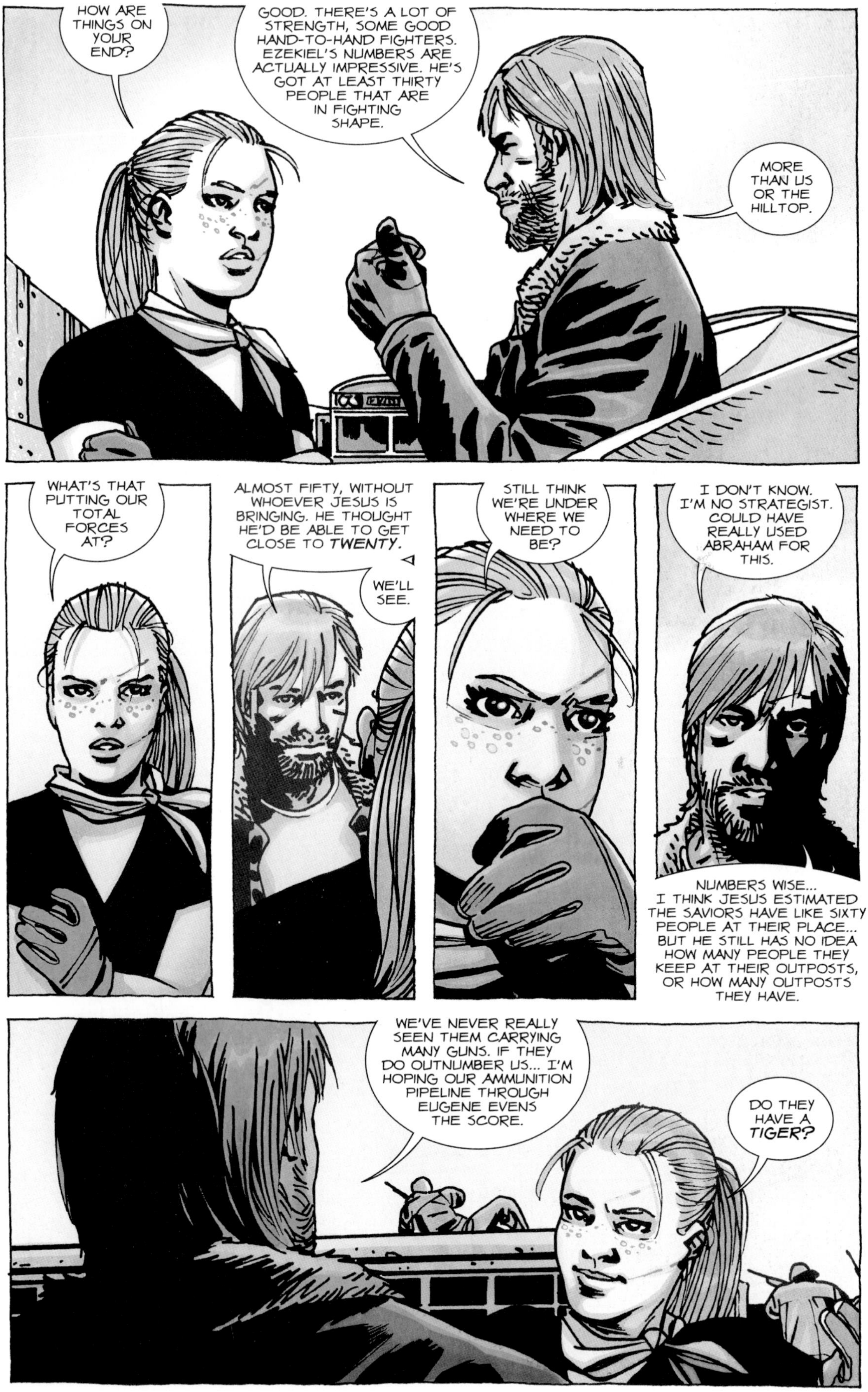
HOW ARE THINGS ON YOUR END?
GOOD. THERE'S A LOT OF STRENGTH, SOME GOOD HAND-TO-HAND FIGHTERS. EZEKIEL'S NUMBERS ARE ACTUALLY IMPRESSIVE. HE'S GOT AT LEAST THIRTY PEOPLE THAT ARE IN FIGHTING SHAPE.
MORE THAN US OR THE HILLTOP.
WHAT'S THAT PUTTING OUR TOTAL FORCES AT?
ALMOST FIFTY, WITHOUT WHOEVER JESUS IS BRINGING. HE THOUGHT HE'D BE ABLE TO GET CLOSE TO *TWENTY.*
WE'LL SEE.
STILL THINK WE'RE UNDER WHERE WE NEED TO BE?
I DON'T KNOW. I'M NO STRATEGIST. COULD HAVE REALLY USED ABRAHAM FOR THIS.
NUMBERS WISE... I THINK JESUS ESTIMATED THE SAVIORS HAVE LIKE SIXTY PEOPLE AT THEIR PLACE... BUT HE STILL HAS NO IDEA HOW MANY PEOPLE THEY KEEP AT THEIR OUTPOSTS, OR HOW MANY OUTPOSTS THEY HAVE.
WE'VE NEVER REALLY SEEN THEM CARRYING MANY GUNS. IF THEY DO OUTNUMBER US... I'M HOPING OUR AMMUNITION PIPELINE THROUGH EUGENE EVENS THE SCORE.
DO THEY HAVE A *TIGER?*

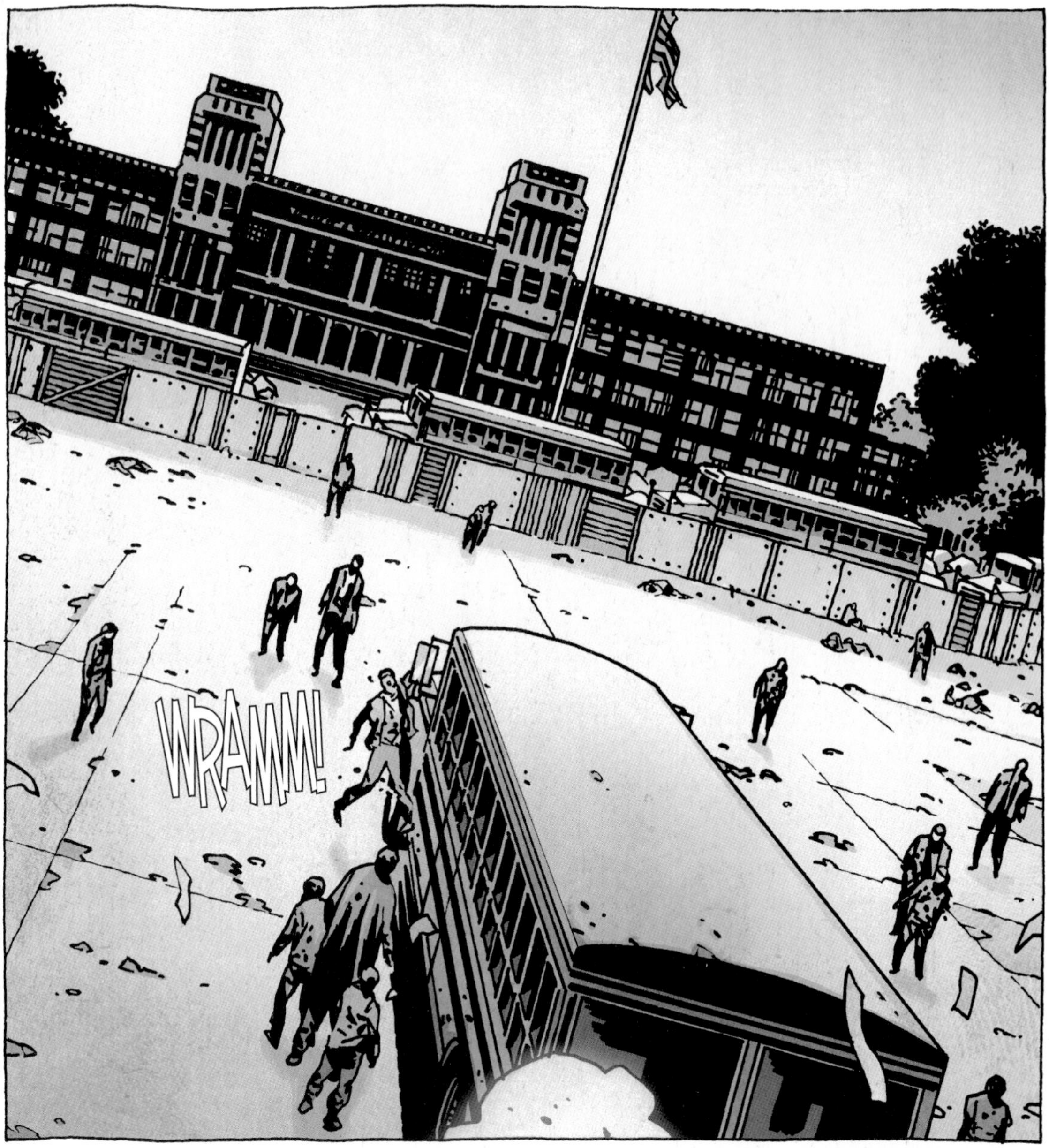
WRAMM!

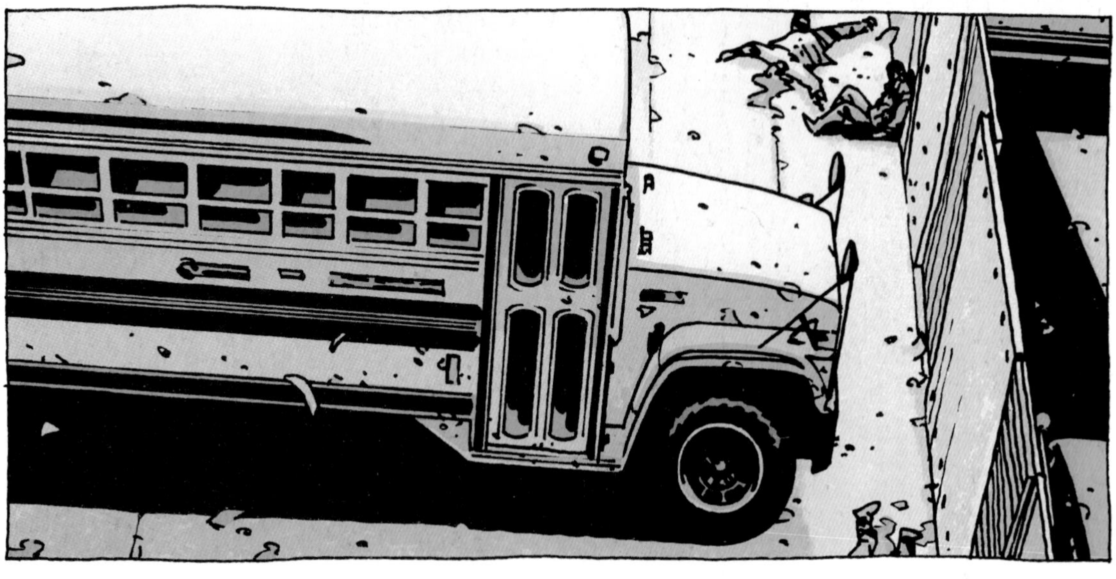

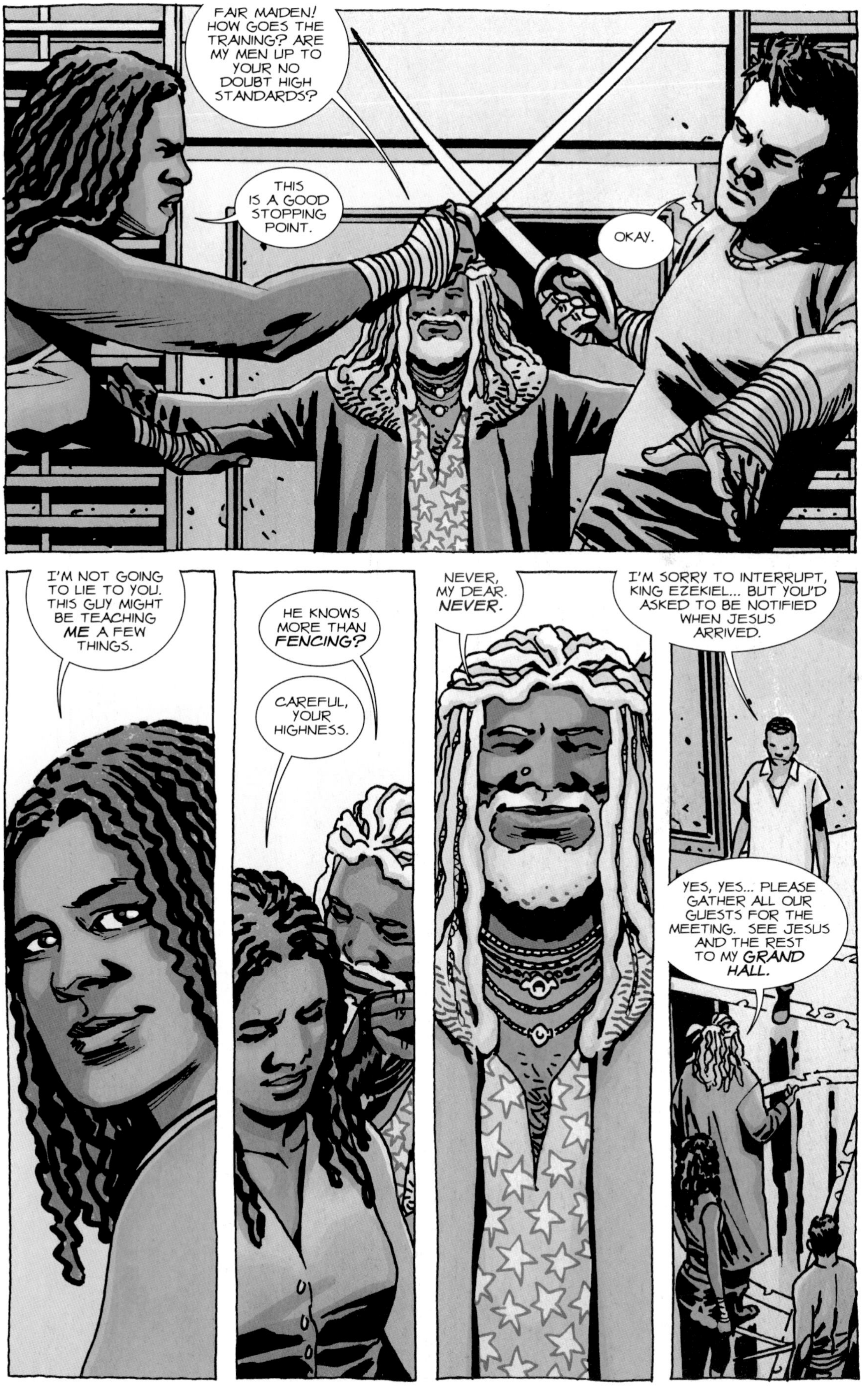
FAIR MAIDEN! HOW GOES THE TRAINING? ARE MY MEN UP TO YOUR NO DOUBT HIGH STANDARDS?
THIS IS A GOOD STOPPING POINT.
OKAY.
I'M NOT GOING TO LIE TO YOU. THIS GUY MIGHT BE TEACHING ME A FEW THINGS.
HE KNOWS MORE THAN FENCING?
CAREFUL, YOUR HIGHNESS.
NEVER, MY DEAR. NEVER.
I'M SORRY TO INTERRUPT, KING EZEKIEL... BUT YOU'D ASKED TO BE NOTIFIED WHEN JESUS ARRIVED.
YES, YES... PLEASE GATHER ALL OUR GUESTS FOR THE MEETING. SEE JESUS AND THE REST TO MY GRAND HALL.

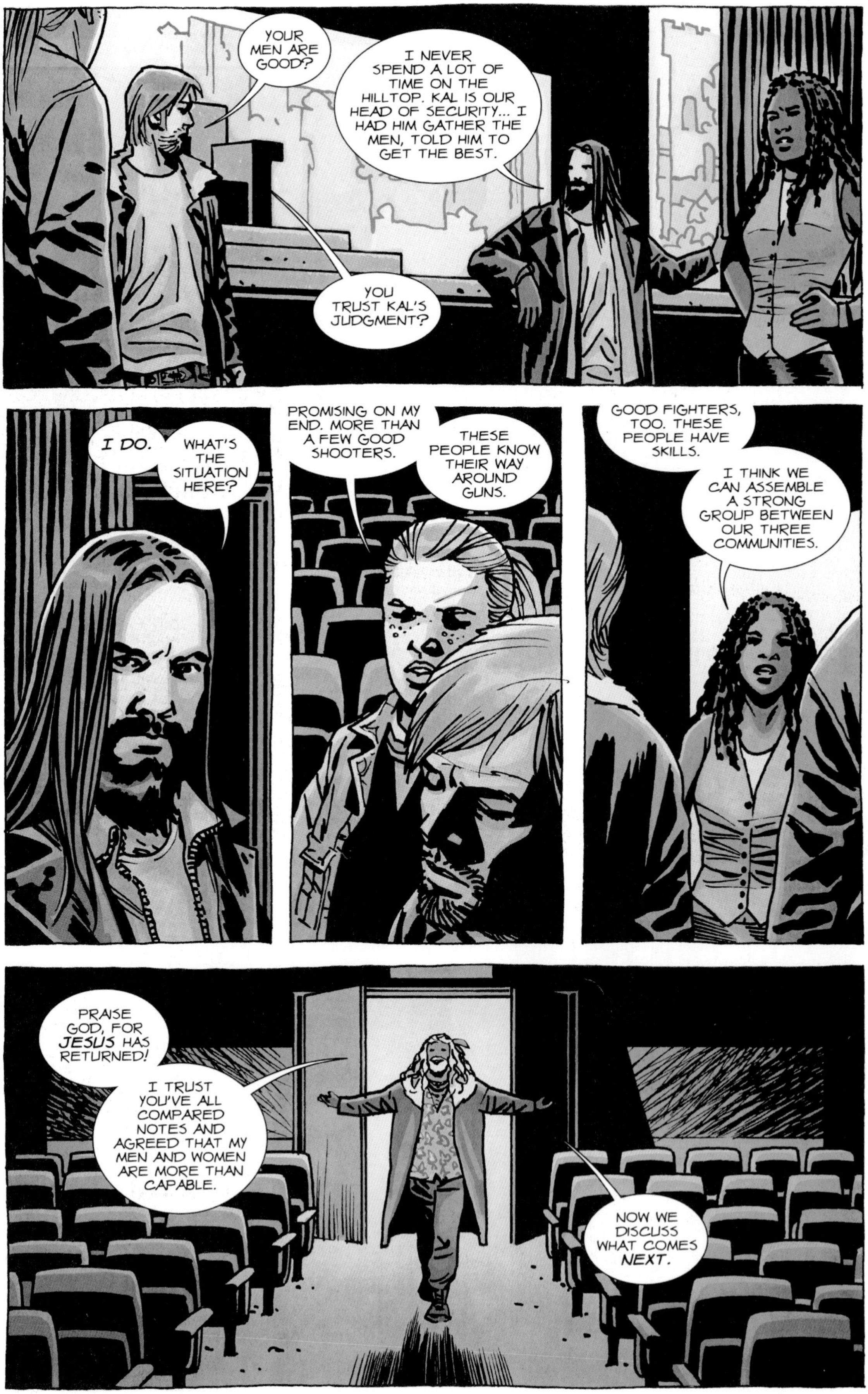
YOUR MEN ARE GOOD?
I NEVER SPEND A LOT OF TIME ON THE HILLTOP. KAL IS OUR HEAD OF SECURITY... I HAD HIM GATHER THE MEN, TOLD HIM TO GET THE BEST.
YOU TRUST KAL'S JUDGMENT?
I DO.
WHAT'S THE SITUATION HERE?
PROMISING ON MY END. MORE THAN A FEW GOOD SHOOTERS.
THESE PEOPLE KNOW THEIR WAY AROUND GUNS.
GOOD FIGHTERS, TOO. THESE PEOPLE HAVE SKILLS.
I THINK WE CAN ASSEMBLE A STRONG GROUP BETWEEN OUR THREE COMMUNITIES.
PRAISE GOD, FOR JESUS HAS RETURNED!
I TRUST YOU'VE ALL COMPARED NOTES AND AGREED THAT MY MEN AND WOMEN ARE MORE THAN CAPABLE.
NOW WE DISCUSS WHAT COMES NEXT.

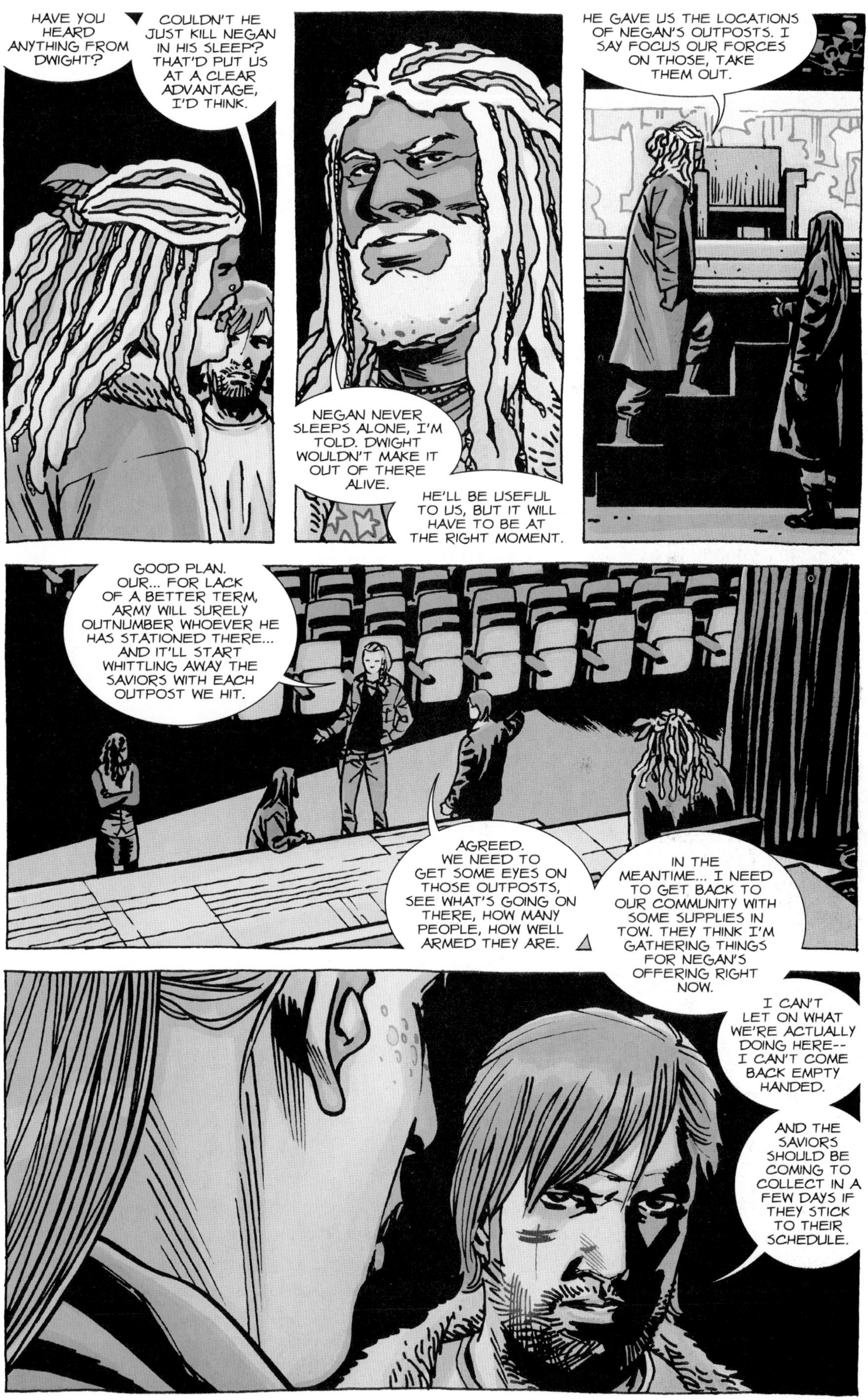
HAVE YOU HEARD ANYTHING FROM DWIGHT?
COULDN'T HE JUST KILL NEGAN IN HIS SLEEP? THAT'D PUT US AT A CLEAR ADVANTAGE, I'D THINK.
NEGAN NEVER SLEEPS ALONE, I'M TOLD. DWIGHT WOULDN'T MAKE IT OUT OF THERE ALIVE.
HE'LL BE USEFUL TO US, BUT IT WILL HAVE TO BE AT THE RIGHT MOMENT.
HE GAVE US THE LOCATIONS OF NEGAN'S OUTPOSTS. I SAY FOCUS OUR FORCES ON THOSE, TAKE THEM OUT.
GOOD PLAN. OUR... FOR LACK OF A BETTER TERM, ARMY WILL SURELY OUTNUMBER WHOEVER HE HAS STATIONED THERE... AND IT'LL START WHITTLING AWAY THE SAVIORS WITH EACH OUTPOST WE HIT.
AGREED. WE NEED TO GET SOME EYES ON THOSE OUTPOSTS, SEE WHAT'S GOING ON THERE, HOW MANY PEOPLE, HOW WELL ARMED THEY ARE.
IN THE MEANTIME... I NEED TO GET BACK TO OUR COMMUNITY WITH SOME SUPPLIES IN TOW. THEY THINK I'M GATHERING THINGS FOR NEGAN'S OFFERING RIGHT NOW.
I CAN'T LET ON WHAT WE'RE ACTUALLY DOING HERE-- I CAN'T COME BACK EMPTY HANDED.
AND THE SAVIORS SHOULD BE COMING TO COLLECT IN A FEW DAYS IF THEY STICK TO THEIR SCHEDULE.

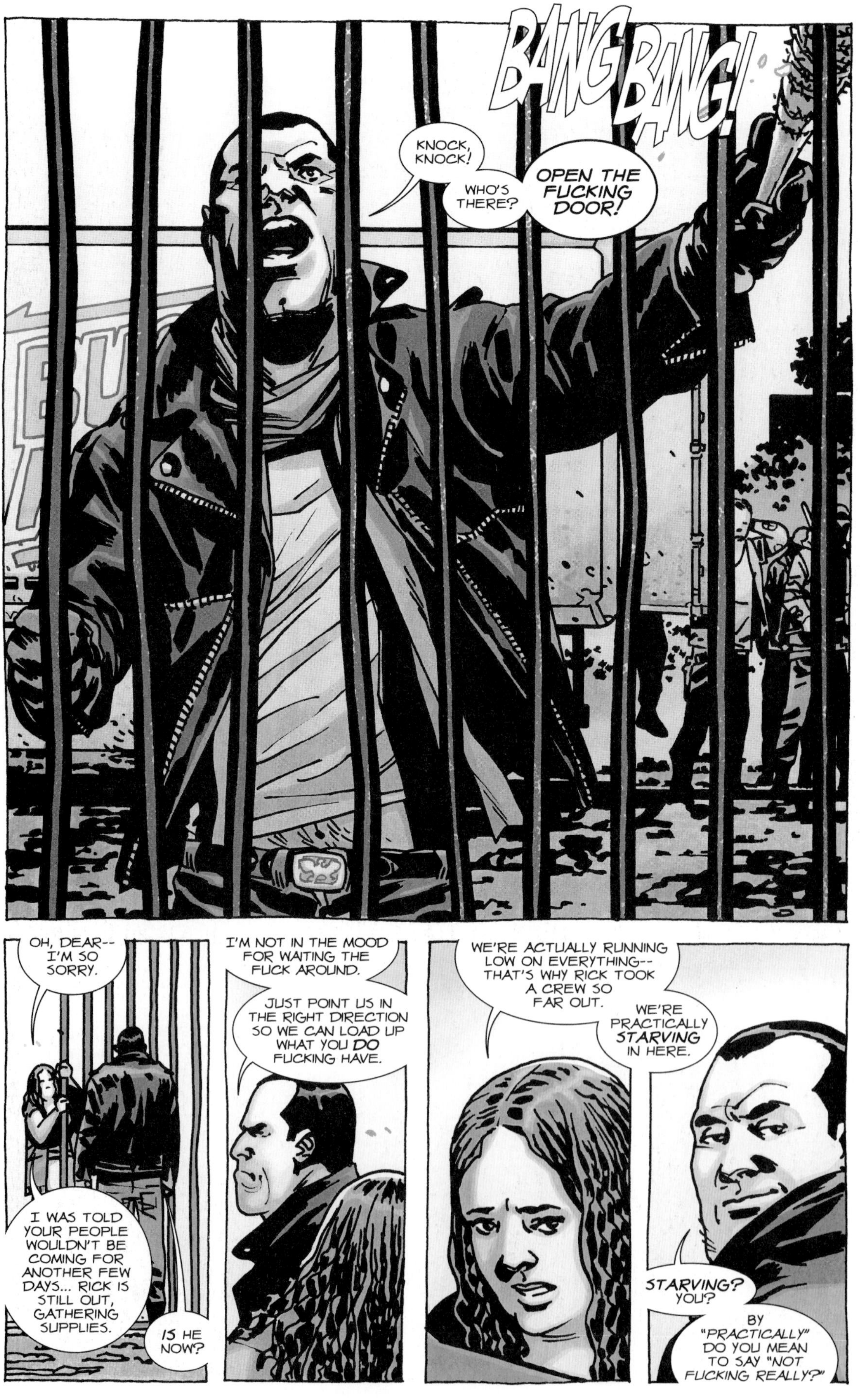
BANG BANG!
KNOCK, KNOCK!
WHO'S THERE?
OPEN THE FUCKING DOOR!
OH, DEAR-- I'M SO SORRY.
I WAS TOLD YOUR PEOPLE WOULDN'T BE COMING FOR ANOTHER FEW DAYS... RICK IS STILL OUT, GATHERING SUPPLIES.
IS HE NOW?
I'M NOT IN THE MOOD FOR WAITING THE FUCK AROUND.
JUST POINT US IN THE RIGHT DIRECTION SO WE CAN LOAD UP WHAT YOU DO FUCKING HAVE.
WE'RE ACTUALLY RUNNING LOW ON EVERYTHING-- THAT'S WHY RICK TOOK A CREW SO FAR OUT.
WE'RE PRACTICALLY STARVING IN HERE.
STARVING? YOU?
BY "PRACTICALLY" DO YOU MEAN TO SAY "NOT FUCKING REALLY?"

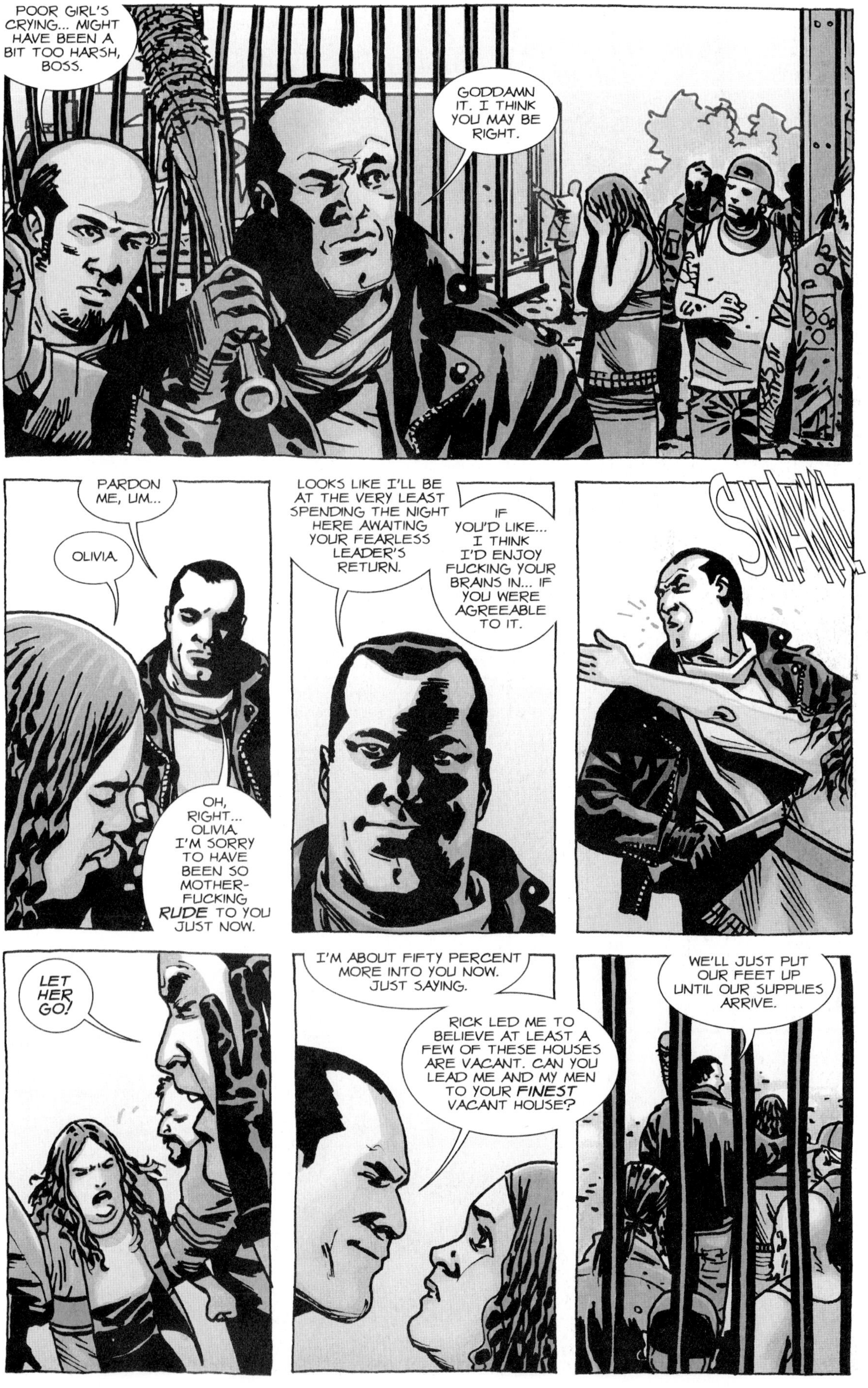
POOR GIRL'S CRYING... MIGHT HAVE BEEN A BIT TOO HARSH, BOSS.
GODDAMN IT. I THINK YOU MAY BE RIGHT.
PARDON ME, UM...
OLIVIA.
OH, RIGHT... OLIVIA. I'M SORRY TO HAVE BEEN SO MOTHER-FUCKING RUDE TO YOU JUST NOW.
LOOKS LIKE I'LL BE AT THE VERY LEAST SPENDING THE NIGHT HERE AWAITING YOUR FEARLESS LEADER'S RETURN.
IF YOU'D LIKE... I THINK I'D ENJOY FUCKING YOUR BRAINS IN... IF YOU WERE AGREEABLE TO IT.
LET HER GO!
I'M ABOUT FIFTY PERCENT MORE INTO YOU NOW. JUST SAYING.
RICK LED ME TO BELIEVE AT LEAST A FEW OF THESE HOUSES ARE VACANT. CAN YOU LEAD ME AND MY MEN TO YOUR FINEST VACANT HOUSE?
WE'LL JUST PUT OUR FEET UP UNTIL OUR SUPPLIES ARRIVE.

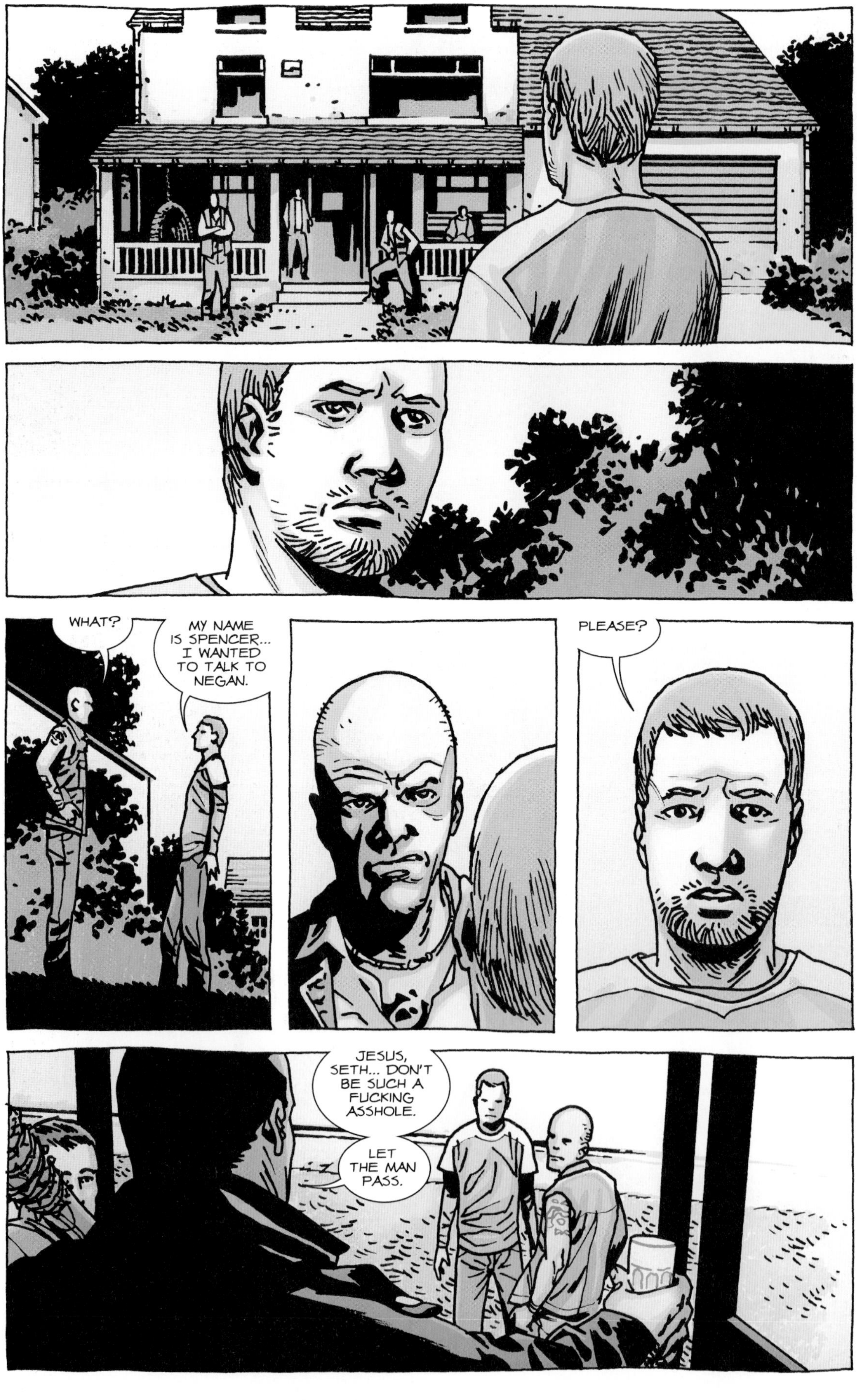
WHAT?
MY NAME IS SPENCER... I WANTED TO TALK TO NEGAN.
PLEASE?
JESUS, SETH... DON'T BE SUCH A FUCKING ASSHOLE.
LET THE MAN PASS.

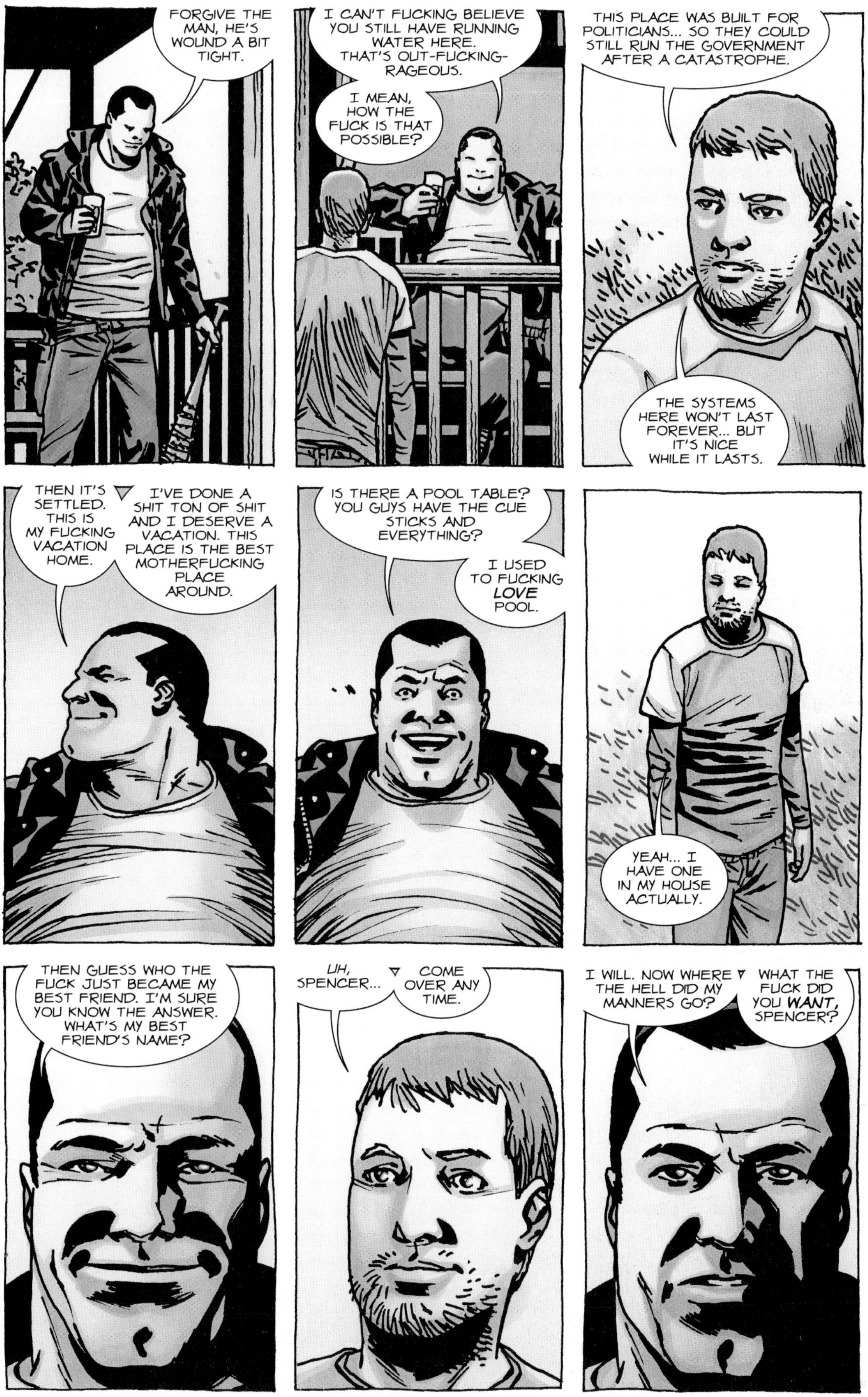
FORGIVE THE MAN, HE'S WOUND A BIT TIGHT.
I CAN'T FUCKING BELIEVE YOU STILL HAVE RUNNING WATER HERE. THAT'S OUT-FUCKING-RAGEOUS.
I MEAN, HOW THE FUCK IS THAT POSSIBLE?
THIS PLACE WAS BUILT FOR POLITICIANS... SO THEY COULD STILL RUN THE GOVERNMENT AFTER A CATASTROPHE.
THE SYSTEMS HERE WON'T LAST FOREVER... BUT IT'S NICE WHILE IT LASTS.
THEN IT'S SETTLED. THIS IS MY FUCKING VACATION HOME.
I'VE DONE A SHIT TON OF SHIT AND I DESERVE A VACATION. THIS PLACE IS THE BEST MOTHERFUCKING PLACE AROUND.
IS THERE A POOL TABLE? YOU GUYS HAVE THE CUE STICKS AND EVERYTHING?
I USED TO FUCKING *LOVE* POOL.
YEAH... I HAVE ONE IN MY HOUSE ACTUALLY.
THEN GUESS WHO THE FUCK JUST BECAME MY BEST FRIEND. I'M SURE YOU KNOW THE ANSWER. WHAT'S MY BEST FRIEND'S NAME?
UH, SPENCER...
COME OVER ANY TIME.
I WILL. NOW WHERE THE HELL DID MY MANNERS GO?
WHAT THE FUCK DID YOU *WANT,* SPENCER?

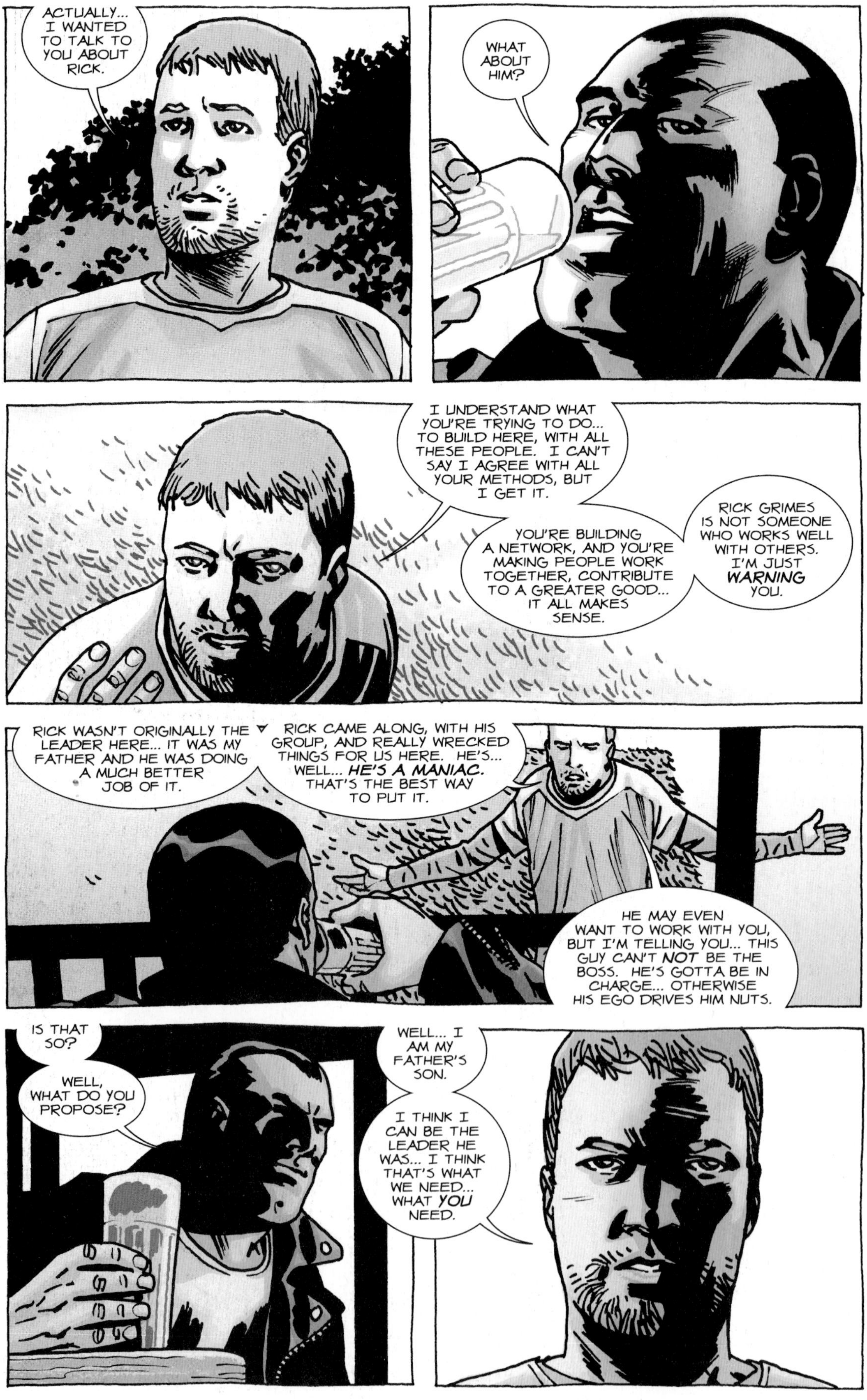
ACTUALLY... I WANTED TO TALK TO YOU ABOUT RICK.
WHAT ABOUT HIM?
I UNDERSTAND WHAT YOU'RE TRYING TO DO... TO BUILD HERE, WITH ALL THESE PEOPLE. I CAN'T SAY I AGREE WITH ALL YOUR METHODS, BUT I GET IT.
YOU'RE BUILDING A NETWORK, AND YOU'RE MAKING PEOPLE WORK TOGETHER, CONTRIBUTE TO A GREATER GOOD... IT ALL MAKES SENSE.
RICK GRIMES IS NOT SOMEONE WHO WORKS WELL WITH OTHERS. I'M JUST WARNING YOU.
RICK WASN'T ORIGINALLY THE LEADER HERE... IT WAS MY FATHER AND HE WAS DOING A MUCH BETTER JOB OF IT.
RICK CAME ALONG, WITH HIS GROUP, AND REALLY WRECKED THINGS FOR US HERE. HE'S... WELL... HE'S A MANIAC. THAT'S THE BEST WAY TO PUT IT.
HE MAY EVEN WANT TO WORK WITH YOU, BUT I'M TELLING YOU... THIS GUY CAN'T NOT BE THE BOSS. HE'S GOTTA BE IN CHARGE... OTHERWISE HIS EGO DRIVES HIM NUTS.
IS THAT SO?
WELL, WHAT DO YOU PROPOSE?
WELL... I AM MY FATHER'S SON.
I THINK I CAN BE THE LEADER HE WAS... I THINK THAT'S WHAT WE NEED... WHAT YOU NEED.

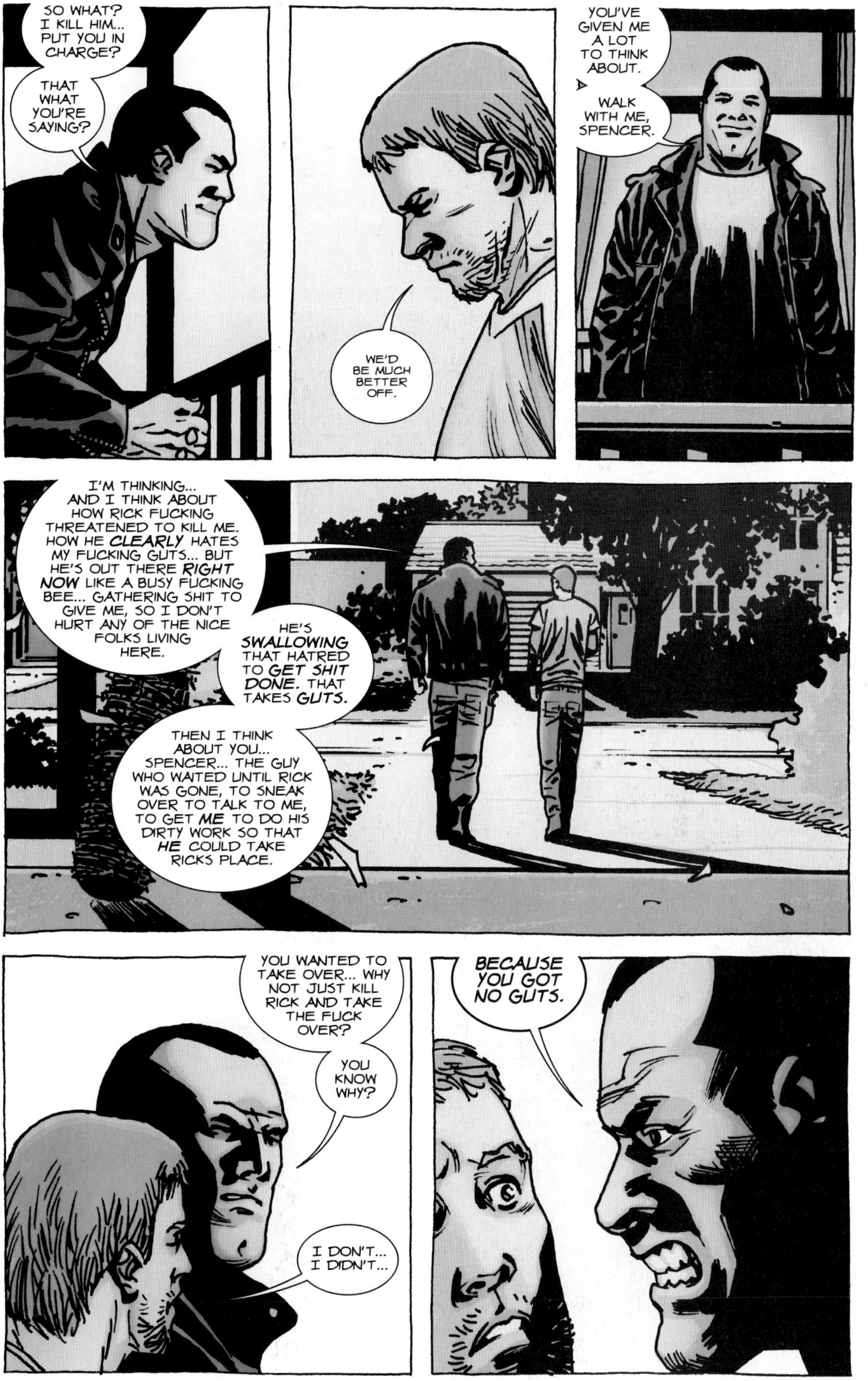
SO WHAT? I KILL HIM... PUT YOU IN CHARGE?
THAT WHAT YOU'RE SAYING?
WE'D BE MUCH BETTER OFF.
YOU'VE GIVEN ME A LOT TO THINK ABOUT.
WALK WITH ME, SPENCER.
I'M THINKING... AND I THINK ABOUT HOW RICK FUCKING THREATENED TO KILL ME. HOW HE CLEARLY HATES MY FUCKING GUTS... BUT HE'S OUT THERE RIGHT NOW LIKE A BUSY FUCKING BEE... GATHERING SHIT TO GIVE ME, SO I DON'T HURT ANY OF THE NICE FOLKS LIVING HERE.
HE'S SWALLOWING THAT HATRED TO GET SHIT DONE. THAT TAKES GUTS.
THEN I THINK ABOUT YOU... SPENCER... THE GUY WHO WAITED UNTIL RICK WAS GONE, TO SNEAK OVER TO TALK TO ME, TO GET ME TO DO HIS DIRTY WORK SO THAT HE COULD TAKE RICKS PLACE.
YOU WANTED TO TAKE OVER... WHY NOT JUST KILL RICK AND TAKE THE FUCK OVER?
YOU KNOW WHY?
I DON'T... I DIDN'T...
BECAUSE YOU GOT NO GUTS.

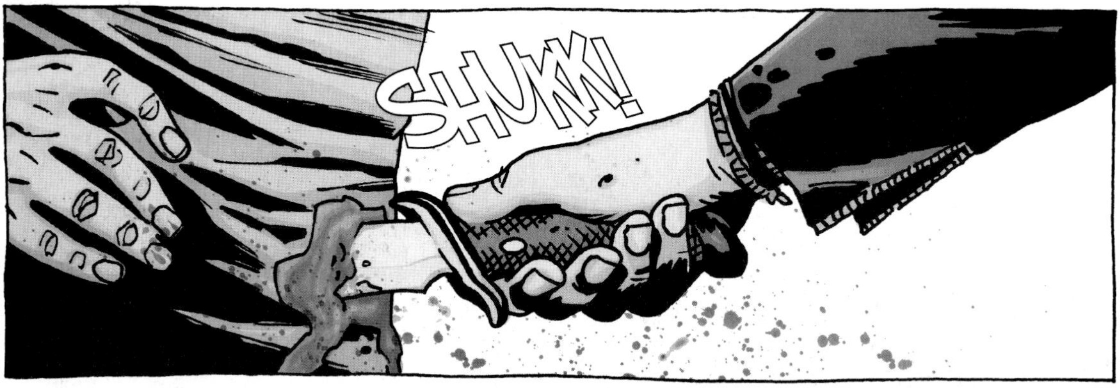
SHUKK!

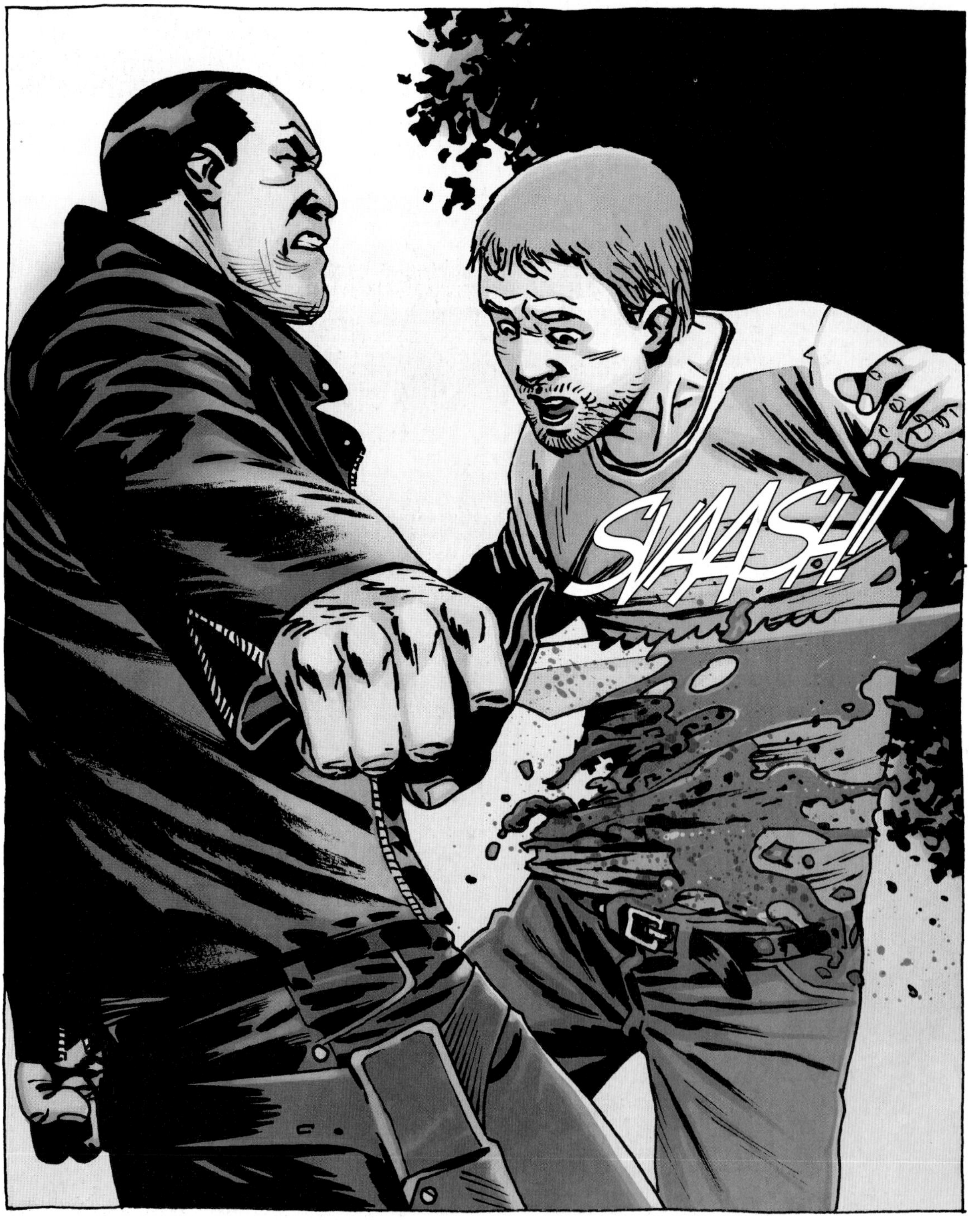
SLAASH!

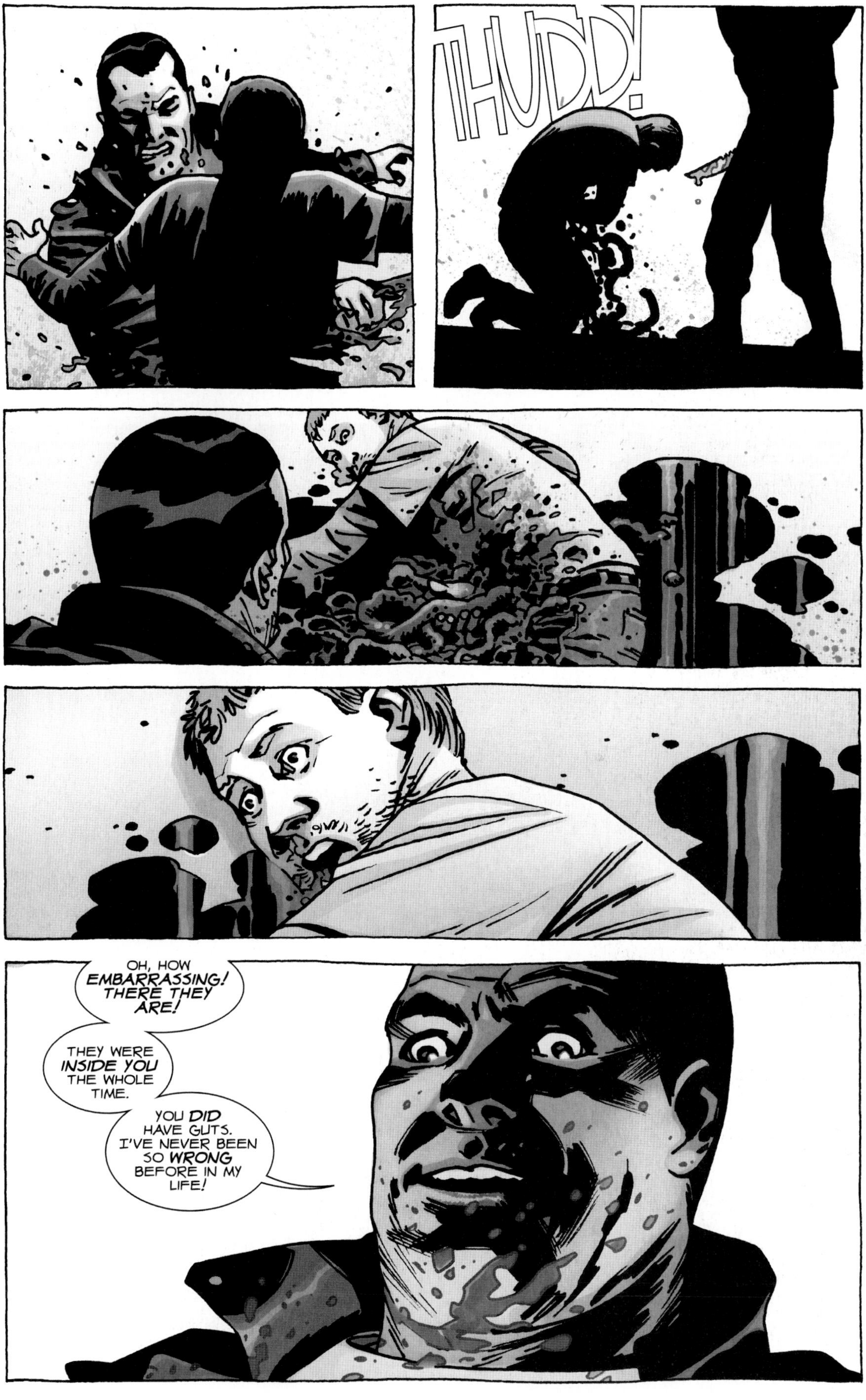
THUDD!
OH, HOW EMBARRASSING! THERE THEY ARE!
THEY WERE INSIDE YOU THE WHOLE TIME.
YOU DID HAVE GUTS. I'VE NEVER BEEN SO WRONG BEFORE IN MY LIFE!

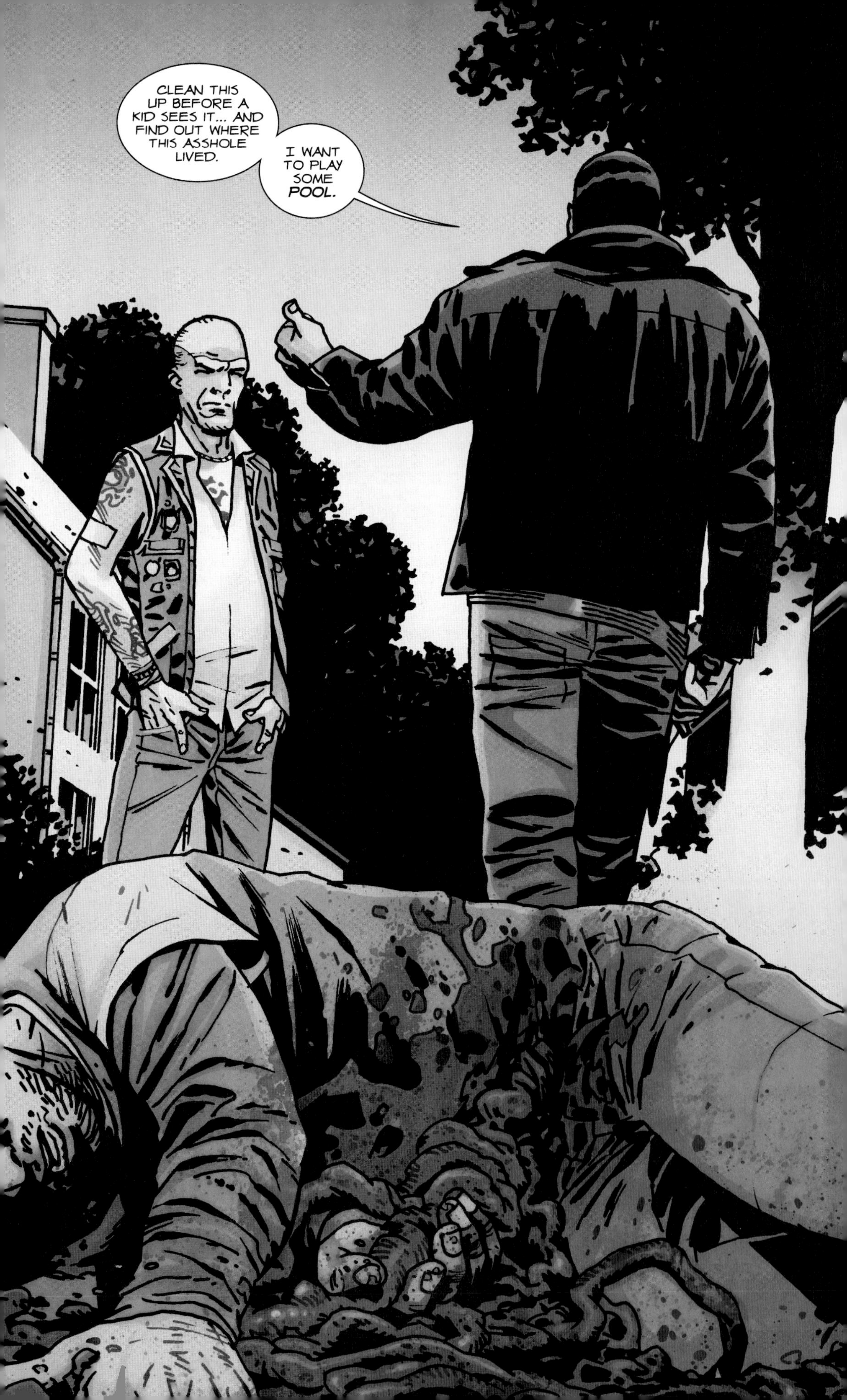
CLEAN THIS UP BEFORE A KID SEES IT... AND FIND OUT WHERE THIS ASSHOLE LIVED.
I WANT TO PLAY SOME *POOL.*

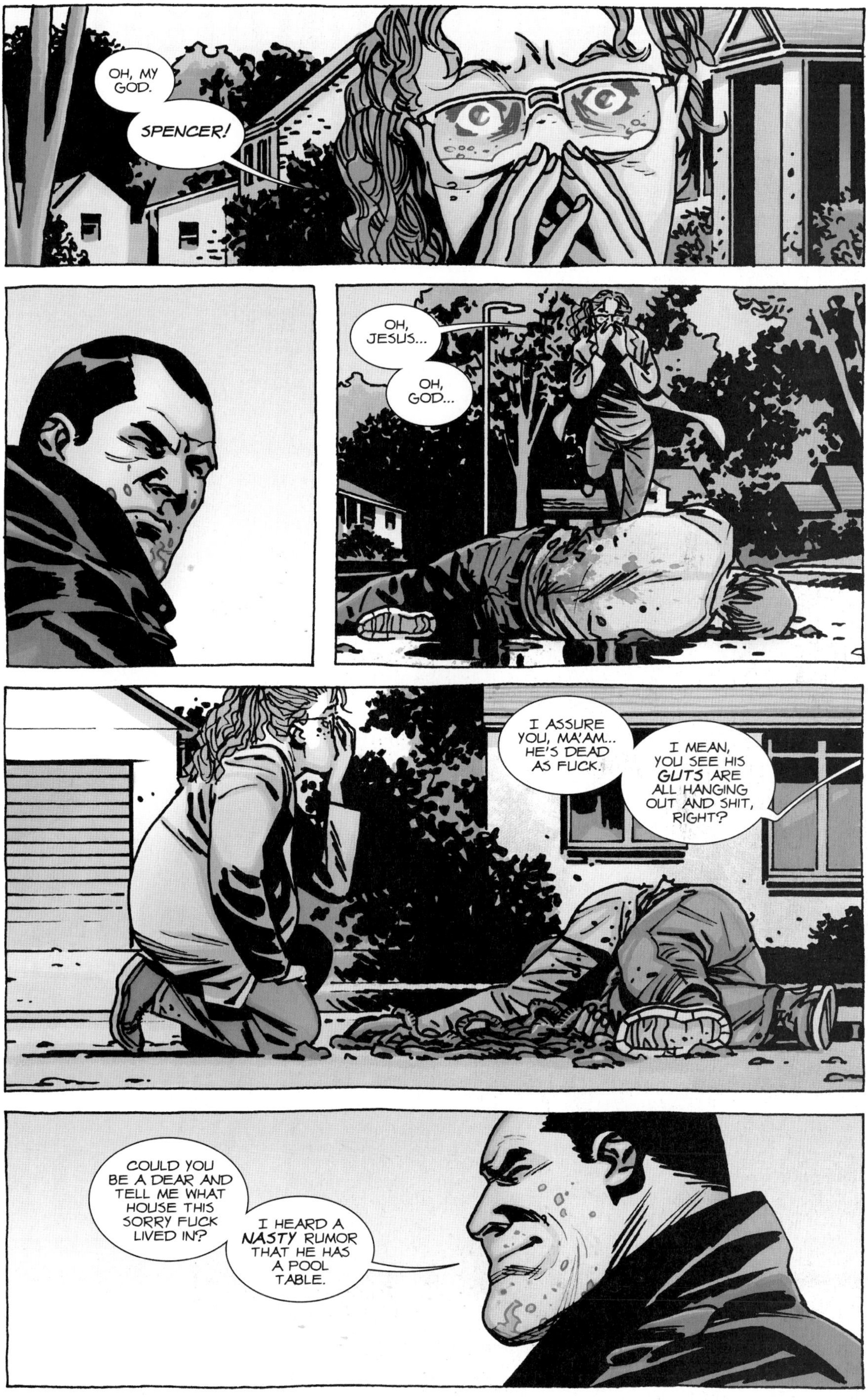
OH, MY GOD.
SPENCER!
OH, JESUS...
OH, GOD...
I ASSURE YOU, MA'AM... HE'S DEAD AS FUCK.
I MEAN, YOU SEE HIS GUTS ARE ALL HANGING OUT AND SHIT, RIGHT?
COULD YOU BE A DEAR AND TELL ME WHAT HOUSE THIS SORRY FUCK LIVED IN?
I HEARD A NASTY RUMOR THAT HE HAS A POOL TABLE.

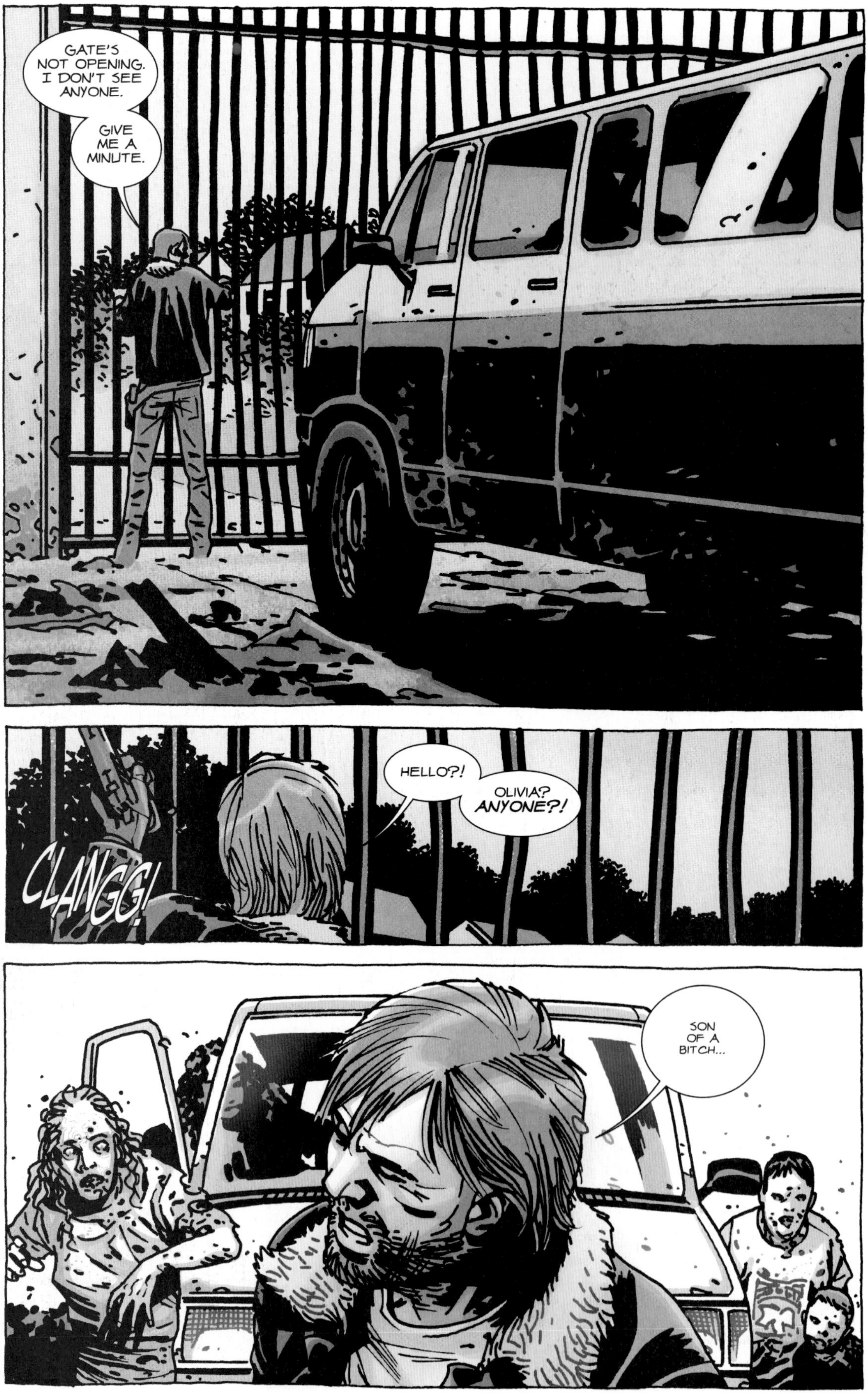
GATE'S NOT OPENING. I DON'T SEE ANYONE.
GIVE ME A MINUTE.
HELLO?!
OLIVIA? ANYONE?!
CLANGG!
SON OF A BITCH...

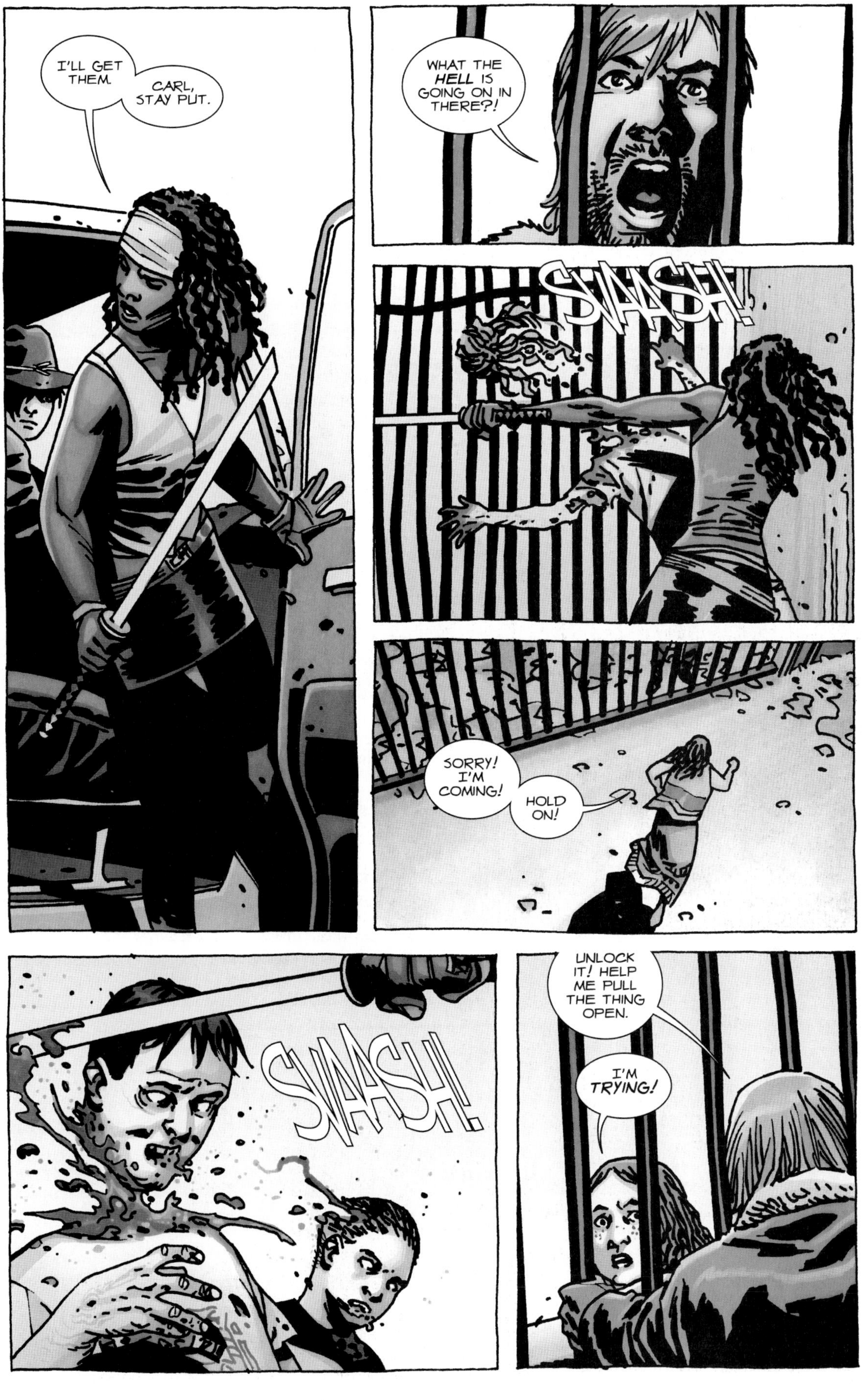
I'LL GET THEM.
CARL, STAY PUT.
WHAT THE HELL IS GOING ON IN THERE?!
SVAASH!
SORRY! I'M COMING!
HOLD ON!
SVAASH!
UNLOCK IT! HELP ME PULL THE THING OPEN.
I'M TRYING!

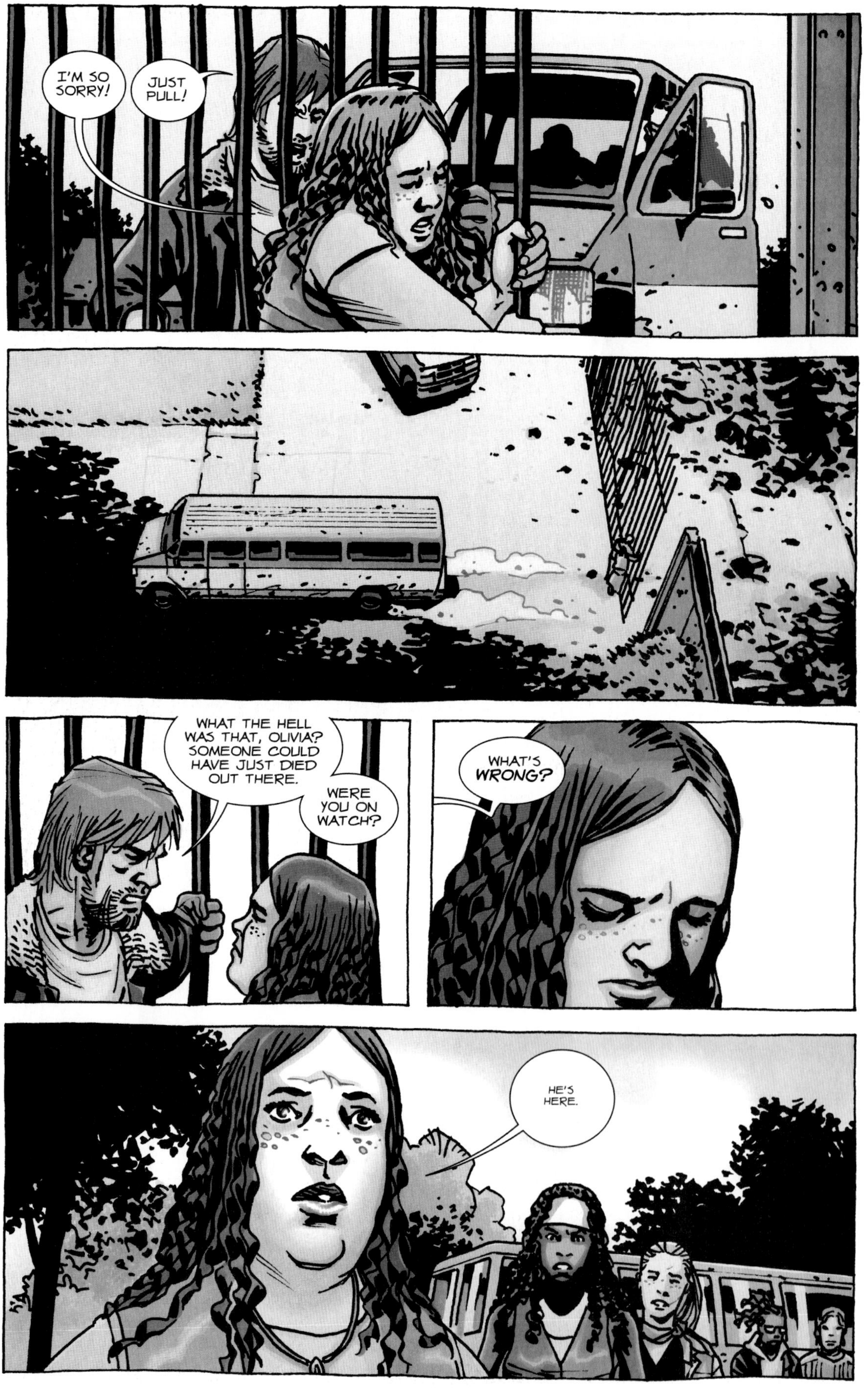
I'M SO SORRY!
JUST PULL!
WHAT THE HELL WAS THAT, OLIVIA? SOMEONE COULD HAVE JUST DIED OUT THERE.
WERE YOU ON WATCH?
WHAT'S **WRONG?**
HE'S HERE.

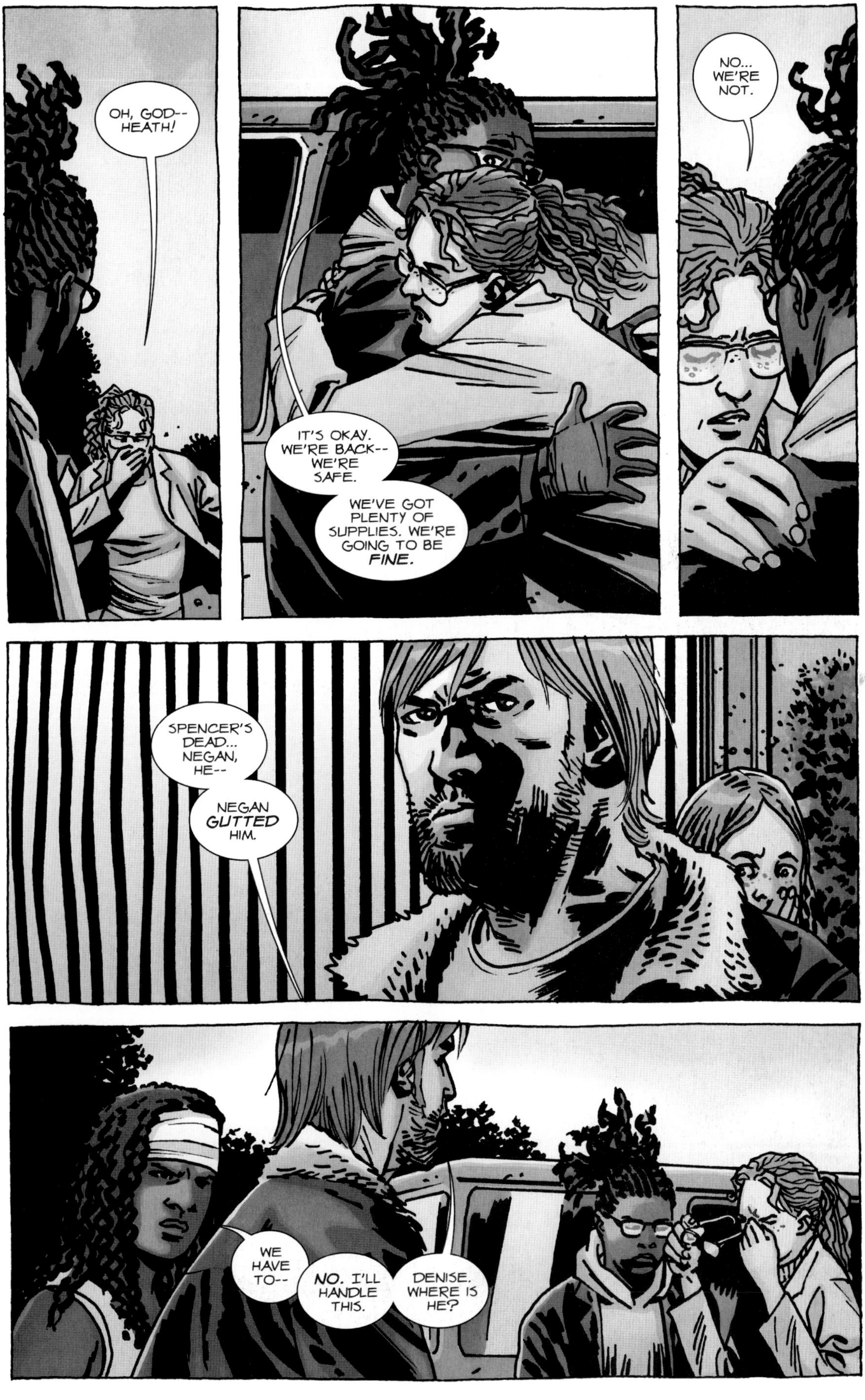
OH, GOD-- HEATH!
IT'S OKAY. WE'RE BACK-- WE'RE SAFE.
WE'VE GOT PLENTY OF SUPPLIES. WE'RE GOING TO BE FINE.
NO... WE'RE NOT.
SPENCER'S DEAD... NEGAN, HE--
NEGAN GUTTED HIM.
WE HAVE TO--
NO. I'LL HANDLE THIS.
DENISE. WHERE IS HE?

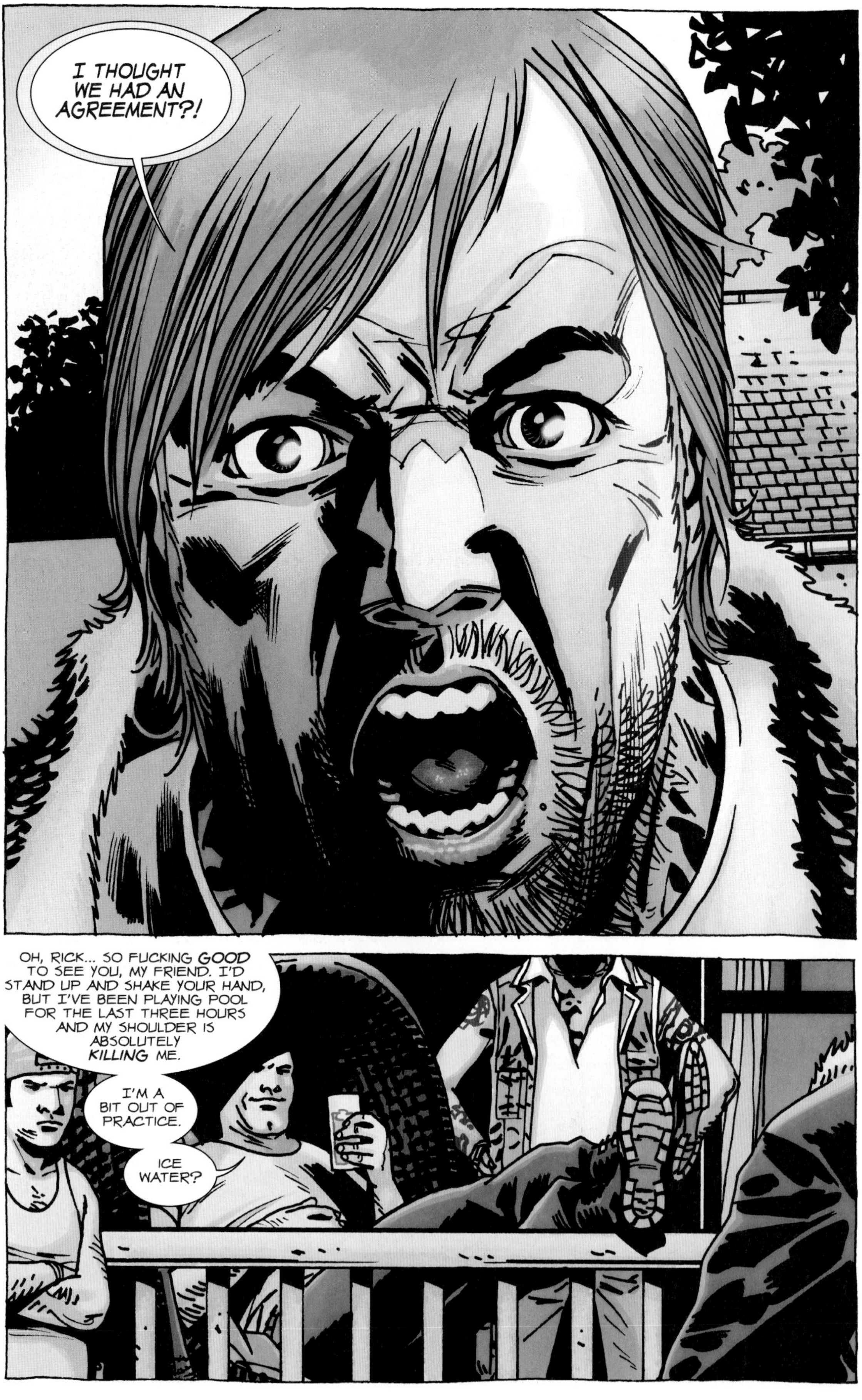
I THOUGHT WE HAD AN AGREEMENT?!
OH, RICK... SO FUCKING GOOD TO SEE YOU, MY FRIEND. I'D STAND UP AND SHAKE YOUR HAND, BUT I'VE BEEN PLAYING POOL FOR THE LAST THREE HOURS AND MY SHOULDER IS ABSOLUTELY KILLING ME.
I'M A BIT OUT OF PRACTICE.
ICE WATER?

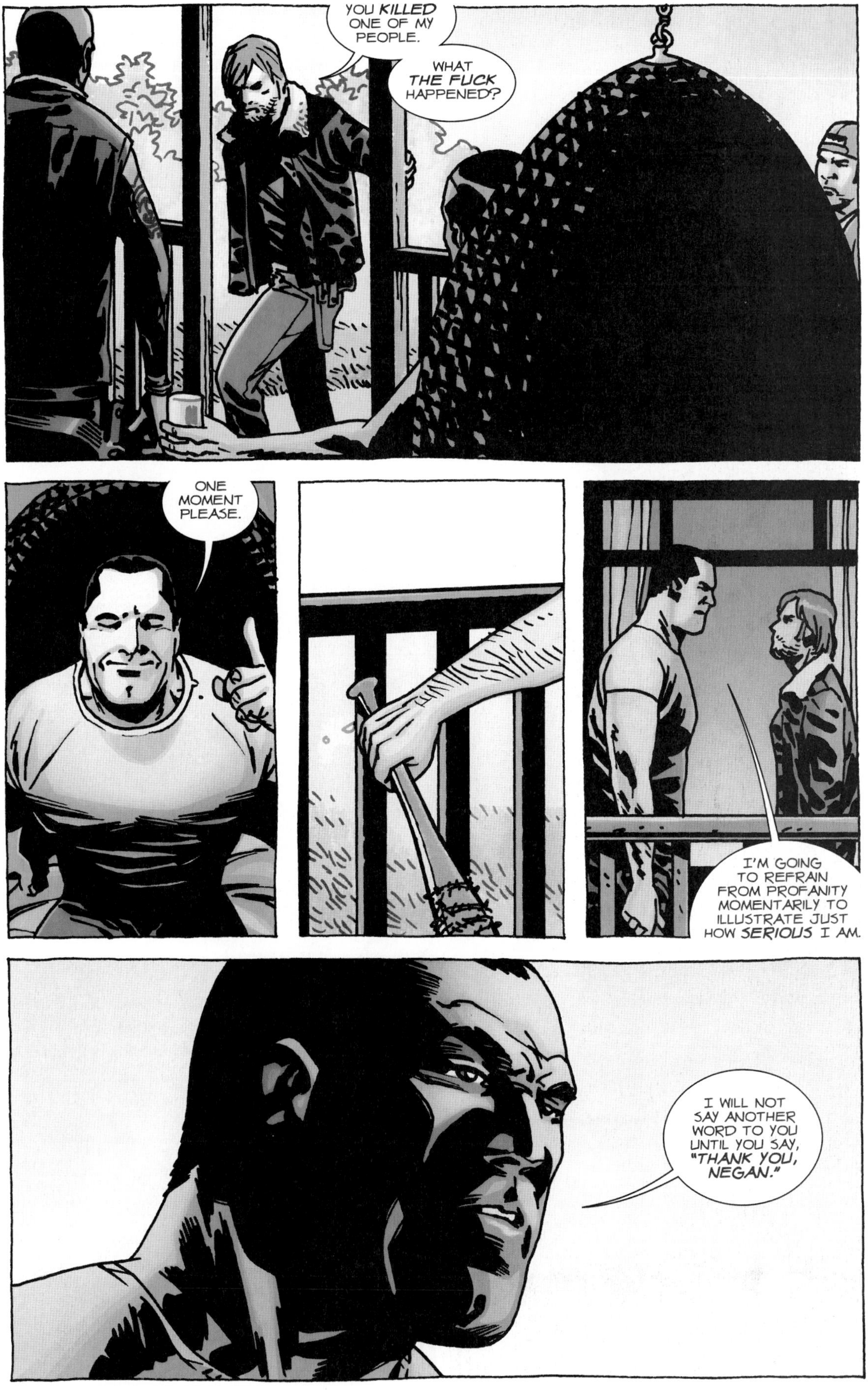
YOU KILLED ONE OF MY PEOPLE.
WHAT THE FUCK HAPPENED?
ONE MOMENT PLEASE.
I'M GOING TO REFRAIN FROM PROFANITY MOMENTARILY TO ILLUSTRATE JUST HOW SERIOUS I AM.
I WILL NOT SAY ANOTHER WORD TO YOU UNTIL YOU SAY, "THANK YOU, NEGAN."

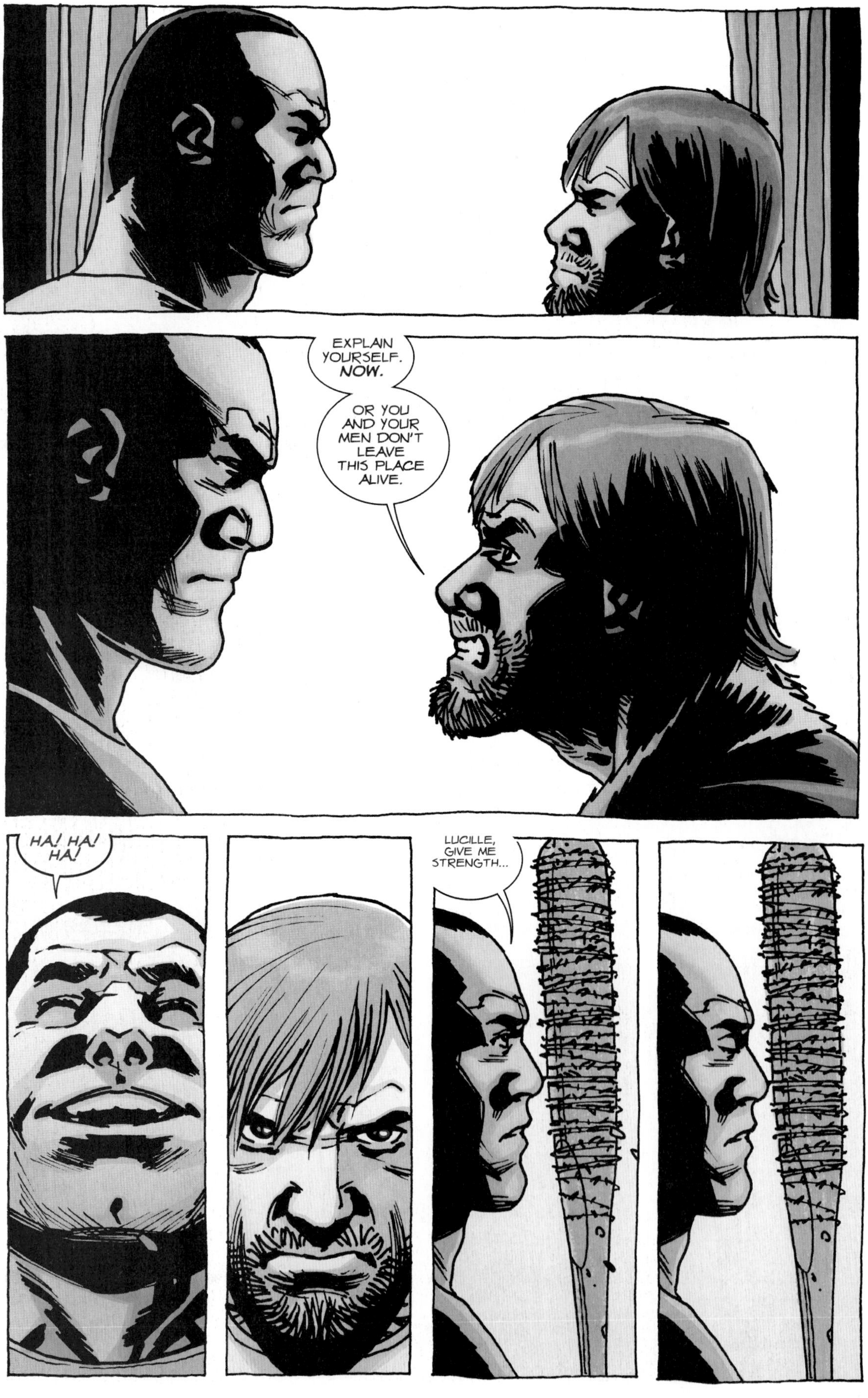
EXPLAIN YOURSELF. NOW.
OR YOU AND YOUR MEN DON'T LEAVE THIS PLACE ALIVE.
HA! HA! HA!
LUCILLE, GIVE ME STRENGTH...

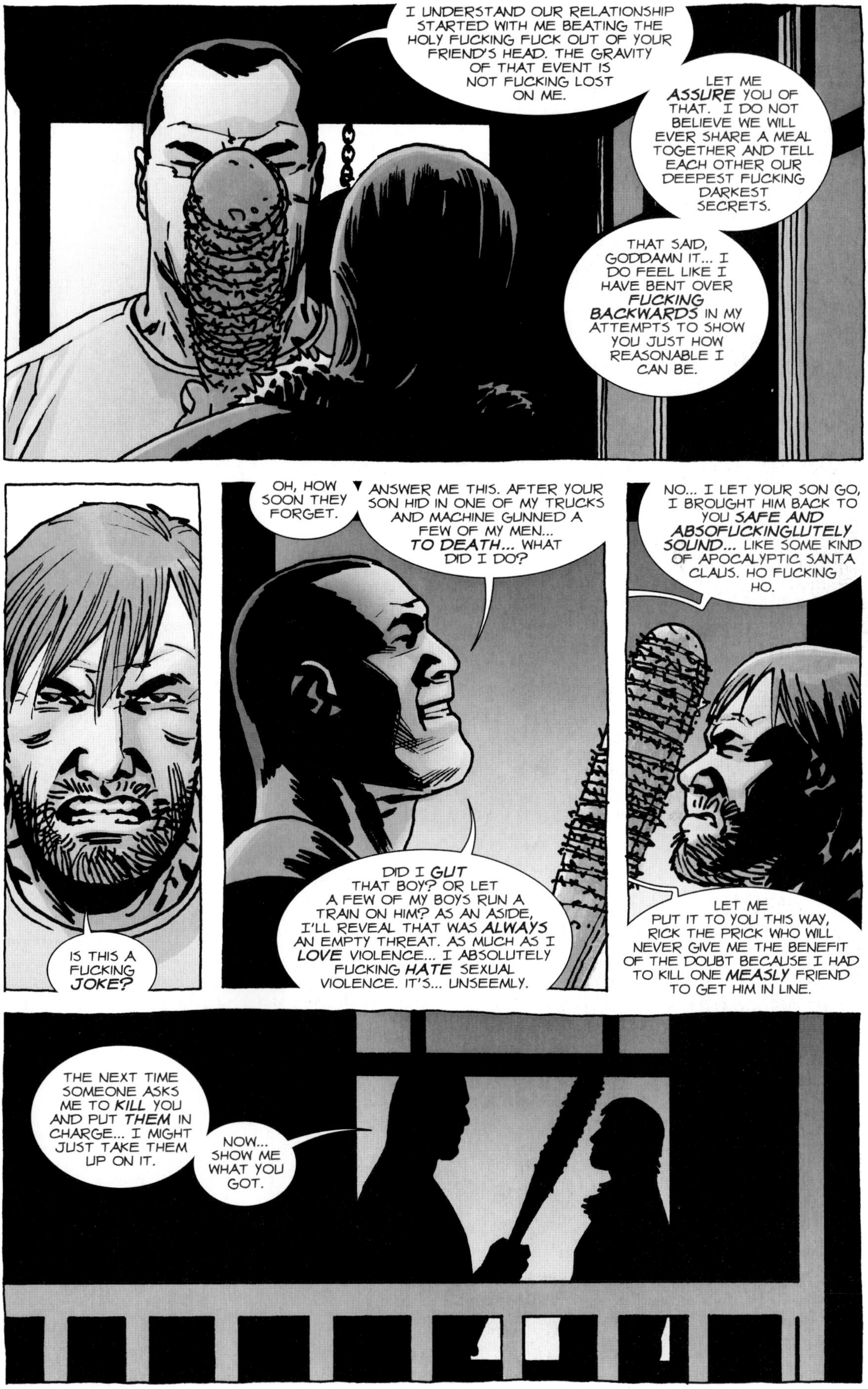
I UNDERSTAND OUR RELATIONSHIP STARTED WITH ME BEATING THE HOLY FUCKING FUCK OUT OF YOUR FRIEND'S HEAD. THE GRAVITY OF THAT EVENT IS NOT FUCKING LOST ON ME.
LET ME ASSURE YOU OF THAT. I DO NOT BELIEVE WE WILL EVER SHARE A MEAL TOGETHER AND TELL EACH OTHER OUR DEEPEST FUCKING DARKEST SECRETS.
THAT SAID, GODDAMN IT... I DO FEEL LIKE I HAVE BENT OVER FUCKING BACKWARDS IN MY ATTEMPTS TO SHOW YOU JUST HOW REASONABLE I CAN BE.
IS THIS A FUCKING JOKE?
OH, HOW SOON THEY FORGET.
ANSWER ME THIS. AFTER YOUR SON HID IN ONE OF MY TRUCKS AND MACHINE GUNNED A FEW OF MY MEN... TO DEATH... WHAT DID I DO?
DID I GUT THAT BOY? OR LET A FEW OF MY BOYS RUN A TRAIN ON HIM? AS AN ASIDE, I'LL REVEAL THAT WAS ALWAYS AN EMPTY THREAT. AS MUCH AS I LOVE VIOLENCE... I ABSOLUTELY FUCKING HATE SEXUAL VIOLENCE. IT'S... UNSEEMLY.
NO... I LET YOUR SON GO, I BROUGHT HIM BACK TO YOU SAFE AND ABSOFUCKINGLUTELY SOUND... LIKE SOME KIND OF APOCALYPTIC SANTA CLAUS. HO FUCKING HO.
LET ME PUT IT TO YOU THIS WAY, RICK THE PRICK WHO WILL NEVER GIVE ME THE BENEFIT OF THE DOUBT BECAUSE I HAD TO KILL ONE MEASLY FRIEND TO GET HIM IN LINE.
THE NEXT TIME SOMEONE ASKS ME TO KILL YOU AND PUT THEM IN CHARGE... I MIGHT JUST TAKE THEM UP ON IT.
NOW... SHOW ME WHAT YOU GOT.

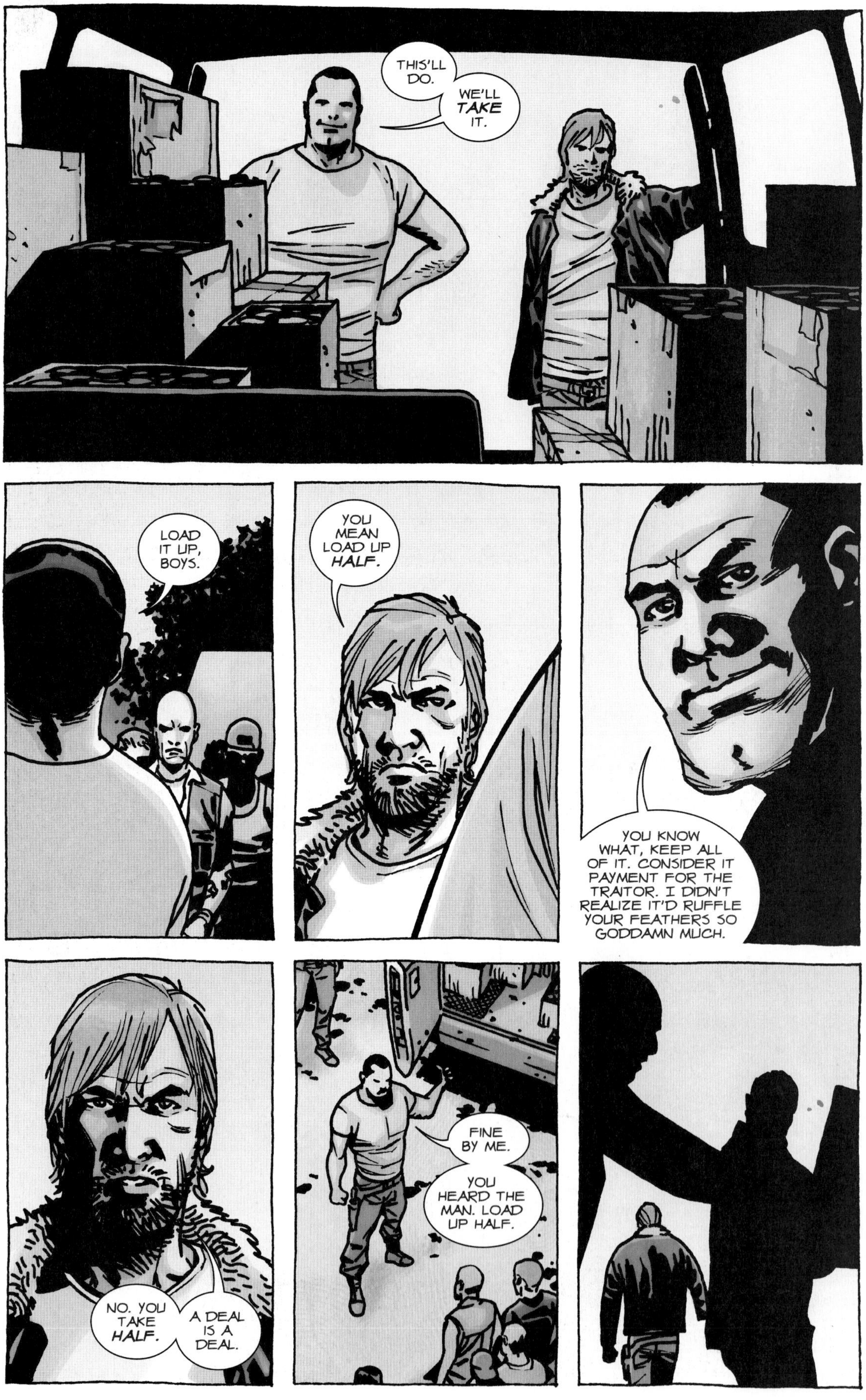
THIS'LL DO.
WE'LL *TAKE* IT.
LOAD IT UP, BOYS.
YOU MEAN LOAD UP *HALF.*
YOU KNOW WHAT, KEEP ALL OF IT. CONSIDER IT PAYMENT FOR THE TRAITOR. I DIDN'T REALIZE IT'D RUFFLE YOUR FEATHERS SO GODDAMN MUCH.
NO. YOU TAKE *HALF.*
A DEAL IS A DEAL.
FINE BY ME.
YOU HEARD THE MAN. LOAD UP HALF.

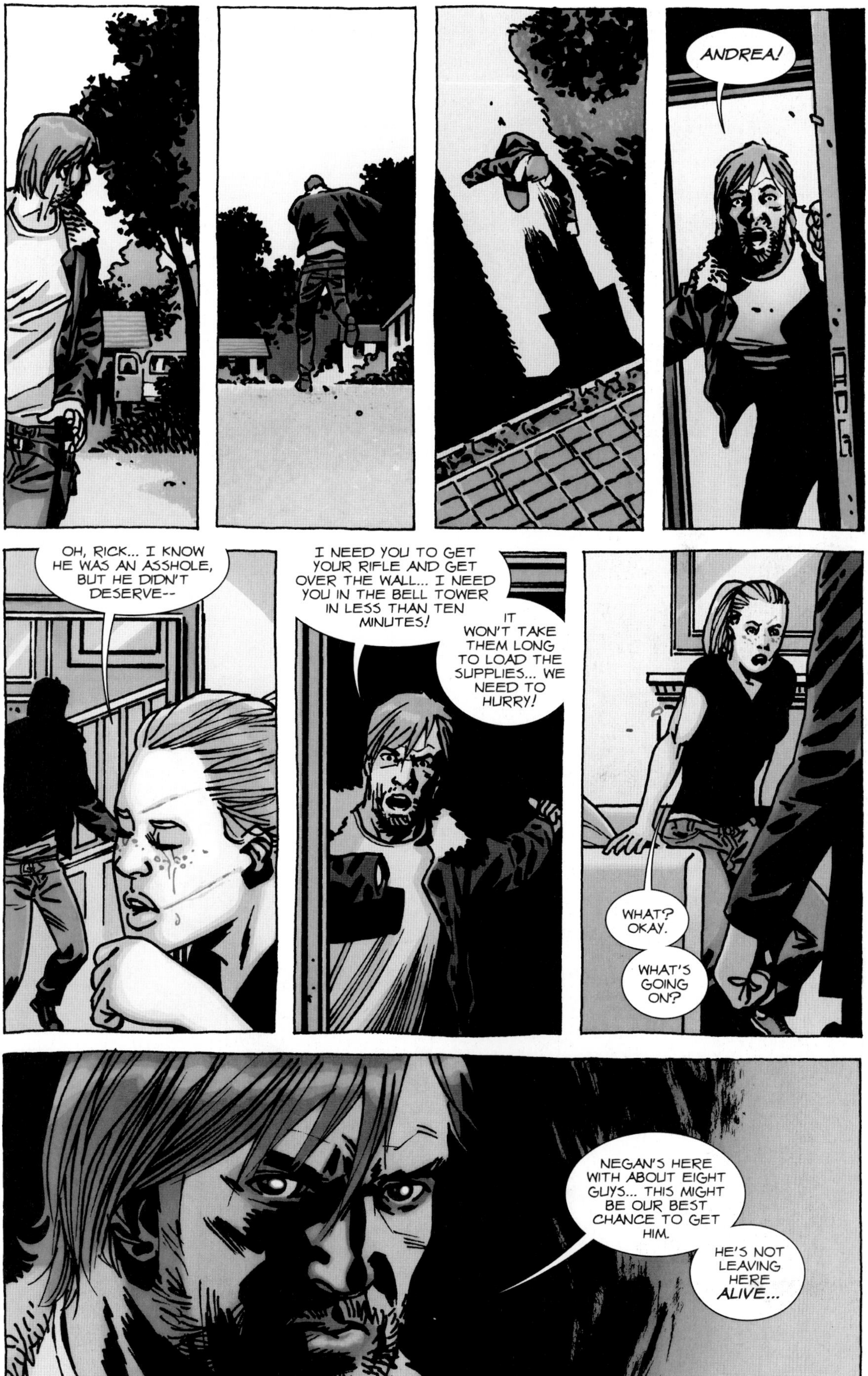
ANDREA!
OH, RICK... I KNOW HE WAS AN ASSHOLE, BUT HE DIDN'T DESERVE--
I NEED YOU TO GET YOUR RIFLE AND GET OVER THE WALL... I NEED YOU IN THE BELL TOWER IN LESS THAN TEN MINUTES!
IT WON'T TAKE THEM LONG TO LOAD THE SUPPLIES... WE NEED TO HURRY!
WHAT? OKAY.
WHAT'S GOING ON?
NEGAN'S HERE WITH ABOUT EIGHT GUYS... THIS MIGHT BE OUR BEST CHANCE TO GET HIM.
HE'S NOT LEAVING HERE *ALIVE*...

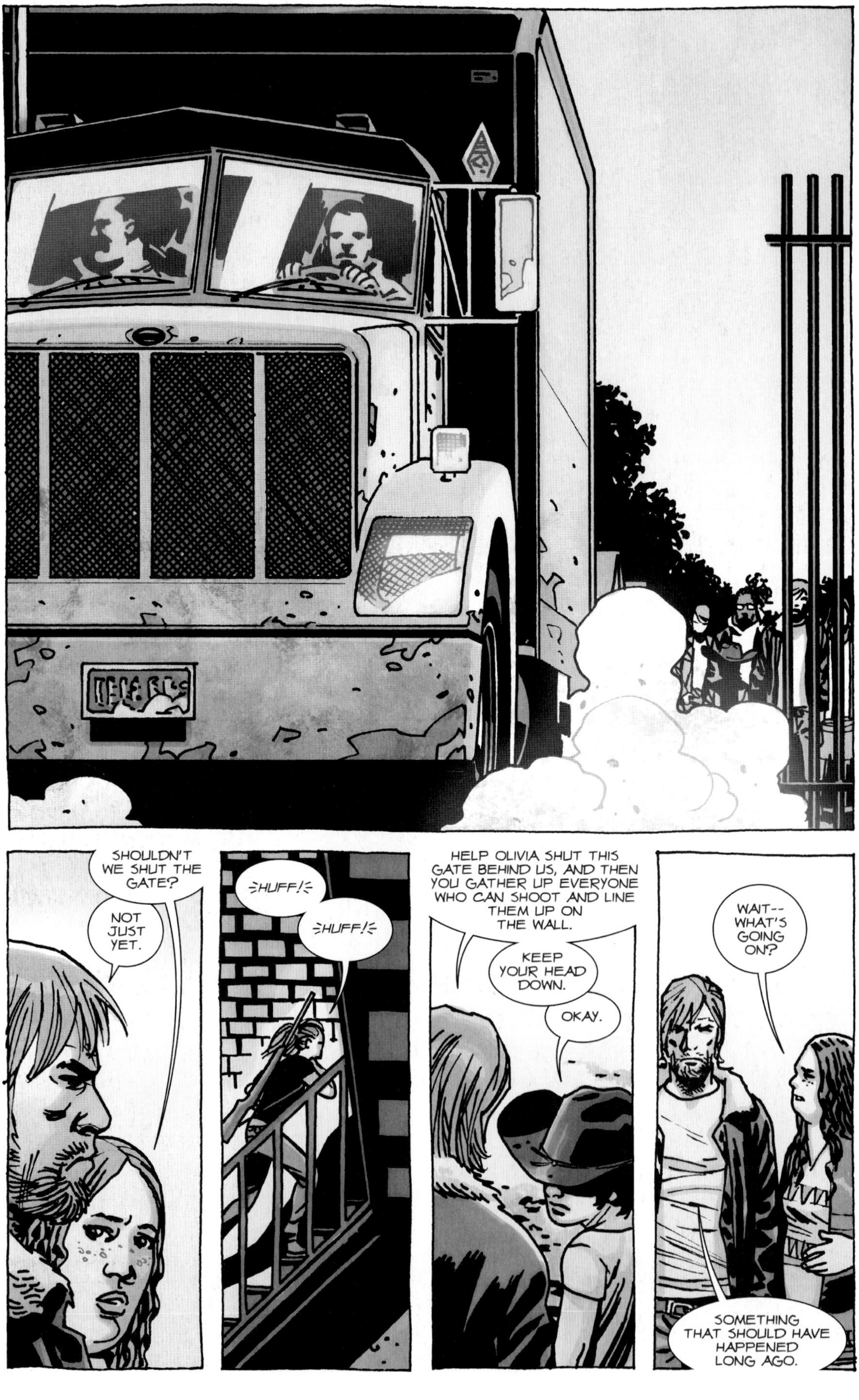
SHOULDN'T WE SHUT THE GATE?
NOT JUST YET.
HUFF!
HUFF!
HELP OLIVIA SHUT THIS GATE BEHIND US, AND THEN YOU GATHER UP EVERYONE WHO CAN SHOOT AND LINE THEM UP ON THE WALL.
KEEP YOUR HEAD DOWN.
OKAY.
WAIT-- WHAT'S GOING ON?
SOMETHING THAT SHOULD HAVE HAPPENED LONG AGO.

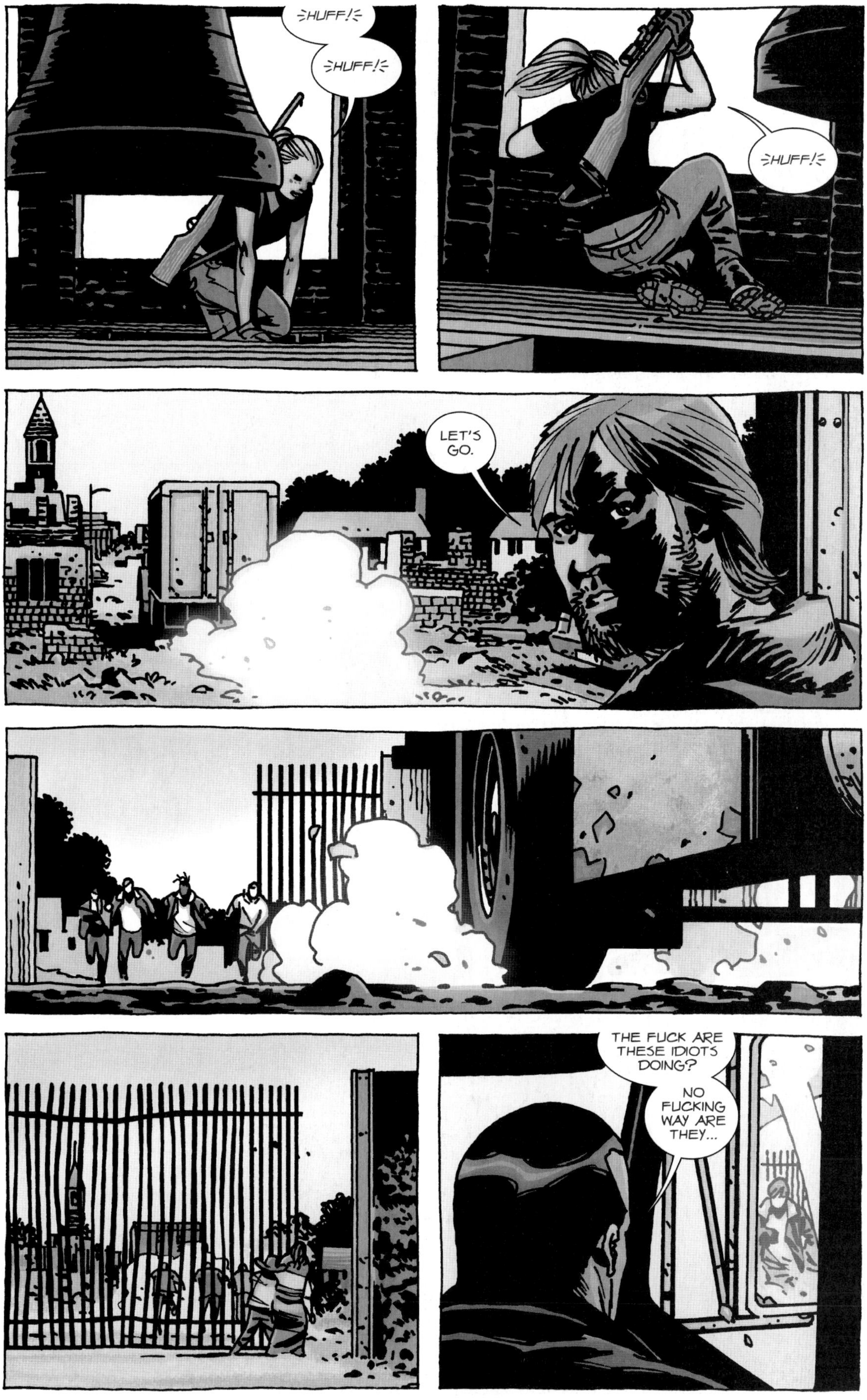
HUFF!
HUFF!
HUFF!
LET'S GO.
THE FUCK ARE THESE IDIOTS DOING?
NO FUCKING WAY ARE THEY...

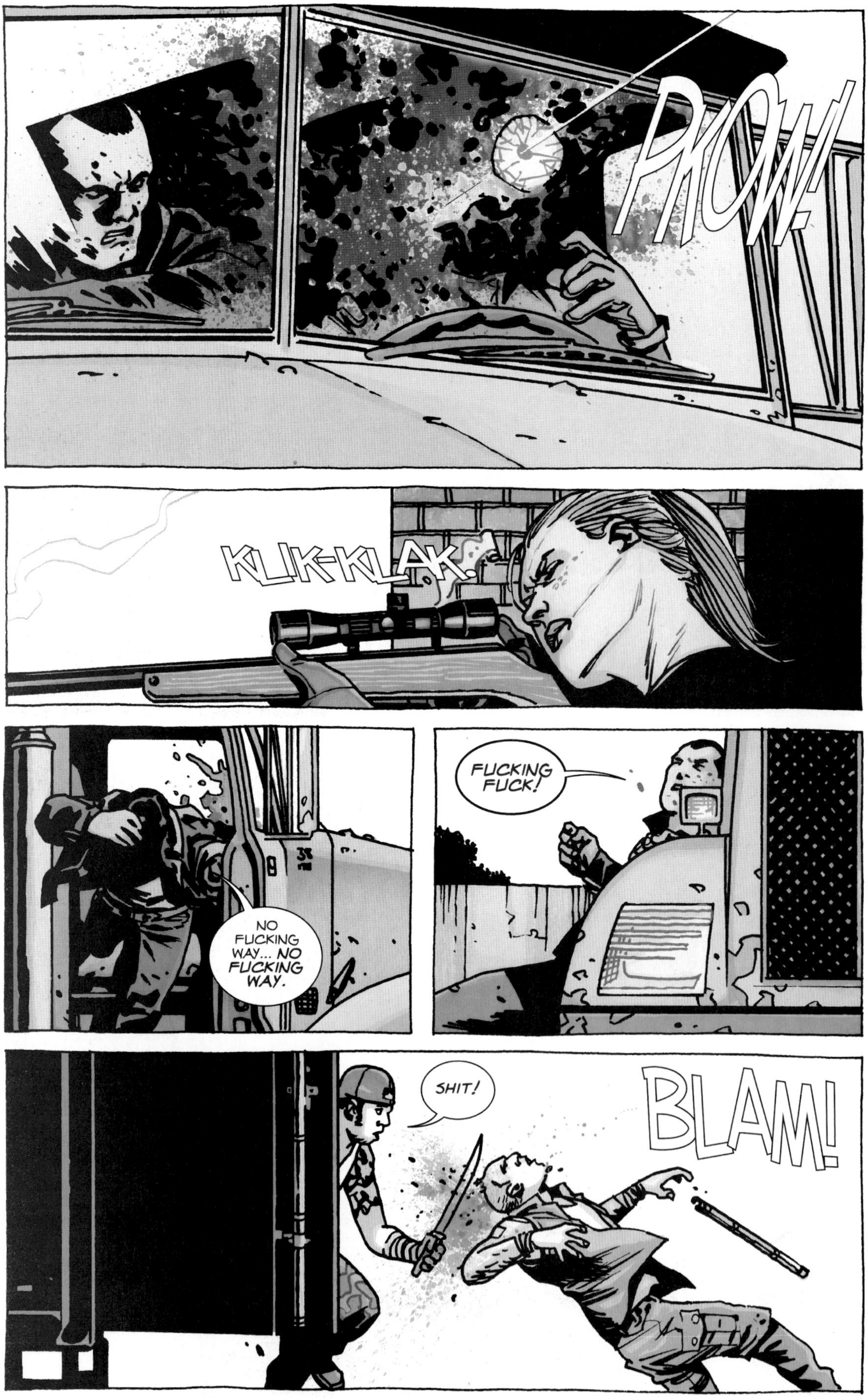
PKOW!
KLIK-KLAK.
NO FUCKING WAY... NO FUCKING WAY.
FUCKING FUCK!
SHIT!
BLAM!

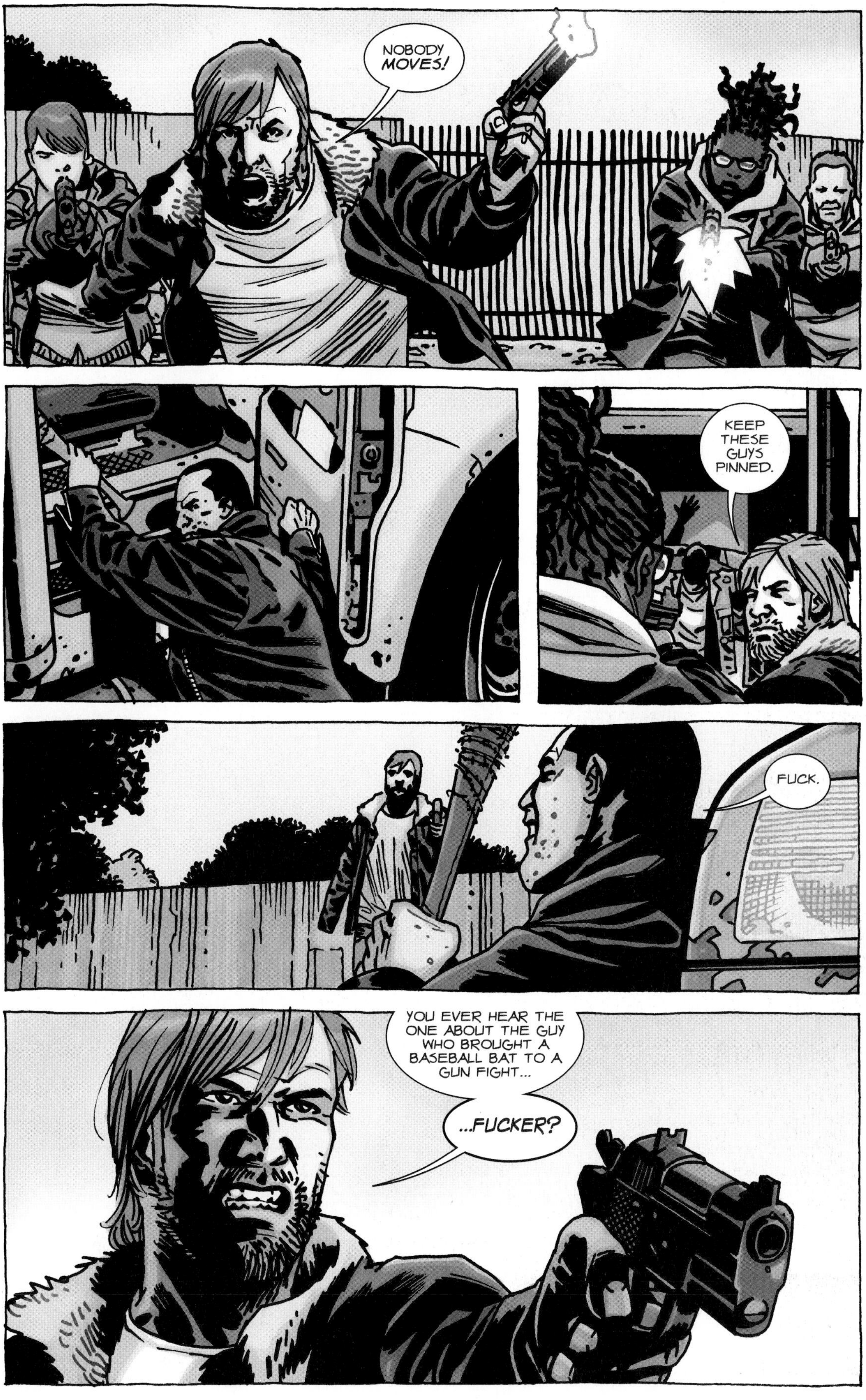
NOBODY MOVES!
KEEP THESE GUYS PINNED.
FUCK.
YOU EVER HEAR THE ONE ABOUT THE GUY WHO BROUGHT A BASEBALL BAT TO A GUN FIGHT...
...FUCKER?

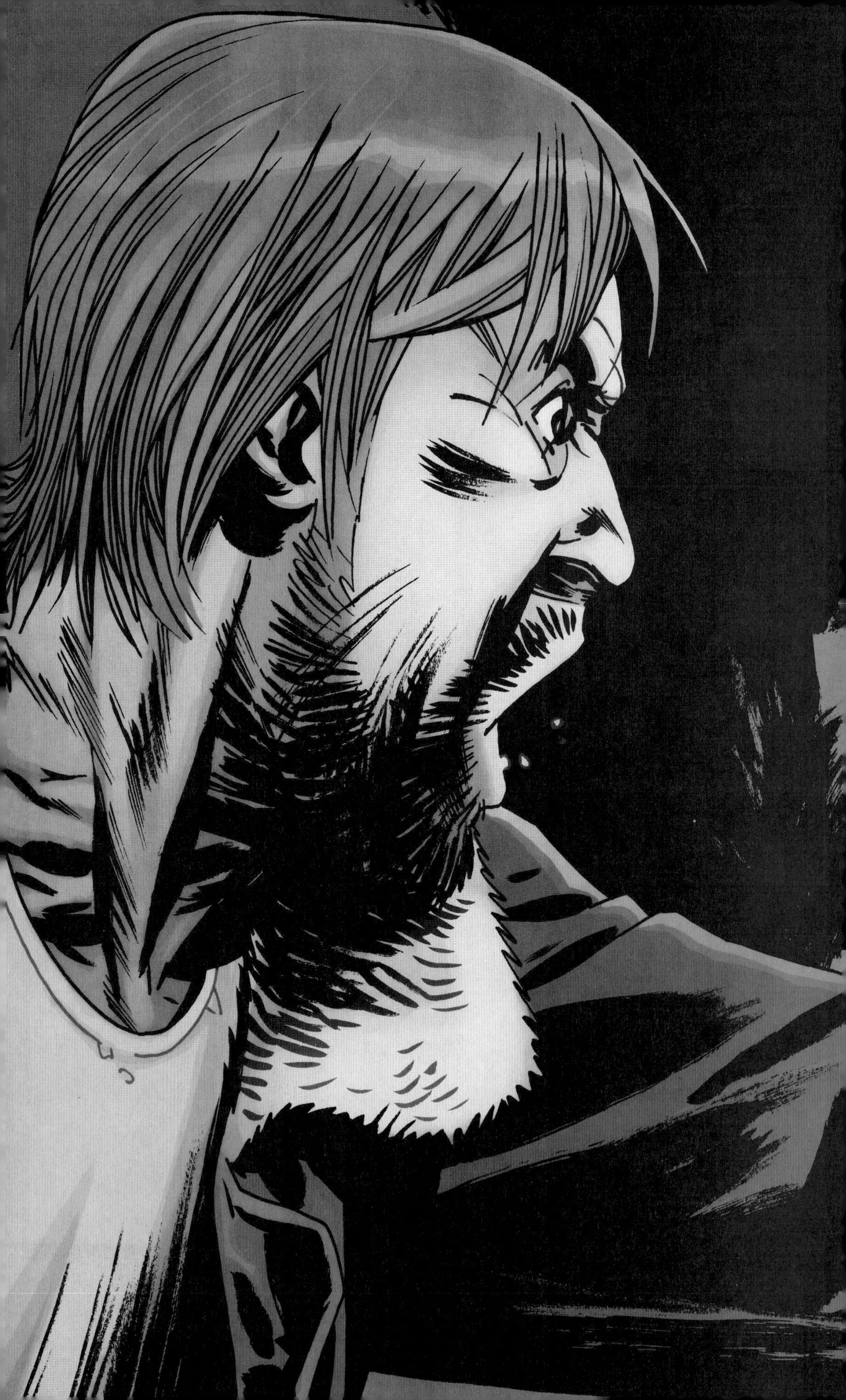

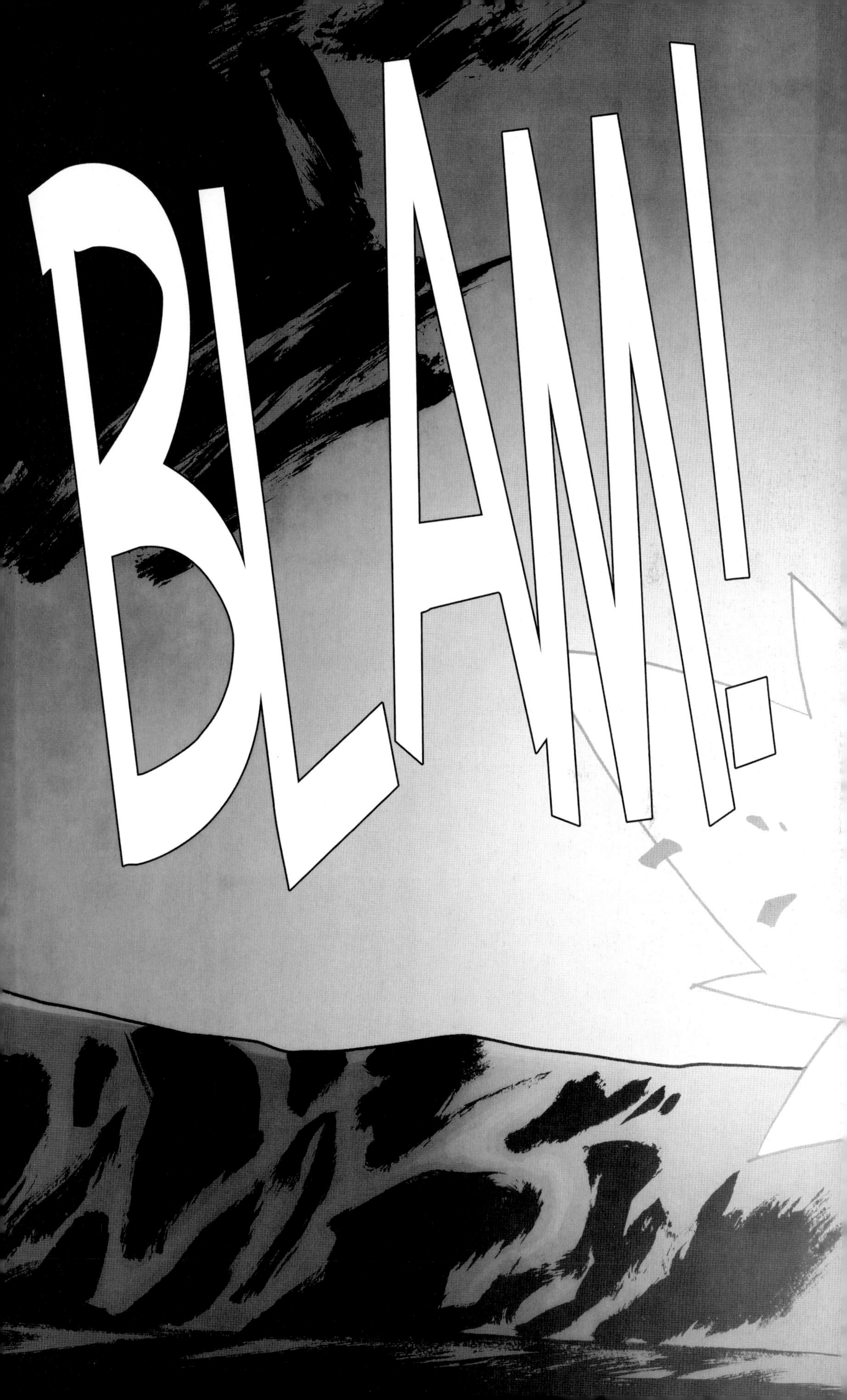
BLAM!

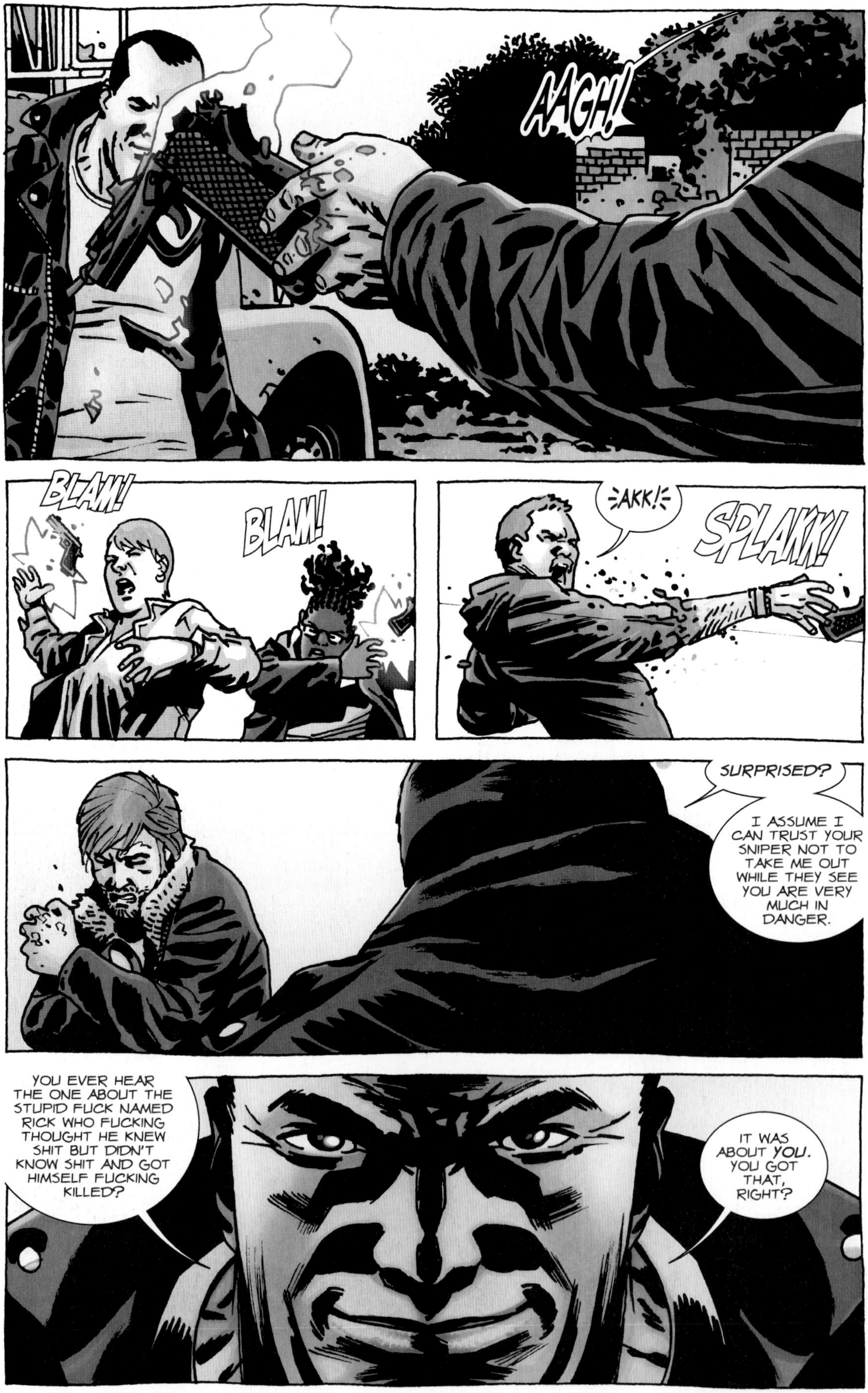
AAGH!
BLAM!
BLAM!
AKK!
SPLAKK!
SURPRISED?
I ASSUME I CAN TRUST YOUR SNIPER NOT TO TAKE ME OUT WHILE THEY SEE YOU ARE VERY MUCH IN DANGER.
YOU EVER HEAR THE ONE ABOUT THE STUPID FUCK NAMED RICK WHO FUCKING THOUGHT HE KNEW SHIT BUT DIDN'T KNOW SHIT AND GOT HIMSELF FUCKING KILLED?
IT WAS ABOUT *YOU*. YOU GOT THAT, RIGHT?

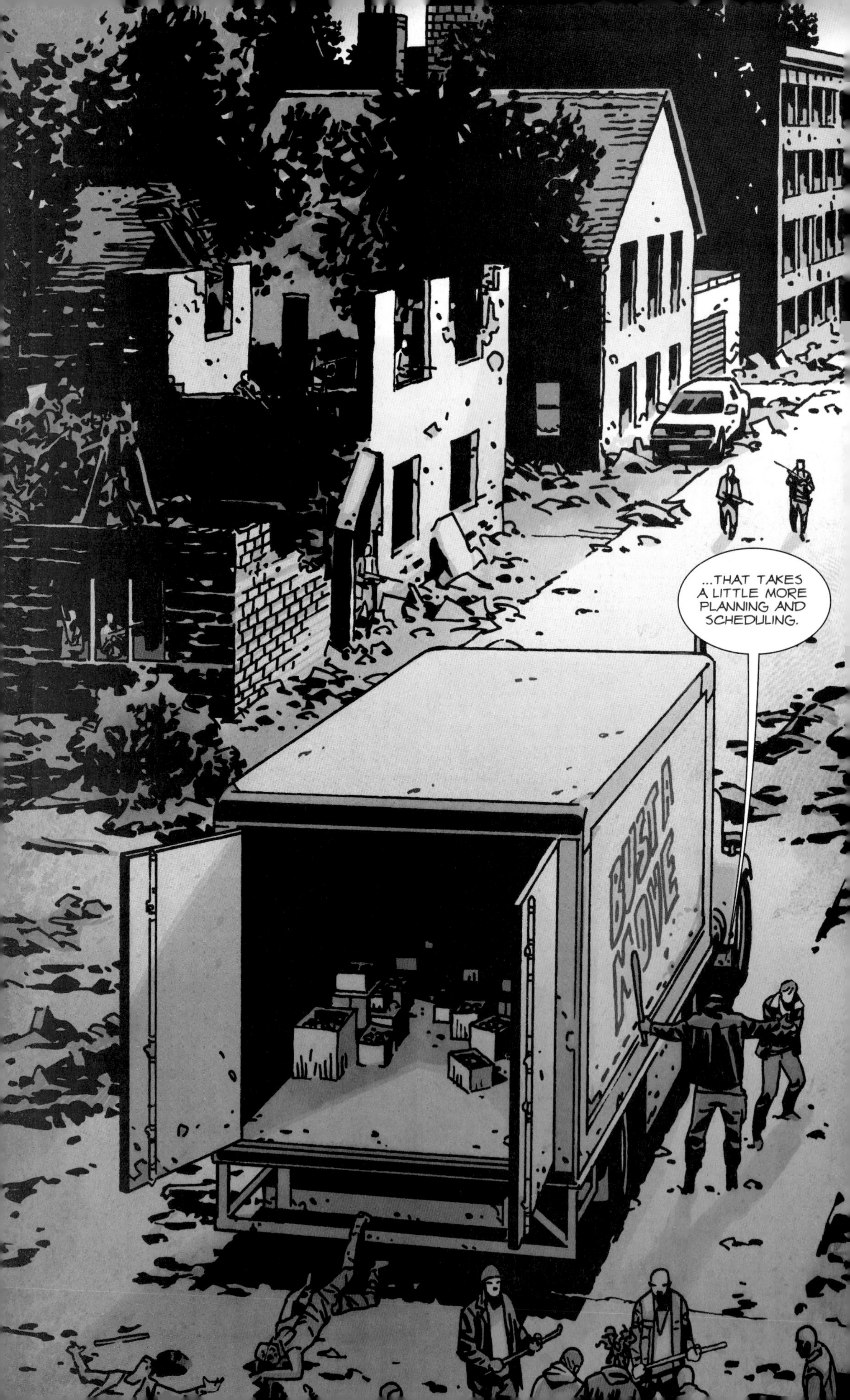
...THAT TAKES A LITTLE MORE PLANNING AND SCHEDULING.
BUST A MOVE

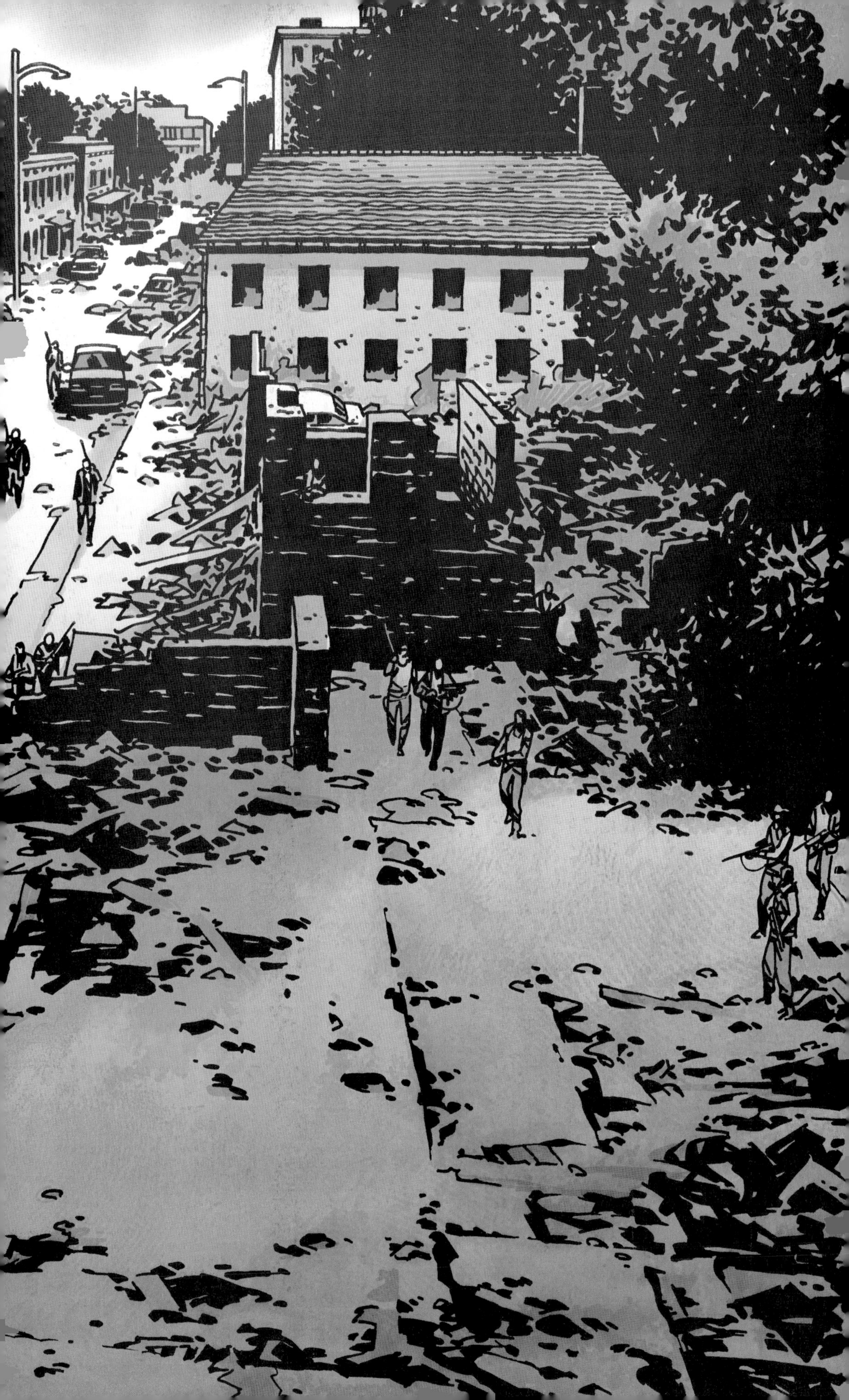

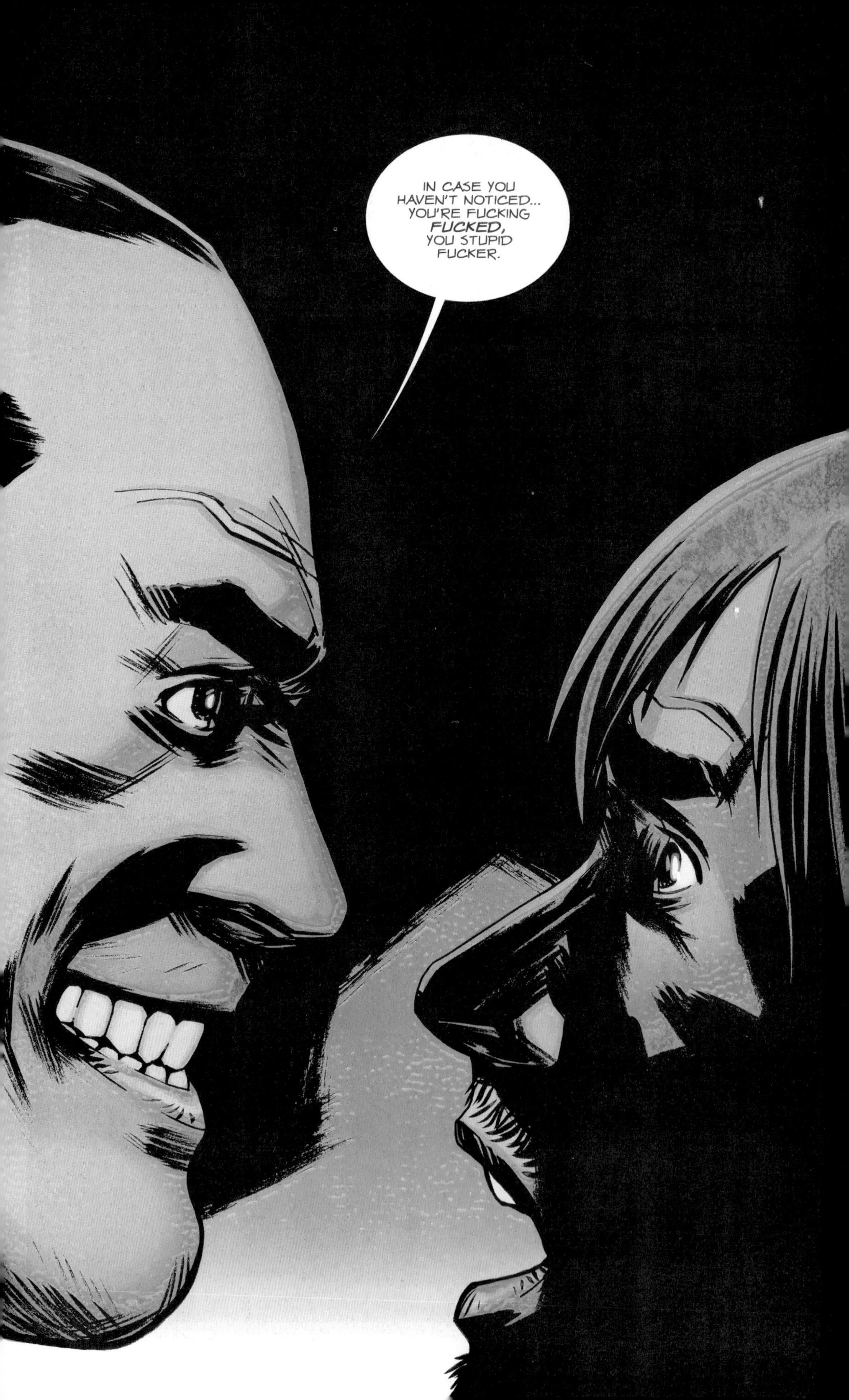
IN CASE YOU HAVEN'T NOTICED... YOU'RE FUCKING *FUCKED,* YOU STUPID FUCKER.

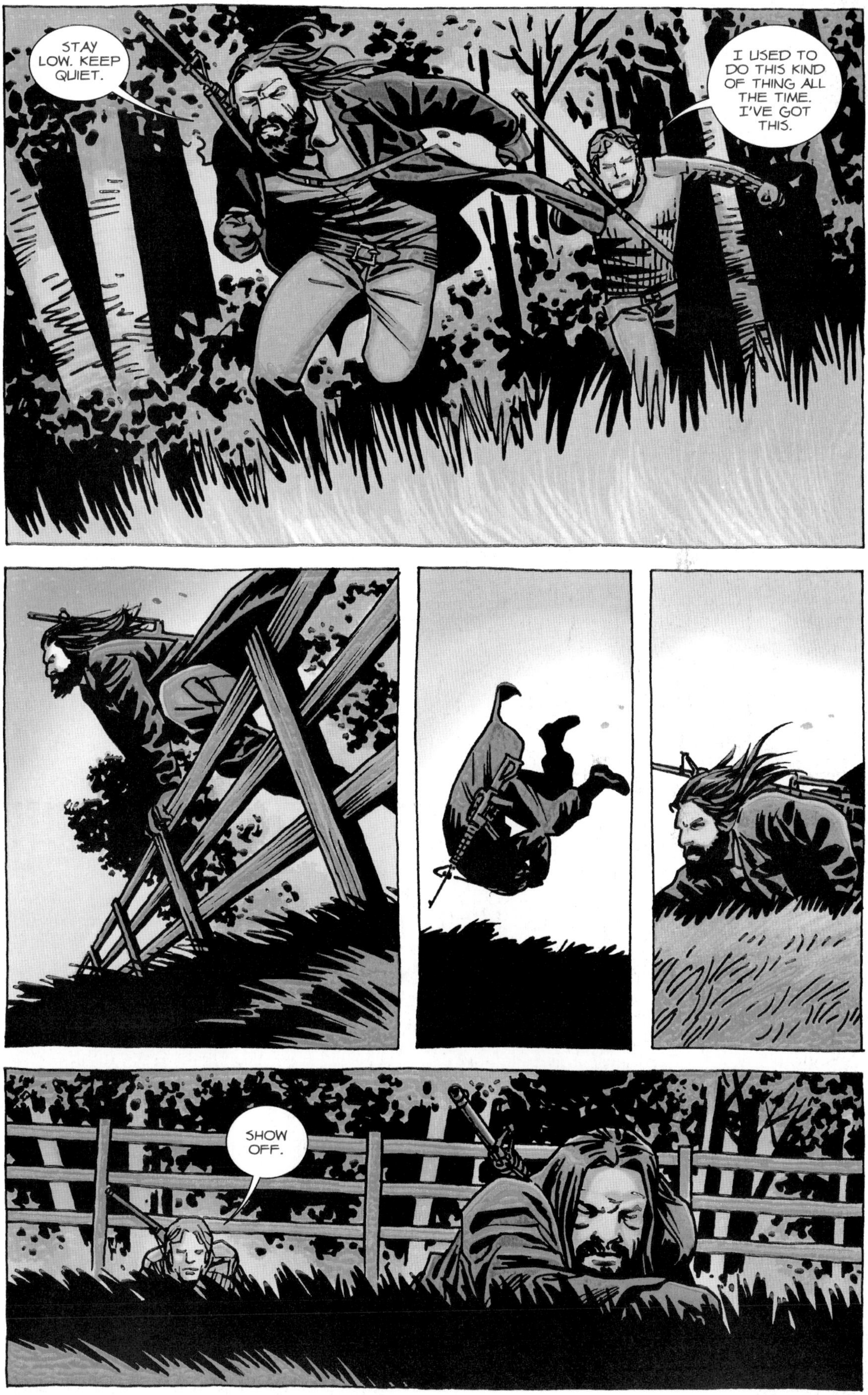
STAY LOW. KEEP QUIET.
I USED TO DO THIS KIND OF THING ALL THE TIME. I'VE GOT THIS.
SHOW OFF.

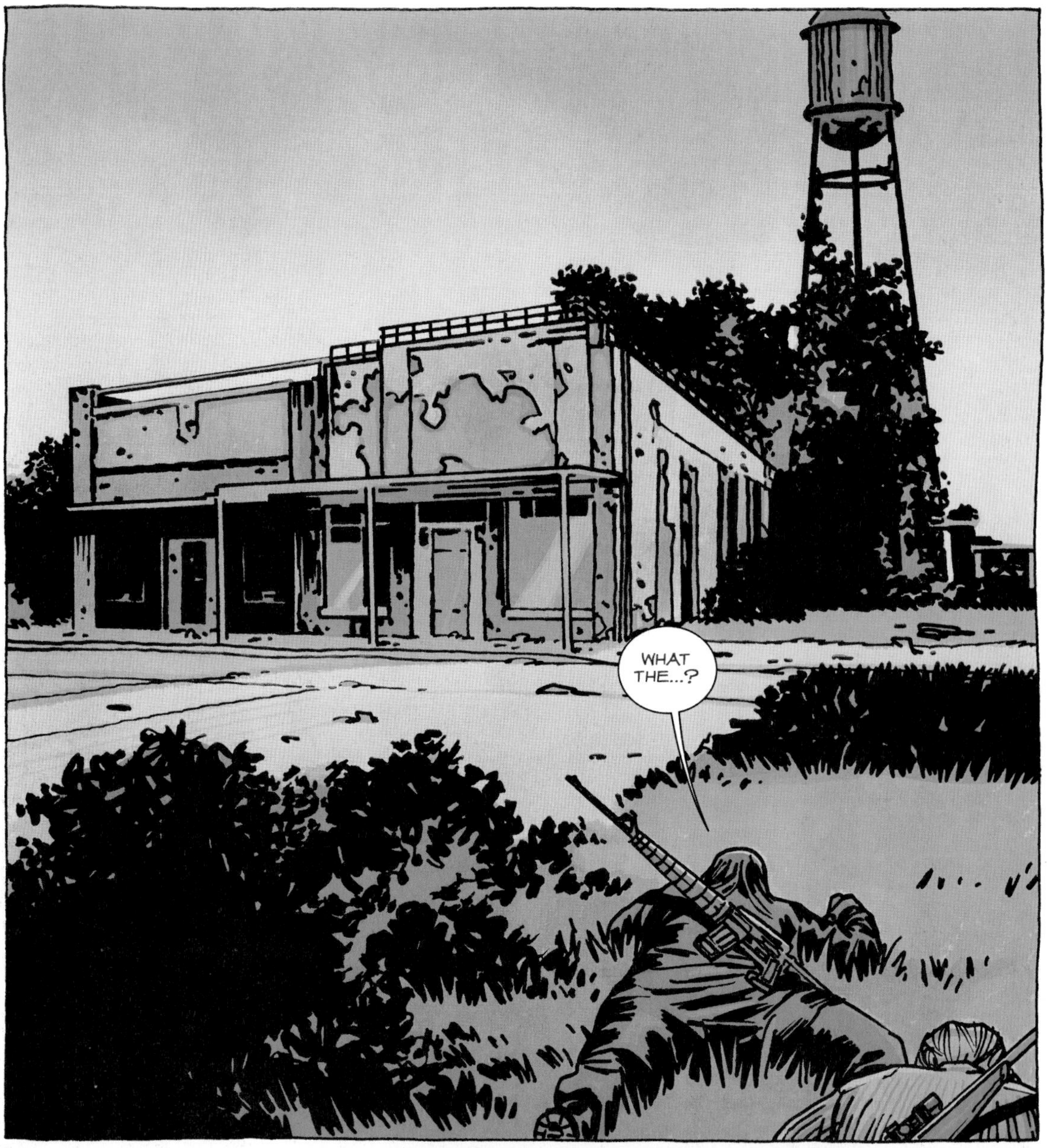
WHAT THE...?

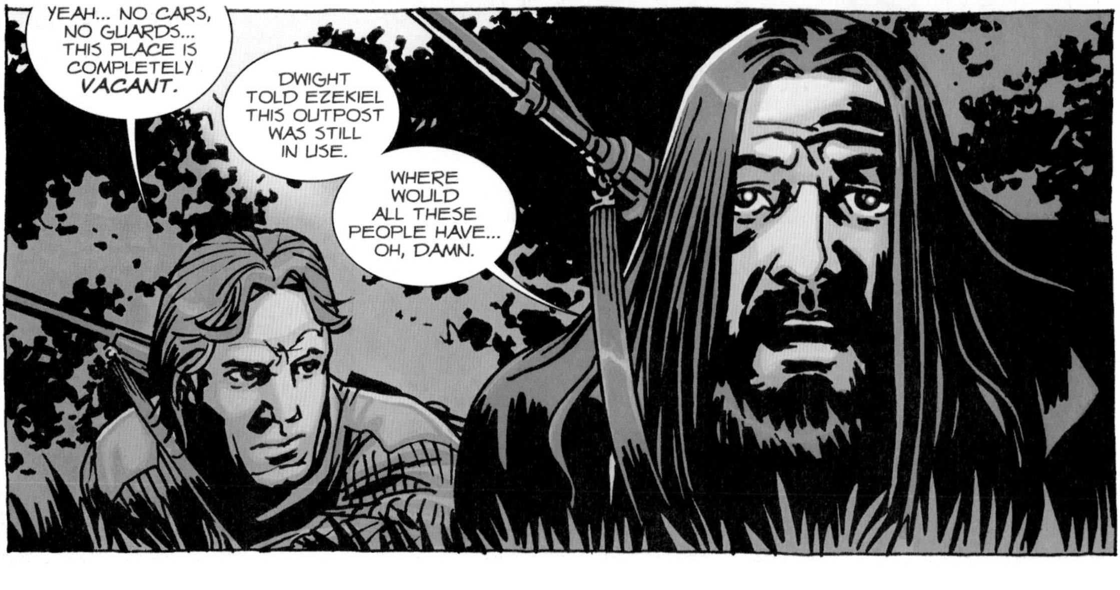
YEAH... NO CARS, NO GUARDS... THIS PLACE IS COMPLETELY *VACANT.*
DWIGHT TOLD EZEKIEL THIS OUTPOST WAS STILL IN USE.
WHERE WOULD ALL THESE PEOPLE HAVE... OH, DAMN.

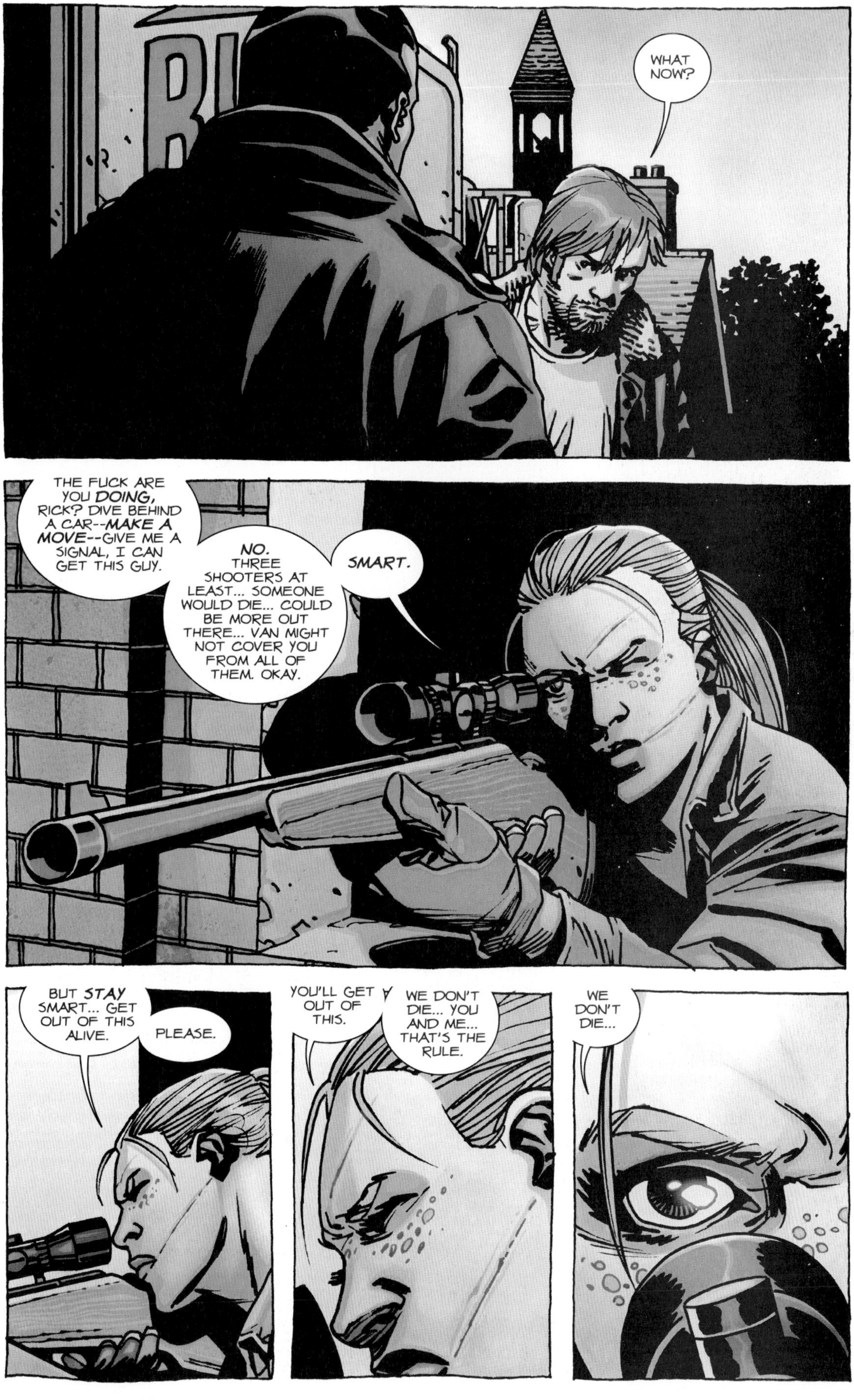
WHAT NOW?
THE FUCK ARE YOU DOING, RICK? DIVE BEHIND A CAR--MAKE A MOVE--GIVE ME A SIGNAL, I CAN GET THIS GUY.
NO. THREE SHOOTERS AT LEAST... SOMEONE WOULD DIE... COULD BE MORE OUT THERE... VAN MIGHT NOT COVER YOU FROM ALL OF THEM. OKAY.
SMART.
BUT STAY SMART... GET OUT OF THIS ALIVE.
PLEASE.
YOU'LL GET OUT OF THIS.
WE DON'T DIE... YOU AND ME... THAT'S THE RULE.
WE DON'T DIE...

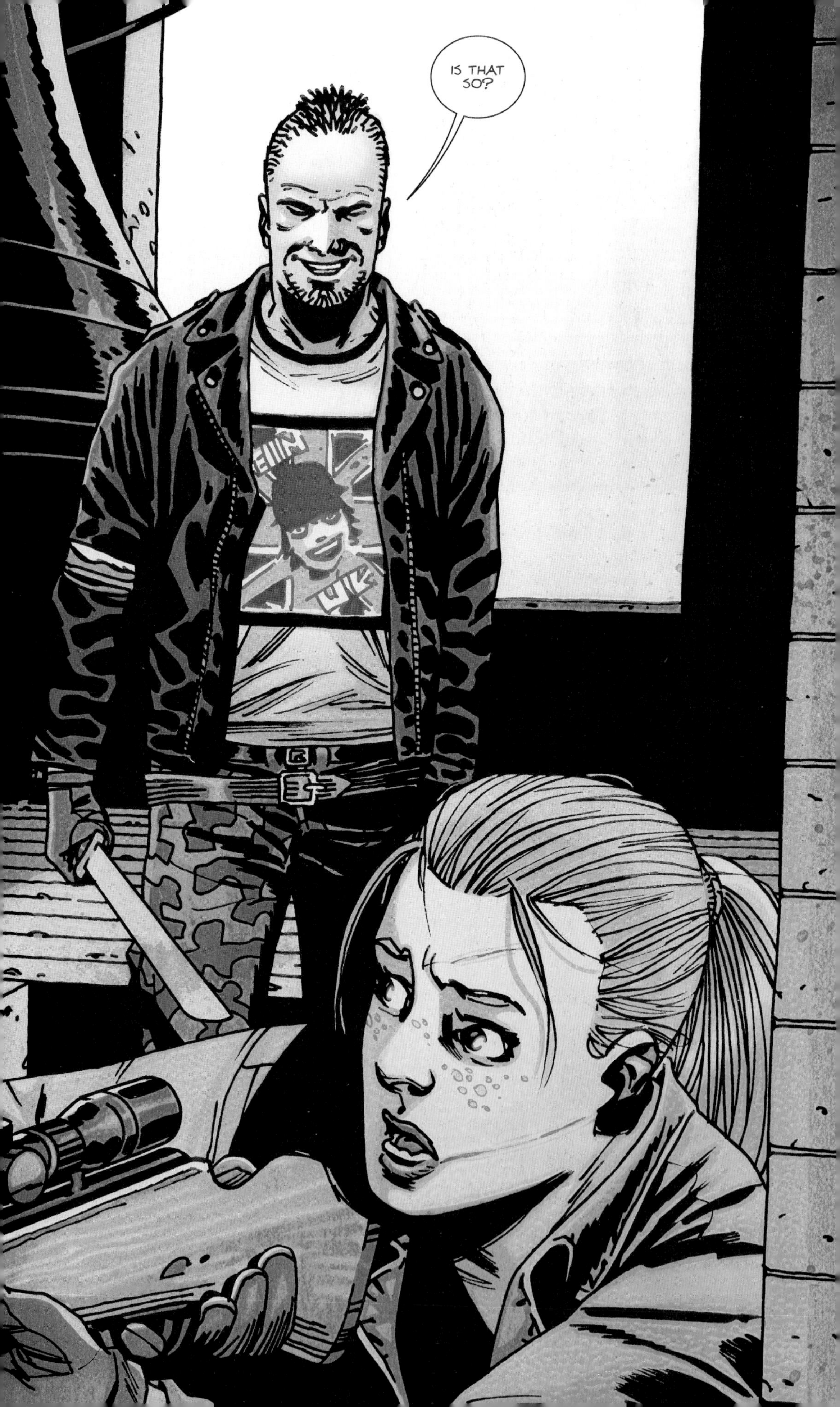
IS THAT SO?

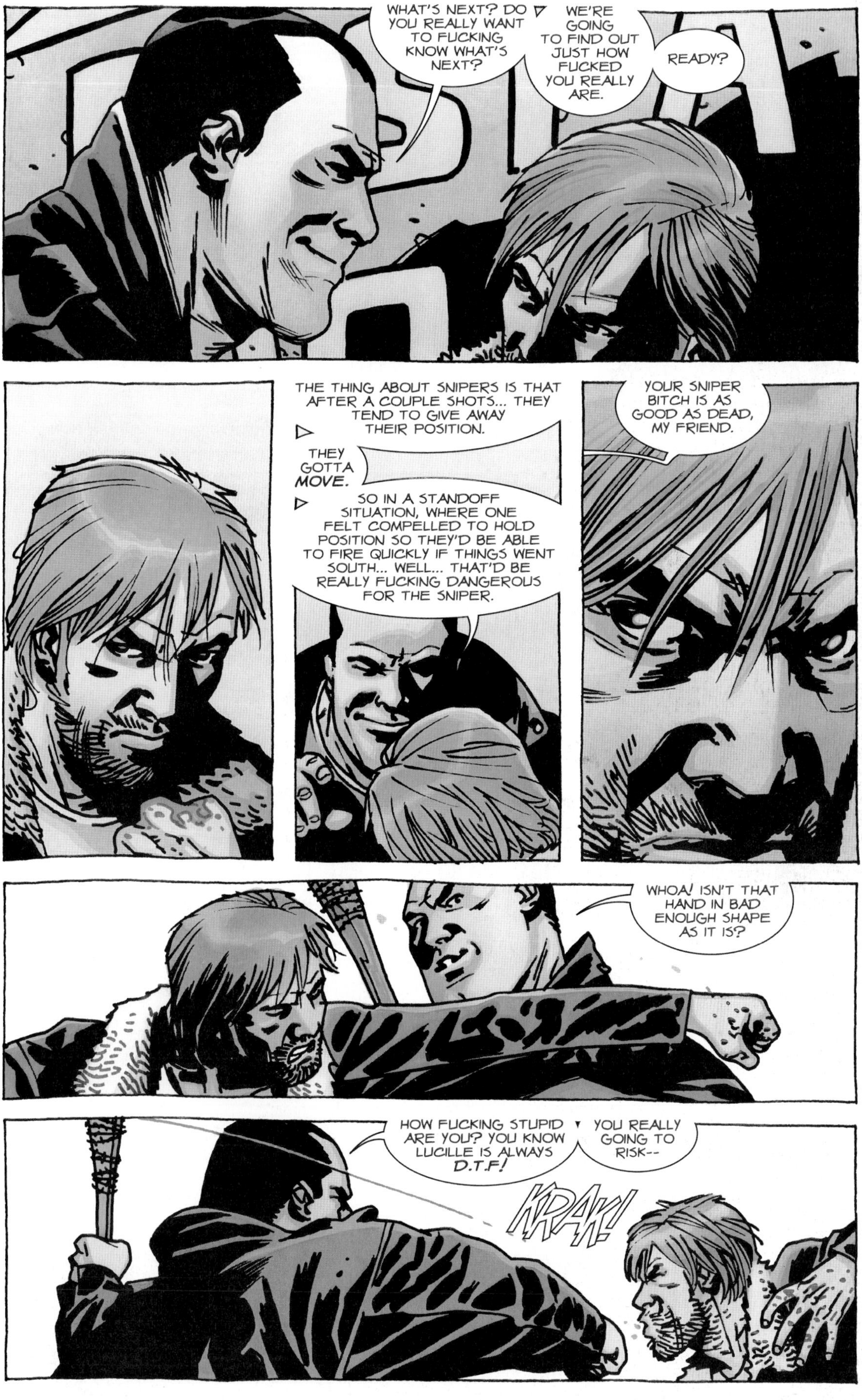
WHAT'S NEXT? DO YOU REALLY WANT TO FUCKING KNOW WHAT'S NEXT?
WE'RE GOING TO FIND OUT JUST HOW FUCKED YOU REALLY ARE.
READY?
THE THING ABOUT SNIPERS IS THAT AFTER A COUPLE SHOTS... THEY TEND TO GIVE AWAY THEIR POSITION.
THEY GOTTA **MOVE.**
SO IN A STANDOFF SITUATION, WHERE ONE FELT COMPELLED TO HOLD POSITION SO THEY'D BE ABLE TO FIRE QUICKLY IF THINGS WENT SOUTH... WELL... THAT'D BE REALLY FUCKING DANGEROUS FOR THE SNIPER.
YOUR SNIPER BITCH IS AS GOOD AS DEAD, MY FRIEND.
WHOA! ISN'T THAT HAND IN BAD ENOUGH SHAPE AS IT IS?
HOW FUCKING STUPID ARE YOU? YOU KNOW LUCILLE IS ALWAYS *D.T.F!*
YOU REALLY GOING TO RISK--
KRAK!

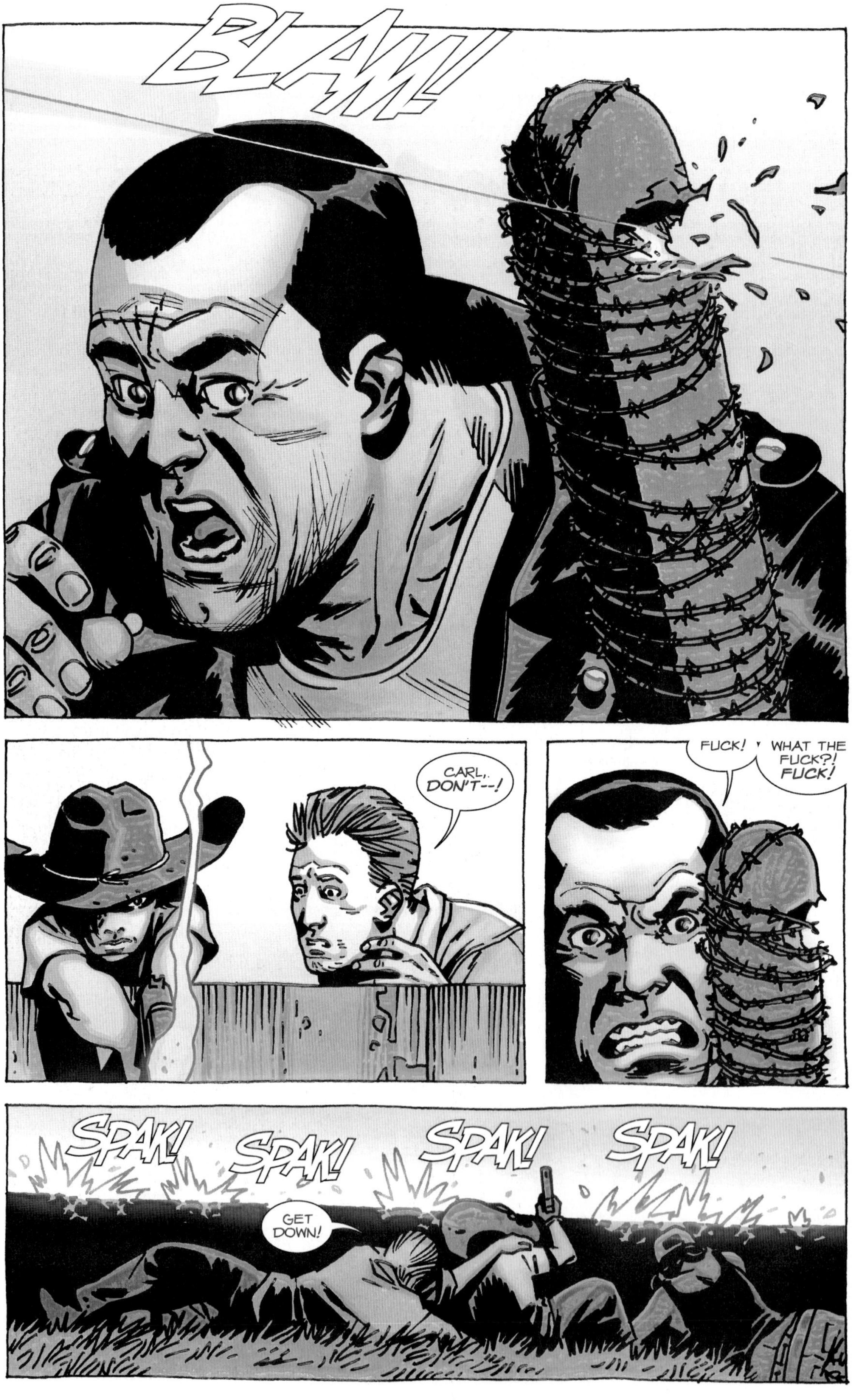
BLAM!
CARL, DON'T--!
FUCK!
WHAT THE FUCK?! FUCK!
SPAK!
SPAK!
SPAK!
SPAK!
GET DOWN!

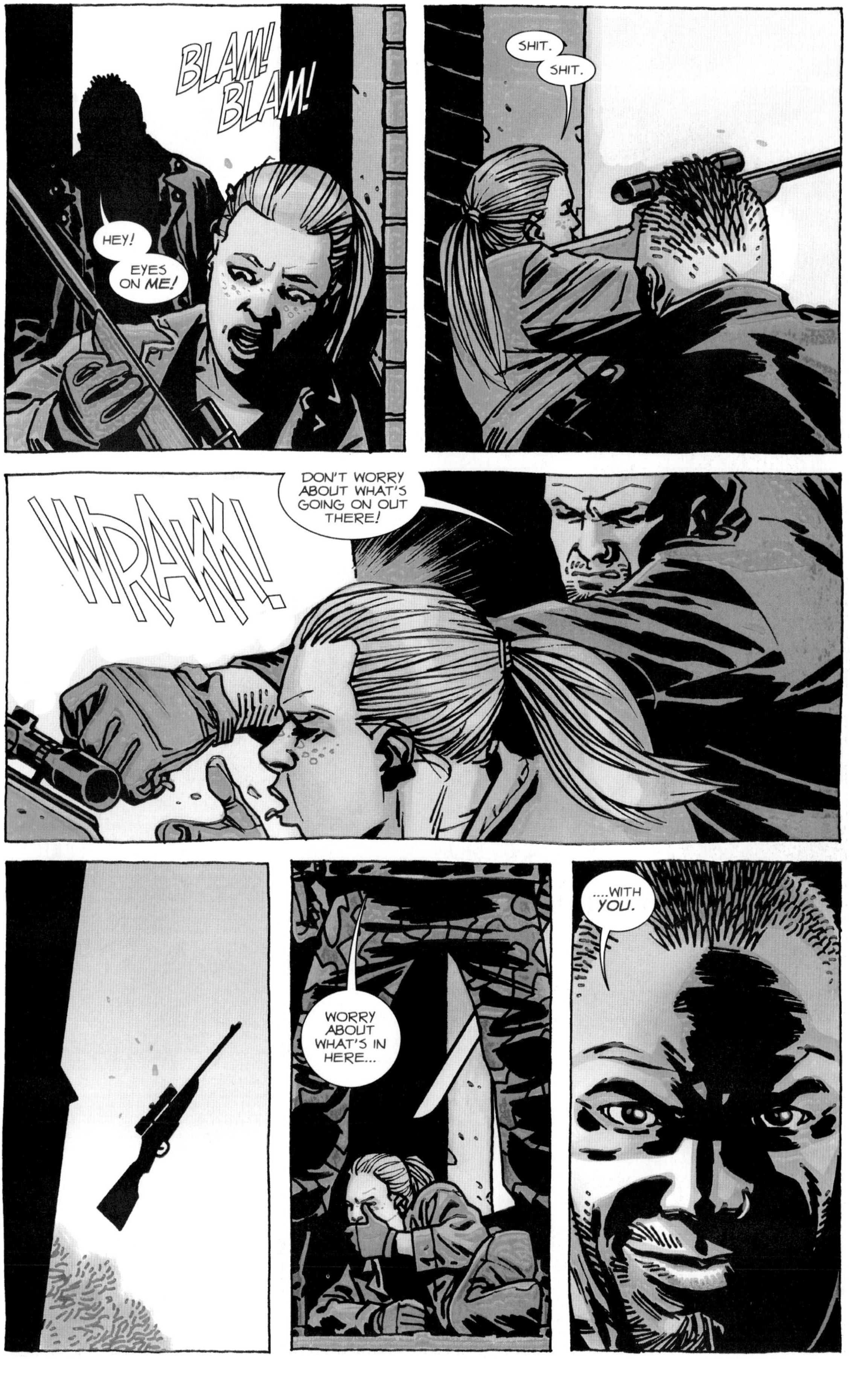
BLAM! BLAM!
HEY!
EYES ON ME!
SHIT.
SHIT.
WRAKK!
DON'T WORRY ABOUT WHAT'S GOING ON OUT THERE!
WORRY ABOUT WHAT'S IN HERE...
....WITH YOU.

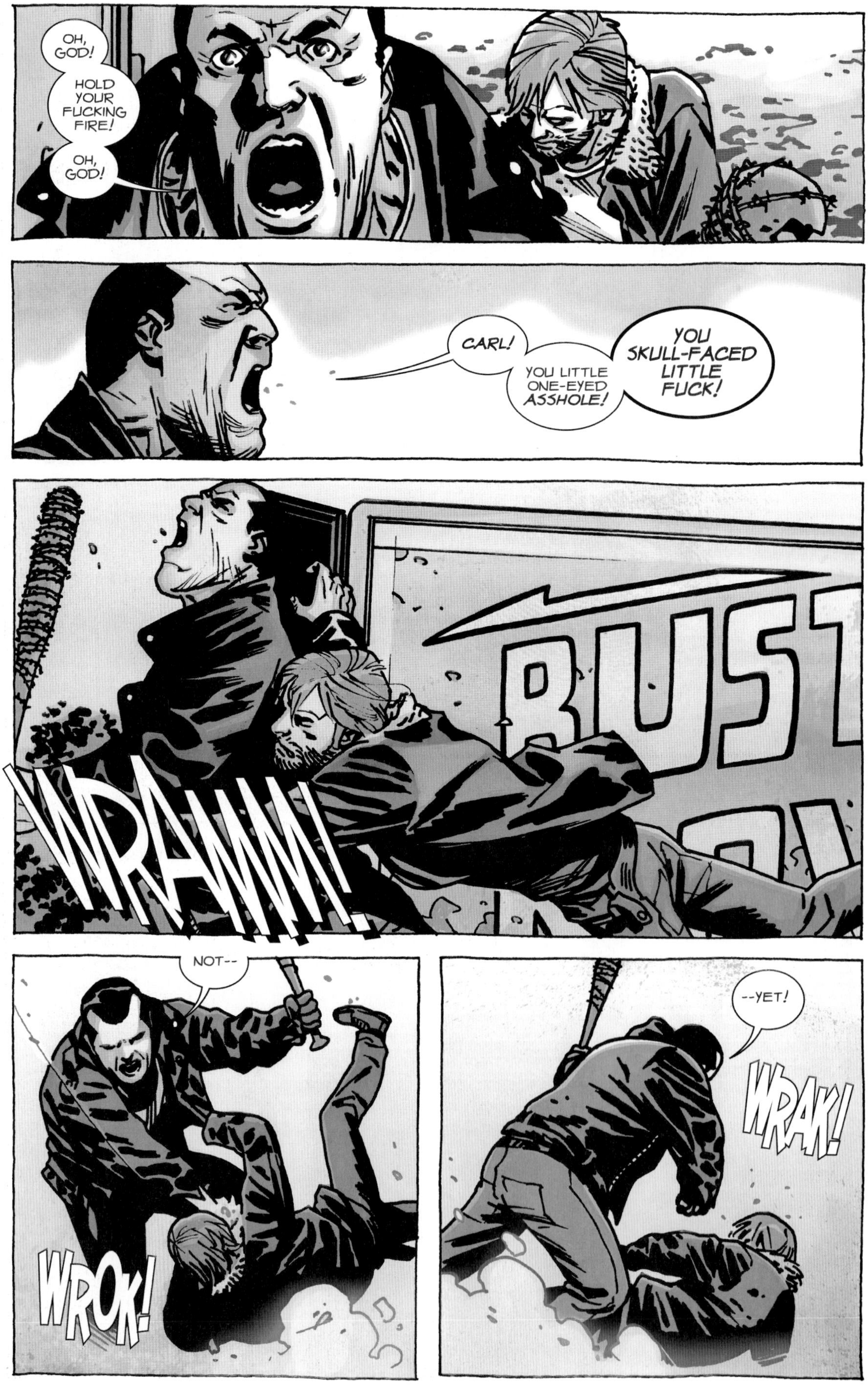
OH, GOD!
HOLD YOUR FUCKING FIRE!
OH, GOD!
CARL!
YOU LITTLE ONE-EYED ASSHOLE!
YOU SKULL-FACED LITTLE FUCK!
WRAMM!
NOT--
WROK!
--YET!
WRAK!

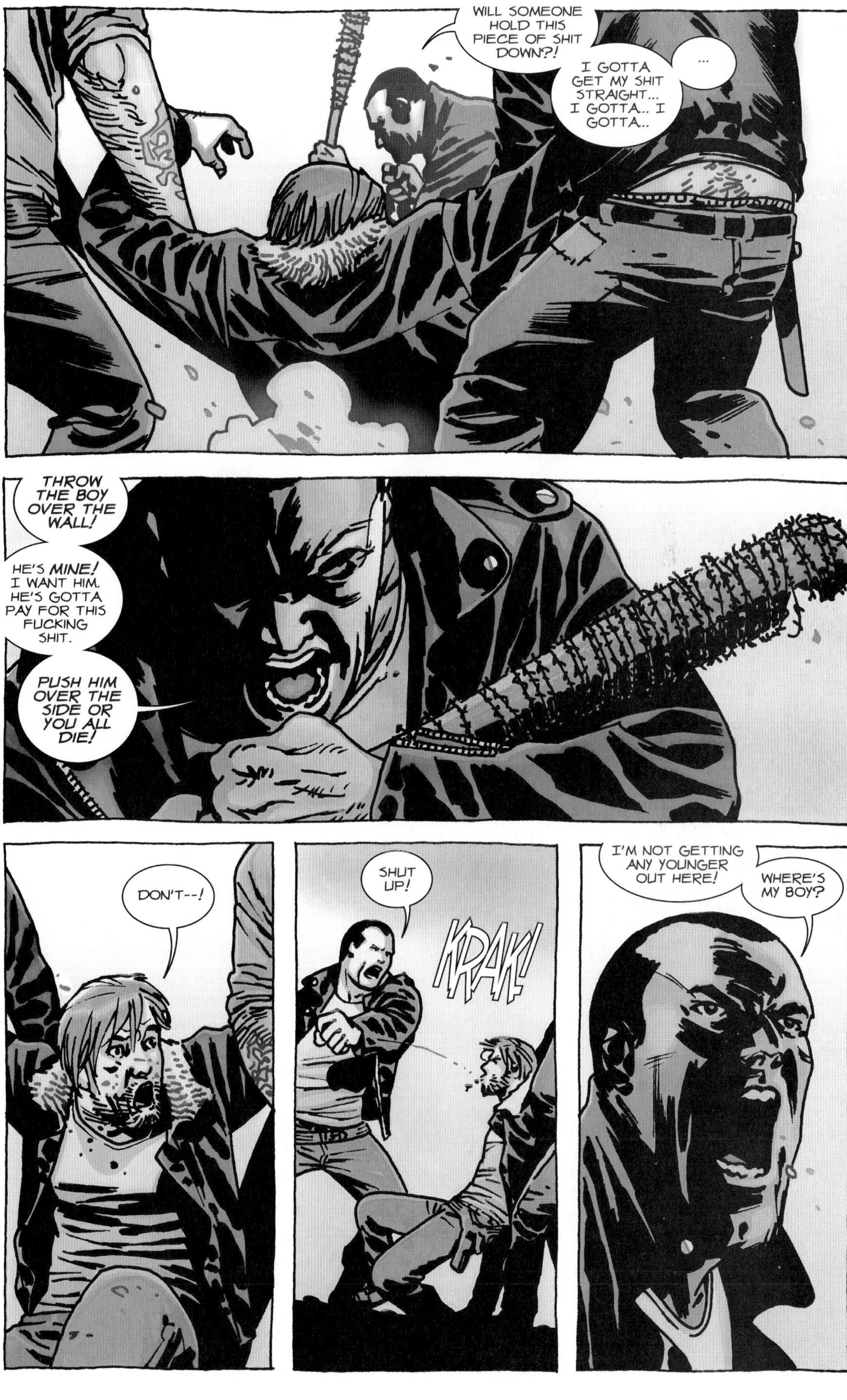
WILL SOMEONE HOLD THIS PIECE OF SHIT DOWN?!
I GOTTA GET MY SHIT STRAIGHT... I GOTTA.. I GOTTA..
...
THROW THE BOY OVER THE WALL!
HE'S MINE! I WANT HIM. HE'S GOTTA PAY FOR THIS FUCKING SHIT.
PUSH HIM OVER THE SIDE OR YOU ALL DIE!
DON'T--!
SHUT UP!
KRAK!
I'M NOT GETTING ANY YOUNGER OUT HERE!
WHERE'S MY BOY?

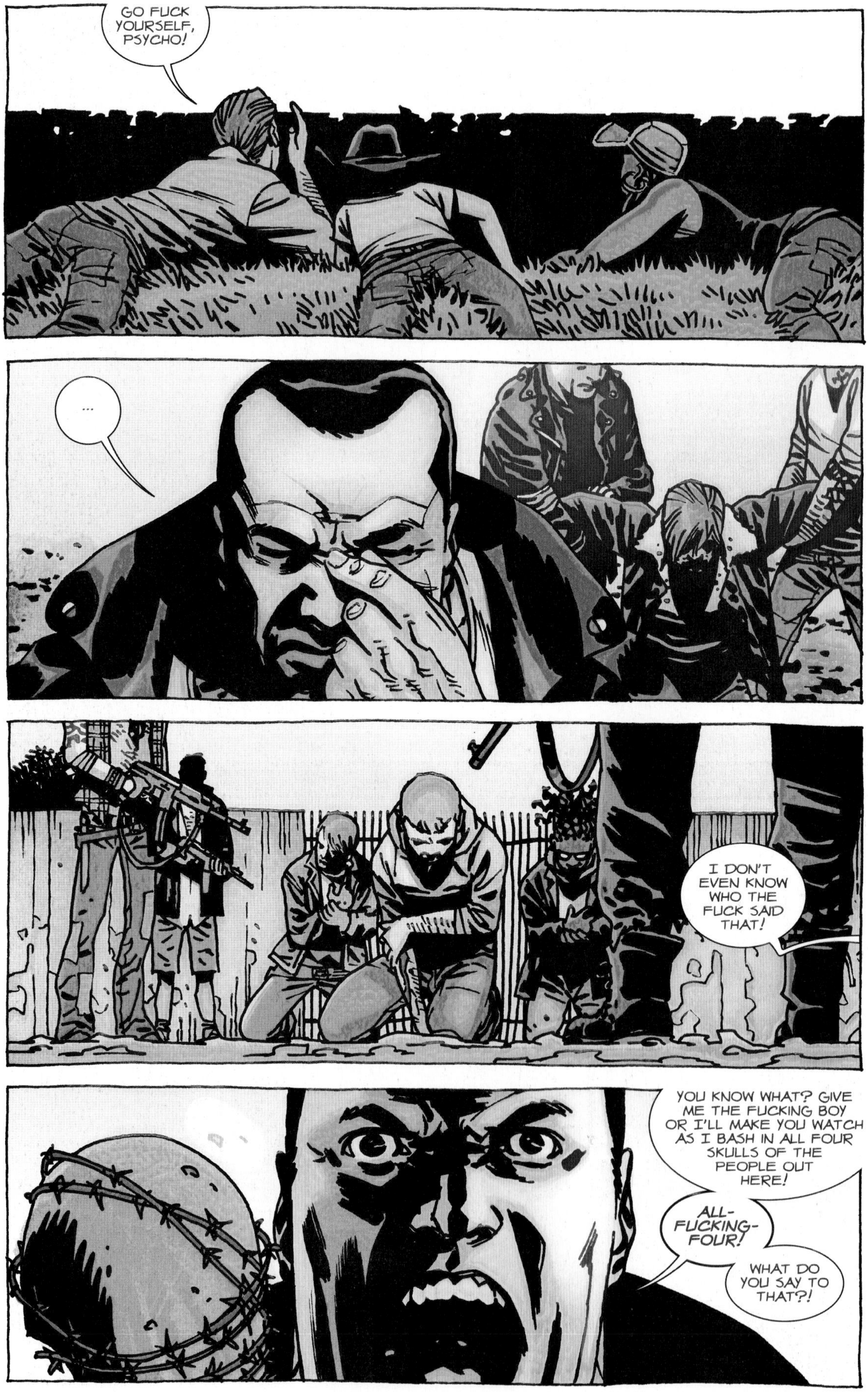
GO FUCK YOURSELF, PSYCHO!
...
I DON'T EVEN KNOW WHO THE FUCK SAID THAT!
YOU KNOW WHAT? GIVE ME THE FUCKING BOY OR I'LL MAKE YOU WATCH AS I BASH IN ALL FOUR SKULLS OF THE PEOPLE OUT HERE!
ALL-FUCKING-FOUR!
WHAT DO YOU SAY TO THAT?!

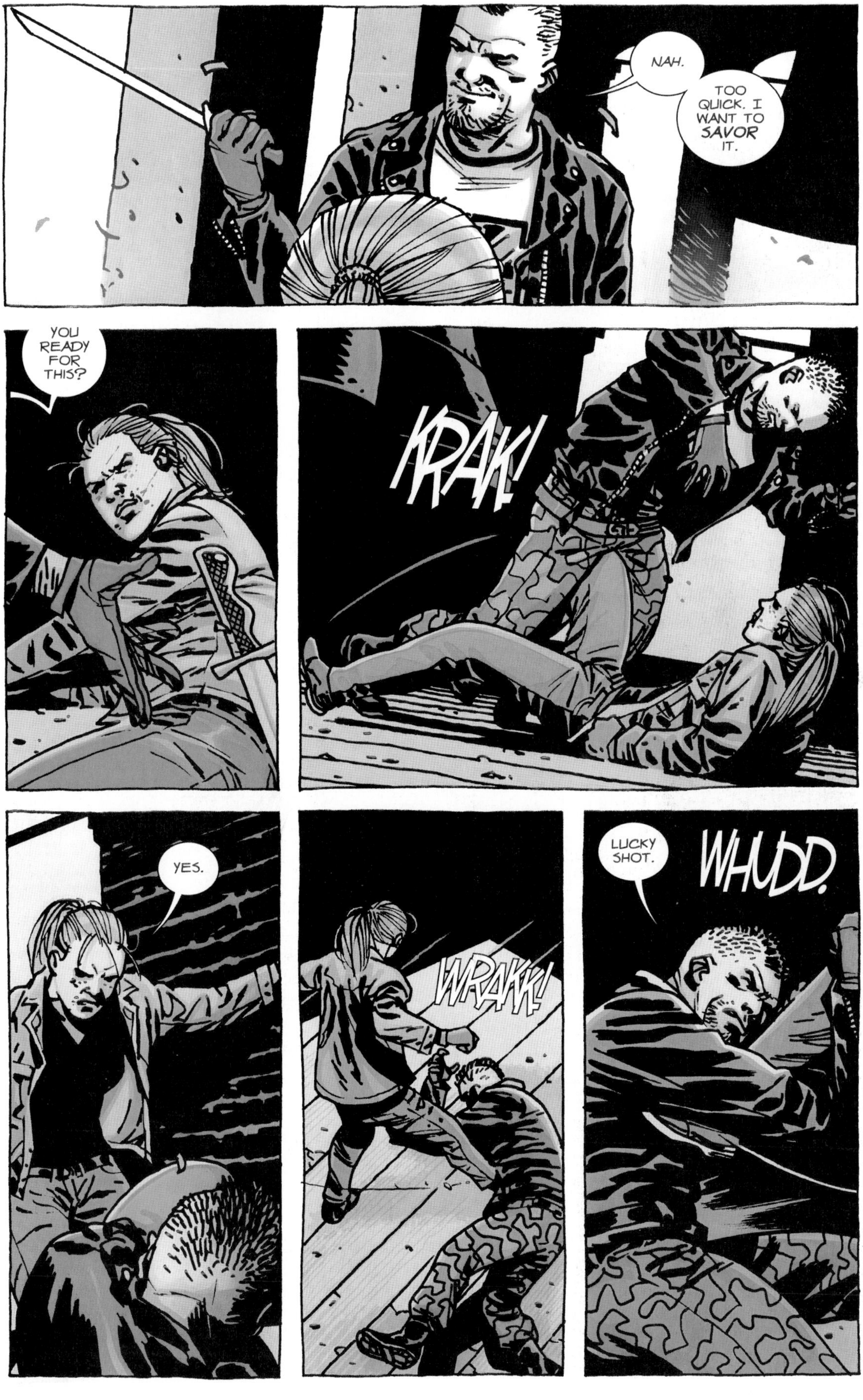
NAH.
TOO QUICK. I WANT TO SAVOR IT.
YOU READY FOR THIS?
KRAK!
YES.
WRAKK!
LUCKY SHOT.
WHUDD.

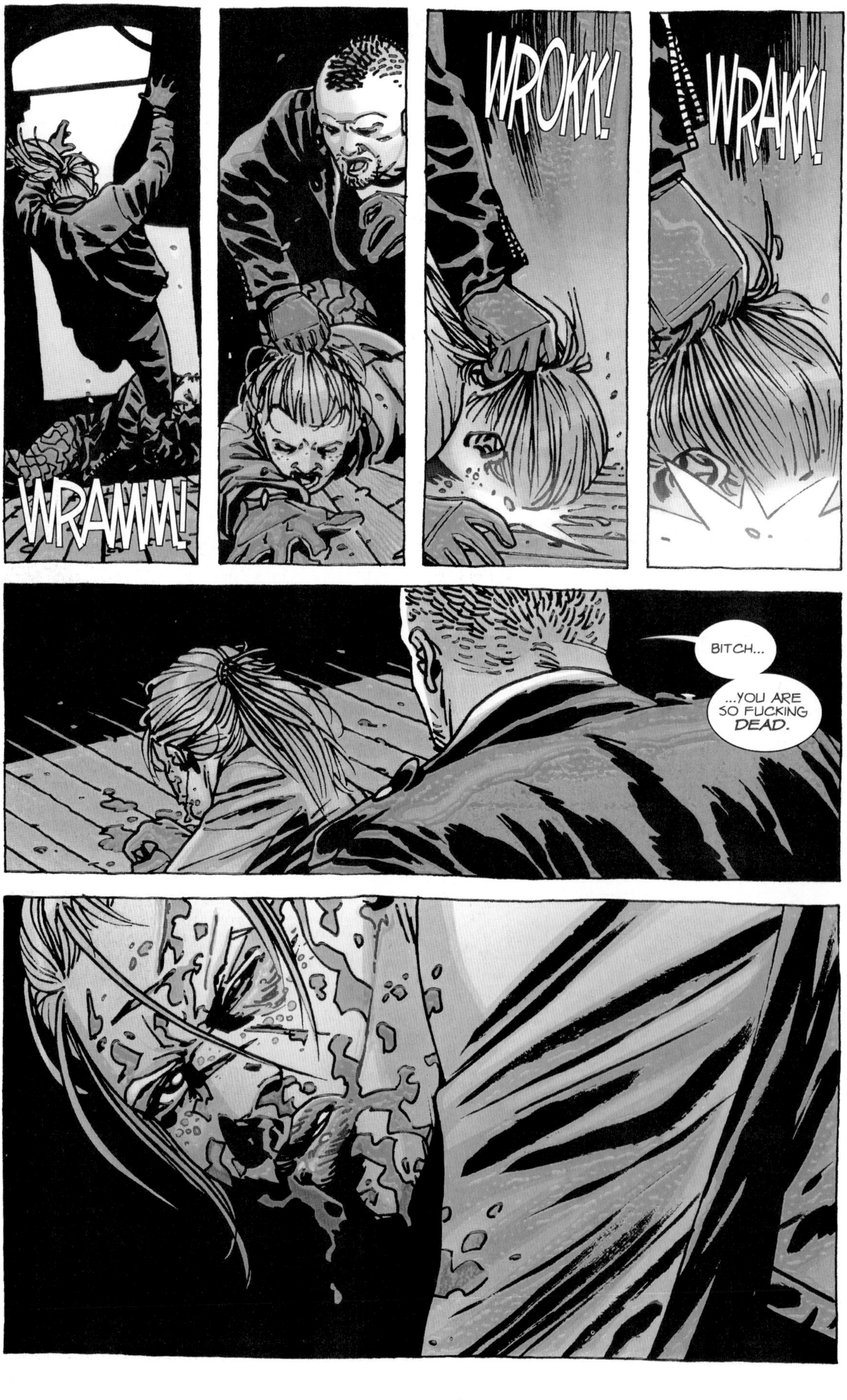
WRAMM!
WROKK!
WRAKK!
BITCH...
...YOU ARE SO FUCKING DEAD.

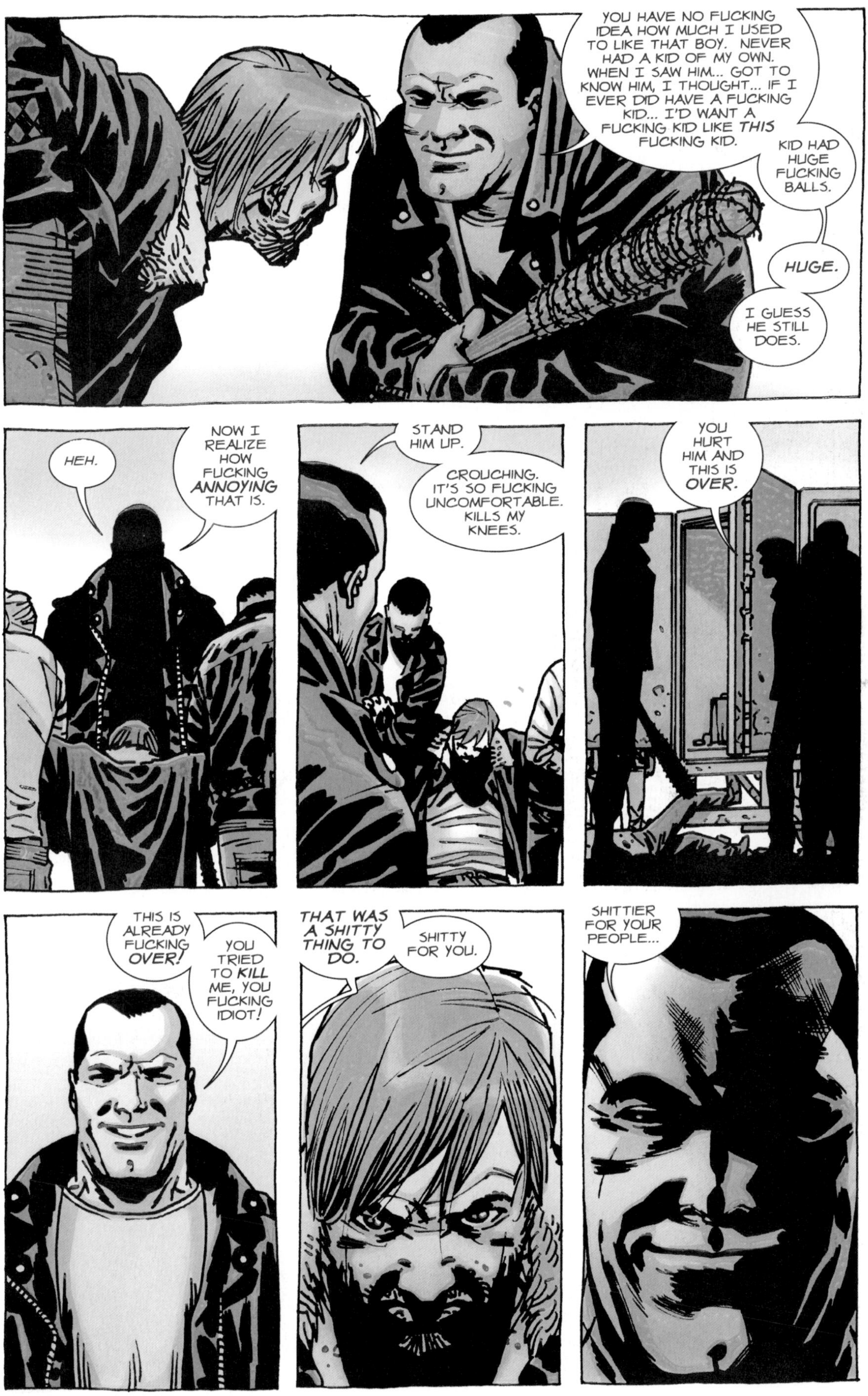
YOU HAVE NO FUCKING IDEA HOW MUCH I USED TO LIKE THAT BOY. NEVER HAD A KID OF MY OWN. WHEN I SAW HIM... GOT TO KNOW HIM, I THOUGHT... IF I EVER DID HAVE A FUCKING KID... I'D WANT A FUCKING KID LIKE *THIS* FUCKING KID.
KID HAD HUGE FUCKING BALLS.
HUGE.
I GUESS HE STILL DOES.
HEH.
NOW I REALIZE HOW FUCKING *ANNOYING* THAT IS.
STAND HIM UP.
CROUCHING. IT'S SO FUCKING UNCOMFORTABLE. KILLS MY KNEES.
YOU HURT HIM AND THIS IS *OVER.*
THIS IS ALREADY FUCKING *OVER!*
YOU TRIED TO *KILL* ME, YOU FUCKING IDIOT!
THAT WAS A SHITTY THING TO DO.
SHITTY FOR YOU.
SHITTIER FOR YOUR PEOPLE...

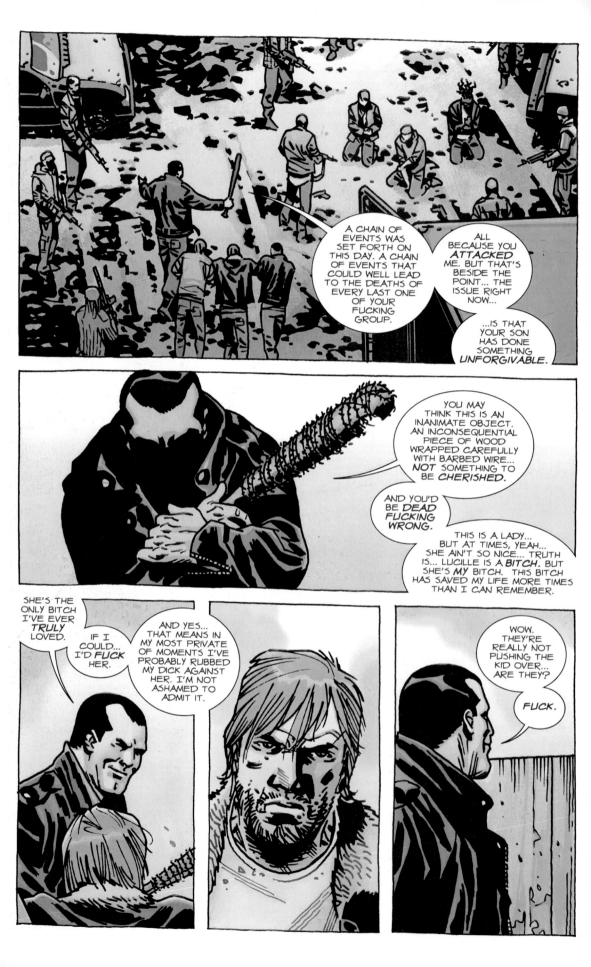

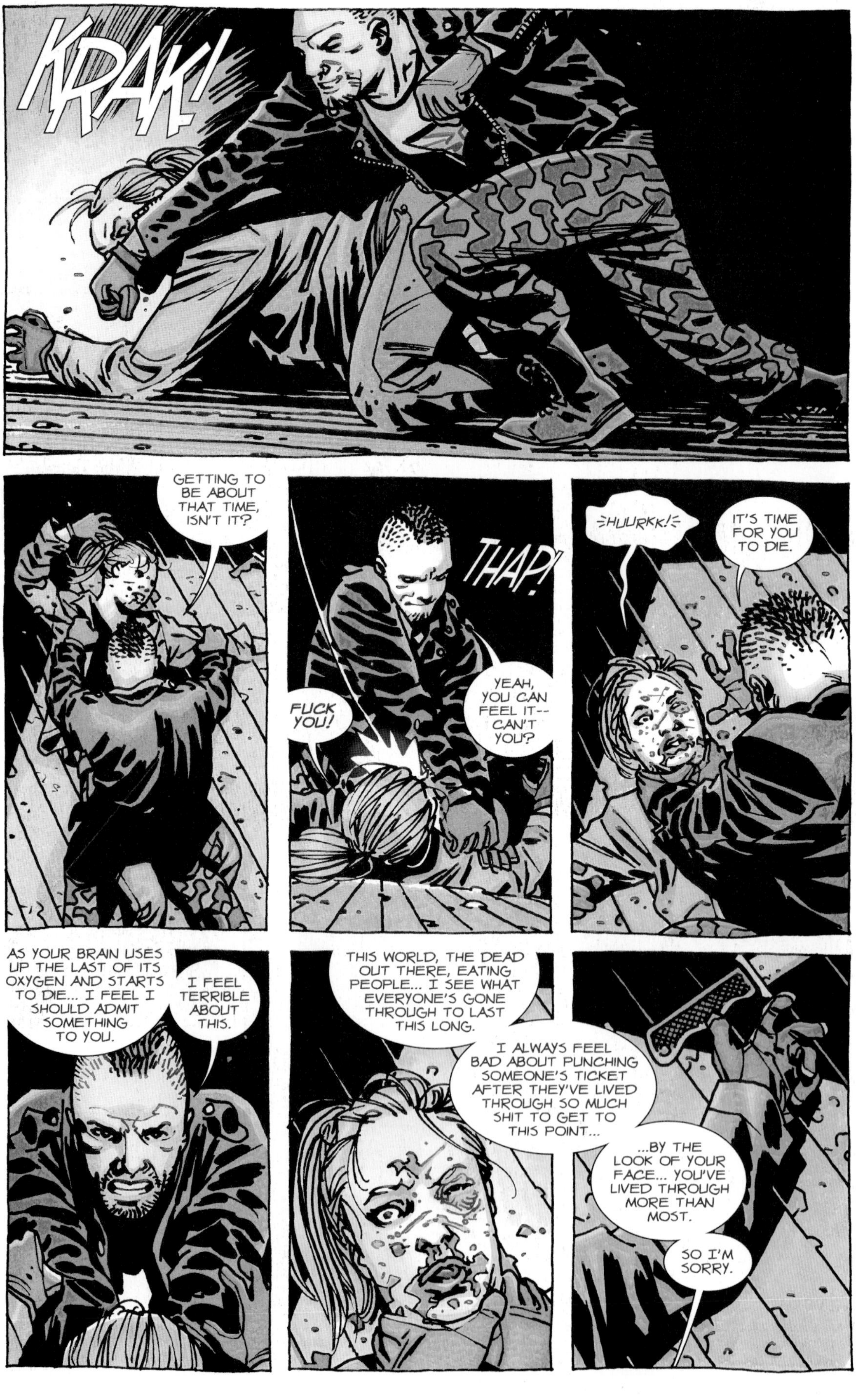
KRAK!
GETTING TO BE ABOUT THAT TIME, ISN'T IT?
THAP!
FUCK YOU!
YEAH, YOU CAN FEEL IT-- CAN'T YOU?
=HUURKK!=
IT'S TIME FOR YOU TO DIE.
AS YOUR BRAIN USES UP THE LAST OF ITS OXYGEN AND STARTS TO DIE... I FEEL I SHOULD ADMIT SOMETHING TO YOU.
I FEEL TERRIBLE ABOUT THIS.
THIS WORLD, THE DEAD OUT THERE, EATING PEOPLE... I SEE WHAT EVERYONE'S GONE THROUGH TO LAST THIS LONG.
I ALWAYS FEEL BAD ABOUT PUNCHING SOMEONE'S TICKET AFTER THEY'VE LIVED THROUGH SO MUCH SHIT TO GET TO THIS POINT...
...BY THE LOOK OF YOUR FACE... YOU'VE LIVED THROUGH MORE THAN MOST.
SO I'M SORRY.

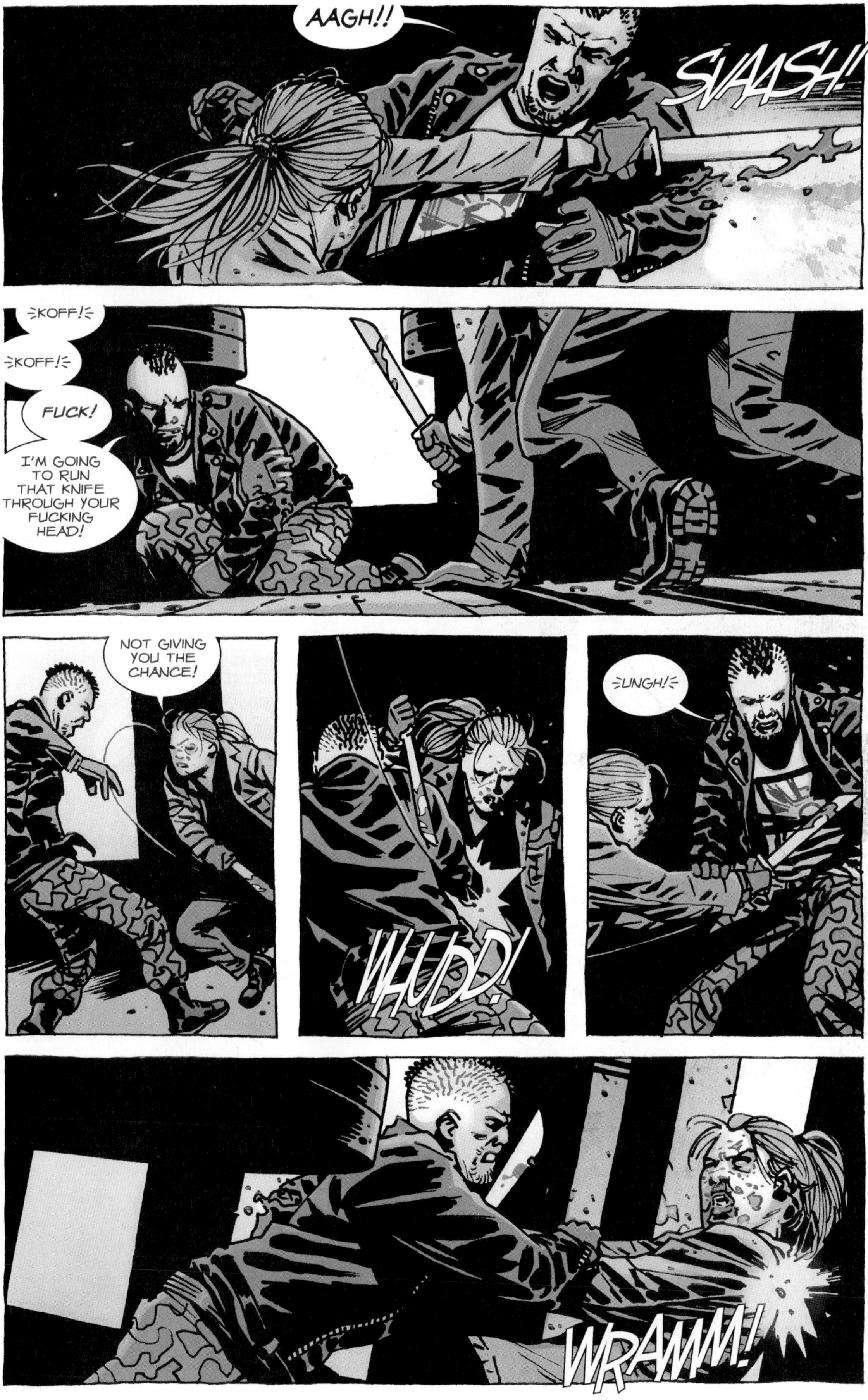
AAGH!!
SVAASH!
KOFF!
KOFF!
FUCK!
I'M GOING TO RUN THAT KNIFE THROUGH YOUR FUCKING HEAD!
NOT GIVING YOU THE CHANCE!
WHUDD!
UNGH!
WRAMM!

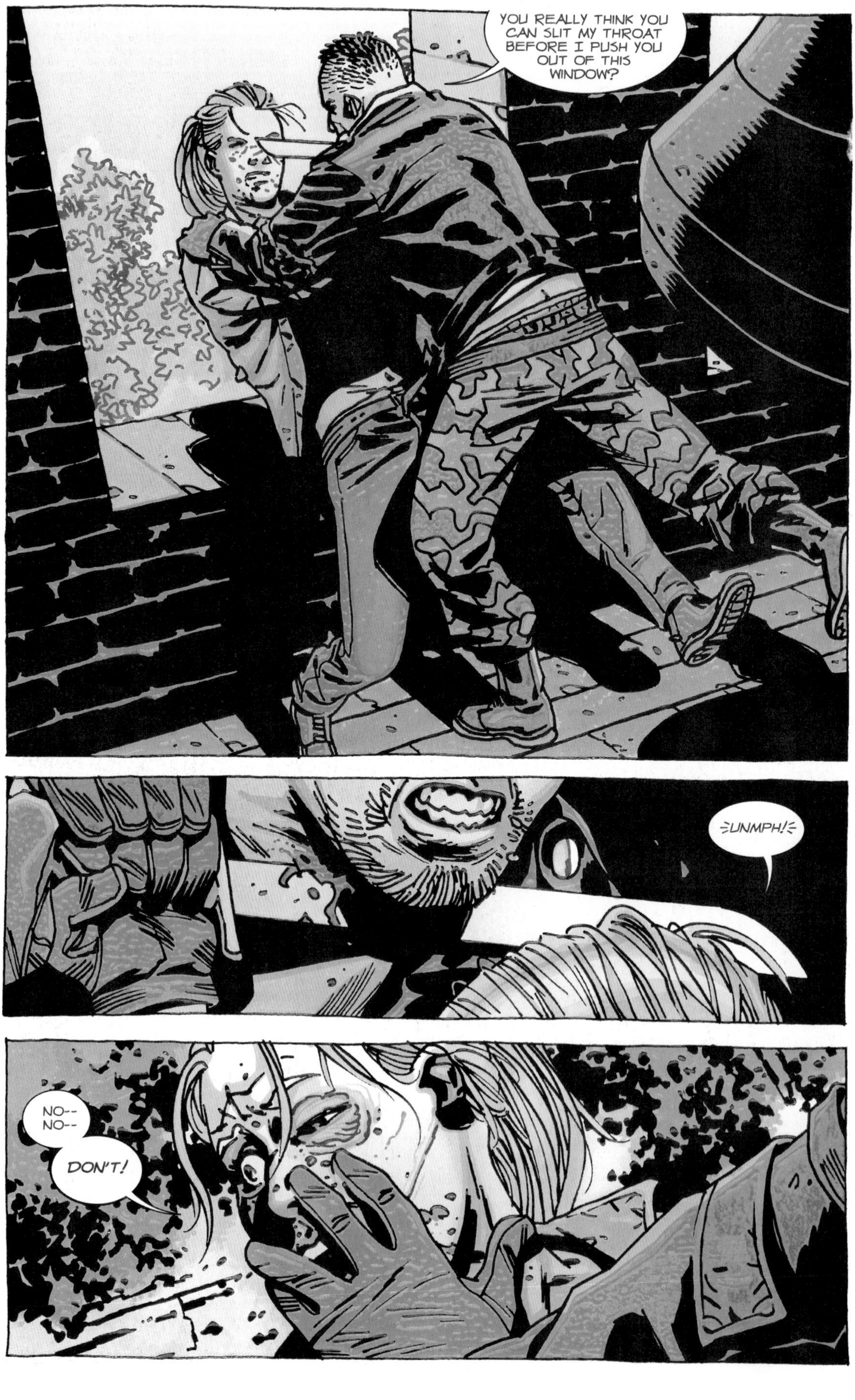
YOU REALLY THINK YOU CAN SLIT MY THROAT BEFORE I PUSH YOU OUT OF THIS WINDOW?
UNMPH!
NO-- NO--
DON'T!

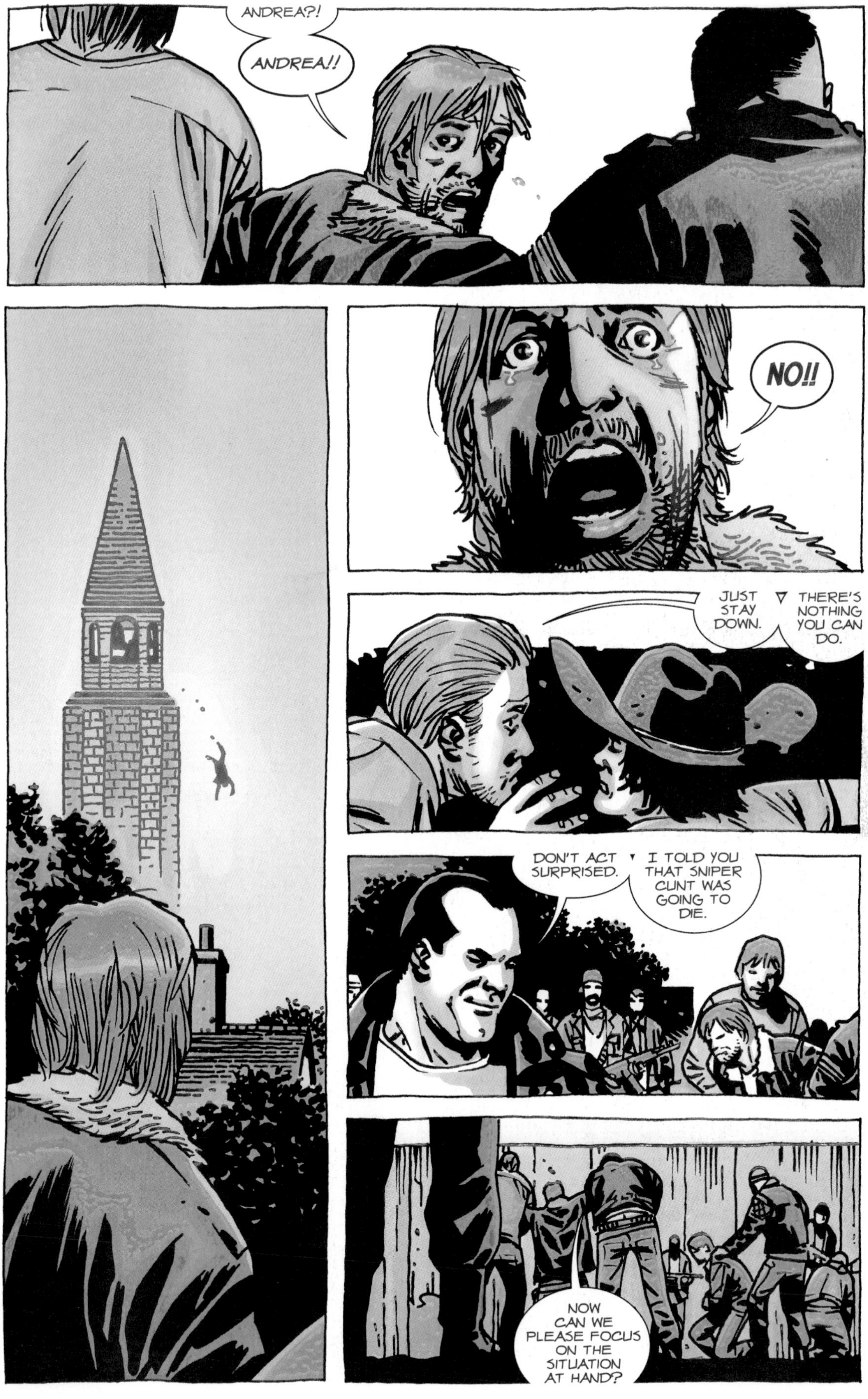
ANDREA?!
ANDREA!!
NO!!
JUST STAY DOWN.
THERE'S NOTHING YOU CAN DO.
DON'T ACT SURPRISED.
I TOLD YOU THAT SNIPER CUNT WAS GOING TO DIE.
NOW CAN WE PLEASE FOCUS ON THE SITUATION AT HAND?

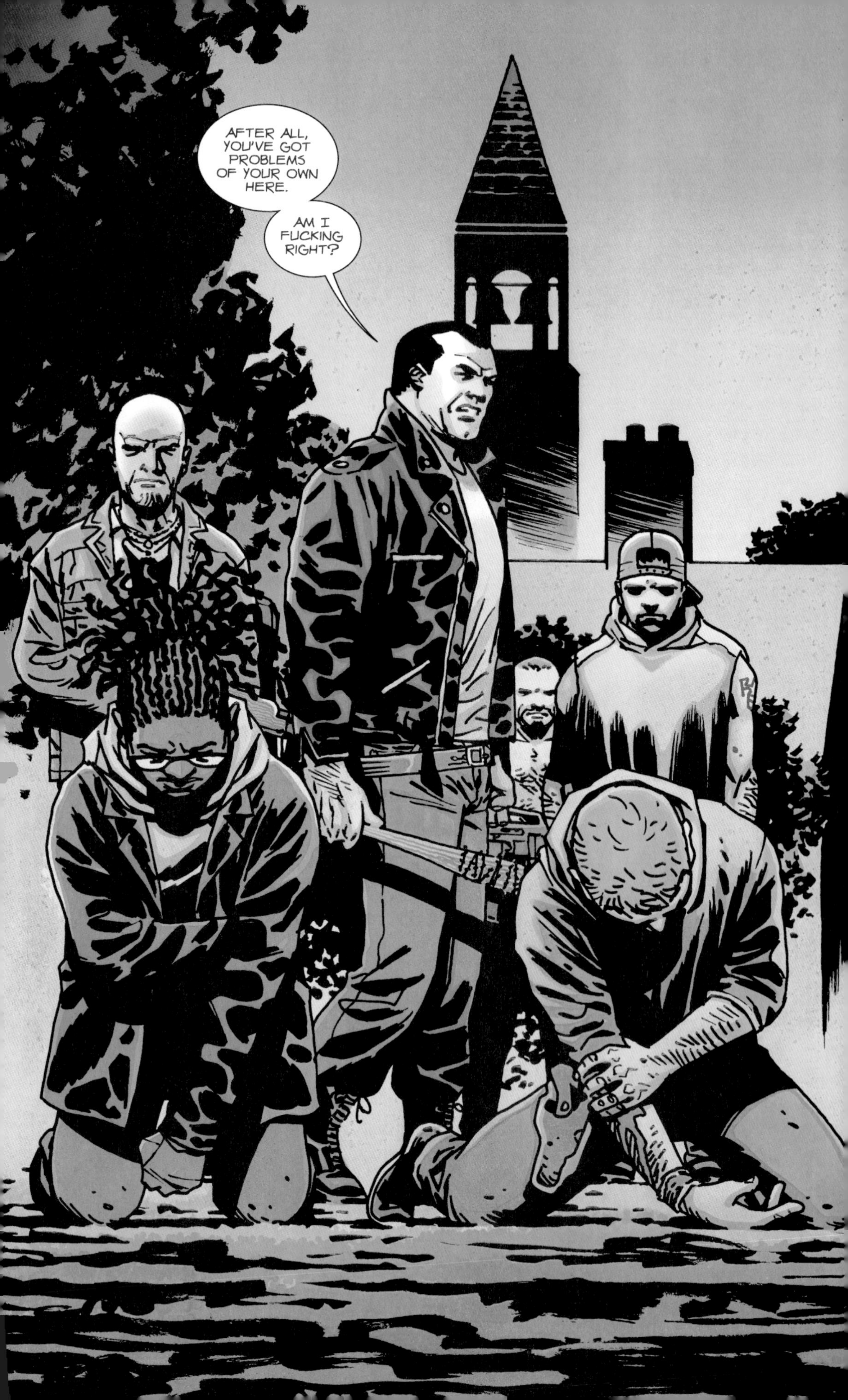
AFTER ALL, YOU'VE GOT PROBLEMS OF YOUR OWN HERE.
AM I FUCKING RIGHT?

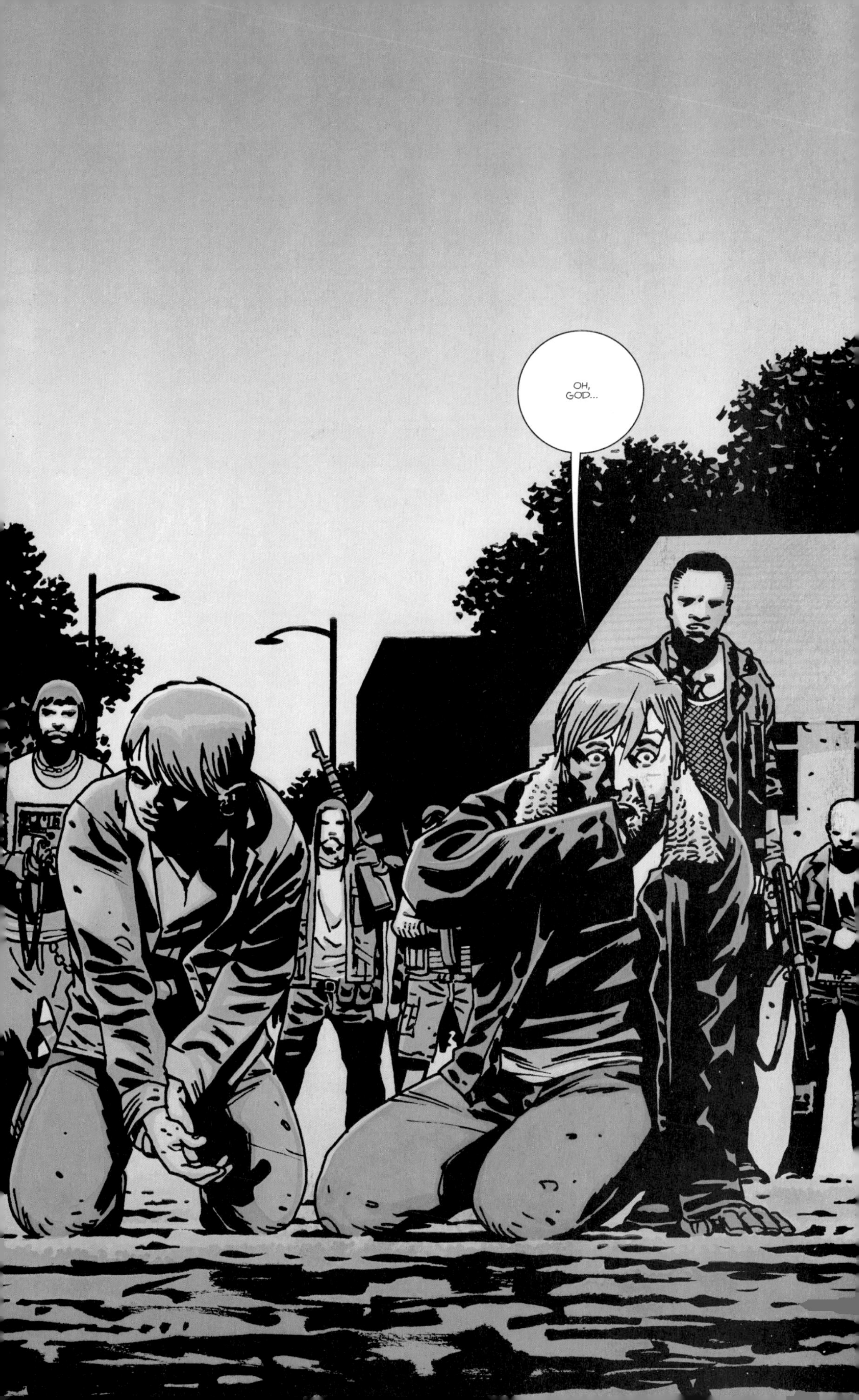
OH, GOD...

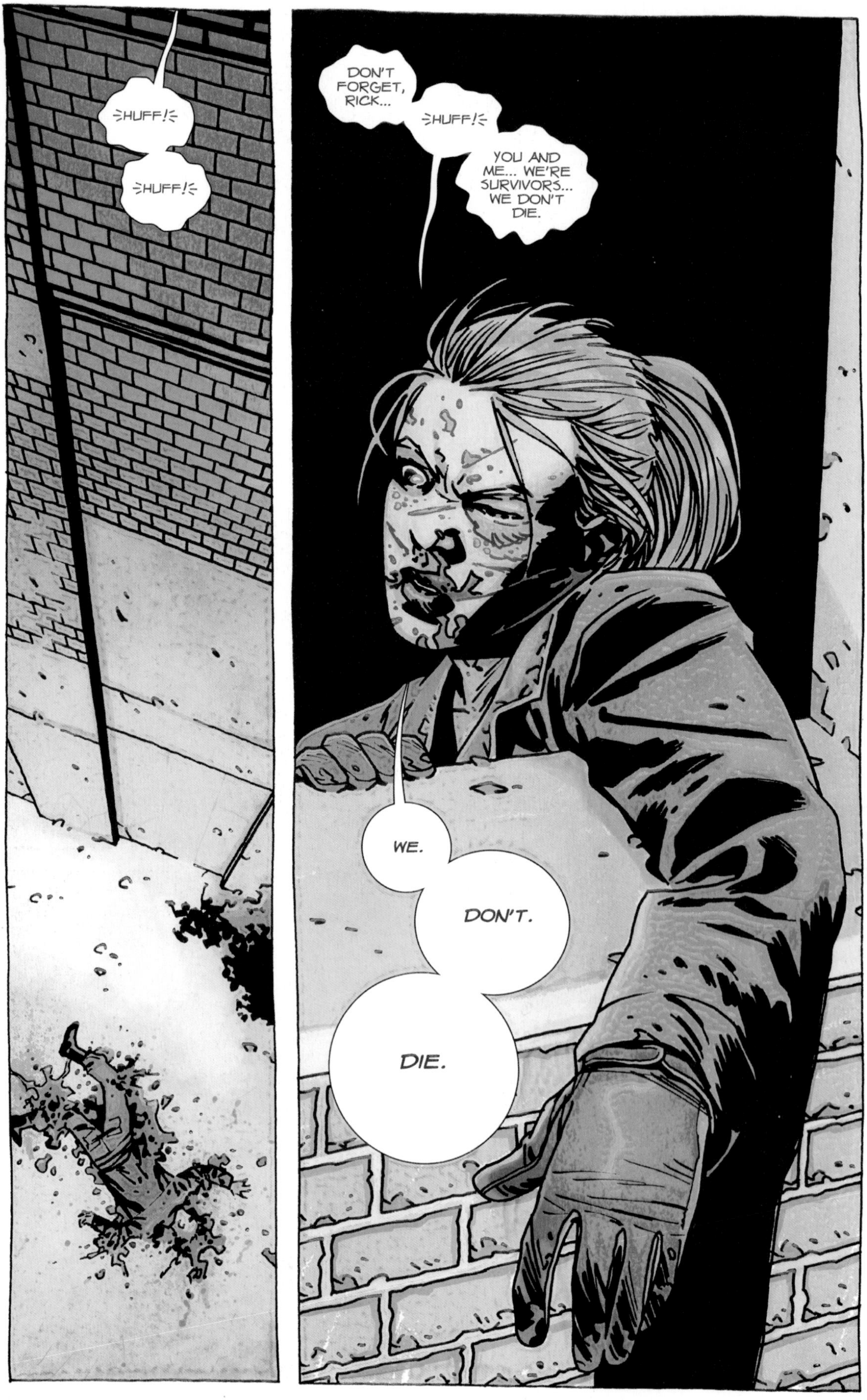

HUFF!
HUFF!
DON'T FORGET, RICK...
HUFF!
YOU AND ME... WE'RE SURVIVORS... WE DON'T DIE.
WE.
DON'T.
DIE.

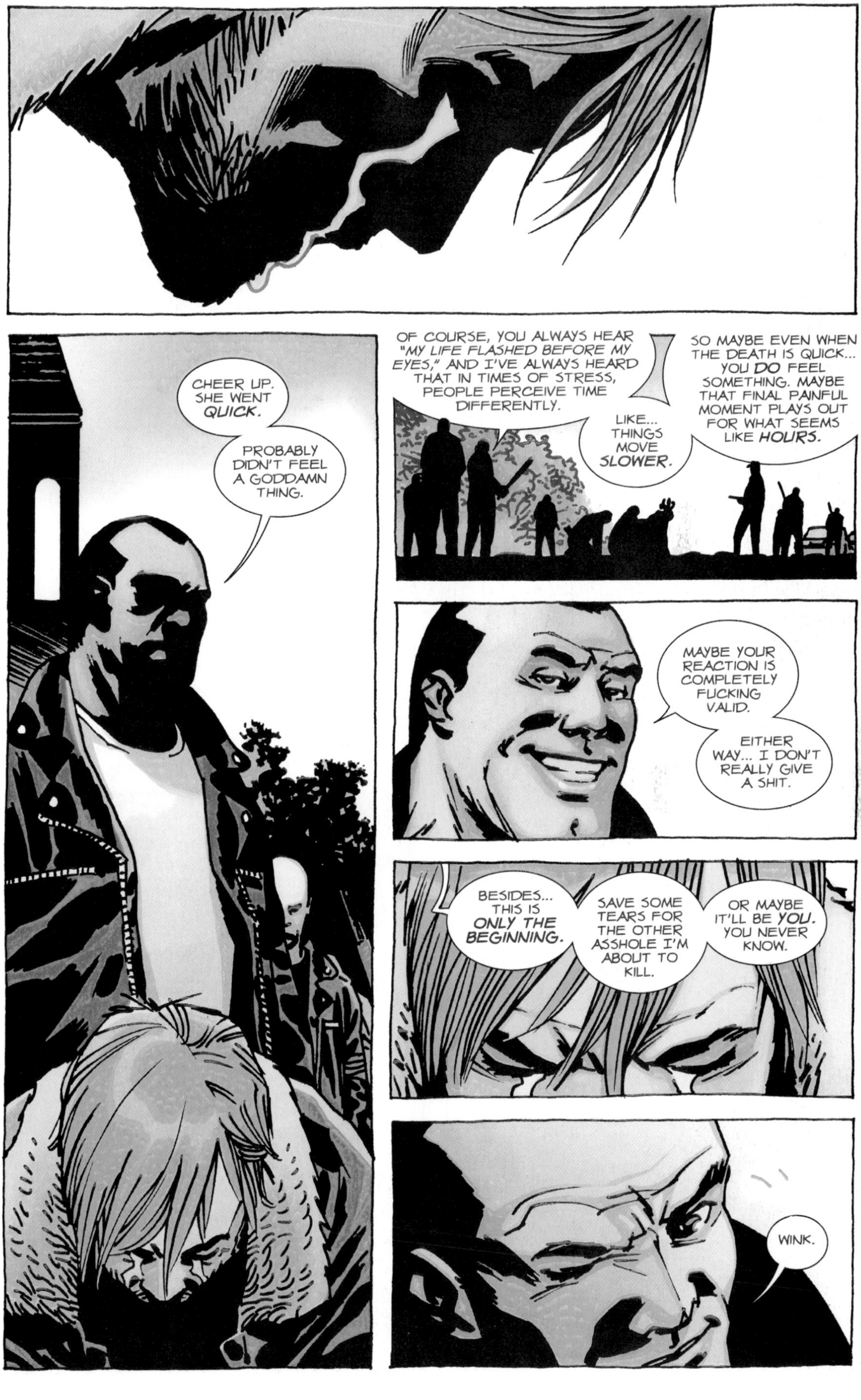

CHEER UP. SHE WENT QUICK.
PROBABLY DIDN'T FEEL A GODDAMN THING.
OF COURSE, YOU ALWAYS HEAR "MY LIFE FLASHED BEFORE MY EYES," AND I'VE ALWAYS HEARD THAT IN TIMES OF STRESS, PEOPLE PERCEIVE TIME DIFFERENTLY.
LIKE... THINGS MOVE SLOWER.
SO MAYBE EVEN WHEN THE DEATH IS QUICK... YOU DO FEEL SOMETHING. MAYBE THAT FINAL PAINFUL MOMENT PLAYS OUT FOR WHAT SEEMS LIKE HOURS.
MAYBE YOUR REACTION IS COMPLETELY FUCKING VALID.
EITHER WAY... I DON'T REALLY GIVE A SHIT.
BESIDES... THIS IS ONLY THE BEGINNING.
SAVE SOME TEARS FOR THE OTHER ASSHOLE I'M ABOUT TO KILL.
OR MAYBE IT'LL BE YOU. YOU NEVER KNOW.
WINK.

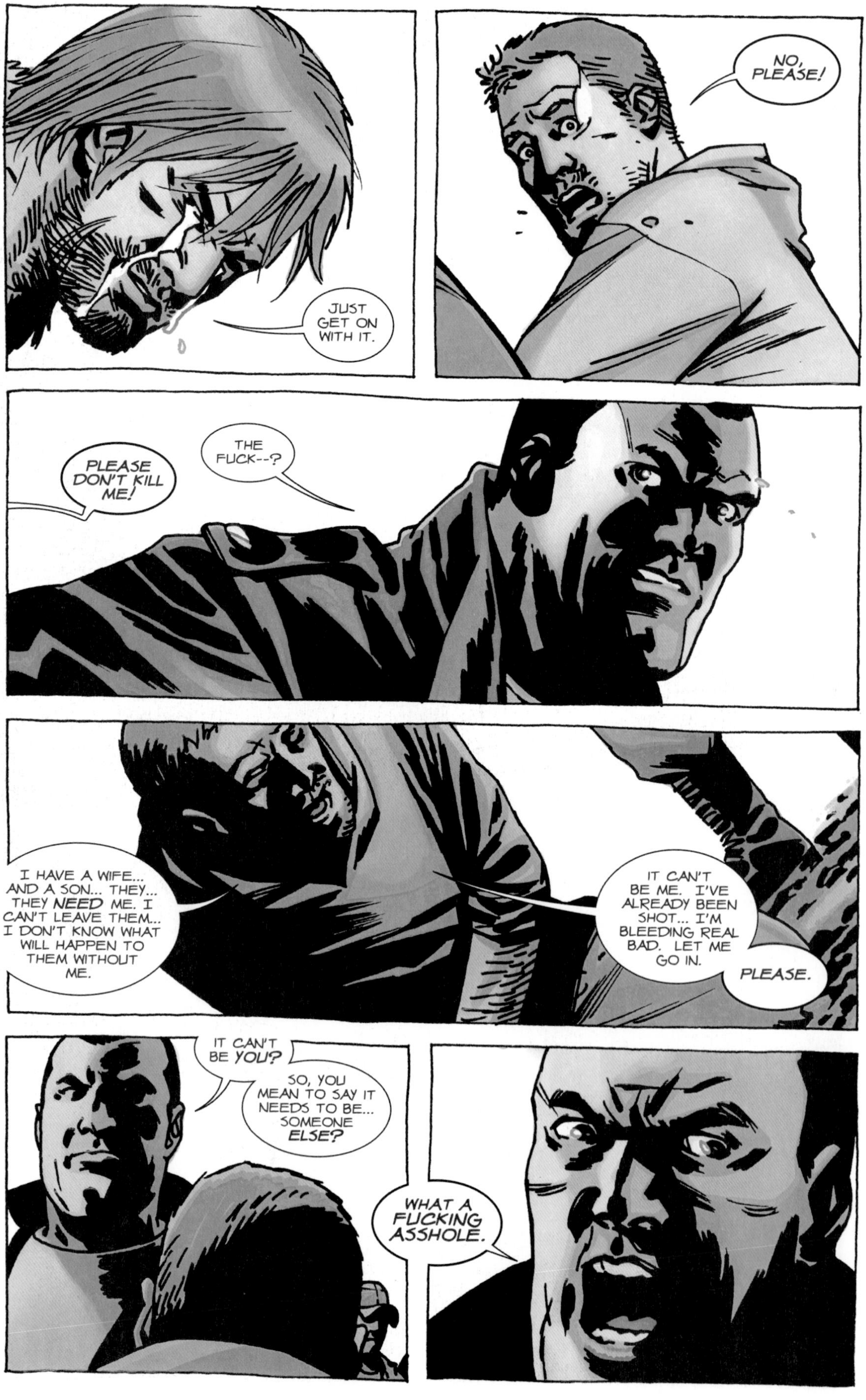

JUST GET ON WITH IT.
NO, PLEASE!
PLEASE DON'T KILL ME!
THE FUCK--?
I HAVE A WIFE... AND A SON... THEY... THEY NEED ME. I CAN'T LEAVE THEM... I DON'T KNOW WHAT WILL HAPPEN TO THEM WITHOUT ME.
IT CAN'T BE ME. I'VE ALREADY BEEN SHOT... I'M BLEEDING REAL BAD. LET ME GO IN.
PLEASE.
IT CAN'T BE YOU?
SO, YOU MEAN TO SAY IT NEEDS TO BE... SOMEONE ELSE?
WHAT A FUCKING ASSHOLE.

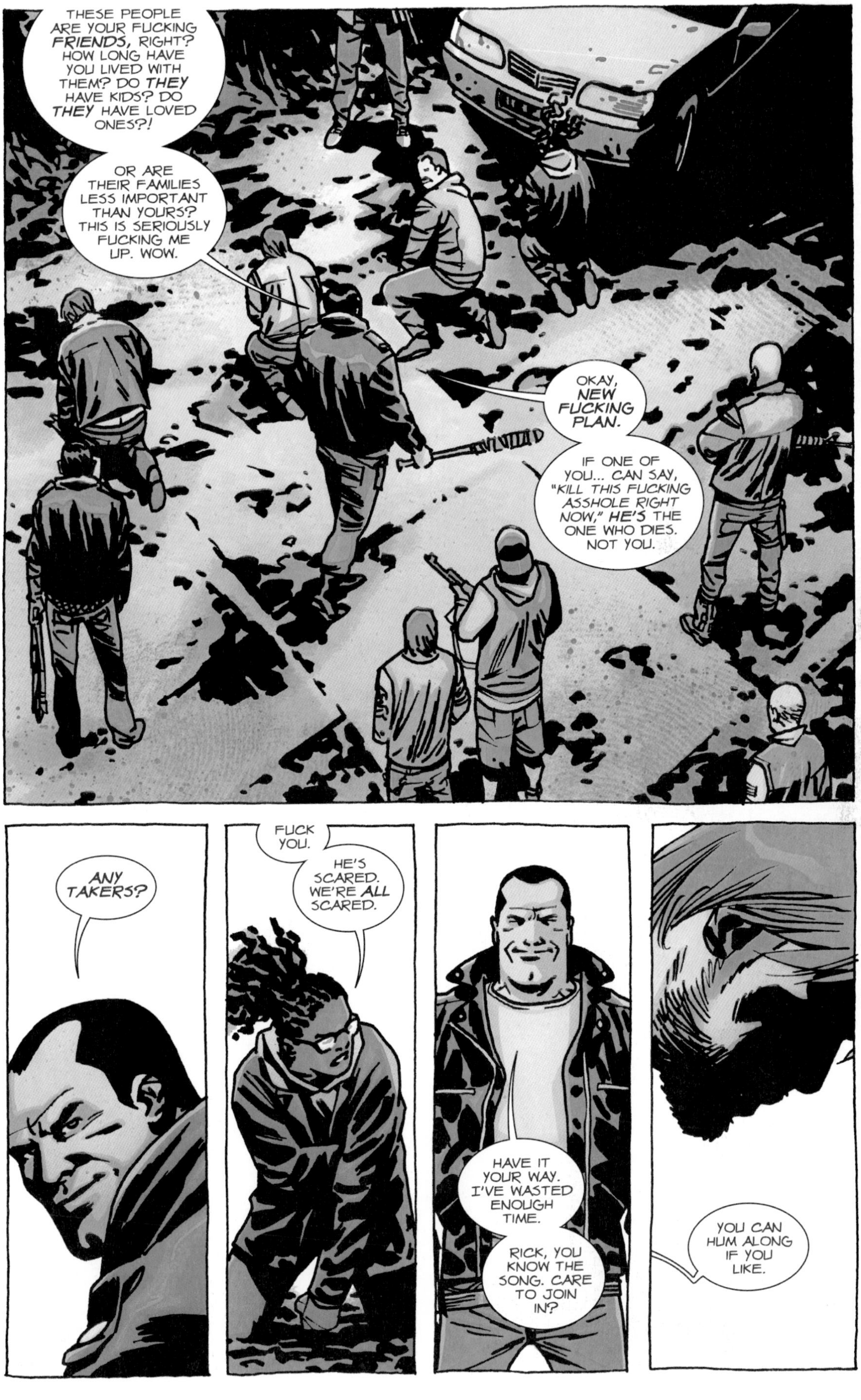
THESE PEOPLE ARE YOUR FUCKING FRIENDS, RIGHT? HOW LONG HAVE YOU LIVED WITH THEM? DO THEY HAVE KIDS? DO THEY HAVE LOVED ONES?!
OR ARE THEIR FAMILIES LESS IMPORTANT THAN YOURS? THIS IS SERIOUSLY FUCKING ME UP. WOW.
OKAY, NEW FUCKING PLAN.
IF ONE OF YOU... CAN SAY, "KILL THIS FUCKING ASSHOLE RIGHT NOW," HE'S THE ONE WHO DIES. NOT YOU.
ANY TAKERS?
FUCK YOU.
HE'S SCARED. WE'RE ALL SCARED.
HAVE IT YOUR WAY. I'VE WASTED ENOUGH TIME.
RICK, YOU KNOW THE SONG. CARE TO JOIN IN?
YOU CAN HUM ALONG IF YOU LIKE.

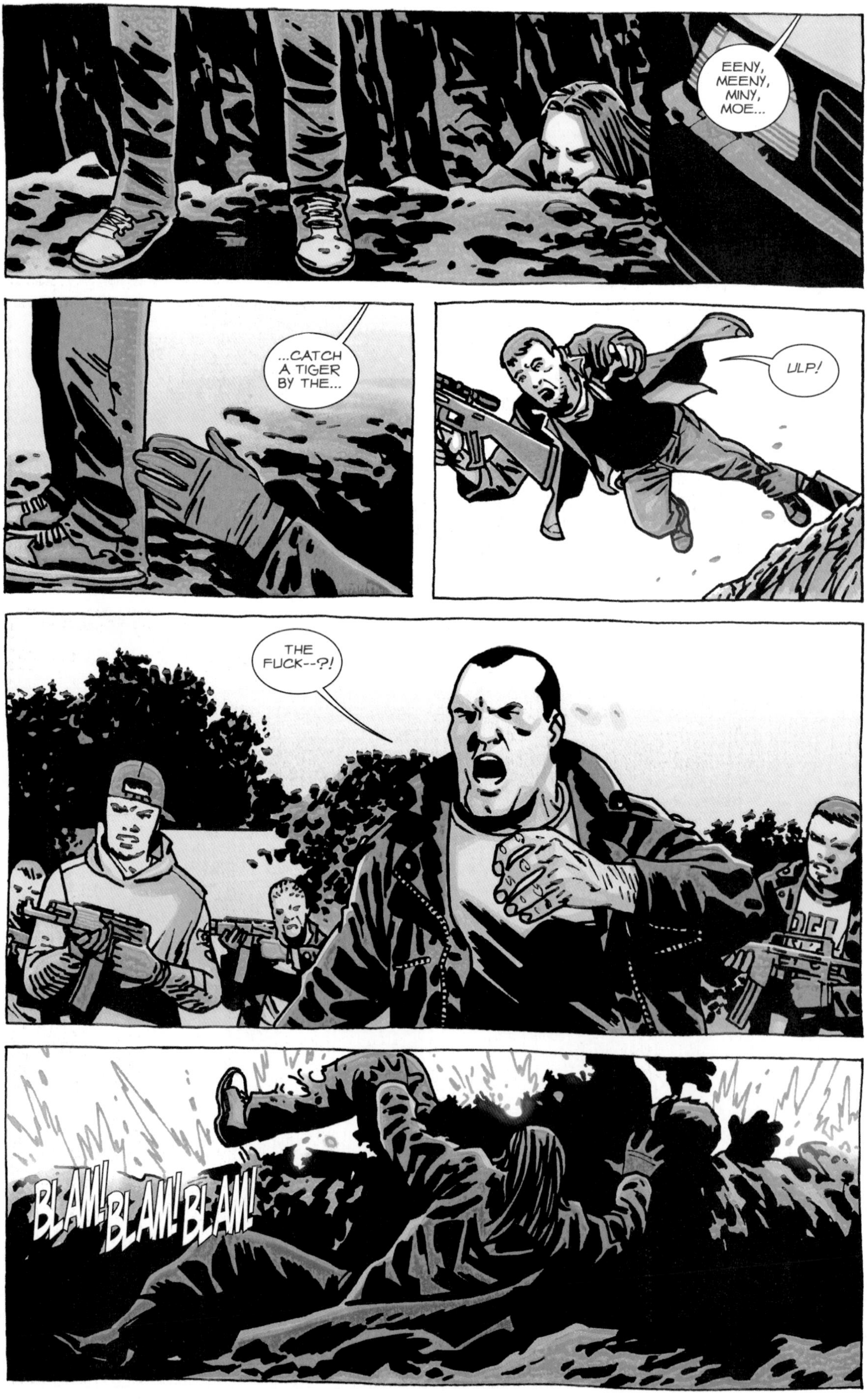
EENY, MEENY, MINY, MOE...
...CATCH A TIGER BY THE...
ULP!
THE FUCK--?!
BLAM! BLAM! BLAM!

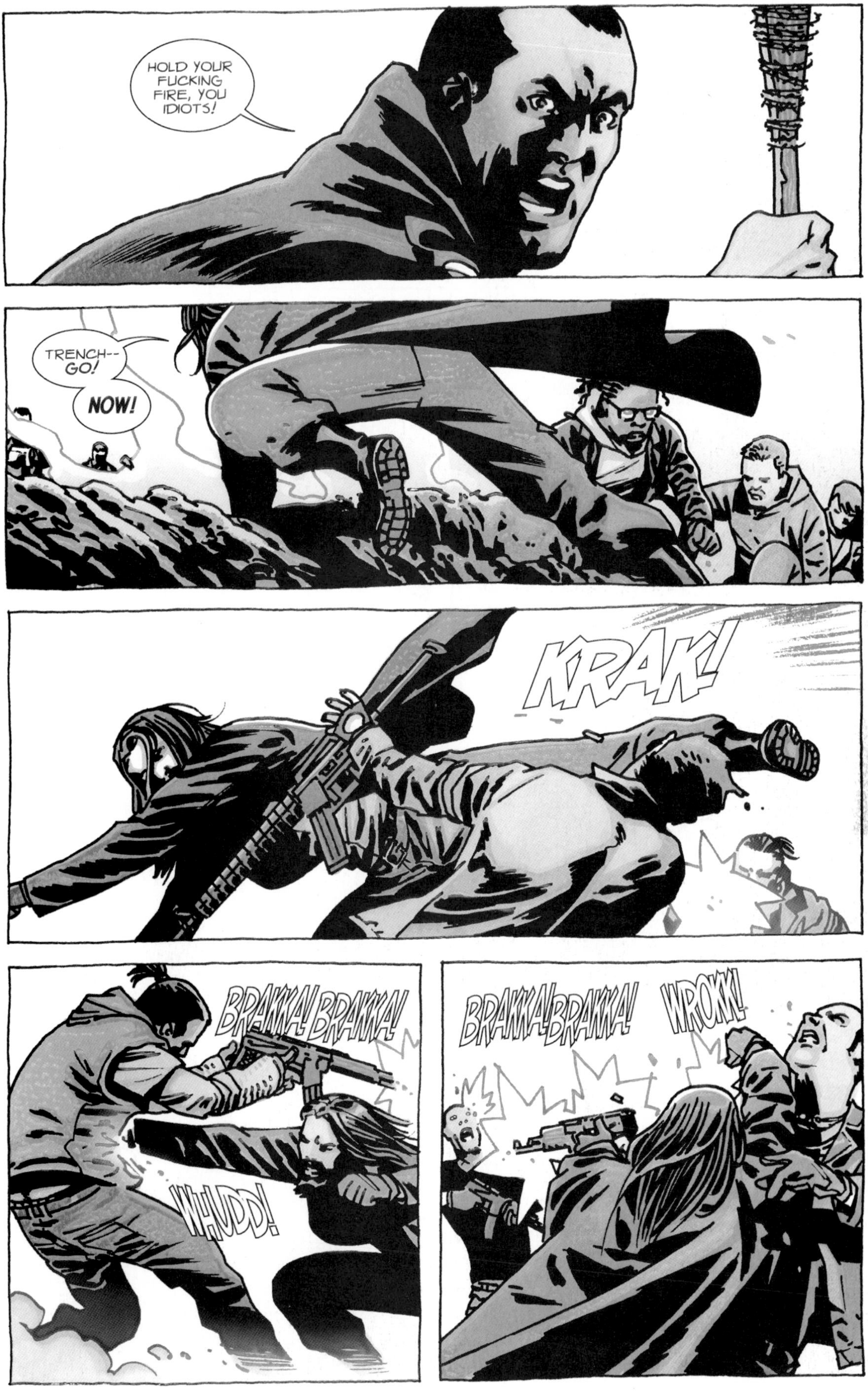

HOLD YOUR FUCKING FIRE, YOU IDIOTS!
TRENCH-- GO!
NOW!
KRAK!
BRAKKA! BRAKKA!
WHUDD!
BRAKKA! BRAKKA!
WROKK!

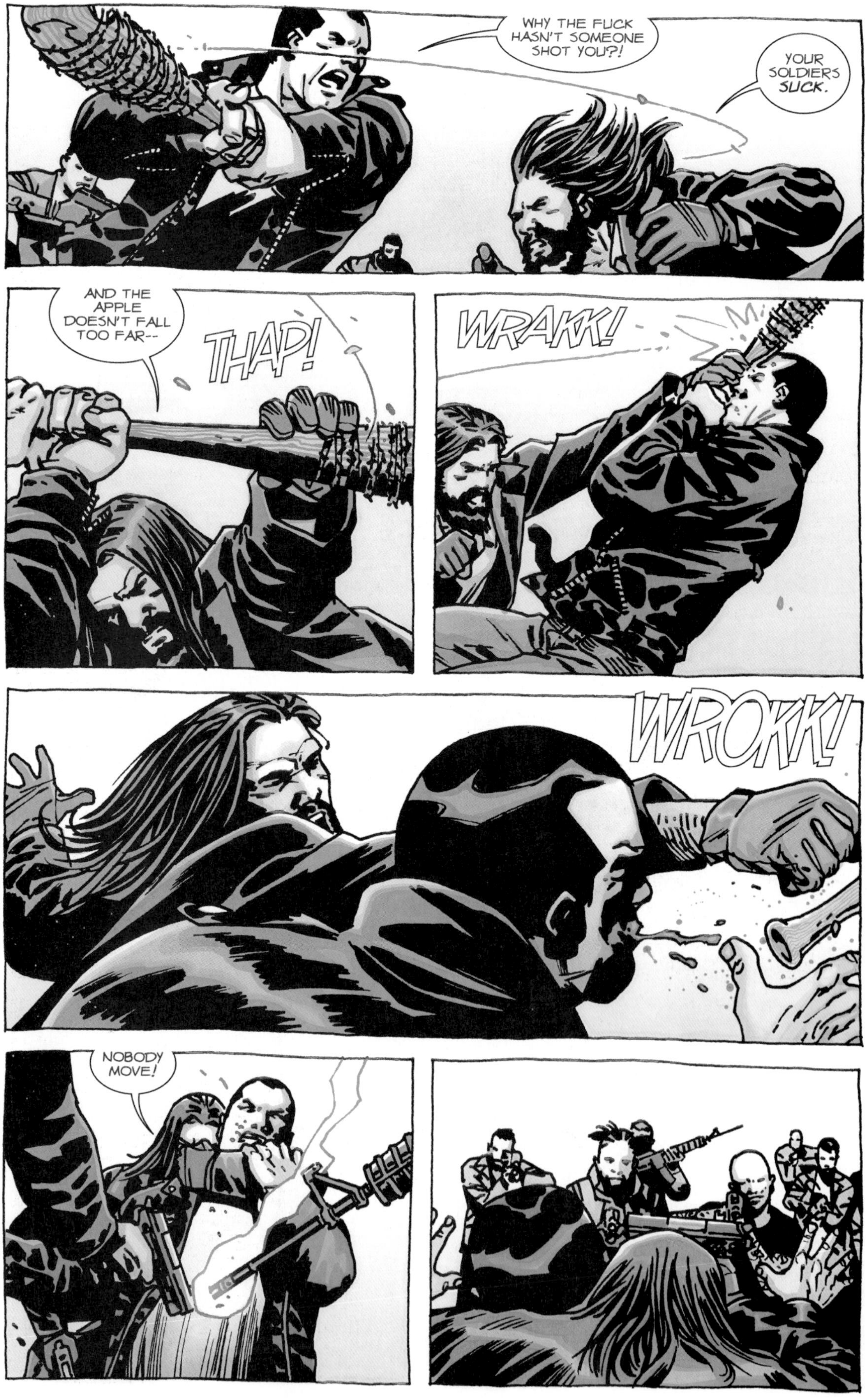
WHY THE FUCK HASN'T SOMEONE SHOT YOU?!
YOUR SOLDIERS SUCK.
AND THE APPLE DOESN'T FALL TOO FAR--
THAP!
WRAKK!
WROKK!
NOBODY MOVE!

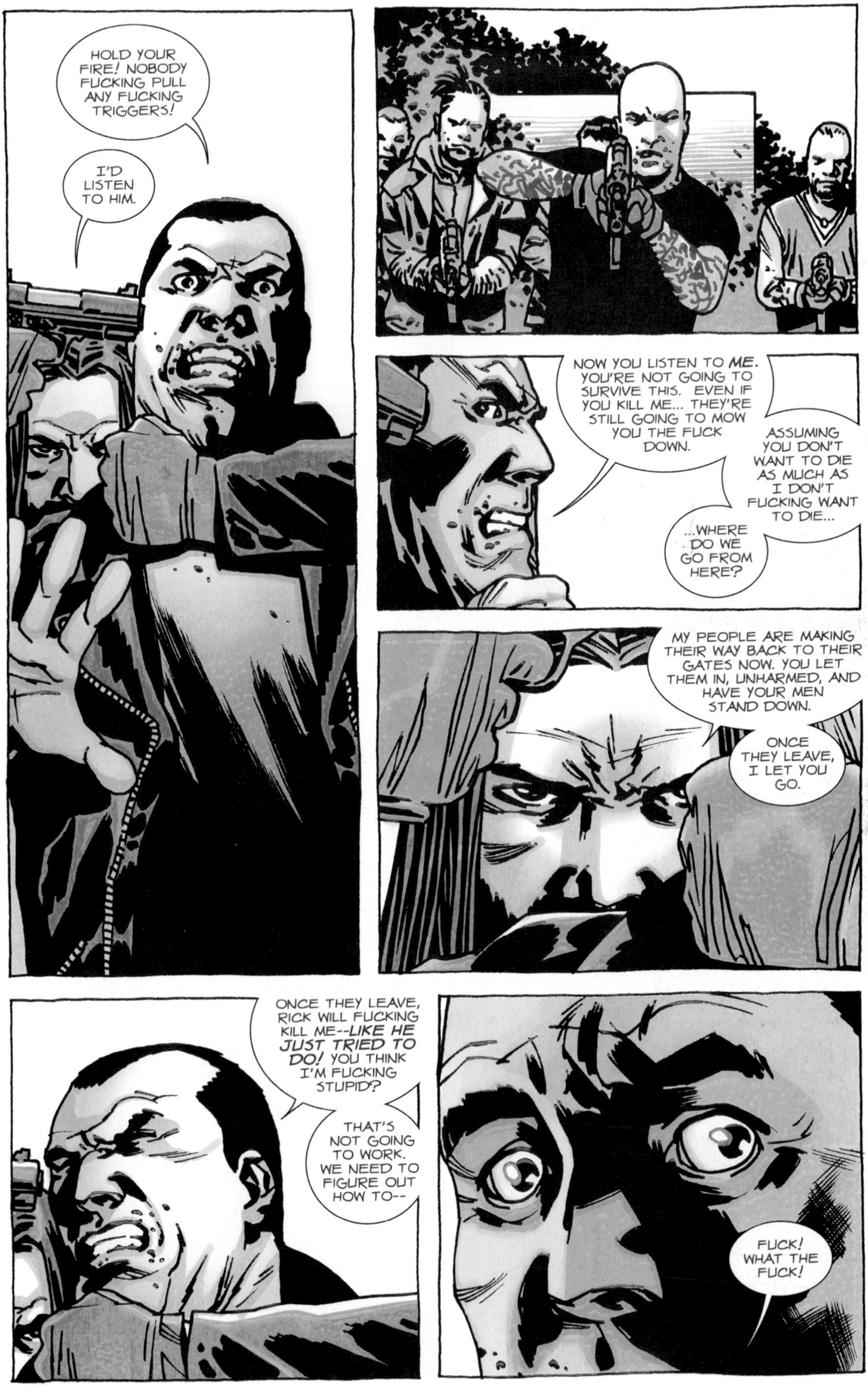
HOLD YOUR FIRE! NOBODY FUCKING PULL ANY FUCKING TRIGGERS!
I'D LISTEN TO HIM.
NOW YOU LISTEN TO ME. YOU'RE NOT GOING TO SURVIVE THIS. EVEN IF YOU KILL ME... THEY'RE STILL GOING TO MOW YOU THE FUCK DOWN.
ASSUMING YOU DON'T WANT TO DIE AS MUCH AS I DON'T FUCKING WANT TO DIE...
...WHERE DO WE GO FROM HERE?
MY PEOPLE ARE MAKING THEIR WAY BACK TO THEIR GATES NOW. YOU LET THEM IN, UNHARMED, AND HAVE YOUR MEN STAND DOWN.
ONCE THEY LEAVE, I LET YOU GO.
ONCE THEY LEAVE, RICK WILL FUCKING KILL ME--LIKE HE JUST TRIED TO DO! YOU THINK I'M FUCKING STUPID?
THAT'S NOT GOING TO WORK. WE NEED TO FIGURE OUT HOW TO--
FUCK! WHAT THE FUCK!

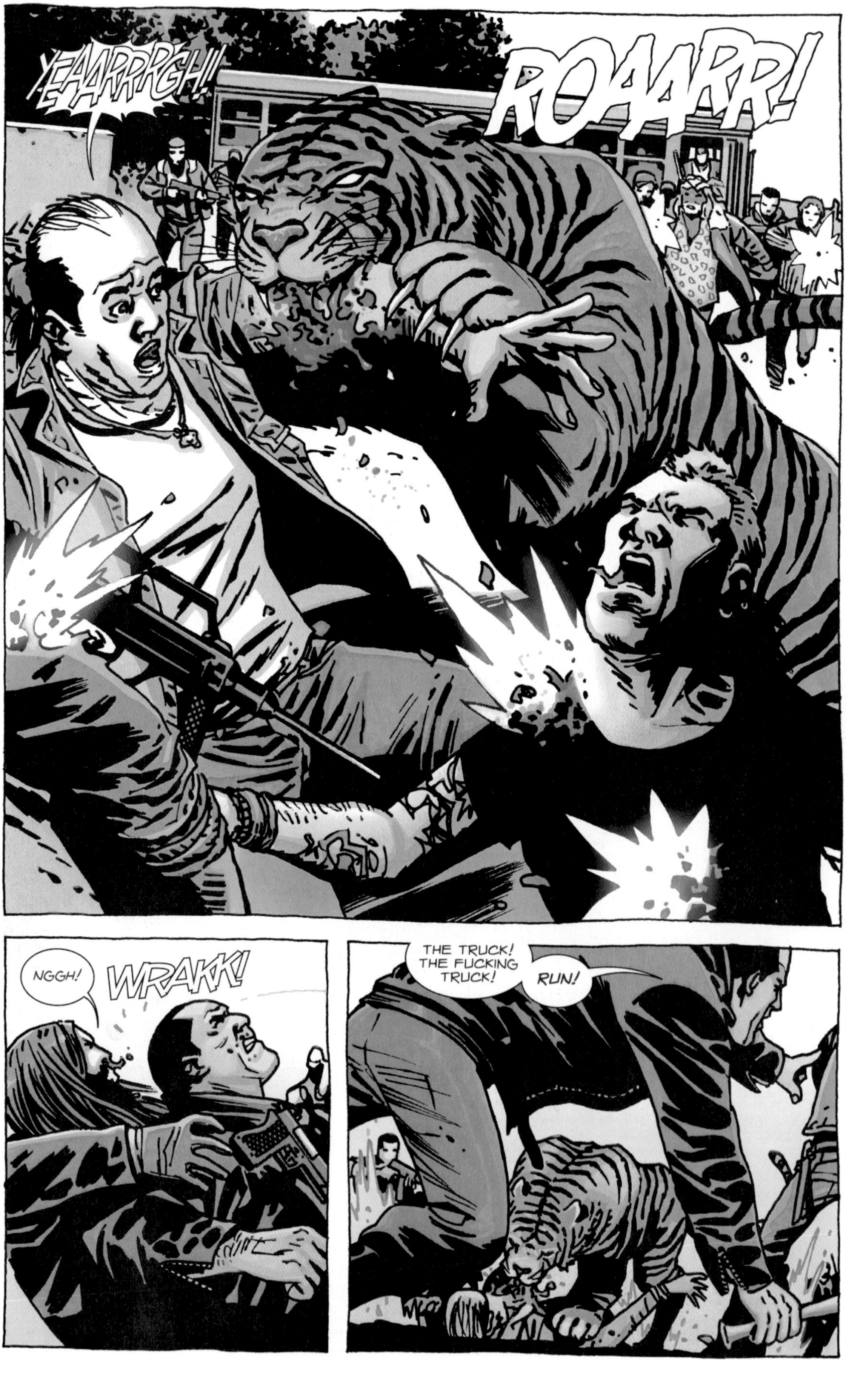
YEAARRRRGH!!
ROAARR!
NGGH!
WRAKK!
THE TRUCK! THE FUCKING TRUCK!
RUN!

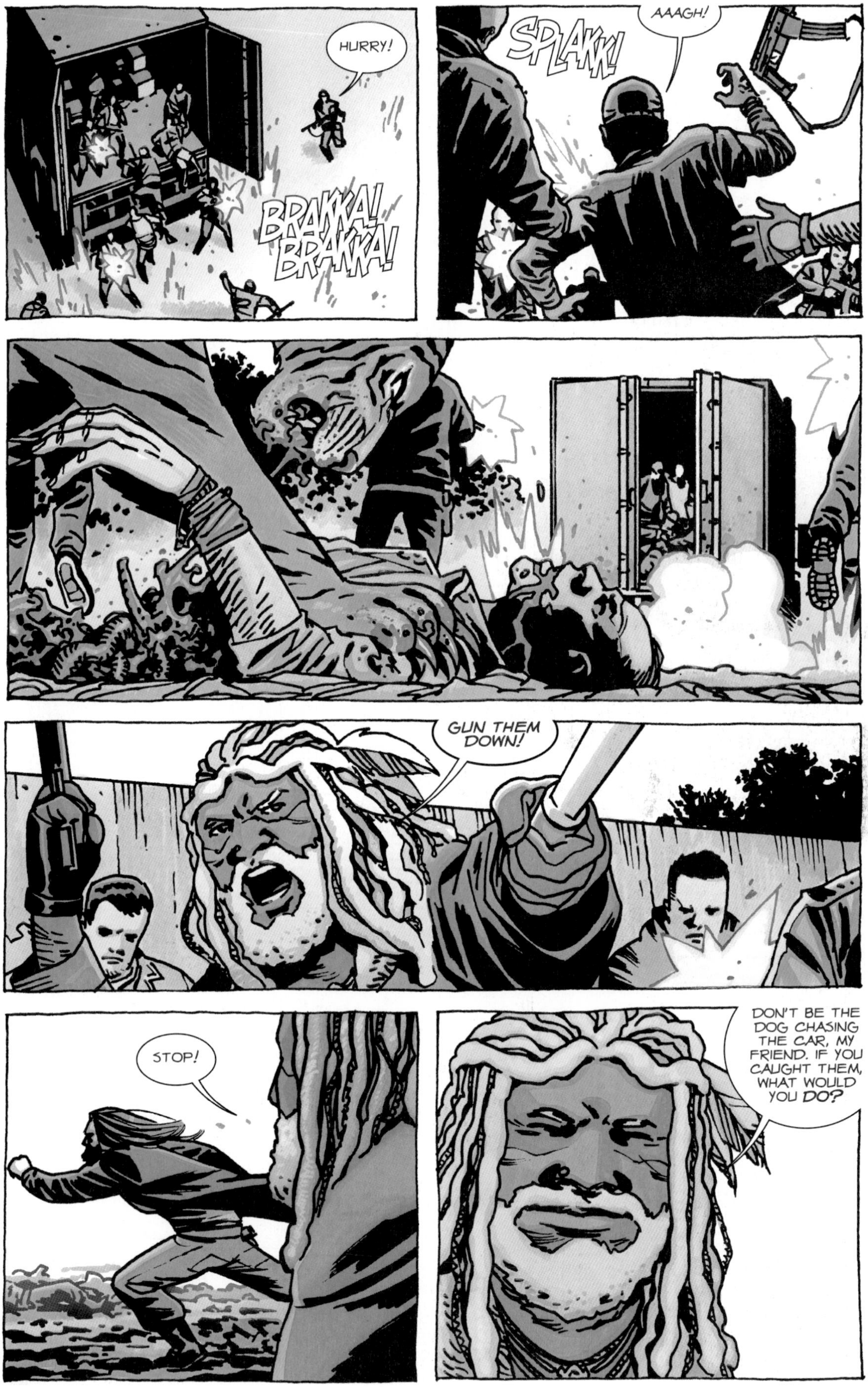
HURRY!
BRAKKA! BRAKKA!
SPLAKK!
AAAGH!
GUN THEM DOWN!
STOP!
DON'T BE THE DOG CHASING THE CAR, MY FRIEND. IF YOU CAUGHT THEM, WHAT WOULD YOU DO?

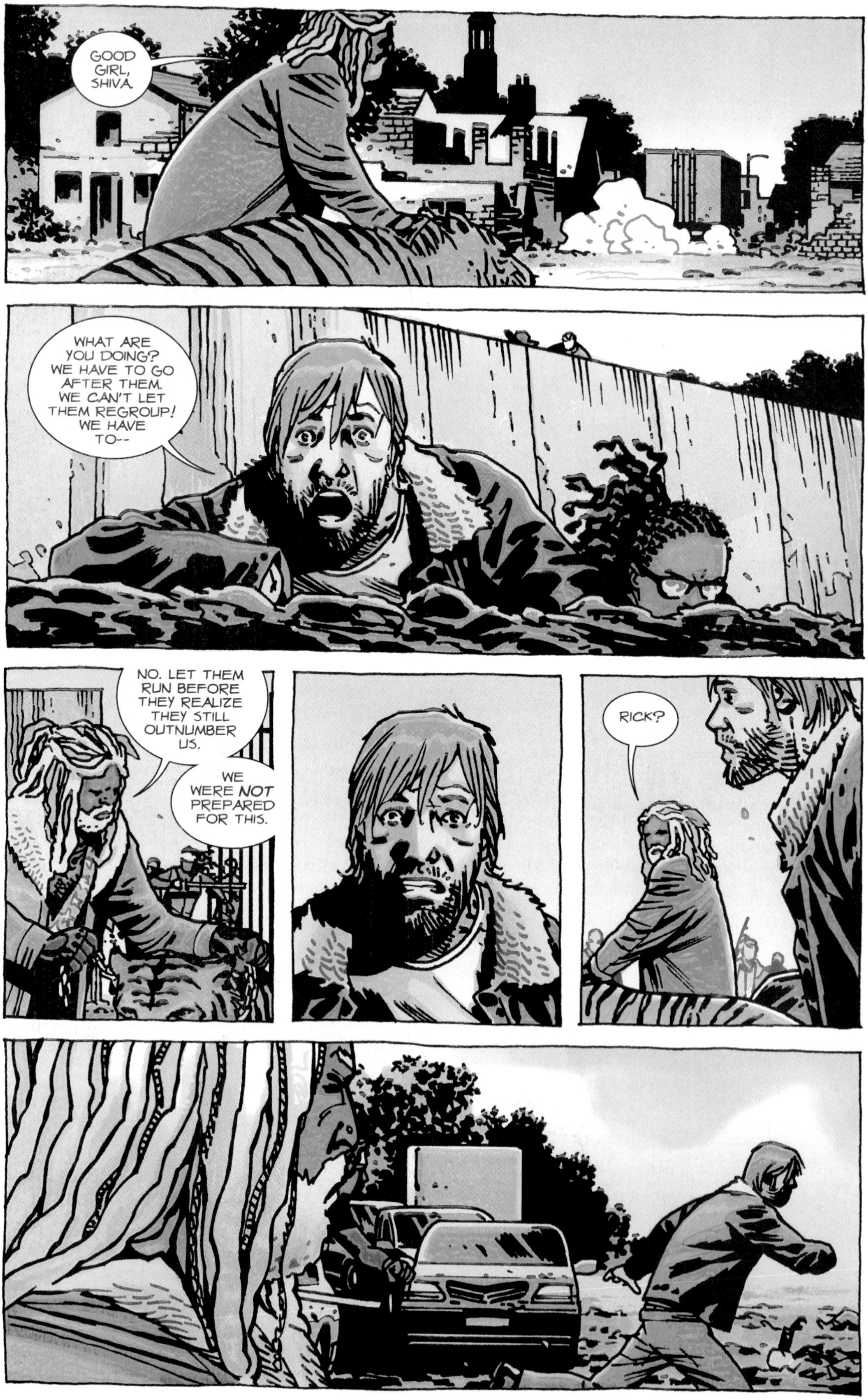
GOOD GIRL, SHIVA.
WHAT ARE YOU DOING? WE HAVE TO GO AFTER THEM. WE CAN'T LET THEM REGROUP! WE HAVE TO--
NO. LET THEM RUN BEFORE THEY REALIZE THEY STILL OUTNUMBER US.
WE WERE NOT PREPARED FOR THIS.
RICK?

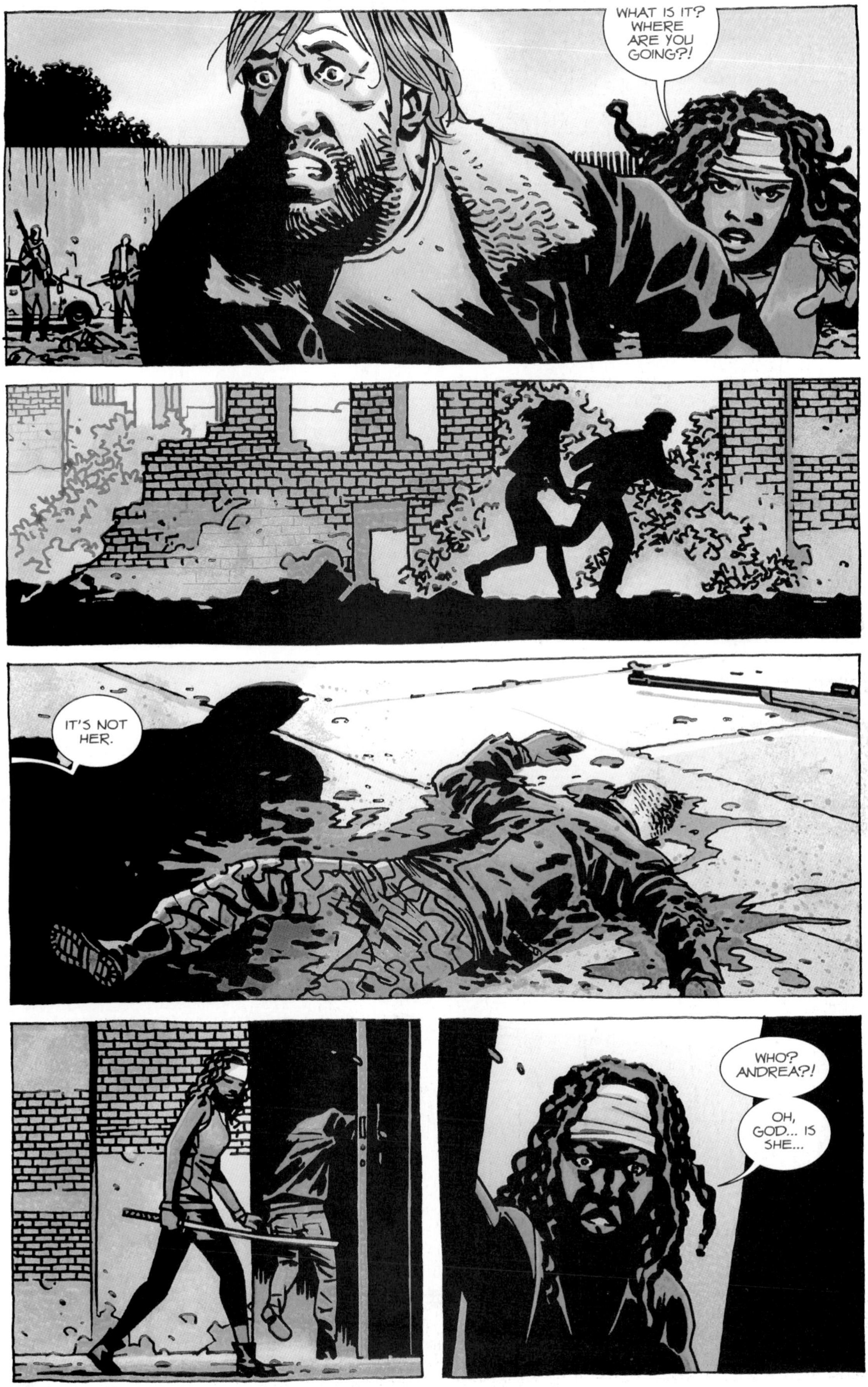
WHAT IS IT? WHERE ARE YOU GOING?!
IT'S NOT HER.
WHO? ANDREA?!
OH, GOD... IS SHE...

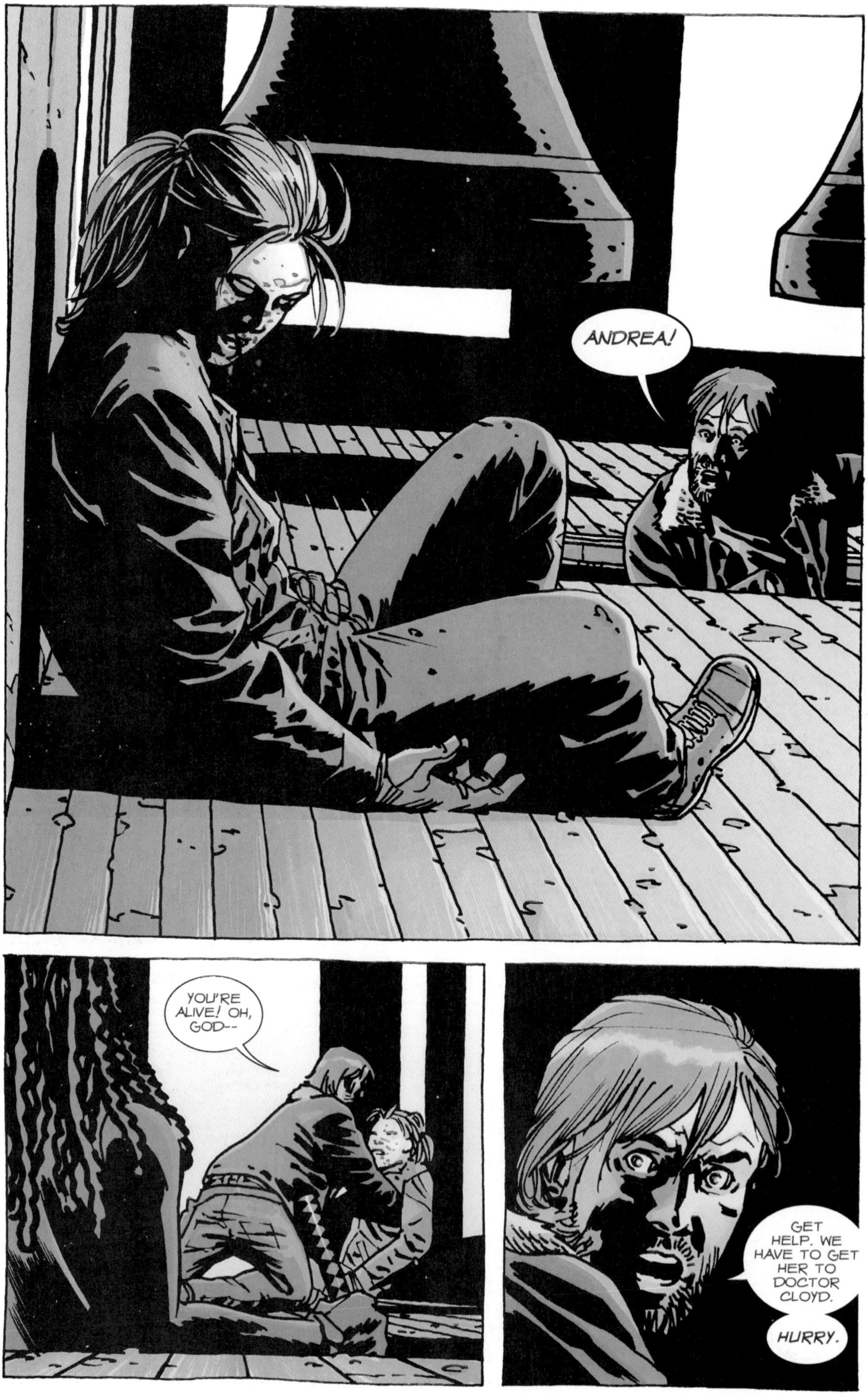
ANDREA!
YOU'RE ALIVE! OH, GOD--
GET HELP. WE HAVE TO GET HER TO DOCTOR CLOYD.
HURRY.

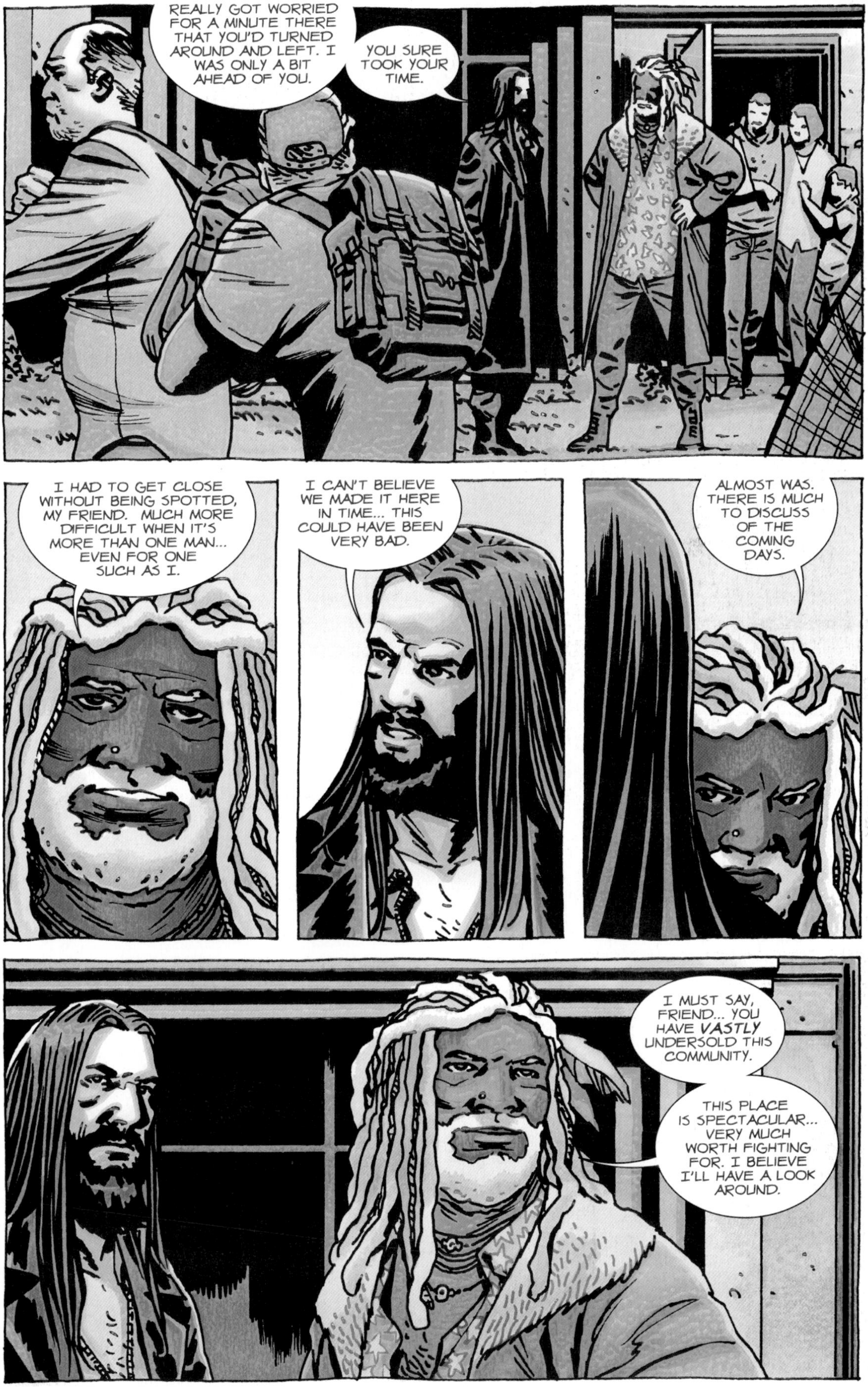
REALLY GOT WORRIED FOR A MINUTE THERE THAT YOU'D TURNED AROUND AND LEFT. I WAS ONLY A BIT AHEAD OF YOU.
YOU SURE TOOK YOUR TIME.
I HAD TO GET CLOSE WITHOUT BEING SPOTTED, MY FRIEND. MUCH MORE DIFFICULT WHEN IT'S MORE THAN ONE MAN... EVEN FOR ONE SUCH AS I.
I CAN'T BELIEVE WE MADE IT HERE IN TIME... THIS COULD HAVE BEEN VERY BAD.
ALMOST WAS. THERE IS MUCH TO DISCUSS OF THE COMING DAYS.
I MUST SAY, FRIEND... YOU HAVE *VASTLY* UNDERSOLD THIS COMMUNITY.
THIS PLACE IS SPECTACULAR... VERY MUCH WORTH FIGHTING FOR. I BELIEVE I'LL HAVE A LOOK AROUND.

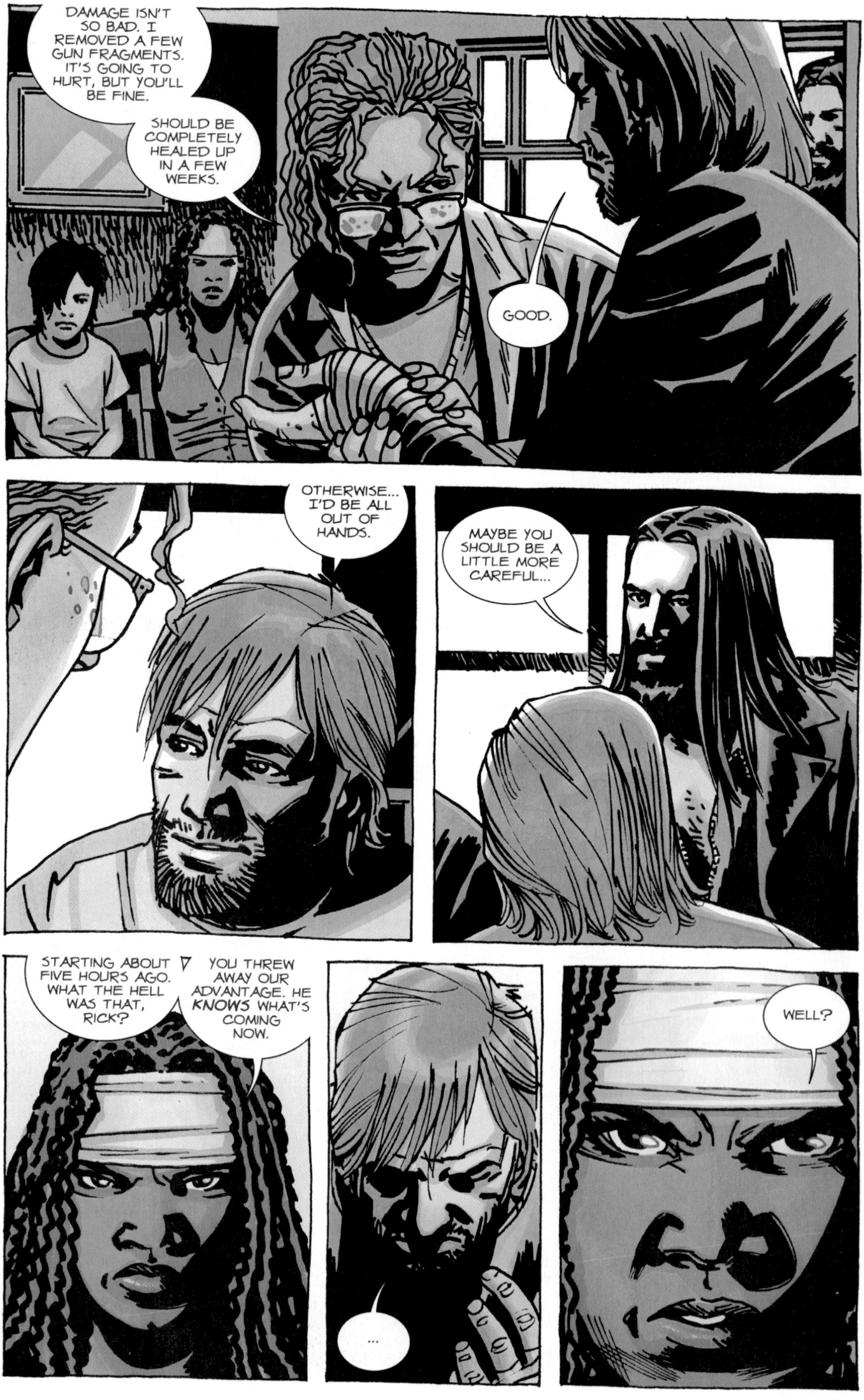
DAMAGE ISN'T SO BAD. I REMOVED A FEW GUN FRAGMENTS. IT'S GOING TO HURT, BUT YOU'LL BE FINE.
SHOULD BE COMPLETELY HEALED UP IN A FEW WEEKS.
GOOD.
OTHERWISE... I'D BE ALL OUT OF HANDS.
MAYBE YOU SHOULD BE A LITTLE MORE CAREFUL...
STARTING ABOUT FIVE HOURS AGO. WHAT THE HELL WAS THAT, RICK?
YOU THREW AWAY OUR ADVANTAGE. HE KNOWS WHAT'S COMING NOW.
...
WELL?

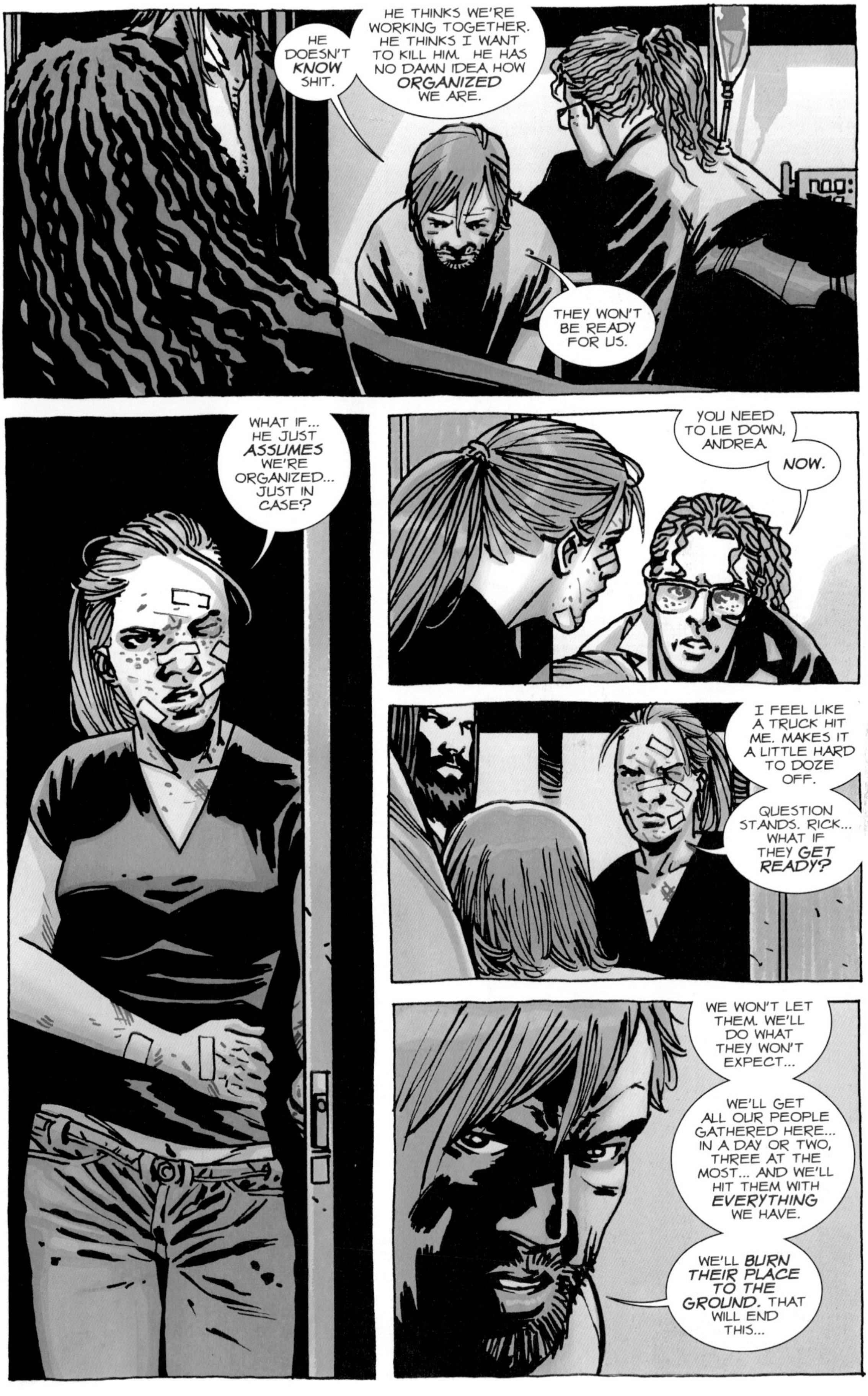
HE DOESN'T KNOW SHIT.
HE THINKS WE'RE WORKING TOGETHER. HE THINKS I WANT TO KILL HIM. HE HAS NO DAMN IDEA HOW ORGANIZED WE ARE.
THEY WON'T BE READY FOR US.
WHAT IF... HE JUST ASSUMES WE'RE ORGANIZED... JUST IN CASE?
YOU NEED TO LIE DOWN, ANDREA.
NOW.
I FEEL LIKE A TRUCK HIT ME. MAKES IT A LITTLE HARD TO DOZE OFF.
QUESTION STANDS. RICK... WHAT IF THEY GET READY?
WE WON'T LET THEM. WE'LL DO WHAT THEY WON'T EXPECT...
WE'LL GET ALL OUR PEOPLE GATHERED HERE... IN A DAY OR TWO, THREE AT THE MOST... AND WE'LL HIT THEM WITH EVERYTHING WE HAVE.
WE'LL BURN THEIR PLACE TO THE GROUND. THAT WILL END THIS...

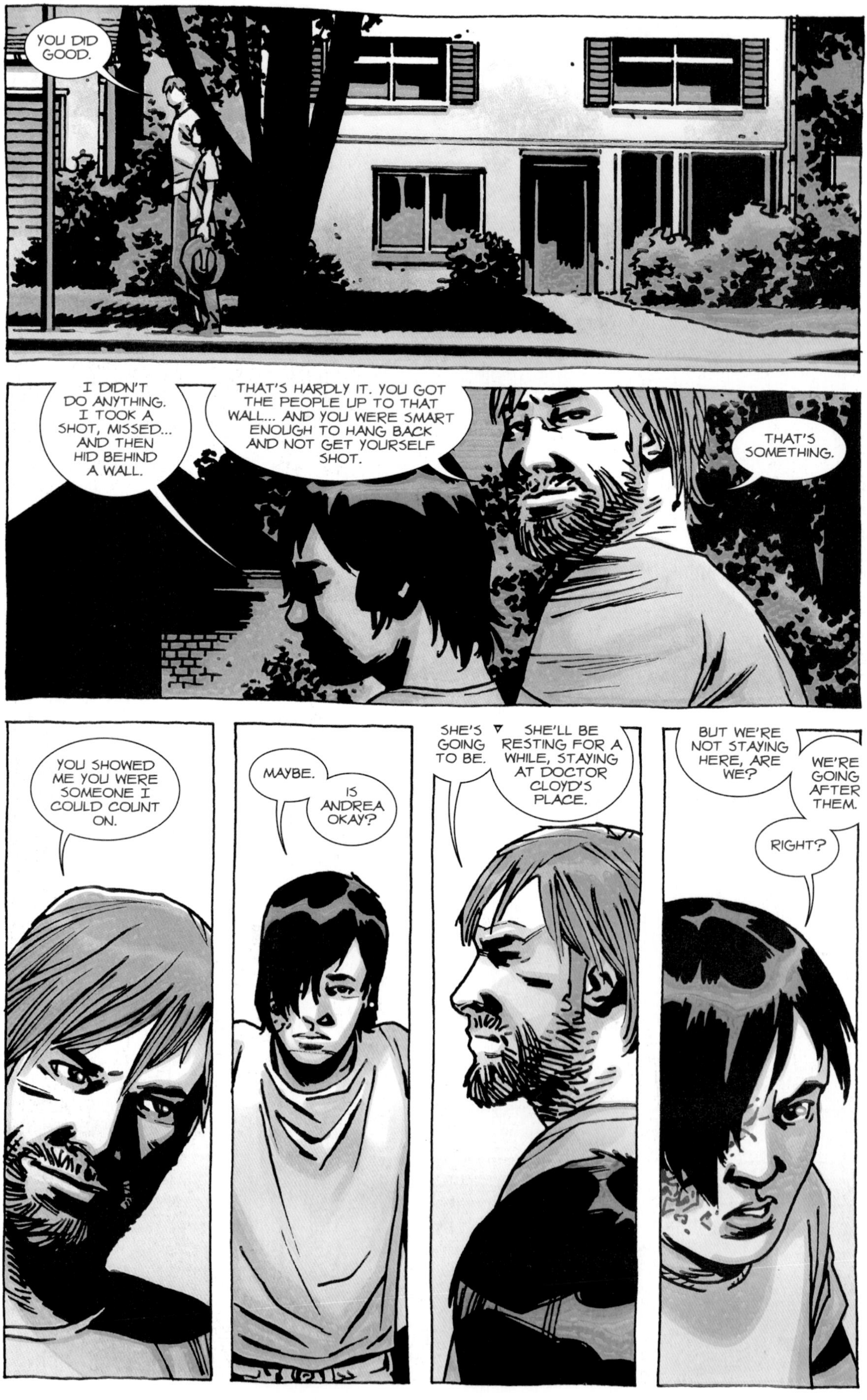
YOU DID GOOD.
I DIDN'T DO ANYTHING. I TOOK A SHOT, MISSED... AND THEN HID BEHIND A WALL.
THAT'S HARDLY IT. YOU GOT THE PEOPLE UP TO THAT WALL... AND YOU WERE SMART ENOUGH TO HANG BACK AND NOT GET YOURSELF SHOT.
THAT'S SOMETHING.
YOU SHOWED ME YOU WERE SOMEONE I COULD COUNT ON.
MAYBE.
IS ANDREA OKAY?
SHE'S GOING TO BE.
SHE'LL BE RESTING FOR A WHILE, STAYING AT DOCTOR CLOYD'S PLACE.
BUT WE'RE NOT STAYING HERE, ARE WE?
WE'RE GOING AFTER THEM.
RIGHT?

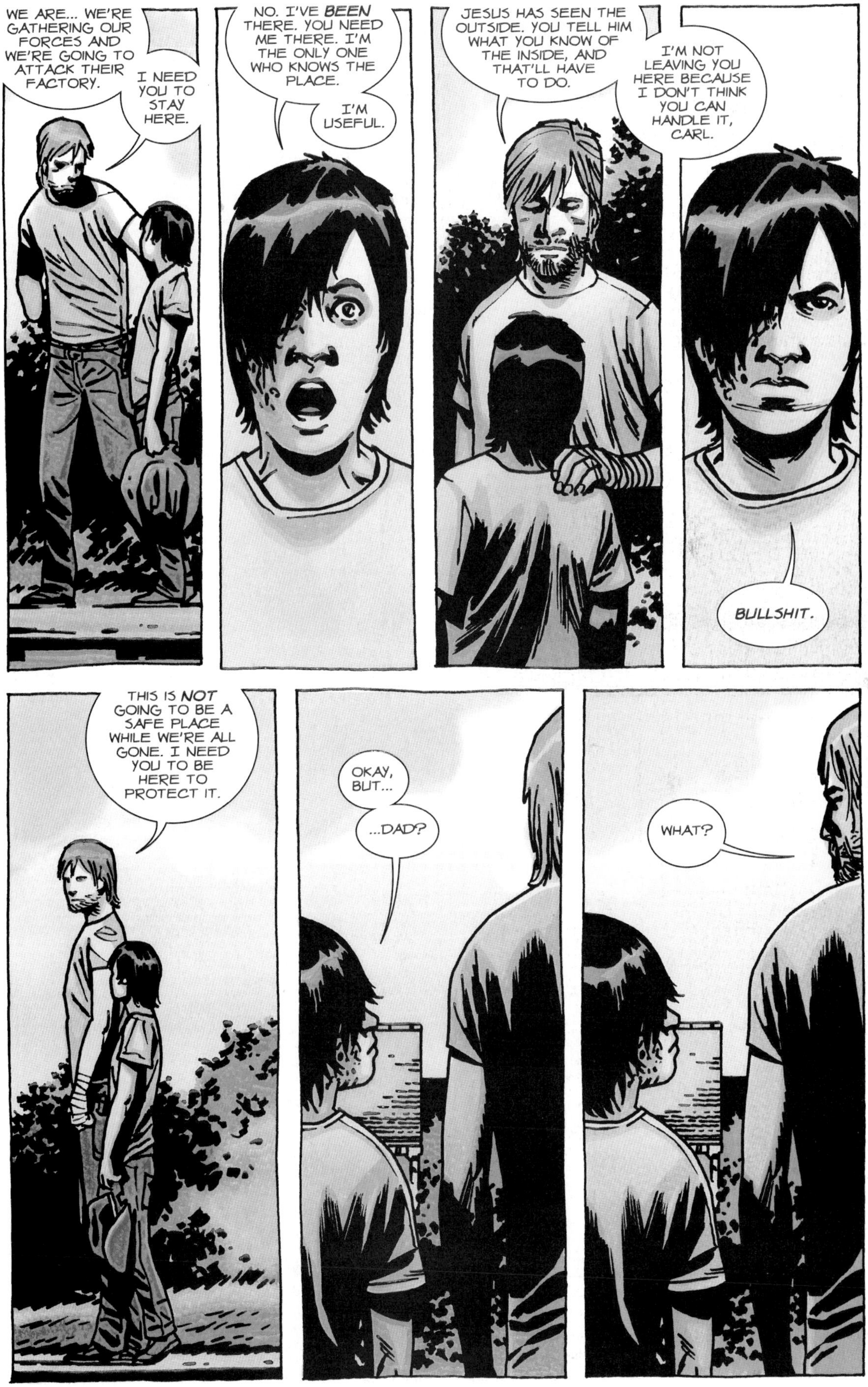

WE ARE... WE'RE GATHERING OUR FORCES AND WE'RE GOING TO ATTACK THEIR FACTORY.
I NEED YOU TO STAY HERE.
NO. I'VE *BEEN* THERE. YOU NEED ME THERE. I'M THE ONLY ONE WHO KNOWS THE PLACE.
I'M USEFUL.
JESUS HAS SEEN THE OUTSIDE. YOU TELL HIM WHAT YOU KNOW OF THE INSIDE, AND THAT'LL HAVE TO DO.
I'M NOT LEAVING YOU HERE BECAUSE I DON'T THINK YOU CAN HANDLE IT, CARL.
BULLSHIT.
THIS IS *NOT* GOING TO BE A SAFE PLACE WHILE WE'RE ALL GONE. I NEED YOU TO BE HERE TO PROTECT IT.
OKAY, BUT...
...DAD?
WHAT?

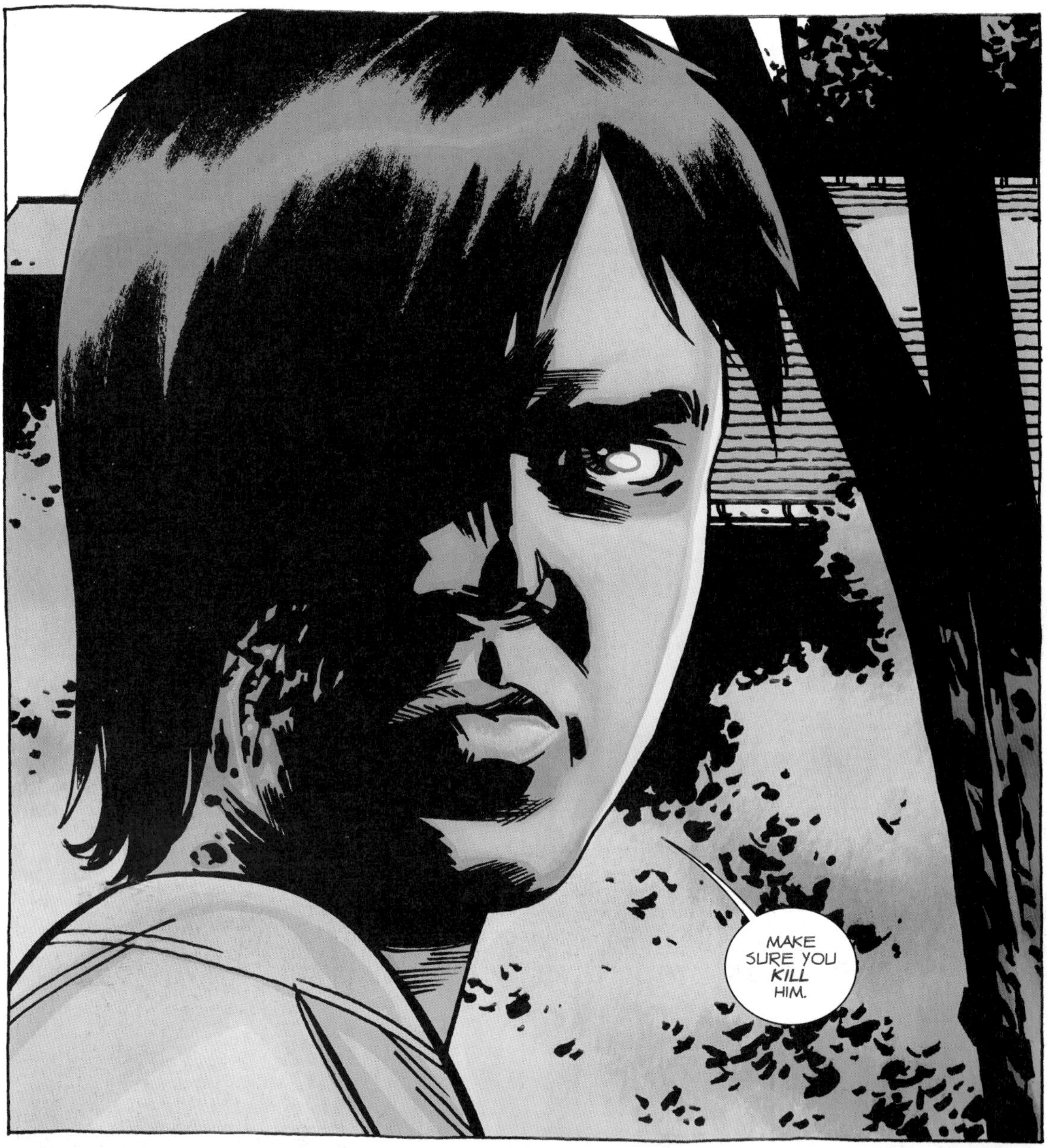
MAKE SURE YOU KILL HIM.

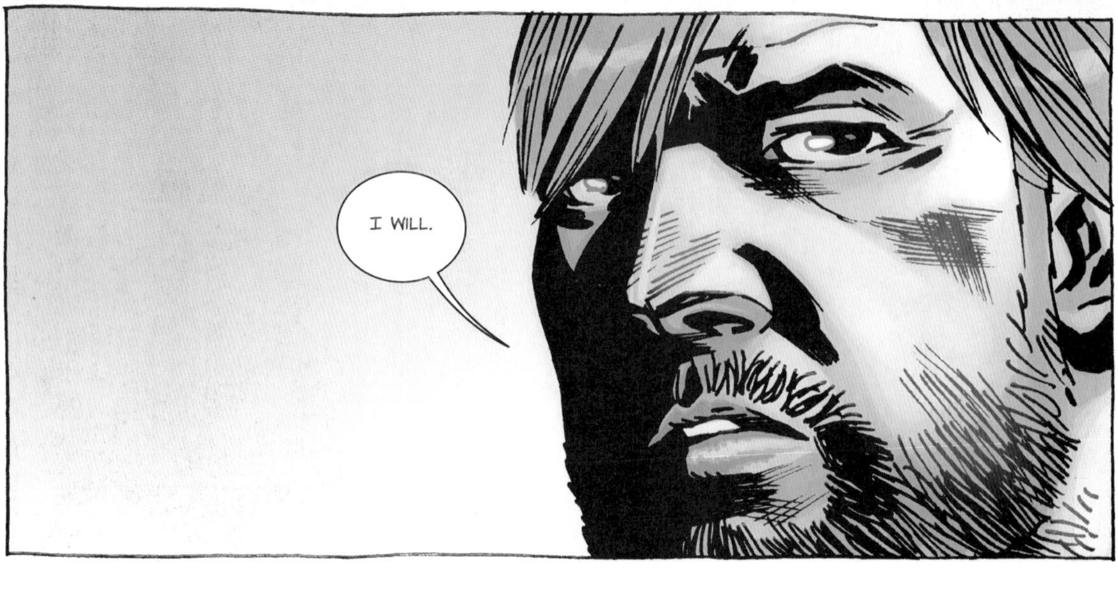
I WILL.

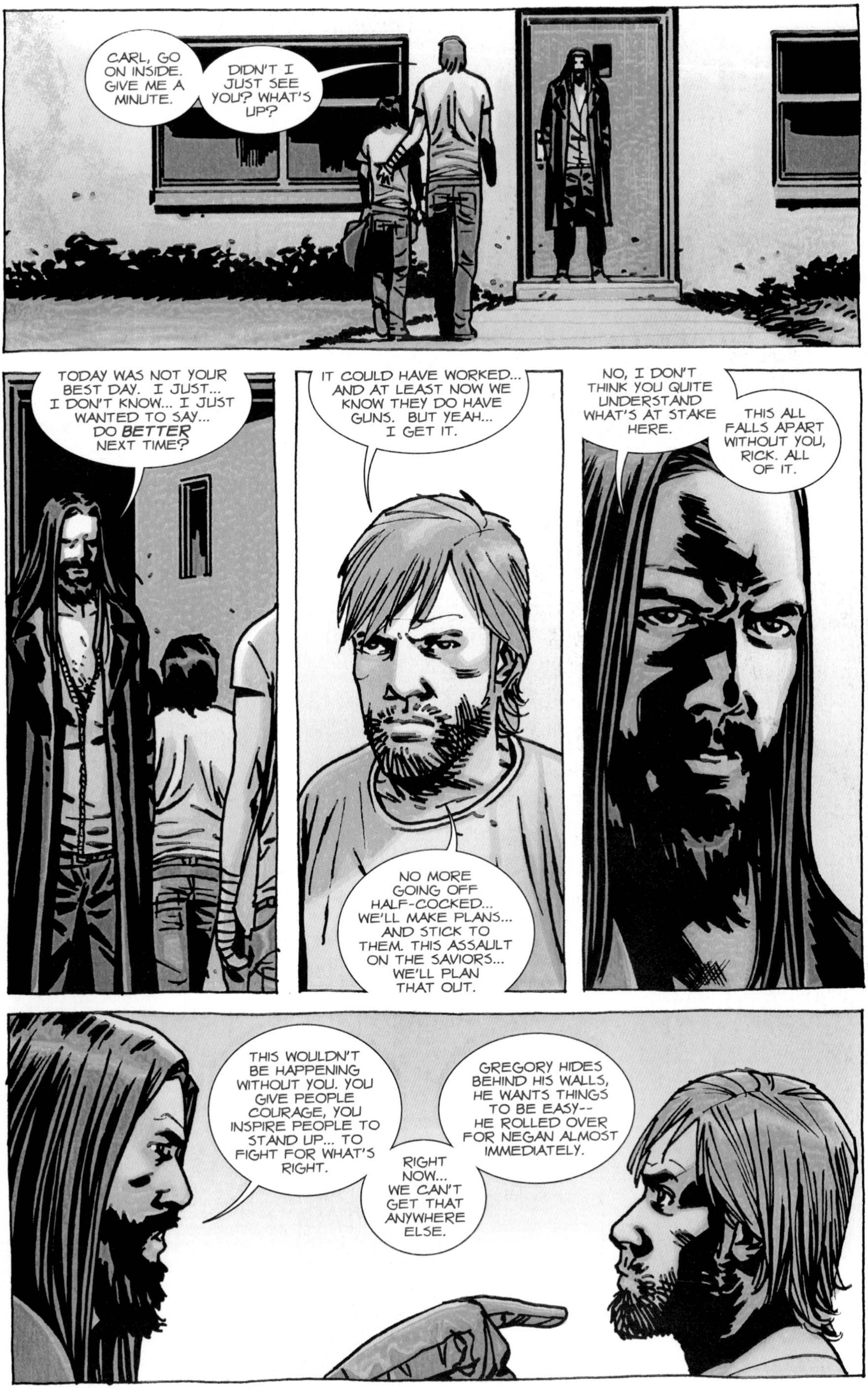
CARL, GO ON INSIDE. GIVE ME A MINUTE.
DIDN'T I JUST SEE YOU? WHAT'S UP?
TODAY WAS NOT YOUR BEST DAY. I JUST... I DON'T KNOW... I JUST WANTED TO SAY... DO *BETTER* NEXT TIME?
IT COULD HAVE WORKED... AND AT LEAST NOW WE KNOW THEY DO HAVE GUNS. BUT YEAH... I GET IT.
NO MORE GOING OFF HALF-COCKED... WE'LL MAKE PLANS... AND STICK TO THEM. THIS ASSAULT ON THE SAVIORS... WE'LL PLAN THAT OUT.
NO, I DON'T THINK YOU QUITE UNDERSTAND WHAT'S AT STAKE HERE.
THIS ALL FALLS APART WITHOUT YOU, RICK. ALL OF IT.
THIS WOULDN'T BE HAPPENING WITHOUT YOU. YOU GIVE PEOPLE COURAGE, YOU INSPIRE PEOPLE TO STAND UP... TO FIGHT FOR WHAT'S RIGHT.
RIGHT NOW... WE CAN'T GET THAT ANYWHERE ELSE.
GREGORY HIDES BEHIND HIS WALLS, HE WANTS THINGS TO BE EASY-- HE ROLLED OVER FOR NEGAN ALMOST IMMEDIATELY.

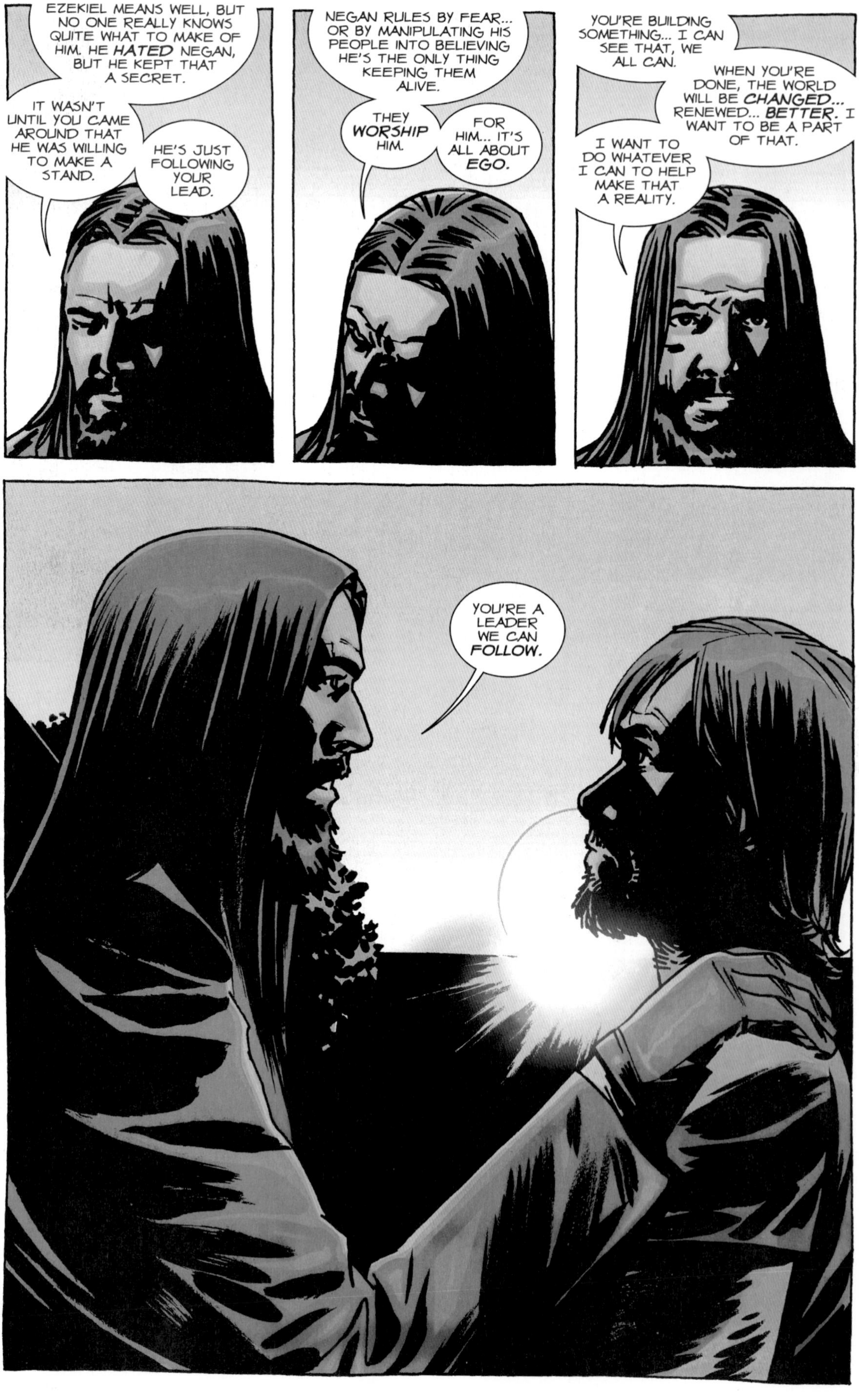
EZEKIEL MEANS WELL, BUT NO ONE REALLY KNOWS QUITE WHAT TO MAKE OF HIM. HE HATED NEGAN, BUT HE KEPT THAT A SECRET.
IT WASN'T UNTIL YOU CAME AROUND THAT HE WAS WILLING TO MAKE A STAND.
HE'S JUST FOLLOWING YOUR LEAD.
NEGAN RULES BY FEAR... OR BY MANIPULATING HIS PEOPLE INTO BELIEVING HE'S THE ONLY THING KEEPING THEM ALIVE.
THEY WORSHIP HIM.
FOR HIM... IT'S ALL ABOUT EGO.
YOU'RE BUILDING SOMETHING... I CAN SEE THAT, WE ALL CAN.
WHEN YOU'RE DONE, THE WORLD WILL BE CHANGED... RENEWED... BETTER. I WANT TO BE A PART OF THAT.
I WANT TO DO WHATEVER I CAN TO HELP MAKE THAT A REALITY.
YOU'RE A LEADER WE CAN FOLLOW.

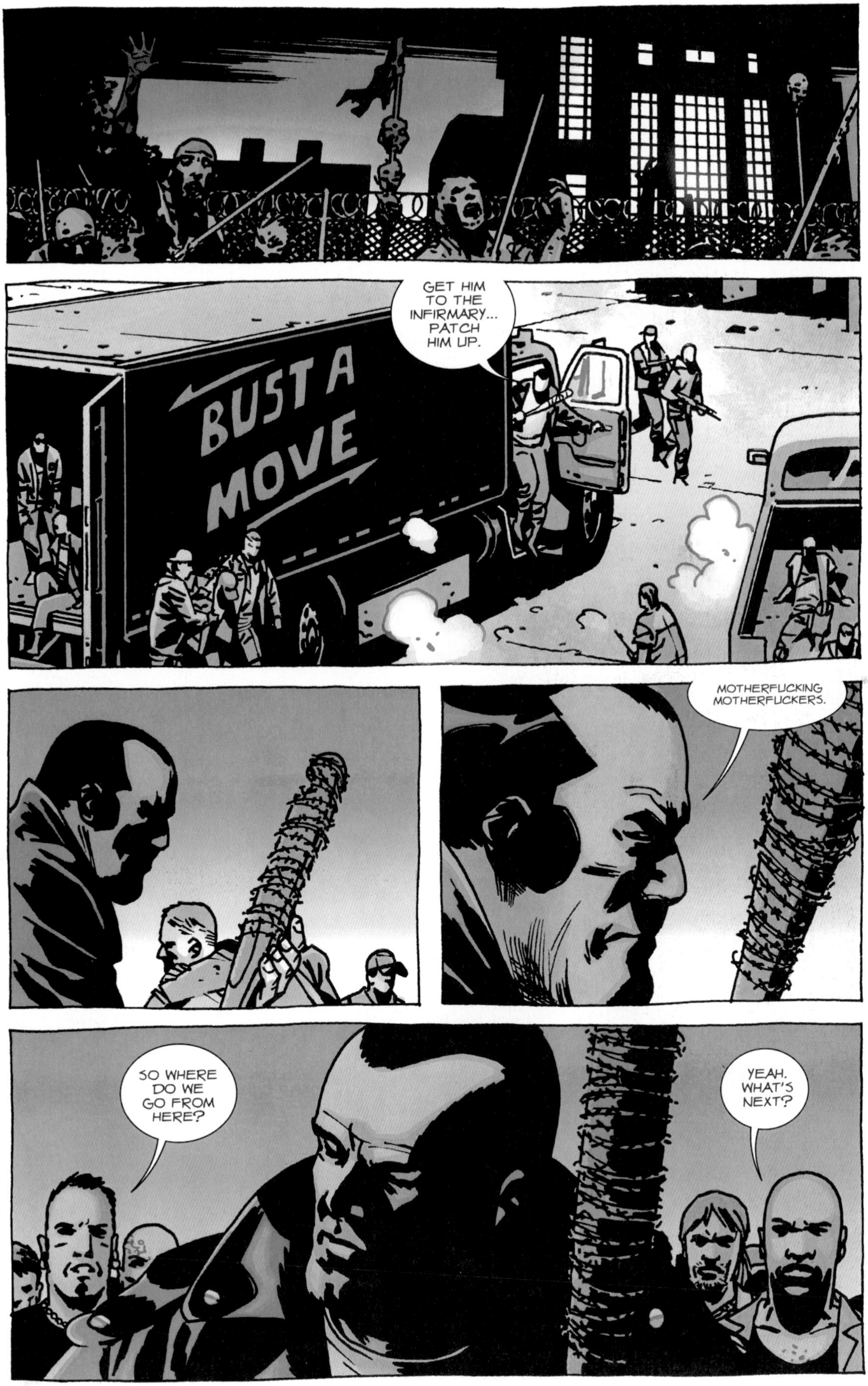
BUST A MOVE
GET HIM TO THE INFIRMARY... PATCH HIM UP.
MOTHERFUCKING MOTHERFUCKERS.
SO WHERE DO WE GO FROM HERE?
YEAH. WHAT'S NEXT?

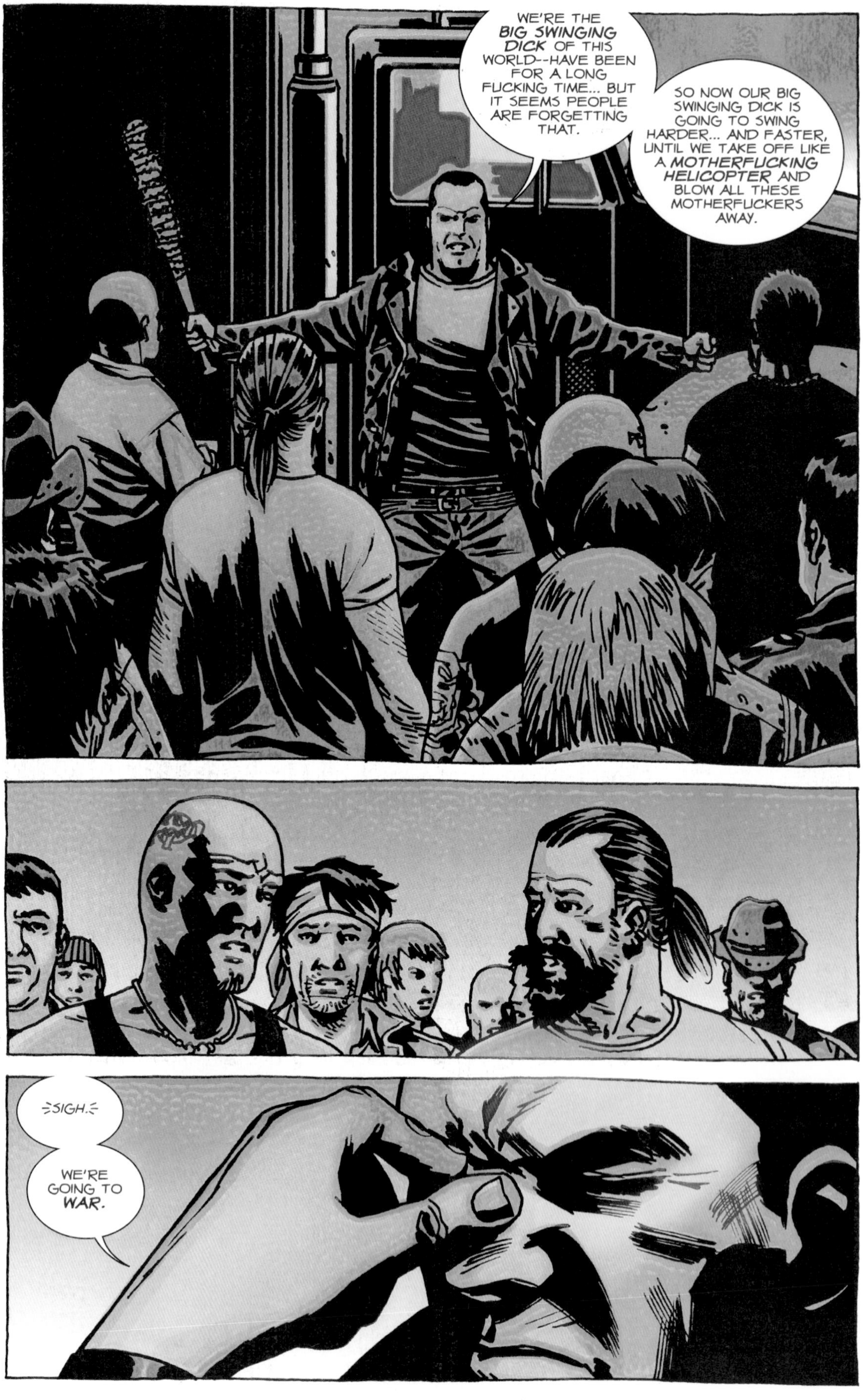
WE'RE THE BIG SWINGING DICK OF THIS WORLD--HAVE BEEN FOR A LONG FUCKING TIME... BUT IT SEEMS PEOPLE ARE FORGETTING THAT.
SO NOW OUR BIG SWINGING DICK IS GOING TO SWING HARDER... AND FASTER, UNTIL WE TAKE OFF LIKE A MOTHERFUCKING HELICOPTER AND BLOW ALL THESE MOTHERFUCKERS AWAY.
SIGH.
WE'RE GOING TO WAR.

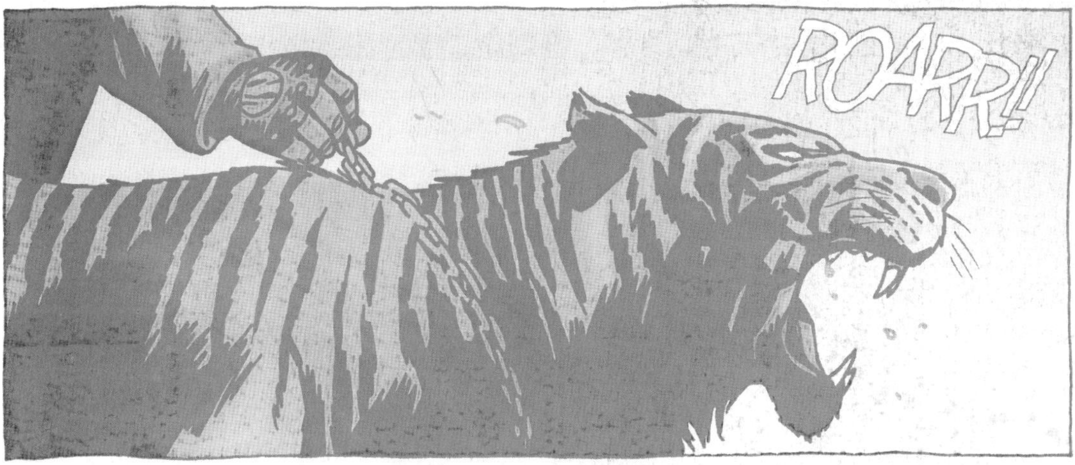
ROARR!!

TO BE CONTINUED...